Bool

UNDYl.

Steel World
Dust World
Tech World
Machine World
Death World

STAR FORCE SERIES
Swarm
Extinction
Rebellion
Conquest
Battle Station
Empire
Annihilation
Storm Assault
The Dead Sun
Outcast
Exile
Gauntlet

OTHER SF BOOKS
Starfire
Element-X

Visit BVLarson.com for more information.

Star Carrier

(Lost Colonies Book #3)
by
B. V. Larson

LOST COLONIES TRILOGY
Battle Cruiser
Dreadnought
Star Carrier

Copyright © 2016 by the author.

ISBN-13: 978-1519008572
BISAC: Fiction / Science Fiction / Military

Star Guard's budget ballooned in the months after I'd first met with the Ruling Council of Earth. The Council was a shadowy group of oldsters who were invisible to society at large, but they possessed tremendous power. They quietly guided events on my home planet from behind the scenes.

Clear evidence of their fantastic influence had appeared in physical form since my last voyage. Seven new spacecraft now hung in orbit over Earth's equatorial belt.

They were battleships all—huge, ugly vessels. They were angular in design and spiked with weaponry. They looked quite distinct from my own ship, *Defiant*.

From *Defiant's* command deck, I reviewed this newborn fleet and went over the relative capacities of the hulking vessels. By the specs, they were slow. They had engines with approximately the same thrust-output as the engines on my own battle cruiser, but they also had three times *Defiant's* mass.

What they lacked in speed and maneuverability they more than made up for in firepower. Their primary cannon batteries outranged my ship's weapons by a million kilometers, and they hit with greater force—at least, they did so in theory.

They were as yet untested ships. They were battlewagons designed to crush an enemy fleet, not to chase down fleeing opponents. Would that design work in open space? It was an unanswered question.

"I don't like it," Commander Durris said.

He was my executive officer, and he stood close by my side as always. He was a well-groomed man whose spine was as ramrod straight as his personality.

"What doesn't meet with your approval?" I asked him.

Durris took a moment to think before replying. He ran his fingers over his console, causing images to shift into wire-frame in the tactical display. A wealth of colored digits appeared all over every vessel.

"They have firepower," he said at last, "but they can't *move*. What if the enemy hits us from multiple fronts? We can't be everywhere at once, and they'll dance away if we chase them with these brutes."

I nodded, as his logic was unassailable. He lacked, however, all the facts that I was privy to.

"That might not be necessary," I said. "This fleet wasn't built to patrol the Solar System."

"What then?" he asked.

His attention left his console, and he fixed me with a sharp stare. He'd asked countless times for more information concerning the strategic meetings the captains of all the capital ships had been attending of late, but I'd given him nothing. I'd been cautioned not to up until our last meeting.

"Previously," I said to him quietly, "we possessed only a defensive force. It's been suspected all along that the Stroj may appear at any moment with an invasive fleet. If they'd done so a year ago, we barely had enough vessels to guard our home space. These new ships are the answer to that dilemma."

"I don't see how," he said, scoffing. "These monsters are too damned slow. What if the Stroj come at Mars or the asteroids? We'd lose everything we have out there. We couldn't even show up at the fight before they erased—"

I lifted a hand to quiet him. "I said that *was* the plan. Things have changed."

"In what way?" he asked, with obvious skepticism.

My XO was competent, hard-working and loyal. He was also suspicious and unwilling to take chances in general. As a result, he made an excellent exec, but he'd been passed up for command repeatedly—even with a dozen new commissions being handed down over the last year.

2

For my own part, I considered the fact he was lingering at his current rank a benefit. I needed an experienced crew, and he was a central part of my team.

"The change involves two specific points," I explained. "Firstly, we now have enough ships to do more than sit here guarding Earth."

He snorted. "We do? Says who?"

I wanted to tell him that the Ruling Council, the oldsters who spun webs of power behind the men and women we took to be our leaders, had done so. But naturally, revealing such a thing was out of the question if I wanted to keep my command.

Instead, I cleared my throat. "Our fleet is more powerful than it may seem," I assured him. "Lay out a course for Mars. We have a mission to perform."

He eyed me tensely for a moment.

"Sir," he said, "I appreciate the need for the utmost secrecy. What with the infiltration of the Stroj among our ranks, I even applaud it. But certain factors would be very helpful when preparing for a voyage. The expected length of our stay, for example...?"

"Assume the worst," I said. "Fill our holds with foodstuffs and emergency supplies. Pack every magazine as if we're going on a lengthy campaign."

He nodded, tapping at his screens with quick fingers.

"What of personnel? What about our marine complement and our—?"

"Get them all back here. All leaves are canceled."

"Yes sir! When do we have to be underway?"

"I'll give you six days. That's all we can afford. Can we be ready to launch by then?"

"I'll make it happen, Captain."

"Excellent," I said. "I know you've kept this ship primed, in the highest state of readiness. I appreciate that, Commander Durris."

He smiled briefly. "Thank you, sir."

That was it. He stopped asking questions, and that pleased me, because I had precious few more answers for him.

I'd been briefed only hours earlier at CENTCOM. Admiral Halsey had kept the affair short and sweet. We were to gather

3

our crews and leave orbit, arriving at the laboratory complex on Phobos within two weeks' time.

I'd promised the admiral I could keep that schedule, and I didn't like to disappoint the brass.

* * *

The fleet slipped away one by one over the following days. There'd been no announcement of intent or statement of purpose to the public.

But they'd noticed—how could they not? The skies were too clear, the fading presence of the heavy, silver-black ships too obvious to ignore. The plumes of exhaust alone formed brilliant streaks as the vessels broke orbit, each like a great comet when seen from the city streets far below us.

"William?" a call reached my mind through my implant. "Captain William Sparhawk, won't you speak with me?"

It was Lady Chloe of House Astra. She and I had a history. We'd been lovers before the war had begun, and I thought of her often still.

Despite these facts, I was reluctant to answer her call. The last time I'd shipped out, she'd contacted me as well—or someone pretending to be her had. I'd been waylaid, and I'd nearly missed my appointment with destiny.

But her voice wouldn't leave my mind. The sweet tones of it rang in my ears as if I was actually hearing them. Despite the fact I knew it was merely my implant playing on my aural nerves, I felt a rush of emotion. Her voice conjured fond memories I couldn't escape.

Sometimes, advancements in technology could be cruel. In the old days, messages from a man's lost love haunted him with mere script or text. They could be more easily and painlessly ignored.

Not so today. Now, I had to endure the lilt of her voice, the emotion in it plain to my senses. It was as if she stood on my command deck and whispered sweetly to me.

Sucking in a breath, I steeled myself for whatever might come from her virtual throat and answered the call.

"Lady Astra," I said formally and with what I hoped was a welcoming tone. "It's good to hear from you. It's been months. What can I do for you and your House?"

"So formal, William!" she said. "May I manifest? Your options are forbidding it."

My cheek twitched. I'd set my implant to allow audio, but to filter out visuals. Releasing a quiet sigh, I willed this to change.

Lady Astra immediately appeared. My mind placed her in an empty seat nearby, one usually occupied by Lieutenant Commander Yamada.

"Excuse me," I told Chloe, "I've been overloaded with documents and reports. They've been cluttering my field of vision lately."

"Perhaps I should go, then?" she asked.

I gazed at her for the span of two heartbeats. I knew I *should* banish her image from my mind—but I couldn't. Not now that I'd laid eyes upon her again. She was as fresh as a flower, as exquisite as a cut jewel.

"Tell me what this is about," I said.

Chloe's eyes crawled around the command deck. She could see what I could see, using my optical channels. She looked at the forward screen, and she gasped.

"It's true," she said, "you're shipping out. All of you. Where are you going, William?"

"I'm not at liberty to say. You know that, Chloe."

"Of course not," she said. "You'd think they'd brief the membership—but not these days. CENTCOM has become positively paranoid."

That was with good reason, we both knew. Stroj assassins had popped up from time to time, and agents had been ferreted out. Some thought we'd gotten the last of them, and none had been discovered for several months.

But how could we be absolutely certain of that? One couldn't verify a negative. The Stroj had proven very resourceful when it came to infiltration, spying and subversion.

Her eyes came back to rest on me.

"You can relax," she said. "I'm not a Stroj agent. Not this time. I'm a worried Public Servant. I'm not calling to beg you

5

to come back to my side or do anything else against your orders."

"Good," I said.

She smiled. "We both know you wouldn't do it anyway. What I'm calling for is information. My House is concerned. The fleet is leaving orbit, and no one seems to know why."

"Someone must," I said, "perhaps you can inquire at CENTCOM?"

She made a snorting sound and a flippant gesture. "As if that would make a difference. They won't even answer my calls. Me, a full-fledged Servant, stone-walled like a salesman! It's astonishingly inappropriate."

"Well, I can't give you anything they won't. Surely, you know that Chloe."

"I do. But perhaps you can tell me a few things that *aren't* classified?"

"Such as?"

"Do you have a full load of supplies aboard?"

I hesitated. There were no orders regarding information dissemination other than not to reveal our mission or our destination.

"I can't tell you that," I said.

"Really?" she asked, more concerned than ever. "That must mean you *do* have a full load. Therefore, they're sending the whole fleet into deep space for a lengthy voyage without informing any of the oversight committees. Unbelievable."

I shifted uncomfortably in my captain's chair despite the fact the padding was more than adequate.

"Please, Lady Astra, don't ask me any more questions. I can't afford to be a source for anything—not even a shrewd guess."

"Do you think I'm a Stroj illusion?" she asked. "Because I'm not. Not this time."

"I'm sure of that, but I have my orders."

She nodded thoughtfully. "I'm sorry for this call. I was asked to do it on the behalf of others. We're in a bit of a power-struggle down here. There are protocols, and they aren't being followed."

"Let me see if I understand you," I said. "Someone felt your relationship with me could be exploited to bypass CENTCOM? I'm alarmed at the thought as well as your participation in this matter."

She sighed and lowered her chin. "I knew you'd feel this way. You're a man of principles, and I must apologize. On a personal note, please contact me when you return home. I'd love to see you again in person, William."

This last statement made me smile. She'd broken my heart some time back and now, here she was again, toying with me. I knew all this, but I'd been captivated by her from the start. She was fickle and aloof at times, but she'd fascinated me from the moment I'd met her.

"I'll do that," I said. "Now, if you could excuse me..."

"Of course. Carry on, and may the stars guide you!"

The channel closed, but my eyes lingered upon her ghostly form until it vanished completely from my mind.

-2-

The trip out to Mars was relatively uneventful, but when we got there, things suddenly changed.

"Excuse me, Captain," Yamada's voice interrupted me. "There's an anomaly on our sensor map."

Sleeping hard in my cabin, the call startled me. I'd left instructions that dictated I was to be awakened immediately upon any kind of threat to the ship. Gasping awake, I slapped at the wall and answered in a rough voice. "I'll be right there."

I didn't bother to ask Yamada what the anomaly was. I simply dressed and rushed to the lift. She knew her business. She wouldn't summon me back to my command chair without good reason.

Linking into the command feed from my cabin was an option, of course. I could have done so while remaining on my back on my bunk, but I passed on that. I'd always believed a captain belonged on the command deck when anything serious occurred.

When I got to my seat and looked over the screens, an ensign pressed a cup of iced caf into my hands. I took it gratefully and sipped the beverage. Stimulants could be over-used, but there were also moments where they were invaluable tools.

The graphics weren't telling me much. *Defiant* was leading the fleet, flying far ahead of the primary formation of battleships. My vessel was quite a bit faster, and we'd naturally taken on the role of scouting ahead.

The sensors displayed a single, large yellow contact about two million kilometers out, orbiting Mars. The color indicated the contact was unclassified but not necessarily dangerous.

As I delved deeper into the data, Durris stepped up to my side to provide his insight.

"We spotted it about ten minutes ago," he said. "I contacted Phobos traffic, and they asked for you by name."

"They told you nothing of the contact?"

"No sir. They only asked for you."

I nodded, wondering what was going on. "Give me details."

"It's about a kilometer wide and four long. She's under power, in a steady orbit."

Frowning at him, I stopped sipping my drink. "Are you saying this thing is a vessel?"

"Yes—it's artificial at least."

"But such size... we've got nothing like it."

"That's correct, sir," he said, giving me a nod.

He retreated, and I was left to ponder the mystery. Why had an unknown vessel parked itself in orbit over Mars? Alarmingly, the ship was so large she dwarfed every battleship in our new fleet.

I sucked in a deep breath and let it out again.

"Have you relayed our findings to Admiral Halsey's ship?" I asked Durris.

As was usually the case, Durris had stood watch during my absence. He made a good XO and rotated shifts with me on a regular basis.

"I have, sir. They acknowledged the report but requested no more information. I'm under the impression that Halsey knows what's going on and doesn't want to talk about it."

"That's a good sign, at least."

"Sir..." Durris said, "perhaps we shouldn't make waves. If the Admiral is aware and unconcerned, is it our duty to—?"

"Yes, it is," I said. "We're flying ahead of the fleet for a reason. The least we can do is make sure we aren't walking our new ships into anything dangerous."

9

Frowning, I brought up a rotating hologram of Phobos. I spun it and reviewed the lab complex on a relatively flat plane, which automatically overlaid all current sensor input with past data. There appeared to be a disturbed region in a crater near the laboratory. But there were no obvious signs of damage or distress. Their power was on and everything appeared to operating normally.

"Yamada," I said at last, "open a channel to Star Guard on Phobos."

"Channel open," Yamada said promptly. "They're requesting your ID, and a private tunnel."

"Provide it."

She slid her fingers over her console for a few seconds, then turned and nodded to me. "Ready, Captain. You can link in with your implant at will."

After another gulp of chilled liquid, I set my cup down and connected to the private data stream Yamada had set up for me.

This time, rather than having the other party appear at my side, my mind was transported to their location.

An unfamiliar chamber took form around me. Bleak and aseptic, the walls were steel and lead-laced to keep out radiation. There were windows, but they were small, triangular affairs with fogged glass. Beyond these apertures, the dull rust-colored light of Mars glowed.

In the chamber with me was an elderly man. He wasn't an oldster—at least, I didn't get that impression. Oldsters were accounted as people who well over a century in age.

"Hello Captain Sparhawk," he said, clasping his hands in front of his lab coat and smiling at me coldly. "I'm Director Vogel, and I'm in charge of this facility. We've been expecting your call. You're the first to detect and identify our project."

"That's only to be expected," I said. "The other ships in *Defiant's* wake aren't within sensor range yet."

Vogel nodded. "They're also poorly designed to detect threats—they're only built to eradicate them."

"You mentioned a project? I can only surmise you're talking about the ship orbiting Mars."

10

"Just so. The *Iron Duke* is our pride and joy. We only launched her yesterday. She'll form the core of Earth's task force when she's ready."

I frowned, despite the fact I was trying not to. "Can you tell me more about this *Iron Duke*, Director?"

Vogel cleared his throat.

"You must understand this is highly classified information," he answered carefully. "I can't tell you anything you don't need to know. I will say, that there's no danger to your fleet. Please approach Phobos and dock at Pier Three. I'm willing to personally entertain you and your questions until Admiral Halsey arrives."

Breaking the connection after the usual pleasantries, I retreated into my own skull and again sat in my chair aboard *Defiant*.

The whole affair was disquieting. Could Vogel be a Stroj agent? Stranger things had happened.

It was difficult in today's climate of secrecy to be sure who to trust. We were all tight-lipped due to our worries about Stroj infiltrators. But that very lack of trust, and the fear that was the root cause of it, heightened everyone's sense of paranoia.

After considering Vogel's offer for a few minutes, I decided to order Durris to dock at Pier Three.

I had little choice. It was my mission to investigate these things to protect the main fleet. I was just going to have to take Director Vogel's word at face value.

Nine hours later we'd completed our deceleration regimen and glided into port near Phobos. The gentle tug of her gravity was only one or two hundredths that of Earth, but we still had to employ stabilizers to keep our ship from drifting down to the surface.

Once we'd docked, I left Durris in charge of the ship and headed to the docking bay.

Pier Three was a long tube of nano-ferrous metal that stuck out like a thin tongue into space. We'd attached ourselves to the end of it, and from the docking bay I rode a capsule down to the surface.

11

Behind me walked Zye and Yamada. Inside the lab complex, we engaged our magnetics. Our boots clicked rhythmically as we made our way down the echoing hallways.

More than just a security grunt, Zye was one of the best among my crew at detecting Stroj influences. I valued her opinions under any suspicious circumstances.

As my science and communications officer, Yamada was a clear choice to round out the team. She could help me to understand this briefing if necessary.

I'd thought about bringing along Marine Commander Morris, but I'd passed on the idea. This was supposed to be a meet-and-greet, not a boarding assault.

A familiar face met us at the end of the first passageway. It was Director Vogel. His hands were laced before his body as they'd been before. He wore an odd smile, and his lips seemed to be too long and sharply curved upwards at the corners.

Reflexively, I smiled in return and nodded to him.

"Welcome to Phobos, Captain Sparhawk," he said. "I see you've brought some of your crew with you."

"Yes. This is Lieutenant Commander Yamada and Lieutenant Zye."

Both women were attractive and Asian in appearance, but they were built on dramatically different scales. Zye was a Beta colonist, a clone hybrid designed to survive under high gravity and difficult conditions. She was taller than I was and built with heavy bones and musculature.

Yamada was much more classic in design. Her straight black hair was several centimeters longer than regulations allowed, but no one had challenged her on that point.

"Excellent..." Vogel said, looking them over briefly. "What a contrast... Come this way, please."

Zye and Yamada exchanged glances, but I didn't respond to his slightly rude behavior.

We followed him into the bowels of the place. Now and then, as we passed various pressure doors and portholes, we spotted more personnel. They were universally dressed in lab coats or vac suits. Everyone seemed very professional and focused on their tasks.

"Director Vogel," Yamada said, speaking up for the first time. "I've checked into the records. There are only six hundred people stationed on Phobos. Are you telling us you managed to build that huge ship out there with such a tiny crew?"

He glanced over his shoulder at her, and his oddly permanent smile lengthened. "Yes," he said, "that's exactly what I'm saying. We have only a small team here, but we've accomplished a great deal."

"Hard to believe," Zye said.

He glanced at her and his smile faded a little. He paused and stopped walking. "Ah, the Beta," he said, referring to Zye. "I've studied you from afar, madam. You're a known deceiver, and yet you're suspicious of all others. Can you explain this combination of personality traits?"

Zye shrugged. She was indeed different from everyone else on Earth, but it rarely seemed to bother her. She didn't bat an eye at the Director's challenge.

"Yes, I can explain," she said. "Someone who has told countless lies to survive also learns to recognize that behavior in others."

Vogel's mouth twitched, but his frozen smile stayed in place. "Pray then, what do you detect from my conduct?"

"Arrogance, mild deception and condescension. On the personal side, a lifetime of academia has apparently led to social disconnection and—"

I cleared my throat and took a step forward, placing myself between the two. "Let me explain, Vogel. Zye is not—"

"Not entirely civilized by Earth standards? Yes, I know. As I said, I've studied her from afar. I'm still fascinated, if somewhat disappointed. Let me show you our work. Perhaps everything will become clear then."

He led us to a chamber with a floor of black glass. It was circular and about ten meters across.

"This is the observation deck. Below us are the construction facilities."

We looked at one another in confusion—but not Zye. She stood near the Director, tense and wary. For once, I couldn't fault her paranoia. After all, we'd been ambushed by people who seemed far less odd than Vogel.

Vogel spread his hands. "Don't you want to see it?"

"Yes," I said, "show me what you're talking about."

The floor beneath our feet shifted. The shift wasn't slow or subtle, it was fast and alarming.

One second, we were standing on a gloss-black floor which was perfectly flat and smooth. The next, we were standing on nothing.

The floor seemed to vanish. As we didn't fall, I could only surmise that it had become transparent. The transparency was so perfect that it seemed as if we were floating in the air.

A very great distance below us was a vast work area. Machine tools of every sort buzzed and whined. The audio had cut in just as suddenly as had the visual.

None of this was more than momentarily alarming. But then we got a closer look at the figures operating the power tools.

They weren't entirely human. Shapes with multiple arms, multiple legs and even multiple heads in some cases were moving down there, working on small craft.

Sleek ships, dozens of them, were all over the factory floor. The odd workers scuttled from one ship to the next, moving with alien dexterity and speed.

"They're all different," Yamada said, gasping.

"The fighters?" Vogel asked in surprise. "Not at all. They're all identical, other than their numbers and state of construction."

"Fool!" Zye growled.

Suddenly, she grabbed Vogel. She gripped him by the neck, actually lifting him into the air so that his feet dangled. Fortunately, the gravity was slight, or he might have been seriously injured.

"She's talking about the workers!" Zye shouted into Vogel's shocked face. "They're all different from one another."

"Specialized, yes," Vogel gargled past Zye's fingers. "They're modified to perform unique tasks. Why has this elicited a violent reaction?" He craned his neck and his wide

14

eyes looked at me plaintively. "Sparhawk, call off your Beta. She's gone mad!"

I stepped forward, placing my hands on my hips. Yamada was still staring down into the factory floor, fascinated and horrified at the same time.

Zye was fixated upon Vogel. I could tell from long experience she wanted to murder him immediately.

For once, I couldn't fault her for her instincts.

"Let me explain our negative reactions, Director," I told Vogel.

His mouth worked like that of a fish, and his eyes bulged in alarm. His insipid smile had vanished completely.

"The creatures below us are all too familiar to me and my veteran crew. They are the enemy. They are Stroj."

Vogel made a choking sound. His slender fingers clawed at Zye's own thick digits.

She relaxed them only enough to let him speak.

"Of course they resemble such creatures," he said. "How else did you think we could build *Iron Duke* in such a short time? Humans couldn't do it. Robots would take too long to be programmed for each task."

I stared down at the floor, my heart sinking. Had CENTCOM gone mad?

"You admit, then, that these creatures are hybrids of humans and machines? Cyborgs? You copied our enemy's designs to speed up production of the fleet?"

He was unable to answer, so I waved for Zye to put Vogel down.

Reluctantly, she released him. He rubbed at his neck and looked at us strangely.

"It was the only way," Vogel said. "It's my greatest achievement. These workers aren't Stroj. I'm not a Stroj."

"If I thought you were, you'd be dead already," Zye growled again. "You're worse than a Stroj. You're a fool."

I nodded, unable to disagree.

"I'd never anticipated such a reaction," Vogel said. "Dignitaries I've brought here have always laughed and applauded."

"That's because they've never met the Stroj face-to-face," I told him.

I was unable to take my eyes from the scene below us. The entire time we'd argued and watched from up here, the creatures below us had remained absolutely focused on their tasks.

They were the ultimate workers, I had to admit that.

-3-

At length, we received a more complete explanation from Director Vogel. The Phobos team had been assigned an impossible task: to come up with a means of multiplying industrial production. Worse, this improvement had to be realized in space, not on any planetary surface. Once the Council had approved the budget to build a new fleet, development of experimental industrial methods had quickly become the sole purpose of the lab complex here on Phobos.

In the past, the academics stationed on this remote outpost had limited their interests to things like asteroid mining techniques for ice and gas reclamation. They'd never been fully-funded or allowed to push the limits of their scientific know-how.

That had all changed after Earth had encountered a serious threat from her colonies. Now, the powerful people who ruled our home world wanted their best minds to produce miracles. Nothing was off-limits. No plan would be rejected—as long as it achieved results.

"So," I said, speaking in the relatively neutral ground of a conference room, "you were inspired by the design of the Stroj. You studied them, took samples, and built your own versions?"

"No," Vogel said, "we did *not* copy the colonist tech. We appropriated the concepts only. In my opinion, we vastly improved upon their primitive, ad hoc designs."

"You think you made improvements?" Yamada asked. "Like what?"

"We've built a variety of highly specialized types, for one. Some are brutes for lifting and placing parts. Others—the ones with numerous small limbs and thin fingers—do the finer work. Still others start off with many optical organs to keep watch on the rest and coordinate the complex manufacturing steps for maximum efficiency."

Pride had crept back into his voice, despite our group's obvious disapproval.

"Who then, Director, approves the final state of these... beings?" I asked.

He shrugged. "Not us," he admitted. "We give them a starting point which consists of one of the basic designs. After working for a time, the variants begin to reconfigure themselves. They seem to enjoy it."

"Variants?" I asked.

"That's what we call them. They're not entirely human, admittedly. They're *variant* humans. People who've been enhanced for the good of us all."

"I see..." I said.

Director Vogel eyed each of us in turn, and he took offense at our dour expressions.

"Look," he said, "we're not monsters. Neither are the variants! For raw materials, we only use volunteers shipped up here from Earth. These people are patriots who wish to forward the cause of Earth's defense. After a minimal mind-scrub, we regrow their basic biologicals and plant them in an artificial chassis. They do the rest, adding mechanical enhancements as they see fit."

Yamada leaned forward. "Do these things *talk* to you? Are they happy? Are they even human anymore?"

Vogel shrugged and avoided her gaze. "They don't speak much—but not because they lack the wit to do so. They don't always need speech. They communicate with packet radio faster than we can with words. They seem happy with their status. Each of them does the work of a hundred trained men. That's a source of great pride to everyone on Phobos!"

Yamada shuddered. I caught that, and I understood it. So far, we'd been unable to get Director Vogel to understand our misgivings. He seemed stubbornly defensive concerning his abominable creations.

"You have to meet them for yourself," he insisted. "You have to witness their incredible efficiency."

Yamada and I exchanged glances, saying nothing, but then Zye spoke up.

She hadn't spoken since we'd first reacted in shock to the variants. Now, she leaned forward and fixed the Director with an unfriendly stare.

"You believe yourself to be wise and powerful, but you're not. You are foolish."

Director Vogel's face reddened. I doubted he was accustomed to having his intellect questioned.

"Zye—" I began, but Vogel waved me off.

"No," he said. "Let her speak. She knows what she means to say, and I'd like to hear it. Accepting criticism of one's own work is the hallmark of any scientist."

"You've created evil here," Zye said. "These beings aren't human—at least, not human enough to trust. They must be destroyed."

"Destroyed? Would you order workers killed after a factory is shut down? Besides, they haven't finished their task yet."

"They've built your ship, haven't they?" I asked.

"Yes, but only the mothership. The smaller vessels aren't all completed. There are thousands more scheduled to be produced over the next month."

"I'm beginning to understand," I said. "That massive vessel circling Mars isn't a battleship, is it?"

"No. It's a carrier, a star carrier. It's an entirely new class of ship, and the largest Earth has ever produced."

"How many fighters can it carry?" I asked.

Vogel shrugged. "That's classified information."

"You mentioned thousands?" I pressed.

Vogel let his smile creep back onto his face. "She is a very large vessel."

"How long?" demanded Zye. "How long will the construction of these fighters take?"

19

"The variants work with amazing speed. They're taking in raw metallic ore constantly and processing it as fast as we can bring it in. We have a shipment from the belt impacting every six hours, around the clock. The refinery workers catch the spheroids of high-grade ore as they impact Limtoc Crater. Each shipment is then processed and sent on to the fabrication crews, and after that—"

"Wait a minute," I said, "you're talking about different teams of variants, right? Multiple teams?"

"Of course."

After further questioning, I leaned back in defeat. Director Vogel wouldn't tell me much about the capabilities of the star carrier, but he was boastful about his shipyard. The labs of Phobos had been turned into a construction facility. There were variants all over this tiny moon, performing countless tasks. The few he'd shown us were only the final assembly team.

"And now," he said at length, "I must bid you farewell. The next tour starts within the hour. This tour is at an end."

"The next tour?"

"Yes. Admiral Halsey is about to arrive. If you want any further information, you'll have to talk to him."

Vogel's attitude had turned sour. He didn't want to talk to us any longer, that much was clear. He'd grown tired of our mistrust and dire warnings.

We were ushered out of the facility with expediency. The long ride back to *Defiant* was a brooding one.

Zye looked out the capsule windows, such as they were. She stared down at the rough, curving surface of Phobos.

Yamada tapped at her mobile computer, and it glowed up into the faceplate of her pressure suit.

"I think they have thousands of these variant creatures," Yamada said, "all over the moon. Probably, there are more of them out in the belt. The old-school belters as we knew them would have a hard time generating all the raw materials needed in such a short time."

"You're right," I said. "The belt represents a nearly limitless source of metals, but they've been supplying the effort to build our battleships in Earth orbit all this time, too."

"I haven't heard of any serious shortage of steel, nickel or radioactives back home, have you?" she asked.

I shook my head. "No," I said. "They must be using variants to raise mining output as well as construction output."

"It only makes sense," Yamada said. "How else could they have increased production so rapidly? With so much orbital construction occurring both on Earth and Mars... they'd have to be producing three or four times their normal levels of mining output to sustain it all."

I stepped to the slit-like windows and looked outside. The reflected light from Mars made me squint a little.

"So, we have to assume they've got these variant things all over the place," I said. "Working faster than men can work."

"They must be out there," she said. "It's a matter of economics. Building starships rapidly has always been problematic. In the old days, they built colony ships as large as *Iron Duke*, but it took several years to construct each of them."

"Right..." I said, recalling my history texts of the past. "It was a massive effort."

"There are two barriers to the rapid production of starships: raw resources and labor," Yamada continued. "If you build a ship in space, that goes a long way to solving the resource problem. Rather than lifting metals from Earth's gravity well one ton at a time, you can move it around much more freely. Asteroids have very little gravity to fight against."

"But humans don't work well in null-G," I said, following her line of reasoning.

"They don't, but I'm willing to bet they solved both problems with the variants. They have teams of them mining at the belt, churning out metals. Construction teams here on Phobos—maybe they're even using them back at Earth, on the orbital platforms..."

"You really think they might have variants working in Earth orbit?" I asked, freshly alarmed by the concept. "Couldn't they have simply built robots to do the task?"

Yamada shrugged. "According to Vogel, these variants get up to speed faster. They self-design to some extent. Pure robots are hard to design and build. You have to plan out every detail of their operation. We haven't done much in the field over the

21

last century. Politics has all but shut down innovation in that direction."

Her words made me somewhat uncomfortable. My own father was the head of the Equality Party. They'd often stifled innovation on the grounds that it killed jobs for their constituents.

"The end result," Yamada went on, "is that we don't have robots sophisticated enough for this kind of labor. A few drones, some repair units with welders, but nothing up to the task of constructing an entire starship. We could develop them in time, of course... but as Vogel said, this was a crash project."

"They've traded an old demon for a worse one," Zye said suddenly. "They have no idea what they've done."

"You might be right," I said. "But these variants don't sound *exactly* like the Stroj. Didn't Vogel say something about scrubbing their minds before rebuilding them into new bodies?"

Zye shook her head. "He also talked about them being volunteers." She looked at each of us for a moment. "Do you really think the previous owners of the brains inside the variants were volunteers when they were sent to Phobos?"

Yamada shook her head. I had to agree.

"It seems unlikely," I admitted, "that anyone would volunteer to have their brains removed from their bodies, processed, and placed inside an abominable construct of flesh and metal."

"And, who volunteers for a mind scrub?" Zye asked. "Would you?"

With grim thoughts lingering in our heads, we rode the rest of the way along Pier Three to *Defiant* in brooding silence.

-4-

After reaching the command deck, I immediately sent an open channel-request to Admiral Halsey. He put me off. No doubt, he was enjoying his tour of the construction facilities.

Nearly an hour later, he finally responded by transmitting a hologram of himself to me as I sat in my command chair. Halsey walked around the place, inspecting my instrumentation.

The rest of the crew couldn't see him, of course. He was a ghost that only existed for my senses.

"Wasn't that incredible, Sparhawk?" he demanded. "I have to tell you, I came out here expecting some surprises, but that Vogel fellow—he's a genius—an absolute *genius*. With characters like him working for Earth, we can't lose this war."

I kept my face neutral with an effort of will.

"Yes sir," I said, "his achievements are startling to say the least."

Halsey stopped pacing on the deck and frowned at me. "Do I detect a lack of enthusiasm? The Director hinted that you had your doubts about his project. He also complained about a sore neck. Do you know anything about that?"

"Well sir… could we take this into my private office?"

"What for?" he growled.

"This project is highly classified."

"Right… Okay, lead on."

His image followed me into my office, and we sat down together. The software made a slight error, probably due to our shift of scenery. He appeared to be sitting on the far side of my desk, but instead of being anchored to the chair, he was posed floating in the air a half-meter above it. As he didn't see anything wrong with my positioning, I decided to ignore the anomaly.

"Admiral," I began, "I do have misgivings."

I proceeded to relate to him all my doubts about using variants.

"You think they're too much like the Stroj, huh?" Halsey asked when I'd finished. "Well, they *are* freaky. I'll give you that. But it's time to man-up, Sparhawk. This isn't just a border skirmish we're involved in. If the Stroj come here in strength, they'll wipe us out. You've seen the projections. Without the ships these monsters have produced, we wouldn't stand a chance."

"I can't deny the truth of your words."

"So then, what would you want to do differently?"

"I think we should build our fleet then immediately close the new facilities," I said.

He blinked at me in shock. "What? Are you kidding? After all this effort and expense? Every Great House on Earth is chipping in. You know that, don't you? They've put down their treasure, and they've spent it all. That includes your family as well, Sparhawk."

"I'm sure that's true, sir. But you asked me what I thought, and I think we should—"

"What would we do with the variants themselves if we closed down their factories?"

"Well... I think we should destroy them. All of them. They pose a danger to—"

Halsey stood up suddenly in agitation. The software was still wrong, and he was now looming over my desk, with his illusory head brushing the ceiling. His finger waggled at my face.

"I've got your number, Sparhawk. I get it. Your family is behind all these misgivings. You Equality types are all alike. You hate progress. You want stagnation and protectionism.

24

Well, your time has passed on for now. This isn't about human labor versus automation. We have to pull out all the stops and use every trick we have to win this war!"

The software managing the admiral's positioning was slowly correcting itself. It now had him drifting downward until his feet touched the floor of my office again. He paced in front of me angrily.

"I don't like to see this kind of thing in my best officers," he said. "Why does politics always have to rear its head when the money begins to flow around in new directions? Can't we all just focus on the joint goal of surviving this war?"

"Admiral," I said, interrupting his tirade, "please understand that I agree with most of what you're saying. But I would ask that you consider how the Stroj developed originally. Did they take the same path we're taking now to solve their problems?"

"Huh? You're not making any sense, man! No one is suggesting that we *all* turn ourselves into variants. A few criminals and social rejects, that's all we have here. I see nothing wrong with pressing them into the service of Earth when she needs them most. They're finally contributing to the social good."

I stared at him for a frozen moment. He was as much as admitting to me that the variants were not volunteers by any stretch of the imagination. I didn't know quite how to respond.

"That's right," he said. "It's hard to be in command of a defensive effort that spans an entire star system. Choices have to be made. Hard calls that don't let a man sleep easily at night—not unless he keeps the consequences of failure clearly in mind."

He went on like that for quite some time, and I no longer bothered to argue with him. He wasn't going to listen, I could tell that by now.

When he ended the call and vanished from my office at last, I headed back to the command deck to check over the status of my ship. All was well for now.

A week passed before we left Mars orbit. The *Iron Duke* came with us when we headed home.

"Course?" Durris asked, looking at me expectantly.

Up until this moment, our destination had been a carefully guarded secret. The officers aboard had a pool going, most of them betting on a return to the nearest colonies such as Tranquility Station at Gliese-32 or the three planets that circled in the Crown system. They were all wrong.

"We're leaving Mars and heading back to Earth," I said. "Take it slow this time, don't lose the battlewagons."

There were a few cheers and a few groans. Those with adventurous dispositions were disappointed.

Rumbold was among those who groaned. He was my helmsman and possibly my best friend. He was also an oldster, boasting a hundred and sixty years of extended life. He'd managed to prove during our previous voyages that he was still capable of piloting a starship past any obstacle.

Oddly, despite his age, he still craved exploration and adventure. He didn't relish battle, but he seemed to be bored by Earth. Perhaps, after another century and a half of existence, I'd find myself feeling the same way.

"Earth?" he asked in a rumbling voice. "Really? What was the point of coming all the way out here then?"

"We came out here to escort *Iron Duke* back to Earth. She's got enough fighters aboard to be effective now, and she'll serve at the core of this task force from now on."

"Who's been given command of her?" he asked. He deftly guided *Defiant* with relatively gentle thrusts into a proper stance before applying the heavy acceleration it would require to escape Mars' gravity well.

"Admiral Halsey has taken personal command of the carrier," I told him.

Rumbold blew out his cheeks and mumbled something.

"What's that, helmsman?" I asked.

"Nothing, sir."

"Please, enlighten us. Do you find Halsey to be a sub-standard commander?"

His red-rimmed eyes slewed around and met mine. His mouth hung open for a moment.

"No, no, nothing like that. Halsey's a good officer, when he wants to be. I'm just irritated that we've been put on parade duty."

I frowned, not quite catching his meaning. The others on the deck were listening as well with frank curiosity.

"Parade duty?" I asked. "How so?"

"Don't you see, sir? Why fly out Earth's entire fleet all the way to Mars to collect this new ship? Why have all of us, flying in formation, return to Earth like a flock of baby ducks in their mother's wake?"

"Perhaps he wants us all to become acquainted with a new battle formation."

"Maybe, maybe... But think of how it *looks*, sir. Think of how the net vids will carry this all over Earth. Admiral Halsey will be returning home with the greatest ship ever built under his fine posterior, surrounded by these big shiny battleships. There won't be a dry eye on the planet."

"Hmmm..." I said, thinking it over. "I do believe you might have a point, Rumbold."

"Damn straight I do. If there's anything the brass is really good for, it's grandstanding. Now, back in my day—"

"That's sufficient commentary, pilot. Carry on."

Muttering a few more inaudible thoughts, he did as I'd ordered.

-5-

Less than a month after we'd set off, we returned to Earth and slid into a low orbit. The task force was clustered around Araminta Station, dwarfing the orbital structure. The star carrier alone was nearly as bulky as the station.

Waiting our turn to dock, we eventually disembarked and found the place thronged with naval personnel. Many of them seemed fresh from boot camp—which they were.

Star Guard had undergone a transformation. Not only was the organization fully funded for the first time in a century, the service was now the beneficiary of a recruiting drive.

Some of the new sailors were veterans from Star Guard's police forces on Earth, summoned back to active duty due to their specialized skill set. A fair number of these people were experienced spacers. But most of them were raw recruits, fresh faces. They were young men and women who'd joined up out of a sense of patriotism or simply to expand their wallets.

The Guard's pay rates, all the way down to the level of those who bore a single stripe, had more than doubled. That simple fact had counterbalanced the grumbling of the oldsters about the snot-noses they were now surrounded by.

"They're not the best," Rumbold said as he walked laboriously at my side, "but at least there are a lot of them."

"They have the energy of youth," I said. "They're anxious to get out there to the stars."

"Damned fools, the lot of them," he muttered. "God bless them and keep them all."

I hadn't seen Admiral Halsey in person since we'd left Earth, and I'd had precious little contact with him during our trip to Mars. It had come as no surprise I'd been ordered to meet with him in his office upon arriving back home at Araminta Station.

After buying Rumbold lunch, during which he polished off two beers in my honor, I took my leave of him and headed to Halsey's office.

There were subtle improvements to be seen even from outside his suite. The doors were more ornate, run through with filigreed platinum and punctuated with starbursts of gleaming gold. I had to wonder if these improvements had come from his own salary or the general fund. I suspected it was the latter.

Inside, the secretary primly escorted me to yet another door and swept it open—an entirely unnecessary gesture. It was formal and courteous, however, so I bowed slightly to her before proceeding farther into the Admiral's lair.

There, in the innermost sanctum, the Admiral sat at his desk. He was in an uncharacteristically good mood and greeted me with enthusiasm.

"Sparhawk! Come in, good man. I hope all's well with you and yours."

"It is, sir," I said, stepping onto a lush royal-blue carpet. The gravity was light on the station, but I sank into the soft rug nonetheless. "May I say, you've upgraded this place quite tastefully."

"I have indeed. Finally, at long last, Earth sees the benefit of the Guard. Good to be the first in line at the budget troughs when they're full, isn't it?"

"As long as our odds of victory improve, there's no expenditure I would vote against."

Halsey paused. His grin faded somewhat.

"There's that prissy attitude of yours again, rearing its accountant's head. Don't you think we should be enjoying things a little? Don't you think seeing their admiral treated appropriately for his rank improves the morale of our spacers?"

29

"I'm sure there are incalculable benefits," I said with deliberate vagueness.

He muttered something, then stood up and came around his desk to give me a hearty handshake.

"Well, let's forget about all that. Years under the penny-pinching Guard of the past has no doubt warped your thinking. Miserly reactions are only to be expected until our people unlearn such conditioning."

Feeling by no means miserly, I felt my mouth opening to object, but then I thought the better of it and clamped my jaw shut. What was the point? It wasn't as if the admiral was going to sell his massive desk or his engravings and buy additional plasma cannons with the proceeds. Pursuing an argument at this point was counterproductive, so I merely nodded and smiled as I shook his hand in return.

"I've done a lot of thinking about our first foray into space," Halsey said, "that's why I brought you here."

"Excellent. What's the plan to retake our colonies, sir?"

He waved toward a massive window of lead-impregnated glass. Outside, the cosmos glittered with cold light.

"We're flying into the unknown very soon now, Captain. I'll be flying with *Iron Duke* at the center of the formation. She'll be my flagship."

I nodded, having gathered that much.

"First, we'll visit Gliese-32 as you did. We'll refuel there and impress them with the might of our fleet. Moving on, we'll eventually recapture the Crown system. Those poor people will be freed from the raids of the Stroj forever. After that, we'll head for the enemy strongholds and destroy them."

Far less confident than he was that such glorious things could be achieved, I nodded regardless. The brass had seen fit to risk everything on a single cast of the dice. To attack, rather than defend. Was it arrogance and hubris, or a wise stratagem? I wasn't certain.

"Will you be taking all seven battleships, sir?"

"Absolutely. There will be a large number of smaller support ships in our wake as well—many of them newly built."

"What of *Defiant*?"

He stepped to my side and put an arm up to touch my shoulder. This act surprised me, as he rarely came so close to subordinates.

Lowering his voice, he spoke to me as we gazed out the window at the ships gently floating at anchor around Araminta Station.

"I have a special role for you, Sparhawk. A critical one. Possibly, it's the most critical mission of all. You're going to stay home and guard Earth."

I felt as if I'd been punched in the gut. With all the talk of glory and flying into the face of the enemy, I'd never seen this moment coming.

Suddenly, many things fell into place. I'd been unaware of many plans. I'd been surprised by everything going on at Phobos. I'd even been kept at arm's length by personnel all over the navy.

Sure, I was a member of a Great House and accustomed to being ostracized for my political connections. Further, I'd managed to embarrass the brass at CENTCOM on multiple occasions. But in addition to those negatives, I was also the most experienced starship commander in living memory.

"Admiral," I began, "I'm not sure that would be the best utilization of my skills."

"Oh now, don't start. I knew you'd be sorely disappointed. I would be too, if I were in your shoes. One after another, we've rolled out battleships. We've even produced our first carrier in more than a century. Who wouldn't become jealous and desire to command a bigger ship?"

"That's not what I—"

"We all have our regrets, Sparhawk," he interrupted sharply. "We all secretly wish to hog the glory. But I think it's high time for you to allow older, wiser heads to take over. Don't you? Let others guide this fleet to victory over the Stroj."

"If that is your wish, sir," I said stiffly. "I will do as you command. What are my exact orders?"

"Sit here in orbit. Go on patrol if you wish, but don't leave the Solar System. If the Stroj show up, destroy them."

"By myself? With a single capital ship?"

"You've done it before. You can do it again. But don't worry. Our attack will seize the initiative. We'll terrify the Stroj and drive them back. You'll sit here and mind the store while we're away."

"It hardly seems like a critical mission."

"On the contrary! Every civilian on Earth is depending on you. Keep them safe, keep them happy, and you'll be just as big a hero by the time we return as I am."

That was it. The Admiral would hear nothing else on the topic.

-6-

Admiral Halsey paused for not more than forty hours before shipping out again. There was a great fanfare on Earth and the station as they left orbit. Seven princely battleships surrounded their queen, the star carrier. Encircling these capital ships were several dozen smaller vessels and a growing cloud of fighters.

The armada floated away into the void, stopping off at Mars to load yet more fighters before heading to the edge of the Solar System to find a breach point. From there, they would enter an ER bridge and exit the star system.

After they'd gone, I was left in a glum mood, unlike the rest of my crew. Most of them were overjoyed to learn *Defiant* was to remain parked in orbit while the fleet journeyed out into the unknown.

I could not share their happiness. I felt I was being left behind, relegated to guard duty just when Earth needed my skills most.

Durris seemed to understand my plight, but he didn't share my sentiments.

"Can't get enough of the glory, can you Captain?" he asked.

"It's not that, Durris. I feel useless here. Admiral Halsey is about to leave the system, but I think he's going to need our experience and guidance once he's gone."

33

"Maybe he will, or maybe he won't, but I guess it's not our place to say."

I nodded in agreement and finished packing a duffel bag. I'd given everyone a further extension of their shore leave, and this time I'd included my command staff. We'd placed stand-ins on *Defiant* for now. There were plenty of green spacers begging for the chance just to fly my ship in circles.

When I was finished, I headed for the station docks. I couldn't help but tap at the walls of my ship as I walked the passages. I'd truly believed we were about to fly her into the unknown once again. It was such a disappointment.

Zye met me on the station decks. She'd obviously been waiting around for me to disembark. I didn't complain as I knew she was nervous whenever we returned to Earth. Too many people here seemed to wish me harm, and as my self-appointed bodyguard, she was keenly aware of this fact.

My implant buzzed as we rode the sky-lift down the umbilical. I checked reflexively for storms or other oddities, but all seemed peaceful this time.

Zye was stoic as usual. Her staring green eyes roved over the environment, suspecting every man, woman and child present of ill intent.

Checking the identification of the caller, I knew in an instant it was Chloe of Astra. I smiled despite myself and answered quickly.

She did not materialize at my side, but rather summoned me to her location. I went with the invitation, and I appeared beside her within the Astra family mansion.

House Astra was richly appointed. There were crests, moving holo-portraits and deep carpets that gently massaged the foot. As I was only a hologram myself in her surroundings, I couldn't enjoy the sensations, but I could hear and see everything else.

Chloe was speaking with two of her house agents. I was glad to see their breed hadn't been wiped out during previous unfortunate encounters at House Astra. The agents were impressive, as always.

Fiercely loyal and bred for the job, they had the bearing of predatory beasts in human form. I knew from experience they weren't thoughtful men. They were more akin to a special breed of dog. They'd been cultivated for nearly two centuries to serve the household with zeal.

They had short dark hair, broad shoulders and expressionless mouths. Wearing midnight blue, their capes hung low and were dripping wet. I could tell they'd been out in the rain.

My ghostly form stood motionless, waiting for her to finish with her agents. Chloe turned away from them at last and stepped toward me.

"Thanks for accepting my invitation," she said.

"I wouldn't think of refusing."

Her lips fluttered as if trying to form a smile, but failed at it.

"What's the matter, Chloe?" I asked.

She licked her lips and stepped close before answering. The two men behind her stood silently. I knew that if they could have seen how close I was standing to her, they would have watched with great disapproval.

"William, did you meet with certain people on Earth—after your last mission?"

I shrugged. "I met with many people."

Her eyes darted around the room then landed back on me. "I'm not sure our words are private, but I must ask you more directly. Did you meet with certain individuals of... shall we say... unusual age?"

This last question caused me to wince slightly. I had indeed met with a grim tribe of oldsters. People who should be, by all rights, long dead. People who our history files no doubt listed as deceased—but who had somehow evaded the reaper.

"I might have," I said cautiously.

The oldsters in question had commissioned the very fleet I'd just seen off to war. They'd exhibited great power over earthly events, and I'd opted to follow their advice and keep their existence a secret.

Chloe was quite possibly the only person I knew who could cause me to talk about something I'd sworn not to. I hated breaking my word in any form, but in her case, I just had to do it.

She nodded knowingly. Her face seemed to tremble, almost as if she was about to cry.

"What's wrong, lady?" I asked. "Tell me."

She compressed her lips and regained her composure.

"Nothing," she said. "I've made a difficult decision, that's all. I'm thinking about resigning my seat at the Ministry. About stepping down as a Public Servant."

"What? Whatever for? You recently devoted your life to the task."

"Yes… but I've changed my mind."

I sensed that she was holding back, that she was concerned we were being listened to, somehow. Over the last year or so, I'd learned our implants could be used for more purposes than I'd understood. They could track a person, certainly, and they could also be hacked.

"I understand," I said. "I know it's your decision, but I would urge you to reconsider."

"I value your advice," she said, eyes downcast.

"May I ask something?"

"Certainly," she said.

"May I come visit you in person? Tonight, perhaps? It's been a long time, and if your reason for ending our previous acquaintance was related to your role as a Servant—"

She smiled weakly. "You've divined my secondary purpose for this call. I'd love to see you tonight."

"Excellent," I said, feeling a surge of well-being despite her odd behavior. The truth was, I'd never felt quite the same way around other women. I'd moved on after our breakup, and I'd assumed she had as well. But now I hoped there could be a rekindling.

"I'll take a car to your mountaintop," I said. "I should be there by nine."

"No," she said quietly. "Can I come to your residence?"

"My…" I began, disappointed. "Of course. I'll be there by eight, in that case."

There was nothing wrong with my ancestral home. We Sparhawks were quite wealthy, if not as rich as House Astra. The trouble was my parents lived there too. Unfortunately, they weren't the sort who excelled at allowing two young people the privacy I was craving right now.

"I'll see you at eight then," she said, and the channel closed.

Muttering, I crossed my arms. "I should have moved out a decade ago."

"What's that, sir?" Zye asked.

"My parents," I said heavily. "They're bound to be asking me a million irritating questions."

She looked at me quizzically. "Were you talking to someone just now? I thought I heard you muttering."

"A private matter. I'm going to have to part company tonight, Zye, if you don't mind. I'm going home."

"Oh," she said disappointedly. "I'd hoped we might share a hotel room and a drink."

There it was. She still hadn't moved past our brief relationship. I'd wondered if that was the case, and it apparently was.

"Well, my parents do have plenty of extra rooms to spare..."

"No, no," she said quickly. "I'll find my own drinking partners. Plenty of crewmen have inquired about my availability on shore leave."

It was probably true. Zye had developed something of a reputation for her appetites—both in drink and men. She also knew from experience that my parents weren't fun at a party.

After climbing into the back of a purring vehicle, I rode home in comfort. The niceties of a Sparhawk air car with a professional driver were luxurious when compared to the simple fare of the Guard.

The man driving the car spoke not a word. Even when I asked him an idle question about the weather, he seemed not to hear it.

Shrugging, I took no insult. People these days often were distracted by having conversations with individuals that weren't visible to anyone else.

On another day, I might have become annoyed with him, but not today. I was in a good mood. Chloe seemed distraught, but she was also interested in seeing me again. I was surprised how much that meant to me even now.

It was only when I saw we were outside the city and drifting down into a wooded area, that I became alarmed. I rapped on the glass between us—there was no response.

Working the controls, I tried to lower the barrier—but it wouldn't budge.

Heart pounding, I reached out with my implant, finding there was no signal, no service. I tried the latch, but it didn't work.

My PAG was in my hand by now, and we were almost on the ground. I aimed the weapon at the back of the driver's head, gave him an ultimatum, then fired a power-bolt.

To my surprise, it was deflected. It spat around the enclosed space, narrowly missing my right knee before it splashed into the velvet-covered door and filled the cab with blue-white smoke.

"Sealed in," I said, coughing.

My eyes were wide and my teeth bared when the car came to a rest. I thought I was prepared for anything when the door finally opened—but I was wrong.

Three striking individuals were standing outside the car. Their type was known to me. Feral in face and attitude, I recognized them as House agents.

They wore black, from their capes down to their gloves and boots. They each carried a PAG in one hand and a powered truncheon in the other. The electric glow around the truncheons matched the gleam in their eyes.

"Step out of the car, Sparhawk."

I lifted my PAG, pointing it at them through the glass. They lifted their weapons in turn. Their lips slid up to display their teeth.

The driver turned to face me at last. I hadn't gotten a good look at him when he'd picked me up at the station. Now, I studied him closely.

"You're one of my father's men…" I said through the intercom. "A traitor?"

"I'm a hired hand, just like the rest. Today, I resigned and took new employment. Now sir, if you would be so kind as to put aside your weapon, I'll unlock the doors."

The agents outside the car stood tensely, watching us.

Their kind was neither bright, nor thoughtful. But what they lacked in personality they made up for in tenacity, loyalty and vigilance.

I thought about various delaying tactics, but I doubted they would improve my circumstances. Since they hadn't seen fit to assassinate me thus far, I decided I might as well find out the nature of their plans.

Placing the gun on the seat beside me, I waved for the driver to proceed.

He shook his head. "The sword as well, sir."

"It's ceremonial," I protested.

He chuckled. "Not for your family, it isn't. If you would please hurry—these agents will soon lose patience."

His words were true. Two of the agents now stood at my door while the other had circled around to the far side.

"You have no honor," I told the driver flatly.

This seemed to cause him a pang. He looked down, avoiding my gaze, but he still watched as I drew my power sword from its scabbard and placed it aside.

The doors unlocked the instant I was disarmed. Both sides were wrenched open. A grasping hand snatched my PAG away. The agent's other hand grabbed for the power sword at the same moment.

I could tell the agent had no experience with this type of weapon. He'd grasped it by the blade in a gloved fist.

When I'd drawn it, I'd thumbed the blade to its lowest power-setting. It was on, but appeared dormant.

A shock of current caused the agent's gloved hand to squeeze spasmodically around the blade. The edge of my sword was a mono-filament and extremely sharp. Three of his four fingers were severed, sending up a wisp of blue smoke.

Before I could take advantage of the moment, two additional sets of hands reached in from the other side to haul me out.

My cooperative mood vanished. I'd never liked being arrested or kidnapped, and I wasn't enjoying the process now. I'd already decided to resist as best I could.

Reaching up to my neck, I activated my cloak. A personal shield sprang into existence around my body.

From inside the effect, the world appeared translucent as if observed through water. Angular planes of force surrounded my body, like moving blocks of clear ice.

Unfortunately, each of the two agents already had a hand inside my shielding. They were able to pull me from the car, snarling.

They dropped their PAGs and pulled out their powered truncheons. They knew a bolt from their guns couldn't penetrate the shield.

An uneven struggle began. They were beating on my shield ineffectually, causing showers of sparks and sounds like that of electrical discharges to fill the night air.

The driver took this moment to emerge from the car and wave to them. "He's got a button at his neck," he said. "Turn it off or tear it free."

I might have spared him if he'd stayed in the car, but in my estimation, he'd gone too far. He was beyond redemption. As the two men struggled to reach the button at my neck, I dropped to the ground and managed to grab hold of a fallen PAG.

The pistol spat fire. I landed a bolt on the driver's chest. He slumped down with a stunned look on his face.

The man with the missing fingers reentered the fray then. He'd come around from the far side of the car and taken aim. He fired his PAG at me, splattering my shield and making it turn a burnt orange. Fortunately, it held.

The two men who had me now were grasping at my wrists, cursing. I managed to line up the gun briefly with the man who was missing three fingers, but I ended up hitting one of the men who were struggling with me instead. He spun around and thrashed in a pile of dry leaves.

My luck ran out after that. The last undamaged agent got his hands to my neck. Rather than throttling me, he managed to turn off my shield by fumbling with the clasp.

Grunting with excitement and fury, he began to rain down blows with his truncheon. Shocked, numb and face down in the leaves, I soon lost consciousness.

* * *

41

I awakened what seemed a short time later. My clothes were gone, except for a light smock of gauzy white.

Inside... I thought hazily, *I'm inside now, not out in the forest...*

I tried to use my implant, to reach out and contact the Guard. There was no response, no signal at all. I'd been cut off from the rest of the world.

A figure stirred by the bed. She stood and laid a cool hand on my wrist.

The woman was elderly in the extreme and gaunt. Her face was like that of someone who had lain in a coffin for years yet still somehow managed to draw dusty breath. I almost recoiled from her touch.

"He's awake," she said. "Call the Chairman."

"You should not stand so close to him, Lady," said an agent with a husky voice. "He's dangerous. He killed two men as we were bringing him in."

Her sallow face smiled thinly. "He's a Sparhawk. You're lucky he didn't kill you all."

The agent shuffled about, uncertain and frowning. I knew he didn't want to leave her alone with me.

"Have no fear," I said to the man. "On my honor, I will not harm this woman."

She made another dismissive gesture, and at last the agent retreated.

"Call if you need us, Lady," he said.

"I won't. This one is true to his word. He's not like your kind."

Slowly, I sat up. I was aching in a dozen locations. I rubbed at my torso, and I found swellings and ridged nano-patches. More patches overlaid my scalp and my cheeks.

"They really worked you over," the woman said, watching me.

"Who are you, Lady?" I asked.

"My identity doesn't matter," she said. "I've passed on, beyond the knowledge of the young such as yourself. *You* matter, however."

"Why have I been forcibly brought here?"

42

"Tell me, do you recall standing before the Council last year?"

"Yes, I do."

"You joined your aunt and made an impassioned plea for us to intervene in events. It's been a long time since anyone has moved the Council to take drastic action."

Pulling my probing fingers away from my bruises, I took a good look at her. Unless I was fooling myself, I thought that I recognized her. She'd been present in the gallery of the shadowy council chambers. She was one of those who ruled Earth in secret.

"I remember you," I said.

"Good. It's a blessing to be remembered. I was once a famous physician, you know. That's why the Chairman sent me here to make sure you survived."

"You've done your job well. But now, I'd like to take my leave. I have an appointment."

Her hand came up, but not in a threatening manner. "Won't you please meet with the Chairman? He's very upset about this. It was all a misunderstanding."

"How so?"

She took in a breath before answering. The sound was like that of a dust broom on flagstones.

"The agents should have told you who had sent them, who you were being summoned by. They wrongly assumed you could be handled like a child."

"I acted in self-defense."

"Yes, of course. They were arrogant. Their instructions were to quietly bring you to us—not to die or abuse you in the process. The agents will be punished."

I considered asking about the nature of their punishment, but I thought the better of it. Something told me I didn't want to know the details.

"A misunderstanding," I said, "such things seem to happen often in my presence."

She shrugged her bony shoulders. "You have to understand, the agents treated you like a Guardsman, not a member of a Great House. The Guard isn't respected here."

43

"A common mistake. I intend to reeducate people on the subject one at time, if necessary."

She made a wheezing sound. After a moment, I realized it must be laughter.

"What is your name, if I may ask, Lady?"

"Dr. Peis," she said, "Ariel Peis."

"Thank you for telling me. It seems to be a big deal to your group to be identified."

She stared at me for a moment. "You've never heard of me, have you?" she asked. There was a wistful tone in her voice. "Outside of this place?"

I frowned and thought about it. "No," I admitted, shaking my head. "I don't think I have."

She nodded and looked away. "It's only to be expected. My achievements were forgotten long ago."

She left me then, and I stood and stretched painfully. I found my clothes and put them on. None of my weapons or my personal shielding device was to be found. That didn't surprise me.

Dr. Peis did leave me with lingering doubts, however. She'd thought I might know of her—of the achievements from her youth. Was she really someone famous? I had no clue. It must be painful to live so long you're forgotten by the public.

When I tried the door, I found it was locked. The doctor had allowed it to snick shut behind her.

I considered yelling and banging, but I thought it would do little good and might even prejudice my captors against me.

At last, another visitor came to see me. No less than six agents with feral faces accompanied him. They watched me the way guard dogs watched visitors they were unfamiliar with.

The visitor was the Chairman. He beckoned for me to follow him.

I exited the cell gratefully. I found the passageway outside to be just as gloomy, however. Shadows seemed to hang everywhere as if two thirds of the lighting had been switched off.

"You might recall that we like it dark down here," he said. "It's due to our longevity. Our eyes and minds can't take the daylight easily anymore. We started extreme biochemical processes so long ago... they've had certain dire effects."

"Yes, my aunt told me about them. Speaking of her... have you seen Lady Grantholm lately?"

He glanced at me with black, calculating eyes. I was deliberately name-dropping to raise my status in this place. We both knew it, but he didn't seem impressed. At least he didn't take offense.

"Yes, of course. She comes here now and again to ask for favors and make reports. William, we must talk seriously."

"Excellent. First, I'd like to discuss your role in today's criminal activity."

He stopped walking and stared up at me. "Are you serious?"

"I'm a Guardsman, sir. I'm always serious when a crime is involved."

He laughed and started walking again. He shook his head. "Your aunt said you were a firebrand. An unbending force of upright duty."

"Be that as it may, your agents illegally detained and abused a uniformed starship captain."

"The results were regrettable for everyone. You must understand that I wanted to talk to you urgently."

"Then why didn't you simply contact me and tell me I should meet with you?"

"That isn't how we operate, Sparhawk. Officially, we don't exist."

I thought about his explanation, and I found that nothing about it pleased me.

"This entire situation is unacceptable. In the future, please send a courier or something. I would have happily come here to talk to you."

"That's what I did!" he protested. "Yes, I agree, they were heavy-handed, but you were as well."

"They didn't identify themselves. How was I to know that you were behind it? Many assassins have attempted such moves in the past."

"Hmm," he said. "I may have miscalculated in that regard. Very well, in the future when my agents come to summon you

45

into my presence, we'll make sure that you are more clearly informed."

Despite my best efforts, I was close to becoming irate. This sort of behavior wasn't an isolated occurrence. Members of the Great Houses treated government officials with similar disdain. They believed they were above the law, and the annoying part was how often they were correct in that assumption. Their behavior was never punished as it should be.

"You said it was regrettable," I pressed, "but you didn't apologize. A man in my employ and another in yours are dead over this, and a third man was maimed."

He generated a dismissive snort. "Don't worry so much about trifling details. You have to keep your eyes on the big picture. Don't you even want to know why I summoned you?"

"Please tell me," I said tightly.

"We ordered Halsey to leave you behind. We wanted you here, in defense of Earth. He argued against it, but the Council thought it was for the best. Does that make you feel any better?"

My eyes narrowed as I took in this information. "I guess it is flattering… in a way. Why would you request something so specific?"

"Because we trust you—more than we trust Halsey or that odd duck Vogel, certainly."

I could well understand that, but I had trouble putting the rest of their motivations together.

"You wanted me and my ship to remain here, standing guard over Earth?"

"Exactly. What if another ship shows up from the Stroj? We're building another task force, naturally, but it might not be finished before they appear."

Nodding, I was beginning to see. "This trust is due to the fact that I was critical in stopping their previous assaults."

"Yes," he said. "Star Guard is as full of cobwebs as my Council. They aren't used to thinking on their feet, to taking difficult, drastic action. If it were left to them, this planet might well be slag by now. You're not like the rest of them. You take action reflexively."

"I thank you for your confidence, sir."

"You're welcome. But as to why you're here... the Council wasn't unanimous. Before Halsey's fleet is allowed to leave the Solar System, they voted to bring you here to undergo a thorough examination. The examination had to be a surprise."

"What kind of examination? For what purpose?"

"To see if you were a Stroj or not, of course. Dr. Peis, who you've already met, performed the medical analysis personally. You'll be glad to hear she's cleared you as one hundred percent human."

"That's gratifying," I said with barely concealed sarcasm.

As we spoke, we'd reached the end of a very long, dim-lit passageway. The only route forward was a broad, curving stairway of cut stone. He began climbing these steps, and I walked beside him.

Looking up, there seemed to be no end to the winding stair. The Chairman was old beyond measure, but his legs carried him upward with a steady, plodding pace.

Behind us, as silent as ghosts, a team of agents followed. They never seemed to take their suspicious eyes off me.

"Chairman," I said as we climbed, "I'm still not clear on how this group is exerting your will over our government. As best as I can understand it, you're a private citizen of Earth. Correct?"

He shrugged and looked bemused. "Technically, yes. I suppose that's true."

"You might be the leader of this private entity, this Council of yours, but there's a government in charge of our planet, an official body of Public Servants."

"Ah!" he said. "Now I understand. You're laboring under a number of misconceptions—that's through no fault of your own, Sparhawk. I don't blame you for this rude display. You simply don't understand the nature of your role in our society."

I blinked in confusion. "Would you care to enlighten me then, sir?"

He appeared to think about it.

"All right," he said at last. "But let me warn you, this level of knowledge comes with grave risks."

"Are you threatening a naval Captain of Star Guard?"

47

He nodded slowly. "Yes, I do believe that I am. You'd do well to listen to that warning and take it very seriously. We wouldn't want our best starship captain to be deleted as an unperson. That wouldn't do at all."

"An unperson?" I asked, baffled by the term. "I've never heard of such a thing."

The oldster leered at me with an odd mixture of amusement and triumph.

"*Exactly*, you young fool! An unperson is precisely that—an individual that has been erased from the consciousness of our world."

"Are you suggesting a death sentence?"

"Death? No, no. I'm talking about something far more drastic. Death is a much less devastating penalty. Insignificant for the worst offenders."

"I don't understand."

The Chairman nodded and worked his mouth for a moment in thought.

"Let me put it this way," he said, sidling another pace closer.

I resisted an urge to back away. The man was menacing in a manner that belied his size and age. Fortunately, he didn't seem to notice my aversion.

"The words of a dead man," he said carefully, "are often remembered. Perhaps they are remembered even more clearly than his words were recalled while he lived. Worse, a dead man's relatives and followers are bound to simmer with resentment."

Thinking that over, I could understand what he was saying in theory.

"Death penalties are tools, certainly," he continued, as if giving a lecture on the topic. "For some individuals, people who have been deemed mundane irritants by society, it's a suitable punishment. But I'm talking about a criminal so dangerous, so disruptive, that they must be removed entirely. In such a case, death is insufficient and even archaic."

"But what else is there?" I asked.

"We have another tool to be used under such extreme circumstances. We can transform a citizen into an *unperson*—a deleted individual who's been eradicated from existence. Such an entity was once human, of course, but they no longer reside in the minds of the population at large."

I wasn't entirely following the elderly man, but what I was getting from his words sent a cold worm of concern through my guts.

Could it be that the Council actually had the power to remove a man from existence? How could such an act be accomplished?

Almost unconsciously, I reached back to the base of my neck. My fingers probed the fleshy bulb of the implant that protruded there.

Those who guided Earth's net traffic had the means to project realities into our minds, I knew that much. At one point last year, the Stroj had even hacked into my implant and used it to lure me into a trap.

We Earthers used our implants as powerful tools. We could communicate at will with anyone on the net. We could do more than talk to others—we could *experience* them.

A person who wished to speak with me could appear at my side, detectable only by my senses. When they did so, they seemed as real as the furniture they sat upon. Earthers were accustomed to this technology, and we took it for granted.

But what if there was another, darker side to it all? What if our minds could be *edited*, as well as presented with fresh input?

I blinked and considered these thoughts. All the while, the oldster at my side watched my face with narrowed eyes and a knowing, thin-lipped smile.

"Yes..." he said. "You *are* the clever one. You're beginning to grasp what I'm talking about. A man in your position would do well to understand the true way of things. But that's not to say you should become an evangelist for new-think. There's no call for that! Secrets are secrets for good reasons. These thoughts you're having now—they must stay within your skull. Do you understand me, Captain Sparhawk?"

"I believe that I do, sir," I said quietly.

The Chairman nodded, satisfied. He brushed the back of my hand with his cold, leathery fingers.

49

"Good... excellent! I knew you were of the best stock. Nothing radical about you! Our hopes have become dependent upon the rise of gentlemen of fiber such as yourself, you understand. We're too frail to return to the stars ourselves."

"Just so, sir," I murmured, watching him as one might watch a venomous snake.

"Now, young William, you may take your leave. Fly your captured ship! Take the role of Earth's guardian while Halsey shepherds the bulk of our new fleet. Nothing less than the fate of the home world rests upon the shoulders of officers like you. And remember, as far as the Council goes, mum is the word. We don't exist. You were never here."

I nodded stiffly, and he left me then. The House guardians who'd been following us like ghosts guided me out of the echoing mansion.

Recalling the coldness of the Chairman's touch and the thoughts he'd left lingering in my mind, I was uncomfortable all the way back to House Sparhawk.

An *unperson*. The term kept rattling about in my head. Had I known any of them? Had I forgotten certain individuals, at one moment or another, who'd risen up to denounce the powers that ran Earth?

I could not recall such a person—but that proved nothing. It didn't mean they'd never existed. Quite possibly, at some point in my lifetime, the Council had gathered and declared a noisy malcontent to be unacceptable. As a result, I couldn't recall anything about them to this day.

Such power! To be able to remove an individual from the minds of everyone on my green Earth... the mere concept was unsettling.

Naturally, I couldn't *know* that this had happened, but I strongly suspected that it had. Why else could Earth's recent past be so dull? In our texts, we'd learned of revolutions and rebellions throughout history. But to my knowledge there'd been no such upheavals for more than a century—not since the days immediately following the Cataclysm.

The impenetrable secrecy of this shadow-council seemed to be proof of their power over the minds of others. How else had

50

they hidden themselves all this time? How had they been forgotten and yet continued to rule?

They clearly ran Earth, but that fact was shrouded from the public. The only way conceivable that such a massive deception could be perpetrated was a tool like the one the Chairman spoke of—a wholesale editing of public knowledge.

Had someone discovered the Council in the past and attempted to reveal them? It seemed highly likely given the number of years and individuals involved.

And yet, up until the point Aunt Grantholm had introduced me, I'd never heard of the Council. The only conclusion was that such people had become "unpersons" for their actions.

The worst part was in *knowing* I'd probably forgotten about such souls. It left me with a feeling of loss and violation.

I doubted I'd ever recapture my lost memories. If at any point an unperson had left an impression upon me, that impression had been forever erased from my mind. It was indeed as if such a person, such a rebel from the past, had never existed at all.

The more I turned these disturbing ideas over in my mind, the more alarmed I became with the concept of an "unperson."

These chilling thoughts would not leave my mind, as much as I wanted them to.

-8-

When I arrived at last at House Sparhawk, it was early morning. I was greeted enthusiastically. Sparhawk Agents were everywhere dressed in forest green. They nodded and gave me wintery smiles before their eyes went back to roving over the landscape, looking for threats.

A woman named Jillian was their leader. Unlike many Great Houses and the Council, we Sparhawks didn't employ specially bred agents. Our people were trained, rather than designed, for their jobs.

"Glad to see you made it home, sir," Jillian said. "We found your air car in the forest—the driver was dead."

"Yes," I said, "I was detained."

"Can you tell me why you were held?" she asked with honest concern.

I thought about that. The Chairman must have known I'd face questioning of this sort. It took me a moment to edit my story in my mind. I was accustomed to telling the truth, but in this instance I'd have to leave out some portions.

"We landed in a forest against my orders. I found myself locked in the back seat and unable to escape."

Jillian looked astonished and upset. "What of the driver?"

"I killed him myself. He was in on it."

"I'm so sorry, sir!"

"So am I. You must scan those in your employ. Remove any suspected of disloyalty."

She nodded and compressed her lips tightly. "I will, sir. Again, you have my apologies. I see bruises... are you injured?"

"I reached another house and was cared for. I'm fine. Now, if you might be so kind as to step aside..."

"One more thing, here are your personal items. They were left at the scene."

She handed me my cloak, my sword and my sidearm. I took them gratefully and put them on. I felt better once I was armed again.

Jillian clearly wished to ask me more questions, but I wasn't in the mood. I strode to the front doors, and they swung open inwardly before me. Jillian followed.

"Have you seen Chloe of Astra?" I asked her. I asked this casually, as I wasn't certain if she was in on this kidnapping affair or not.

"She arrived last night saying she was here to meet you. She waited the night."

"Ah, excellent. I'll have to apologize for missing our appointment."

"Uh, sir—you have another visitor."

I swung around, pivoting on the heel of my boot.

"Who?"

"Lieutenant Zye of Star Guard. She heard about your disappearance and—well, we couldn't say no to her."

"I'm not surprised. Thank you, Jillian."

Dismissed, but clearly agitated, I left her at the entrance. It was her job to make sure I was protected while on Earth, and I could tell she wasn't happy about failing at that task. Still, I thought it better to move on and not get near the details of my visit with the Chairman. The risks were too great.

My parents were glad to see me and made an effort to be welcoming. They interviewed me with worried glances tossed to one another. Interestingly, neither of them asked much about where I'd been during the night which made me wonder if they knew about the Council.

How could they not? My father had been a Public Servant for six decades. My mother had been at his side during a hundred political campaigns. All of us danced around the details, and I thought that was probably for the best.

"Such an ordeal…" my mother said at last. "Perhaps you should retire immediately to your quarters."

"I thought you were heading to Asia…?" I said questioningly.

"We heard of your disappearance and returned."

"Of course," I said, wondering how things had really gone. "What of Lady Astra? Is she here waiting for me or not?"

They traded glances again. Their eye-contact was very brief but very telling. They'd been together for so long, it was almost as if they had a single mind when they were busy manipulating events.

"She's here," my father admitted. "But we were under the impression that you two had broken off your affair."

There it was, out in the open. I looked from one of them to the other, aghast.

"You haven't told her of my arrival, have you? Were you hoping I'd come home so fatigued I'd flop into bed and forget she existed?"

"Let's not be dramatic, William, please," my mother said.

Standing and walking away from the plush settee I'd been sitting on, I exited the room. I wasn't in a good mood. I'd been abused by the agents of people who shouldn't exist, and I wasn't interested in entertaining my parents' incessant scheming.

Ignoring their calls behind me, I strode up the stairs. I headed directly to the guest quarters, automatically selecting the suites reserved for the most important persons.

After tapping on the door, I tried the handle and found it unlocked.

Stepping inside, I called for Chloe.

"Lady Astra, are you here?"

I heard a splashing sound from the bathroom. The door stood ajar. She came out, dripping wet, holding a towel to herself. It covered only the essentials.

Both of us eyed one another in surprise. I knew I shouldn't be looking at her lovely skin, but I couldn't help myself.

"William! I had no idea you were home."

"I'm sorry," I said, "I would have called, but my implant isn't functioning. I'll wait outside until you're dressed."

"Nonsense. Come in, come in."

Awkwardly, I found a chair and perched on it while she vanished into the bathroom and dried herself off.

During this time, the door to the suite cracked open, and Jillian poked her head inside. I waved her off crossly and closed the door again. She tapped at it, but I locked it in response. After a time, she went away.

She'd probably been sent up here by my parents bearing some message designed to distract me. I wasn't interested. Jillian had had her chance to affect today's events, and as far as I was concerned, she'd failed to do so.

When Chloe came out at last, she was informally dressed but undeniably lovely to behold. Her hair was tied back and unadorned, but I barely noticed. Her gown caught the light, as it had no doubt been designed to do, reflecting the chandeliers with a sparkling effect. I was unable to tell if the gown was enhanced with optical effects or made of spun gossamer. Either way, I found it enchanting.

She smiled at my admiring gaze.

"Do you like it?" she asked. "It's a new style from the orbitals."

"I love it. Would you like to go out with me?"

She paused and blinked. "Now?"

"Yes. Immediately. I find this environment oppressive."

She cocked her head to one side and looked mischievous. "You're doing this to distract me. You don't want to tell me where you've been. It won't work. I want to know everything."

Hmm, I thought to myself. It was going to be difficult to avoid any kind of explanation for my absence. I suspected my parents knew what was happening—but I was just as sure that Lady Astra didn't.

"That wasn't my intent," I said honestly. "I'm annoyed with my parents, and I'd rather leave the House."

"In that case, you can take me out to dinner tonight," she said. "But first, you must tell me who you spent the night with. Was she pretty?"

"Not in the slightest," I said, thinking of the ghastly Dr. Peis. "It wasn't like that, Chloe. Really."

She looked baffled now. She shook her head. "So all this talk of being waylaid by rogues from a rival House is true? I had no idea. I'm so sorry! Do you know who they were? Is there a feud brewing?"

I thought about the Chairman and the other Council members. I doubted they came from any particular House. They were a collective of people who'd passed on from the public eye. I had no doubt they were somehow related to all of us—but they no longer circulated among even my elite slice of society.

"I wouldn't want a feud with them," I said truthfully.

She came close then, and she ran her hand over my cheek. She looked concerned. She discovered my swollen flesh, which had been masked by sprays and treatments, but some of the injuries were still visible under scrutiny.

"You've been injured!" she said in surprise and outrage. "This is about your position in the Guard, isn't it? Sometimes I hate my own peers."

"Sometimes I do as well. I can't talk about it. Please understand."

She nodded slowly. "I do, unfortunately. Politics… It ruins everything. We have so much wealth and power, but we still mistreat one another."

I noticed then that her hand had stayed in contact with my face. Her nearness was intoxicating. I moved on her then, without thought or plan. In truth, I'd never fallen out of love with Chloe of Astra.

She allowed me to kiss her lightly, but after melting for a few moments, she suddenly stiffened, and I felt her small hands pressing me back.

I retreated a half-pace. My breathing was accelerated.

"I know you to be a man of your word," she said. "I trust that in you. Tell me one last time, did you spend the night with some painted girl from the city?"

"I most certainly didn't," I said with a decisive tone. "I've enjoyed nothing about my return to Earth thus far."

56

She eyed me critically for a few seconds, then nodded and pressed herself against me.

"I believe you," she said, "and I'm going to change your luck right now."

Events proceeded rapidly. I found she was wearing nothing beneath that flashy gown, which made me think she'd suspected how our meeting might conclude.

We made love gently at first, then with urgency. At last, I found I was glad to be back on Earth.

Some hours later, when we tried to sneak out, we were waylaid by my mother.

"William," she called. "Lady Astra!"

We paused, and her smile bathed us in false warmth. "Are you two trying to escape so soon?"

"Not at all," I said. "We were merely stepping out to the city. I'm sure you understand, mother."

Her eyes slid back and forth between the two of us, gathering information like two searchlights.

Chloe looked slightly embarrassed. We were holding hands, and my mother's gaze lingered on our intertwined fingers.

"I see," she said. "No one is interested in our Chef's finest? We're having—"

"No, mother," I said firmly. "We want to go out. I've only just returned."

"I understand," she said with a sigh. "Home is always boring to the young. All right then, I won't trouble you further."

"I'm so sorry, Lady Sparhawk," Chloe gushed. She clearly wasn't used to being in the role of a girl dragging a son away from his mother.

"Don't be, Chloe. I was just like you eighty years ago. Enjoy yourselves—I'm sure you will."

I glanced at her sharply as she spoke these last words. They seemed to be delivered in a sarcastic tone. She had to be aware I'd spent hours in Chloe's quarters alone with her. Perhaps she was annoyed at the fact.

Deciding not to take the bait, I forced a smile and pressed on. Chloe's hand was still in mine, so she was swept along after me.

At the door to the carport on the roof, my father sat in his hover-chair. I swallowed, knowing that brushing by him might be even harder.

"Hello father," I said, "good of you to see us off."

His eyes were calculating and concerned. "May I have a private word before you go, son?" he asked.

That last caught me by surprise and stopped me in my tracks. He rarely referred to me directly as his son. He'd never been completely happy with my career choices. Among the rich and powerful of Earth, military officers had long been considered of low rank.

"I'll wait in the car for you," Chloe said, hurrying out into the afternoon sunshine.

I watched her go wistfully, and I saw that she was escorted into the back of our finest vehicle. My parents rode in it personally when they attended state affairs.

"What's the problem, father?" I asked.

He beckoned for me to lean close. I glanced around, not seeing an agent within easy earshot, but I crouched beside his hover-chair and leaned close.

"I know where you've been," he said in a low voice. "I know who you've spoken to."

Not knowing how to respond, I said nothing.

He nodded. "Yes, I see in your eyes you understand your peril. Listen to me, William of Sparhawk. You're my only offspring, and I don't want to create a new one at my age."

He reached out a hand and squeezed mine. "I don't want to forget a son. Not again."

My mouth fell open, then I closed it again.

"That won't happen, sir," I said.

"Good. See that it doesn't. Be careful about Lady Astra as well. She's a politician now, remember?"

I left him in his chair without responding. I didn't know what to say. Could he be right? Could Chloe be renewing our love affair for political reasons? The thought was disheartening to say the least.

But far more disturbing than that were his hints concerning the past. Had he once conceived an heir and lost him? Had such an individual been erased from public memory?

My parents were both about a century old while I was only thirty. It was unusual for people to wait so long to have a child, but it wasn't unknown. Curiously enough, I'd never considered that there might have been another...

To think that I might have had a sibling... Had there been such a person? A person wholly unknown to me who'd been expunged years ago, probably before I was born? It was difficult to get my mind wrapped around the concept.

Many things did fit, the more I considered the possibility. My father had been so stern, so driven to see that I followed in his footsteps with lockstep motions. Had all that been due to his regrets concerning a past failure?

Climbing into the back of the air car, I was pleased to see Chloe's shining eyes. She seemed not to notice my distraction and proceeded to speak animatedly about an itinerary of shops, cafes and shows she wanted to visit with me. I acquiesced to them all, barely hearing any of it.

Our top House agent, Jillian herself, piloted the air car. This made me smile briefly. She wasn't about to let anything happen to me again tonight.

While Chloe showed me flashing images from her computer scroll and discussed each possible entertainment in detail, I found my eyes wandering out the window.

I saw the city laid out beneath us, like a carpet of glowing, moving lights.

My mind was churning. I'd learned so much over the last twenty-four hours about my world and how it really operated.

Deciding to seize the moment and enjoy it for what it was I turned back to Chloe, who was staring at me.

"You look like you've seen a ghost, William," she said.

"I'm just glad to be home."

She beamed then. "You see? I managed to change your moping attitude!"

We laughed together, and we kissed. It was good to have Chloe back no matter what the future might hold for us.

"What about your resignation from public service?" I asked her in a quiet moment. We'd both been avoiding the topic.

"I… it would make it easier to spend more time with you," she said.

"Now, that I believe. Have you made a decision?"

She licked her lips and avoided my eyes. "No, nothing final yet."

"Okay then," I said, not wanting to press her harder. I could tell she was holding something back, but I figured she would tell me about it when she felt the time was right.

-9-

After a few days of blissful reunion, Chloe and I had to part ways again. We weren't a couple, not like before, but we'd certainly enjoyed one another's company. We'd never again brought up her possible resignation from public service, but I felt her backing away from the idea.

By the end of my visit, she left to return to her duties. Satisfied with this, I didn't say a thing.

For me, the whole vacation together provided a sense of closure. After our breakup a year or so ago, she'd remained in the back of my mind. Both of us had had a number of affairs, but we'd still felt something for one another that we'd never found with anyone else.

"Well, this is my last day of leave," I said. "I need to return to *Defiant* by tonight. I'll miss you."

"I'm so glad you're assigned to defend Earth now," she told me at breakfast. "We can see each other more often—can't we?"

"That's indeed possible, but you should keep in mind that it's also possible I'll be sent to the stars at any moment. That's the life of a Guardsman."

She glanced at me in surprise. Looking back down, she played with her coffee cup.

"But... your parents told me this assignment would be permanent. They were quite adamant about it."

I froze. In that moment, a number of inconsistencies knit together in my mind. Why would someone as important as the Chairman insist a particular captain be kept close to Earth to guard her while all the rest flew to the stars?

Because of politics, that's why. My parents had already demonstrated they were aware of the Chairman and the Council. They weren't without their own influence. Perhaps, as a favor from a loyal patron, they'd requested that I be shackled here.

"...like a dog on a leash..." I muttered.

"What's that, William?"

"Nothing, love. I was merely regretting that I must depart."

"So soon? I thought you had until this evening to report—"

"A captain's duties never cease."

Reluctantly, she let me go. We embraced warmly and parted ways. I paid the hotel bill, despite her complaints. It was true she was a dozen times richer than I was, but as a starship captain whose pay had recently been doubled, I wasn't without resources.

I also possessed an access chip to my family accounts. After a moment's hesitation, I used it to pay the bill. If my parents or their accountants wanted to complain, I would counter with a list of my own complaints.

Angry, I took public transport back to my parents' estate. I didn't want them to know I was coming.

But along the way, I lost heart and redirected the pilot to the spaceport. After all, what was I going to say to them? Would I demand they stop meddling in my affairs? I knew they wouldn't. Should I suggest they get over the idea of trying to protect me? That too, would be fruitless.

The office of a Public Servant was a lifetime appointment, and since I was my father's seventy-percent clone, I'd already been elected according to current law.

That particular law had always troubled me somewhat. It seemed unfair. A lifetime appointment, I could grasp that. But the idea that such an important office should become *permanent*, passing down from parent to clone...

It occurred to me as I rode the sky-lift up to Araminta Station that others must have complained about the injustice of that law in the past. How could they not have? But even so, I couldn't recall a serious public debate on the issue during my lifetime.

A cold chill ran through me. Could the Chairman and his Council of oldsters truly wield that much power? Could they edit what people knew to be their history? Had people protested in the past and been expunged?

By the time I reached *Defiant*, I was thinking about just how such a thing might be accomplished. Where might the equipment reside, and who operated it? The location must be a deep secret. Whoever had control of such a device effectively controlled Earth.

"Captain?" Yamada greeted me as I stepped onto the command deck. "I got an alert that said you were coming up the sky lift, but I disregarded it. We weren't expecting you until this evening."

"Just as you keep tabs on me, I like to keep an eye on all of you," I said, giving her a smile. "Is Zye back yet?"

"No. Haven't you checked her location with your implant?"

The truth was I'd made a point of not using it. Implants traced the wearer with every use. After being kidnapped and beaten, I was reluctant to make things easier for any possible future assailants.

"I haven't been using it," I admitted.

She gave me an odd look then assumed my unit must be operating incorrectly. "Well, report to me later in the labs. We'll have it serviced in the science module."

"All right," I said. "What about Zye then? No word?"

"None, sir. Should I alert her and call her back to duty?"

"No need. She'll be here tonight, I'm sure."

Despite my easy-going attitude, before I left the deck I saw Yamada tapping at her screen and whispering to unseen people. Doubtlessly, she was warning my staff of my early return.

I paused and looked at her thoughtfully. "Yamada, how are your hacking skills?"

"They're better than Zye's—but don't tell her that."

"She wouldn't believe me if I did. Hmm, maybe you can help me with something. Can you accompany me to the science module right now?"

She called an ensign to sit at her post, and we left the deck together. We reached the labs, and when I told her what I wanted, she was surprised.

"I guess it's possible," she said. "But why would you want to shield your implant?"

"I'm afraid I'm too easy to track," I said. I told her then about the abduction on Earth and the misdirection of my air car into a secluded forest.

She was stunned. I'd left all the details out, naturally, concerning who the actual perpetrators were. She spent a few fruitless minutes trying to pry these elements from me, but she soon gave up.

"You always lead an interesting life," she said. "I'm glad I'm not a member of a Great House. The wealth doesn't seem worth it if you have to look over your shoulder all the time."

"Well said. Do you think you can do it? Hack it, I mean? Without making the alteration obvious or setting off any tampering alarms?"

She thought about it for a moment.

"Normally, I'd use my implant right now to search for a how-to on the process," she admitted. "But that would leave a fingerprint I don't want on my record. I'm going to have to invent this hack all on my own. Can you give me a few days?"

I smiled. "You're officially assigned to weapons research until further notice. I'll inform your replacement crewmembers you're off the duty roster."

She thought that over then smiled. "Good. I can use a few days off my station. I'll let you know if I think I've got something. In the meantime, weren't you here to get your implant operating again?"

I considered her suggestion and passed on it. "Not today. Let's see what you come up with first."

"That bad, huh?"

"You don't want to know, trust me."

Walking out, I knew she was staring after me, but I didn't look back. I couldn't afford to involve Yamada deeper in this matter than I already had. It would be unforgivable if, as her friend and commander, I endangered her without letting her know what she was getting into. I couldn't do that.

In the morning, I asked if everyone had made it aboard. Yamada assured me that they had. My crew had gathered aboard and settled back into their duties. The rotation of essential people on and off the ship had ended. We were officially on patrol.

On the command deck, most of the primary crewmembers were there except for Yamada and Zye. I knew Yamada was working on my hack, and I figured Zye must be off-shift. Shrugging, we took the ship out of orbit and began our patrol.

We proceeded to perform a series of sweeps of the inner planets. Our orders were to stay within a twenty-four hour flight of Earth which limited how far we could go. The asteroid belt was beyond our reach, as was Mars when she was on the far side of the Sun.

The next day I was becoming as bored as my crew appeared to be. Yamada herself contacted me using the ship's intercom system in the early morning hours. It seemed as if the walls were talking to me.

She sounded breathless, and I climbed out of bed before she'd done more than identify herself. My first thought was that she'd discovered a hack—or worse, someone else had discovered her actions and reported them.

"You really have to get your implant working again, sir," she said. "I had to have the ship track you down using your bio-rhythm signature."

"It can do that? Never mind... what's the problem?"

"A single ship sir—it just appeared out beyond Neptune. Obviously, it came through a breach out of hyperspace, and—"

"What kind of ship?" I demanded, fighting with my jacket. I shook the auto-buckles so they cinched up on their own and ran my fingers through my hair.

In my private bathroom mirror, I saw the display splashed in all four corners. It was a ship all right—a battleship. "It looks like one of ours."

"It is, sir. It's *Victory*, and she's sustained heavy damage."

"Where's the rest of the fleet?" I demanded of Yamada's disembodied voice.

"I don't know, sir."

"Where's Admiral Halsey and that carrier of his?"

65

"Unknown."

Her voice continued ringing from the walls of my quarters, but I'd already left and begun hurrying up the central passageway to the command deck. I had a very bad feeling about this.

One ship crawling home damaged? Could the unthinkable have occurred? Could Earth be in jeopardy?

-10-

Commander Durris was my XO, but when I was personally on the command deck he functioned as our chief navigator. He performed both tasks equally well.

To prove the point, he'd already worked out a flight path to intercept the ship should it become necessary.

"Take us out just past the Moon, Rumbold," I said, talking to my pilot who'd slid his large rear end into the chair in front of me. "Keep us close to Commander Durris' recommended flight path."

"What's our final destination, sir?" the helmsman asked.

"Just get us moving," I said.

Rumbold shrugged, and I felt the powerful ship surge under my feet.

"Captain," Durris said, "If we head for Luna at half-power, we can use the gravity-well to slingshot us in the direction of *Victory*—if they give us clearance to do so."

I nodded and asked Yamada to open a channel to Star Guard.

My heart racing, I checked with the ops team on Earth. They were as in the dark as we were. What little intel they had was relayed to me, and we played it on our screens and holotables.

It didn't take long before the duty officer in charge came online to talk to us. He was an elderly looking gentleman, Vice Admiral Perez. He was skinny and red-faced. The years hadn't been as kind to him as they'd been to others, but due to heavy use of Rejuv, he appeared to be energetic enough.

"Where do you think you're going, Sparhawk?" he demanded in a slightly high-pitched tone.

"I'm leaving close orbit in case *Defiant* needs to take action."

"No one here on the ground gave you permission to do so."

"Excuse me, Admiral," I said. "My orders permit me latitude when facing a possible threat."

"Yes, but they don't allow you to abandon your post! Earth needs you, man. There's no other vessel of size in the system."

I wanted to point out that the situation wasn't of my making, but I didn't see how it would help to do so.

"What are your orders, Admiral?" I asked.

"That's better. Get out to Luna and circle that rock until we know if *Victory* has been compromised or not."

"But that's what I… Yes sir. We'll be in touch."

Yamada closed the connection, and I cursed under my breath.

"Is Perez really in charge down there?" Rumbold asked in a marveling tone. "Lord help us, he was a dotard when I was swabbing decks."

"Seniority isn't always the best way to make promotional decisions," I agreed. "But old habits die hard."

"Huh!" Rumbold complained. "We'll all die hard if CENTCOM doesn't step it up. Too many oldsters are still in charge. They need to let some younger people take key posts— and I'm saying this as a man who's served a century and a half in the Guard!"

Rumbold was always prone to exaggeration, but I knew for a fact he *had* served for a hundred and thirty long years. It was in his service record. Without continued service, he wouldn't have had the personal wealth to continue his longevity treatments—which meant compulsory retirements were akin to death sentences.

It was just the sort of situation we were faced with on a daily basis in the Guard. We'd been called upon to defend Earth, but our world had become so bureaucratic and tied up in

68

political concerns it was difficult to cut through it all and do our jobs.

"Yamada, where *is* Zye?"

She looked at me worriedly. "I sent you a report—but your implant is out, isn't it? She never made it back aboard, sir. In fact, I've been unable to locate her."

That concerned me. There were very few reasons Zye would fail to keep her commitments—an untimely death being high on that list.

"Alert CENTCOM. It could be related to this situation somehow."

"You don't think Stroj agents are coming out of the woodwork again, do you sir?" Rumbold asked. He spun his chair around and his eyes bulged at me.

"I'm not making any predictions," I told him. "Durris? How long until we reach orbit over Luna?"

"About twenty minutes more."

"All right, let's start a full equipment check."

"Weapons check?" Durris asked.

"Yes. Let's start there."

Defiant wasn't an Earth ship. She'd been built by Betas, a group of colonists who'd long been estranged from the home world. They were all like Zye—at least the smarter ones among them were.

Unimaginative people, but practical and determined, they'd over-built every aspect of this vessel. If something needed a rivet, they made it a rivet as thick as a man's thumb and probably applied ten of them where one would have sufficed.

That heavy design had been carried through to her engines, fortunately, or the ship would have wallowed in space. As it was, she was heavy, but her engines were well up to the task of pushing her around with terrific force. *Defiant* was the most heavily armored and fastest ship in our service. Only Halsey's battleships could rival her when it came to taking a punch, but they couldn't rival her acceleration.

We waited tensely, orbiting Luna over the next half hour before Admiral Perez saw fit to contact us again.

"Stand down, *Defiant*," he said. "That battleship isn't dangerous—not to anyone, apparently."

"Who's in command of her?"

"Admiral Halsey himself. He's lost his carrier it seems."

That last bit of information made me feel ill. "Can I speak with him directly, sir?"

"I don't see why not. Maybe it's a good thing for a man to feel shame in a situation like this."

The channel closed, and I was left in an uncertain state. It wasn't like Perez to suggest another admiral—especially his superior officer—needed any form of shaming.

It could only mean one thing. We'd lost our fleet, and Halsey was limping home with the last vessel in his once-great armada.

After dithering for several minutes, I moved to my private office and opened a channel to Halsey's ship. He didn't answer right away, partly due to distance involved.

After waiting for several minutes, the screen that was my desktop suddenly brightened.

"Is that you, Sparhawk?" he asked. "Why aren't you using your implant?"

"It's disabled sir," I said, not mentioning that I'd done the disabling myself. "I have to use traditionally transmitted video."

"Well, get that fixed," he complained.

He looked the worse for wear, as my elderly Aunt Grantholm might have said. His uniform was dirty and frayed, his hair was unkempt, and his eyes wandered around the scene of my office as he spoke.

"Are we alone? Can anyone else hear this?"

"No sir," I said. "They can't."

He leaned forward with sudden earnest intent. "Sparhawk, listen to me, the variants took my ship from me. They took my command. You have to warn Earth that *Iron Duke* is still out there—"

Then he made an odd sound. Blood exploded from his neck and showered the vid pickup.

Astounded, I half-rose from my seat. I watched helplessly as the transmitted feed continued. Blood had formed a thick film on the lenses, but it slid away revealing a horrid scene.

Halsey was gargling and wrestling weakly with pinchers that held him upright.

"Speak as you were commanded to do," said an odd voice. It didn't sound quite human to me.

The pinchers shook him again like a doll. His neck flopped, and his eyes rolled up into his skull.

"You've damaged him too greatly," said another voice off-camera.

"These creatures are as fragile as ice crystals," complained the first voice.

I stared at the scene, transfixed. I couldn't believe what I was seeing. The variants had clearly captured Halsey and forced him to speak on their behalf.

At length, a leering visage came into view. Staring at me curiously, it had clearly been designed to resemble a human face, but it had drastically failed in achieving that goal.

Instead, it was like looking into the face of a doll with cameras for eyes. It wore a permanent grin, possibly an attempt by the designers to make the thing appear friendly. The expression was oddly misplaced, even hideous, when seen up-close through a film of oozing blood.

Then the variants closed the channel, and I knew Admiral Halsey was dead.

-11-

The moment the channel closed I stood up, determined to act. My first thought was to forward the video captured on my desk to CENTCOM. Next, we'd plot an intercept course and head out to meet *Victory* in open space. Better to fight her there, where she couldn't easily strike at Earth.

But then I paused. The details of my brief conversation with Halsey were sinking in.

Why had he requested a private communication with me—just me? He had to know that once he deviated from whatever script the variants had given him, they would slay him.

Under such circumstances, if I'd been the one forfeiting my life to warn Earth, I would have done so with as many eyes in attendance as possible. So why had he chosen to warn only me?

I felt an urge to disregard this detail—to set it aside and proceed according to the book. The brass had to be alerted. They had to be warned.

Didn't they?

What if, my mind whispered quietly to me, *there are more enemies in our midst?* We'd sent out seven battleships and one monstrous star carrier. Had all their crews been overcome? It seemed unlikely, but the evidence indicated that was exactly what had happened. The other ships were missing, not chasing this one to do battle.

Unsure of my situation, I saved the video capture and set the file to forward itself to CENTCOM in one hour from now. Then I locked my desk with new biometric passwords and returned to the command deck.

In the event I was about to lose my ship as Admiral Halsey had lost his, the warning would go out long before *Victory* could reach Earth. The battleship was at least forty hours out, and I felt I could afford the time. With luck, the enemy would reveal themselves in other ways.

Walking onto the command deck, my eyes slid over the crewmen who turned toward me. Most were familiar faces, but not all. There were new people aboard.

Durris stepped out of my chair, but I didn't replace him immediately. After nodding vaguely to his inquiries, I moved to Yamada's side and leaned over her so that my voice wasn't easily overheard.

"Lieutenant Commander," I said, "could you pull up a roster of new crewmembers?"

She did do, looking at me quizzically while I examined them. They seemed legitimate at first glance.

"Are you looking for someone in particular, sir?"

"Anyone new, anything unexpected."

She frowned, then her face brightened. "Oh, you must be talking about the variants. They're all down in the main hold. They work like machines—faster I think."

I froze, and then I stared at her in shock. My heart rate accelerated, but I made an effort to appear calm.

"Variants? You mean like the ones we saw on Mars?"

"Almost the same, sir. These units are a little more sophisticated. They can talk and interact almost like humans."

I considered that statement. Not until that moment had I recalled what Director Vogel had said on Phobos: that the variants didn't speak. Could it be that only his construction units lacked that capacity? Did the more humanoid types use speech? I was certain now that they did. I'd heard them talk, plainly, even as they'd murdered Admiral Halsey.

Reaching over her shoulder, I tapped on the "more information" icon. The documents for the transfer of those hideous things were immediately displayed. Running my finger down vertically, I caused the screen to jump to the last page.

"Is something wrong, Captain?" Yamada asked.

Before answering, I read the name at the bottom of the assignment order. None other than Admiral Perez had signed off on the documents. The man was either a dupe or an enemy agent. The effect either way was the same for now.

"I'm just curious," I told Yamada, which was a half-truth. "I was unaware we were carrying any of these... variants. How many are there, when did they come aboard, and why wasn't I informed?"

"There are three, sir. They came aboard during your shore leave period on Earth. I didn't think to discuss it as *Victory* only appeared this morning. Really, I thought you must have known. Very strange that CENTCOM would send these units without informing the captain."

"Yes... strange indeed," I said.

Internally, my guts were knotting themselves up. We had three of these monstrosities aboard *Defiant*? As I recalled, precisely that number had encircled Halsey before they butchered him.

Had Halsey known they were on my ship? Had he suspected?

It suddenly made more sense why he'd requested a private channel. If he'd broadcast the warning in the clear, perhaps the variants on *Defiant* would have overheard and stepped up their plans.

I stared at Yamada's screens while she frowned up at me in confusion. After several long seconds, I came to a fateful decision.

"First Officer Durris," I said loudly. "Has *Victory* done anything interesting out there?"

"She has, Captain. She's adjusted her course slightly. She was heading directly for Earth—but now it looks like she's headed here to Luna."

Unsurprised, I nodded. They were coming to meet my ship, to kill the man who'd been tipped off.

"I see. That's not a terribly dramatic change. Please take command chair again. I'm going below to investigate some new items of interest."

"New items?" he asked. "Oh, you must mean the variants. They're freaky! Last night I took a peek in the hold myself. They move so *fast*."

With an effort, I managed to repress an outburst. Had everyone aboard gawked at these possibly deadly constructs without bothering to inform their captain?

Regaining my composure, I reminded myself they'd all naturally assumed I knew about the variants. After all, the creatures possessed every qualifying document conceivable. The transfer had been legitimate and had gone unchallenged. That was one of the problems with any bureaucratic organization. They tended to follow the rulebook and ask too few questions.

As I left the deck, I found Yamada following me discreetly.

"Yes, Lieutenant Commander?" I asked in a clipped tone.

"Captain, I made some progress on that special project you assigned to me."

After blinking twice, I remembered what she was talking about. "My implant malfunction?"

"Yes. Here, use this."

She handed me a slip of what appeared to be ordinary plastic. "This must make contact around the base of the implant before it's attached to your spinal cord. It will require a bit of improvising, but it should mimic the sanitized covering film. There's no way around the procedure. You'll still need a tech for the insertion."

I looked at it dubiously. It appeared to be nothing more than a clear, plastic candy wrapper. Possibly, it was even less substantial.

"Won't the technicians remove it before—"

"Yes," she said, "they will, but only when they're ready to root the implant. At that point, the code in this wrapper will have infected it with my handiwork."

"Ah," I said, "that's what this is. A vector for the transmission of a virus."

"Right. I can't get access to implants from my terminal. I can only reprogram them through contact. The virus was very easy to write, but gaining access to the implant before the technicians insert it without anyone noticing? That's the tricky part."

Impressed, I took the slip of plastic and put it in my pocket. I thanked her and headed down to the main hold.

Before I reached the hold to see the variants in action, I was waylaid again.

"Captain?" asked Marine Lieutenant Morris.

I turned to face him. He was standing in front of two other marines. All of them were wearing their sidearms.

That wasn't unusual aboard *Defiant* when we were underway on a war footing, but I raised my eyebrow in any case.

"What is it, Lieutenant?" I asked sternly.

"I'm really sorry about this, Captain," he said. "But we've been ordered by CENTCOM to escort you to medical."

"And why is that?"

"Something tripped up one of the desk-jockeys down there, I'm sure that's all it is. They've noted that you don't have an active implant. Apparently, that's against regulations."

Nodding, I suddenly understood. "Right... it is, actually. No Star Guard officer can proceed into action without having been connected to the local net at least. It's considered a dereliction of duty."

"Right. That's what CENTCOM said. Well, can we go fix this? Again, I really want to apologize."

"There's no need," I told him. "In fact, I want you to do something for me as we comply with this order."

"Anything sir, anything."

"Order your full complement of marines to go on alert. Get them into separate, isolated locations distributed around the ship. Place one team at each location, fully armed."

He stared at me in surprise.

"Has this got anything to do with *Victory*, sir? Or is there anything else I should know about?"

"Yes. We're in danger. All of us. You're not to tell that to anyone—nobody. Just quietly mobilize and disperse."

76

Fully alert now, Morris was lifting his com set to his chin. I put my hand out and pushed his wrist back down.

"No," I said quietly, making eye-contact with all three of them. "Do it quietly, pass the message only by word of mouth. No implants. No intercoms."

"You mean walk around the ship and tell every marine in person?" he asked.

"That's exactly what I mean."

He looked at me as if I was crazy for a second, but then he nodded.

"Sir," he said in a husky whisper. "If we're in trouble, we can postpone this thing with the implant. I'll report it was done. I owe you that."

"No," I said, shaking my head. "I want it done. They must know their will has been imposed upon me."

"Who are you talking about, sir?"

"No one," I said thoughtfully. "No one you've ever heard of, anyway."

We headed down to medical then. Morris was too agitated and concerned to watch me undergo the implantation. He left his marines to witness the event and moved off to walk the passages alone.

One at a time, I knew, he was pulling his marines aside and giving them private orders.

-12-

The implantation process was painful and messy, but I managed to briefly handle the item in question before they inserted it.

That was the hardest task of my very long day. I'd never been good at sleight-of-hand. In fact, I could not recall ever having attempted such a thing before.

"What are you doing, Captain?" a tech asked me.

"I've never held one of these things in my hand, nurse," I said, thoughtfully. "Isn't that strange? To spend my whole life with one rooted in the back of my—"

"If you don't mind, Captain," she said, taking the implant from me.

She examined it closely, frowning with intensity. She didn't like what she saw.

"This hygienic wrapper has been damaged," she complained. "It's curled up in several places. We'll have to sterilize it."

"Don't worry about it. Just put it in."

"I'm sorry sir," she said, shaking her head. "It probably isn't sanitary now. You don't want an infection, do you?"

"Nurse," I said sternly. "I'm doing this to satisfy the bureaucrats down on Earth. Our entire fleet has apparently been destroyed, save for this vessel and one other. I don't have time to fool around. Get on with it, and give me a shot of antibiotics if it makes you feel better."

"All right, all right," she said, chastened and sullen. "No need to get huffy. You must realize that there have been nasty cases of meningitis from accidents like this."

"Then give me a *big* antibiotic booster if it pleases you."

She sniffed, but she did it. The implant wriggled into place, with a cold slippery feeling. When it bit down and connected with my spinal cord, I felt an electric shock run through me. I gritted my teeth and hissed.

"At least you didn't damage it," she said. "Looks like a good bite. Now for the antibiotic."

She got out what had to be the largest needle on the ship. She held it aloft, filling it with magenta fluid. I suspected she wanted to make sure I had time to admire it before she plunged it into my neck.

The automated bulb on the end of the syringe pumped rhythmically, and I felt the fluid injecting. My veins ran cool, then warmed again as the drug was delivered.

"Is there anything else?" she asked innocently after yanking the needle from my throbbing neck.

"No," I rasped out. "I should think you've done quite enough."

She put her fists on her hips and frowned as I climbed painfully off the gurney and left her office. The marines, faces twisted up at what they'd witnessed, followed in my wake.

"Go find Morris," I told them. "No transmissions—don't forget."

They trotted away, and I leaned against the wall of the passage for a moment to catch my breath and steady my stomach. The implant reinsertion procedure had left me feeling off-balance.

When I had my wits and equilibrium back, I attempted to interface with the unit.

There was a fuzzy moment. I was informed via projected text printing on my retina that the implant was updating...

Could that be Yamada's virus altering the software? In retrospect, my scheme now seemed somewhat hastily planned and ill-advised. It wasn't a crime to hack your implant, as far as I knew, but I felt sure the Chairman and his Council, should they learn of it, would take a disapproving view.

Straightening my spine, I decided I didn't care what they thought. If at some point they decided someone I knew was an embarrassment, I would still be able to remember that individual. They would never become an "unperson" to me. That was worth a great deal of personal risk.

Eventually, the implant began functioning normally. I didn't want to overuse it just yet, but I tried to access the ship's central data core. The first thing I did was turn off the auto-forwarding option on the vid file I'd captured that showed Halsey's execution. I didn't want CENTCOM to know I was aware of his fate. Not yet.

New information from the data core began to flash up visually. To prevent impairment, it was designed to only display text and vid data on one retina. When you got used to the effect, you learned to shut out input from one eye or the other, shifting your focus entirely onto the one that you wished to deal with at that moment.

The ship was on course, curving and accelerating as she swung around Luna. We were preparing to move toward *Victory* and intercept her.

This plan evidently was obvious to those at CENTCOM, and it didn't meet with approval at the highest levels.

A channel request blinked. It was from Admiral Perez. I accepted it as I had no choice.

"At least you have your implant online again," he said, glaring at me from under his sparse white curls. "I see you're walking. Come to my office when you stop. You have five minutes to do so."

By "come to my office" he meant I should use my implant to visit his location.

He closed the channel before I could ask what this was about. I didn't have to guess. He knew I was moving to engage *Victory*. The question was: why did he want our meeting to be conducted in private? Did he already know what had happened to Halsey?

Deciding I'd best comply and step carefully, I moved to my office and sat down. A quick look at the data from the ship indicated we wouldn't leave Luna's orbit for another ten minutes. I had time.

Using the implant, I reached out to connect to Perez. At this distance, there was a significant propagation delay of a few seconds, but it wasn't too bad.

The net hummed on hold, but at last Perez appeared. He was in his office as well. No one else was present.

The connection placed me on a low couch in front of his desk. From my perspective, he seemed to tower over me. I didn't know if that was purposeful, accidental, or some kind of glitch in the visual-placement layer of the software.

"Sparhawk? Can you hear me?"

"Loud and clear, Admiral."

"I want to know what you're up to out there. You were ordered to move to Luna and take up a patrol position. Reports have you preparing to leave orbit."

"I'm exercising my prerogative under Admiral Halsey's orders, sir."

He stared at me in alarm for a moment. "You've been in contact with Admiral Halsey?"

"I didn't say that, sir," I pointed out. "I'm talking about my orders as per May 28th—"

"I don't care about that!" he shouted suddenly. "You're disobeying *my* orders. I may just have to relieve you of duty, replacing you with…" Here, he consulted a document. "First Officer Durris. He'll soon have full command of *Defiant*."

Slowly, I shook my head. "I'm sorry sir," I said, "but you're mistaken. Admiral Halsey is now in-system. He out ranks you—I'm sure I don't have to point that out. I'm following my standing orders from him. If you want to get them changed, I suggest you either get the Joint Chiefs to override Halsey, or talk to Halsey yourself and get him to inform me."

He stared at me venomously. At that point I suspected he knew what had happened to Halsey—but I couldn't be sure.

If he *did* know the truth, he knew he couldn't get Halsey to countermand anything he'd written previously because he was stone dead.

With an effort of will, I kept my face and tone neutral. I didn't want him to think this was anything more than an argument about the chain of command.

"You always were a cocky one, Sparhawk," he said at last. "Very well, I'll get the Joint Chiefs to alter your orders one way or the other."

The connection closed with disconcerting suddenness. My world went black for a moment until my real surroundings took precedence and settled in around me.

He'd given me much to think about, but I didn't have time to ponder it all. I had my own pressing problems.

I almost made a mistake then. I almost contacted Marine Commander Morris via my implant. It was a reflex that was hard to avoid.

Instead, I stepped out into the passages of the ship and marched off in search of him. With any luck, I'd find him in the vicinity of the engineering section on the lower decks. The troop module and the primary armory were located down there.

The main cargo hold and our odd new friends known as variants were also on that same deck. That should make this entire affair come to a conclusion soon after it began if events went according to my plans.

-13-

Morris and his troops met me outside the cargo hold.

"It's them, isn't it?" he asked. "Those freaks inside? I knew they'd be trouble the second they came aboard."

Nodding, I didn't try to deny it. I hadn't been specific about the nature of the threat previously because I didn't want him to spread the word about the details. It seemed likely these creatures would find out if we did.

He tested the swivel-cannon on his body-shell and seemed satisfied.

"We're good to go, Captain," he said.

I stepped to the hold and reached out a hand to open the hatch. This made Morris flinch as he'd never liked to see me put myself into danger.

"My plan isn't to go in guns blazing," I told the marines who leaned closer around me. "Everyone, back up. Stay here until I give you a signal. I want to see if they're in a talking mood first."

"They don't *talk*," Morris said. "At least… that's what I heard."

"We'll soon learn the truth."

I touched the hatch, releasing the lock. It opened and squealed, grinding metal against metal. The hatch was powered and swung open fully. Inside, it was brightly lit and full of equipment.

There was no immediate sign of the variants, but I could hear them. They were generating a sound that reminded me of beating wings heard in close proximity.

Frowning, I stepped cautiously into the hold and looked this way and that. After another ten steps in, Morris hissed behind me.

"Captain?"

I glanced back toward the open hatch. Morris and his men were nothing if not disciplined. They were clustered at the hatchway where they'd been ordered to remain.

Signaling them to enter, I stepped farther into the hold. The peculiar fluttering sounds were irregular now, and they grew louder.

It turned out these odd noises were coming from the embodiment of inhuman efficiency. I came around a six meter tall rack and found them there, all three of the monstrosities, working at a frenetic pace.

It's hard to describe what variants are like close-up to anyone who hasn't met them personally. They move with amazing precision and speed. Their arms—each had at least six of them—were almost like the blades of a helicopter. They flashed and thrummed in the air, taking items from one another and the shelves around them with blurring speed.

Their whipping arms were long, too. They could grab things from the top shelf or the bottom one without stretching. In contrast to the speed of their upper bodies, the group glided much more slowly on their feet. Overall, they gave me an alien feeling while I watched them.

Their lower bodies were like those of an insect's thorax. They had six legs each, and they moved every leg as slowly as their arms were moving quickly. The difference between the two was unnatural and disturbing as everything else about them.

They didn't bump along when they walked the way that humans do. They seemed to glide—like a trio of spiders doing a slow, methodical crawl as a group. It was only their whipping arms that moved with startling rapidity.

Their heads swiveled with odd, precise movements as they worked to watch everything they were doing at once. Some parts of the heads were flesh as were the trunks of their bodies. But those *arms*... they had to be enhanced with plastic and metal. I wondered if there was anything like meat and bone inside them.

"Variants," I said loudly. "I must ask you to stop what you're doing and talk to me."

None of them reacted much. I thought they may have twitched, glancing in my direction during their frantic activities, but that was all.

"Variants, you are crewmen here on *Defiant*. I'm this ship's captain. You will obey me now."

This got the attention of one of the three. His arms slowed and moved at a waltz when compared to the flailing speed of the others.

"You are the captain?" he asked.

"I'll be damned!" Morris exclaimed behind me. "They *do* talk!"

"I am the captain," I repeated. "Now, if you would be so kind as to—"

"We have no need of direction. We're behind schedule."

Frowning, I considered the creature's statement. As far as I knew, they were done with their major assignment, which had been to load the ship with equipment and supplies.

"If you do not listen to me, you'll be confined," I announced.

This got the attention of all three. They kept working, but they slowed down to listen and consider my words.

"Impossible," said the second one. It had the number R-77 emblazoned on its chassis. The third one, number Q-161, spoke next.

"We're getting further behind. Perhaps its goal is to delay us?"

"If so," said the leader, number K-19, "it has already succeeded. Captain? Is that your goal?"

Putting my hand on the hilt of my sword nonchalantly, I considered the creature's question. "I only want information."

"And yet you threaten force," the leader said, one tube-like eye focused on my sword.

"This is my ship, and I'm in charge here. I need to know what's going on in order to pass judgment on your actions."

"He's unaware," said R-77.

"Do not enlighten him," piped Q-161.

But despite their suggestions, K-19 turned to look me over. "If we explain ourselves, will you leave us to perform our duties?"

"If I'm satisfied you're acting under orders from CENTCOM, then yes."

"Very well. We're assembling a weapon."

"What kind of weapon?"

"It must be mounted externally, on the hull. It's a heavy impulse laser projector. We're constructing the magnetics now."

Peering in alarm, I saw they were forming what appeared to be a tube strung with wires.

"What's the purpose of all this?"

K-19 looked at me for a moment. "Are you aware this ship is under threat?"

"Yes, of course," I said. "You're talking about the battleship *Victory*. Correct?"

"He is aware!" said R-77, glancing at the others.

"This ship lacks armament powerful enough to puncture the enemy hull," Q-161 said.

I noted that Q-161's voice was higher than the other two. Could it have been a female, originally?

"We're working to construct a short range, high intensity lance that can do the job," she said.

Stepping a few paces closer, I looked over the thing they were building. It *could* be a laser—a heavy one.

"I'm surprised," I said. "You want to help us build a weapon to stop *Victory?* It's your kind who have mutinied and taken control of that ship."

"That's insulting," Q-161 said.

"How so?" I asked.

"We're not machines. We're individuals."

"I see, and I stand corrected." For some reason, the variant's miffed responses made me smile. Perhaps there was some humanity left in these creatures after all, no matter what they looked like.

"Captain?" Morris said from behind me. "You aren't suggesting we should trust these freaks, are you?"

"Please, no insults Lieutenant," I said sternly. "Stand down."

Morris had waved his men forward, and they were advancing with weapons lifted. Reluctantly, he signaled for them to halt. They stepped from foot to foot uncertainly. Every one of them wore a frown.

"We're behind schedule, Captain," K-19 repeated. "Will you leave us to our work?"

"No, not yet, I need to know more."

"Please speak with Director Vogel in that case. He's on Phobos. He'll inform you concerning the situation better than we can."

Nodding, I decided to follow K-19's suggestion. "All right. Morris, let them work but watch them. Report to me before you take any action against them unless they threaten you directly."

"But Captain…"

"Are my orders clear, Lieutenant?"

"Yes they are, sir."

"Good. I'll be back shortly."

Leaving the hold with long strides, I found my mind was whirling. I returned to my quarters and privately reached out with my implant. I engaged the ship's network and then went beyond it to the Solar System-wide transport layer.

The contact should be untraceable if Yamada had done her work well. I saw several pop-ups warning me about this transgression as I attempted to drive a private tunnel to Director Vogel. I waited a full minute, then another, with growing impatience.

Finally, Vogel answered me.

"This is an illegal correspondence," he said. "I will report this after I identify the criminal behind it."

"Then there is no need to speak," I said.

We had only a voice connection with no visualization. Still, the signal was clear.

Vogel hesitated. "Who is this?"

"Did you place three variants aboard my ship?"

"Captain Sparhawk? Why can't I identify you if it is you?"

I noticed he didn't deny my assertion. Further, he'd recognized me by the inference alone. This allowed me to make two quick assumptions: first, that Vogel had indeed sent the variants. Second, he'd programmed them—if that was the appropriate term with hybrid creatures—to help me.

"You're not the only one with a technical team," I said to him. "This conversation can't be traced or recorded by anyone but me. Now, please tell me what's going on. My marine commander is itching to destroy your variants."

"No, he mustn't do that! Control your dogs, Sparhawk."

"Give me a reason to do so."

"I did send them. After I learned of the misuse of my creations, I felt I had no choice. They're only a small force… I did what I could."

His words confused me, but I was intrigued as well.

"You'll have to explain with greater clarity."

"There isn't time. Your proxy technology is impressive, but you shouldn't think it will stop CENTCOM for long. This conversation will be hacked or disconnected soon. All I can tell you is that you should allow my variants to work. They're efficient and loyal. They will not be turned."

Before I could ask for further information, Vogel's predictions came true. The connection grew fuzzy, the tunnel collapsed and failed entirely.

I put a hand to my chin, mind racing. Who should I trust? Who should I suspect? It seemed that I was in a compromised position. I didn't know how to proceed.

-14-

When I returned to the hold, I ordered Morris and his men to withdraw. They did so with poor grace.

"They'll make hamburger out of you, Captain."

Eyeing him sternly, I waved him out. They all withdrew.

"K-19," I said, "I've spoken with Vogel. He tells me I should trust you."

"Excellent. I hope this means you'll allow us to work at full capacity."

I watched their flashing limbs for a moment. "Are you saying you're performing sub-optimally now?"

"Yes. This hold is pressurized. It would be better if it was not. Gas is like liquid to us, it hampers our movements. The air resistance slows every motion and introduces complex force-application problems our software must continuously compensate for. The additional friction alone—"

"But if I depressurize the chamber, you won't be able to breathe."

Q-161 made a twittering noise. I took it for laughter.

"We don't breathe—not precisely," K-19 explained. "Our organic components are fueled with oxygen artificially. Our vocalizations are generated by speakers for your convenience."

"I see... Very well then, I'll close the hatch and allow you to depressurize the hold."

"Thank you," K-19 said without so much as glancing in my direction.

I couldn't feel bad about that as they were clearly very focused on their work.

"I'll be back in one hour," I said, "expecting a report on your progress."

"We'd prefer a window of ninety-four minutes. We should be finished by then and in need of assistance with the next step."

Agreeing to K-19's terms, I left the hold. I found myself giving an involuntary shudder when I closed the hatch doors.

What had Vogel created? Whether they were working for *Defiant's* defense or not, I felt a sense of unease and even revulsion in the presence of these variants.

The variants' claims concerning *Defiant's* inability to stop *Victory* concerned me. To investigate, I moved to the command deck and consulted my Exec.

"Durris," I said, "have you used the tactical table to game out an encounter with *Victory*?"

He looked at me sharply. "Is that likely to happen, sir?"

"I hope not, but it's best to prepare, isn't it?"

He gave me a nod. "I came to the same conclusion, sir. Accordingly, I've been gaming out various scenarios. The results aren't good."

He proceeded to show me how events were projected to go.

"You can see here," he said, "we'll meet and engage at a range of about two million kilometers."

"Our beam weapons don't reach that far," I pointed out. "Are you supposing we'd fire missiles at that point?"

"That's speculation. What isn't a guess is the effective range of one of these battleships. They can hit us at nearly double our longest reach—two million kilometers."

"I see," I said.

In the long history of naval warfare, the effective range of weaponry had often determined the victor. Battleships had been built bigger and bigger to carry larger guns. Larger weapons could hit an enemy ship before the target could fire back. Eventually, aircraft carriers had been invented to extend this range even farther, making battleships largely obsolete.

The same principle applied in space but even more so. Beams and projectiles fired in space met little to no resistance

90

and thus traveled great distances without losing their punch. In the case of beams, there was a limit as the focus of any radiation tended to spread and thin with every kilometer traveled. Projectiles didn't dissipate in killing power, but the odds of the target being where you thought it would be lengthened with distance. As a result, tracking missiles and beams were favored weapons at long range.

These battleships we'd built had been designed to reach farther than other ships could. The primary method used was to goose-up beam power so a given burst of fire kept its potency even at great distances. Bigger beams required larger generators, and therefore, larger ships.

"I hadn't realized the battleship specs were this good," I said. "No wonder CENTCOM wanted to build these big bastards to go after the Stroj."

"Indeed," Durris said. "There is some good news: The battleship is damaged. She's maneuvering slowly, and her acceleration arc is way off specs. I'd say there are weak points in her armor as well, judging by the state of the hull."

"Do we have targeting data? Points to hit hard with our weapons at close range?"

"Definitely. We know a lot about them, and they know a lot about us."

"Has CENTCOM designated the ship as hostile yet?"

He gave me a quick up-down glance. "No. Not yet. They're marking it yellow on the boards, meaning it's an allied ship."

"Allied? Meaning it isn't an enemy... but not quite a friend?"

He nodded.

"They know something is up," I said, staring at the data. "Someone down there knows. It might be Perez."

"Knows *what*, sir?"

I glanced at him sharply. I wanted to take him into my confidence, but I wasn't sure that I should. So far, I hadn't dared to do so with anyone other than Morris.

"I believe *Victory* has been compromised," I told him in a quiet voice.

He lowered his voice to match mine.

"Is this confirmed, Captain?"

"Not officially… but yes."

"How did you come to this—?"

"It doesn't matter," I said. "We have to prepare to defeat *Victory*, but at the same time, we can't let on that we're doing so."

Durris looked upset. He was a rules-follower and a worrier to boot. This gave him a natural dislike of all off-script activities.

"I don't like this, Captain," he complained. "For the record—"

"I understand your dismay. Unfortunately, I've found over my years as a commander that I've often been forced to deal with reality, rather than a fabrication that I'd prefer to be the truth."

He looked down and nodded his head. "You can count on me, Captain—to a reasonable point."

That was a warning, and I knew I'd best heed it. Durris would contact CENTCOM if I went too far. He'd have to be convinced more directly.

Sighing, I stepped away from the tactical displays and waved for him to follow me. He did so with some reluctance.

When we reached my office, I played the vid recording depicting Admiral Halsey's death. He watched it all, until the final moments when Halsey was torn apart by the variants.

"What is this?" he sputtered. "Has this been reported?"

"Not by me, no," I admitted.

"But it has to be, sir!"

"Not yet. I don't know who else might be compromised."

"Who's doing this, sir? Who's behind it all? Are these variant things planning to kill every human in the system?"

"At first, I suspected they might be. But now I'm of the opinion they're tools, nothing more. The ones aboard our ship seem to be building a weapon to destroy *Victory*."

I told him then about K-19 and his fellow variants.

"I have high hopes the weapon they are creating will do what they say," I said in summary.

"Huh…" Durris said. "That's very odd…"

"What's odd?" I demanded.

"I hadn't yet gotten to the end in my tactical breakdown with you, but my simulation predicts we'll lose this upcoming fight with the battleship. We'll lose because of their thick hull. My entire counter-plan revolved around getting close and penetrating one of the pockmarks in their hull. If those craters go deep enough, and this heavy lance can hit hard enough…"

"We might be able to puncture that big slow ship and take her down?" I asked hopefully.

"Maybe…" he agreed, "provided we aren't blasted out of space during our approach."

We put our heads together then and began to plot in earnest.

Long before Durris and I could set into motion our plans to deploy the lance, I was summoned by another call from CENTCOM.

This time, they didn't bother going through Yamada. They contacted me directly via my implant.

The interface alerted me as to the source of the unwelcome intrusion. It was Admiral Perez, and he was projecting himself to my location.

I hesitated before opening the channel. Was Director Vogel's warning coming true already? Had they detected my hacked implant and moved to discipline me?

There was only one way to find out. I couldn't ignore this caller for long, and I couldn't head out into open space to face *Victory* without convincing CENTCOM it had to be done. My crew was loyal to me, but they weren't mutineers. They'd refuse to follow my orders if they conflicted with the brass unless I had a damned good reason.

As the call buzzed irritatingly in my head, I rushed to my office. Sucking in a deep breath, I conjured up a neutral face and opened the channel.

"Is this something important, Admiral?" I asked immediately. "I'm quite busy at the moment."

He snorted. "No doubt."

He examined his surroundings before speaking further. This time, his avatar was perfectly placed. He was standing on the far side of my desk. He paced the floor, his feet matching the surface of my deck almost as if he was truly present.

93

"Sparhawk," he said, "I'm going to break protocol with you. We've had trouble contacting *Victory*."

"You don't say?"

He removed his gaze from a case containing my service decorations and glanced at me sharply.

"Yes, I *do* say. You're probably aware of more than you're letting on, but you're wary of CENTCOM interference."

"If you have any evidence of my improper—"

He put up a hand to stop me. "Forget it. Your recent actions don't matter. We're in an emergency situation. I've gotten word from abroad that things aren't well. Our fleet has done more than fail—it has damaged Earth's diplomatic status."

"I'm not sure what you're saying, sir."

"I'm saying that Halsey did more than hunt for Stroj ships. He destroyed settlements, trade ships—everything he encountered."

At a loss, I shook my head. "I've known Halsey for a decade. He's never shown any capacity for wanton destruction."

"I agree, but in any case, I've been trying to contact him for hours. He won't respond. *Victory* won't answer anything we're throwing at it. What's more, their course has changed. Instead of heading into orbit over Earth, they're now moving to intercept you at Luna."

"We've calculated the same thing, sir."

He nodded. "What are you doing about it?"

I hesitated. I hardly wanted to tell him I'd been setting my marines all over my own ship in case of an internal threat, while allowing variants to build a weapon to destroy *Victory*, should the need arise.

He laughed. "You don't trust me? Good! Your instincts are sharp. You *can't* trust everyone down here. Unfortunately, I won't be in command for much longer. I've shared the duty on a rotating basis, and it should be mine for another month—but the politicians have seen fit to speed up the process. They're changing the guard."

My eyes narrowed. "Who is going to replace you?"

"They haven't told me. Ever since recent events, they've become quite paranoid about their own commanders."

94

I knew what he was talking about. Several times, it had been revealed that our upper echelons in Star Guard had been penetrated by Stroj agents. It only made sense they would be suspicious with a new crisis brewing.

If the Stroj had dealt us a serious blow by infiltrating the ranks of our leaders, they'd done it by making people mistrust one another. The entire culture of Star Guard had shifted over the years. Everyone looked at everyone else with suspicion.

Each time we uncovered a Stroj agent, their technology had become superior in nature. They were disguised not just in clothing but in flesh. They were cloning our leaders and editing the clones to create nearly perfect matches. Undetectable, in most cases, until they performed their final duties.

"What are your orders, Admiral?" I asked him.

"These are my final standing orders: Destroy *Victory*. Blow her out of the sky. I don't know who's in command of that ship, but I'm willing to bet it's not Admiral Halsey. At least, not the Halsey you and I once knew."

He watched me closely as I digested this information. I was surprised as I'd begun to suspect Admiral Perez himself wasn't what he seemed.

Now, in retrospect, his behavior was more understandable. He'd been just as paranoid as I was all along—how could he not be? After learning the fleet had been lost, he'd come to believe that his superior officer was dead, or worse, allied with the enemy and flying *Victory* toward Earth.

That had put him in a desperate situation. As *Defiant* was the only ship capable of intercepting the incoming battleship, he'd had to rely on me.

But could he trust me? Was I another plant, disloyal and hiding my true nature until a critical moment?

I could see that his new orders were a test of sorts. If I refused to follow them and attack, he could surmise that I was indeed in league with this threat. Fortunately, I wasn't inclined to refuse. I'd been hoping for just such an order.

Looking up again at Admiral Perez, my mouth formed a thin, stern line.

"Very well, sir," I said. "I concur with your judgment. I will meet *Victory* in open space and defeat her."

"Excellent! Don't bother to transmit the details of your attack plan down here to CENTCOM—further, if you're required to do so by my replacement, give them false tactical data. I don't trust anyone right now. This is too important."

I considered telling him what I'd seen of the variants on *Victory*. I almost did—but again, paranoia struck me. I didn't know if I could trust Perez—or whoever else might be listening.

Nodding, I agreed with his orders. We both signed off, and the channel closed.

Leaning back in a creaking chair for a few moments, I pondered the surreal situation I now found myself in. It was unenviable in the extreme. CENTCOM might or might not be turning against me. *Victory* surely had.

As far as I could determine, I was flying the only loyal capital ship Earth had left.

-15-

We left Luna's orbit quietly and powered out into open space, heading toward the outer Solar System.

"According to our predictions," Durris said, "we'll intercept *Victory* here… approximately one hundred ninety five million kilometers out from the Sun."

"We'll be close to the orbit of Mars," I said, looking over the data.

"Yes, but far from the planet itself."

The plan had been approved and reviewed. We were now examining the enemy reaction. So far, there had been none. They had maintained their course and speed, heading directly toward us.

"We'll do battle in this region," I said, outlining an ovoid in space some ten million kilometers across. The shape glowed into being on the planning boards after I touched the controls.

The predictive software provided us two critical pieces of information regarding our plans. First was the timing element, which displayed as a fast-ticking digital clock floating over the ovoid. We'd reach the battleground in thirty-one hours' time.

The second piece of information was far less encouraging. The battle computers were predicting a grim loss, and no less than the destruction of *Defiant*.

"Have you updated the scenario with the addition of the variant's lance to our arsenal?" I asked Durris.

"Yes... The problem is the simulation software doesn't think we'll make it in that close to the enemy ship. According to the computer, we'll be destroyed several hundred thousand kilometers outside the lance's range."

I stared at the screen. A few staffers circling the far side fell silent. Durris and the software were both calmly predicting our destruction.

"The trouble is," I said, going over the stages of the simulated conflict, "we're heavily outgunned too far out. We can't even fire back until we're badly damaged."

"That's correct, sir," Durris said stiffly. "I was hoping... well..."

"What?" I said, turning to him. "Now isn't the time to be shy."

"It doesn't matter. My hopes haven't materialized."

"Ah," I said, looking at him. "You were hoping CENTCOM would commit the rest of the fleet to fight at our side, right?"

He nodded.

"Give me the best predictions you have in that case."

He quickly edited the scene. More green contacts appeared, dotting space on our flanks. Every destroyer and pinnace we had flew with us in the new model.

The ovoid now displayed an amber shade.

"Still predicting defeat?" I asked.

"Yes. But not with one hundred percent certainty."

"It does seem like a better play for Earth. *But*," I said this single word loudly, "we're not her last play. CENTCOM surely has gamed this all out as well. They're hoping we'll damage *Victory* badly. Maybe they dare to hope we'll get lucky and destroy her, as she's in an unknown state after clearly having been battered in your simulation."

"That's right, but if they'd only give us support—"

"No," I said, "they won't. They plan to hold back and marshal their final ships around Luna. They're putting together every missile and ship they have. They'll wait there to win or lose in a final desperate effort."

"Perhaps we should be standing there with them. What good will it do to lose *Defiant* in a hopeless struggle?"

The staffers were now staring at us with wide eyes. They'd been largely in the dark concerning the desperate nature of our situation. Even Rumbold and Yamada had stopped working and begun listening closely.

I didn't care. I no longer thought it necessary or productive to maintain a secretive air among my own command staff. If there were spies, let them hear what we had to say. There were only a few hours left in any case.

"It may buy Earth time. If we can damage *Victory*—"

Durris shook his head and threw up his hands. This was a wild display of emotion for him.

"So what if we do slow her down? She can hold off and repair. She can roam around the outer system destroying our mining facilities at the asteroids and our labs at Mars. Earth won't be in charge of anything other than the home world."

"That's true, but there is hope," I said. "Remember the eighth battleship? She's been under crash construction since the fleet left. They've stepped up her production rate by several months. She should be able to fly with a green crew and the majority of her systems working in a week or two."

Durris stared at me. Slowly, he smiled.

"Ah," he said. "I get it at last. We're a speed bump. We're to die well and buy Earth a few weeks' time."

"If so," I said loudly, "it's a sacrifice I'm willing to make."

Then I turned to regard my crew. My eyes met theirs one at a time. Most of them stared back determinedly. A few dropped their eyes, but no one objected.

They knew the stakes. They hadn't signed on to live forever in Earth's service—well, that may have been the original intent of some. But most had known the dangers and accepted them from the outset.

"Good," I said, after having taken their measure. "Now, let's see if we can devise a way to beat the odds."

I sat back and listened while my various officers gave me what they had. Not many suggested anything useful.

It was the usual stuff—editing our armor to the forward section of the ship to help deflect incoming fire captivated one group. That would give us more survivability as we approached, but nothing to protect our engines after a single pass. It would be a do-or-die one-shot attack.

There were other ideas, but all of them were lacking.

At last, when I was about to give up hope, aid came from a most unlikely source.

"Excuse me, Captain," Rumbold said. "I know it's not my place to—"

"No, no," I said, "speak up, man. We could use wisdom from a spacer who's seen more years of service than the rest of us combined."

"Well, it's like this, I think we need something to hide behind. Something that will stop a beam at least."

Durris frowned at him. "What do you suggest, oldster?"

Rumbold didn't ruffle up at the term oldster, although many of his peers might have been insulted.

"I've been checking the scans," he said. "There are a few rocks out here. Nothing big, mind you, but some that are in the neighborhood of a hundred meters in diameter."

Durris laughed. "Are you serious? Are you suggesting that we slow down, capture a rock, and throw it ahead of us in hopes it will catch some of the enemy fire? We'll be crawling, and we'll be more vulnerable for it."

Rumbold's eyes were narrowed as he looked over the planning table. He shook his white-haired head. "Not exactly, son. I'm not suggesting we fly behind a rock—I'm suggesting we turn it into gravel. Sand is even better, if you can manage it."

They all stared at him. Durris opened his mouth then closed it again with an audible snap. He leaned over the table with sudden intensity.

He worked the controls, bringing up menu after menu. Finally, a small cloud of debris appeared in front of *Defiant* on the simulator.

He engaged the software engine, which did its magic, predicting likely hits and misses.

At last, the scene changed. The ovoid had gone from yellow to blue. That meant the software thought we had a chance.

100

"Forty percent?" Durris asked aloud in amazement. "That's a thirty point jump…"

He reached for Rumbold's shoulder and slapped it hard. "You've done it, man. We've got to move fast, however. There's a window for grabbing a boulder. How far away we are will change everything. We'll end up meeting the enemy closer to Earth, at lower speeds… so many variables!"

He set off to work on his simulator. In the meantime, Rumbold and I came up with a course that would allow us to intercept the rock he'd found and work with it. We'd have to change the rock's course, speed it up, and blast it to bits right before we reached *Victory's* effective range.

"Well done, Rumbold, old friend," I told him an hour or so later. "You've pulled us all out of the fire."

He snorted and lowered his voice, speaking only to me.

"They're all like kids at Christmas," he said. "Never seen such a pack of fools so happy to learn they're facing only a sixty percent chance of death."

"You miss the key point," I said back in a whisper. "What you've really given them all is hope."

Rumbold nodded. He at last smiled and relaxed, accepting everyone's praise. It did my heart good to see it.

At least my crew wouldn't die in a state of cold despair.

-16-

Due to our diversion to intercept the asteroid, it was nearly forty hours later when we faced *Victory*.

The battleship was huge. It was impossible to describe how unnerving her presence was. Somehow, the fact it had been built by Earthmen made it all the worse. The fact we were going to be destroyed by our own sister ship seemed positively unfair.

In the final moments before we came within range of the big enemy guns, we had a final scare. The railgun lance wasn't ready.

The only workers we had who could lever the weapon out onto the hull and attach it to the power cables were the variants themselves. It wasn't encouraging to see them slowly scuttling over our hull carrying their burden like a bizarre trio of pallbearers carrying a massive cylindrical coffin.

"We'll have to use exposed cables," Rumbold complained for the hundredth time.

"I know," I said patiently. "There's no help for it. We've got to make do with what we have."

"Exposed cables…" he muttered again, as if he hadn't heard me. He shook his head slowly. "They'll be cut sure as shit the moment the enemy burns through our gravel shield."

"Again, I'm well aware of this."

It wasn't in my heart to reprimand Rumbold. The crew had been working to the point of near exhaustion. They'd taken only short breaks when ordered to. For all that, they seemed alert enough, if a little glassy-eyed.

At three million kilometers out, a million outside of our enemy's maximum range, we blasted apart the asteroid we'd flung ahead of us.

Defiant's primary cannons hummed, then buzzed, then sang. The asteroid came apart in slow motion. Molten chunks drifted away from the central mass—but there was no helping that.

"She's breaking up, Captain," Durris said. "Just like the simulations."

"Keep working the central chunk, and have the point defense weapons try to guide some of the large chunks back toward the core. There are bound to be holes in this defensive screen. Keep them from growing too—"

"Captain!" Yamada shouted suddenly. "The enemy ship is firing. *Victory* is firing, sir!"

My mouth hung open and my eyes roved the screens.

"We're still too far out. What are they doing?"

"Maybe they're trying to burn the screen..." Durris suggested.

The enemy fire lanced out and punched a hole in our improvised shielding. Yamada gasped.

"They don't have that kind of range," she said. "They *can't* have that kind of range!"

The debris field we were hiding behind began to crumble. I felt like a charging spearman huddling behind an upraised shield with a crack in it.

"Durris, take more off the hard core of the asteroid. Patch that hole."

"The algorithm is punched in... firing on full automatic."

The ship shuddered as our secondary guns sent streams of slugs toward the asteroid shielding us. Fresh rock split and crumbled. Computer-guided aiming systems trimmed more mass from the core of the asteroid to create a larger debris field. This went smoothly, but my mind was elsewhere.

"Durris," I said, "how's it possible for the enemy to have this kind of range? Earth built those cannons. We should damned well be able to plot their reach."

103

"I agree, sir," he said, working feverishly over a screen full of calculations. He was adjusting the simulation to reflect the unexpected changes in the enemy capabilities.

The ovoid on the screen grew. We were now well within it. The field had also changed to orange, indicating we had about a twenty percent chance of survival.

He turned to me slowly when he was done. He had an odd look on his face.

"Captain, come examine the raw data. I have optical probes out on our flanks flying with us. We can see the enemy hull in detail now."

I moved to do as he suggested. What I saw there made little sense. *Victory* looked… odd. Her central hull region had thinned out as far as I could see. It was as if the ship had gone on a crash diet.

"Could she have been damaged so severely?" I asked.

"No sir, I don't think we're looking at damage. In fact, I don't think she's been damaged at all. We made an error in our assumptions."

Frowning at him and the scope, I began to understand. An idea was dawning within my mind. Unfortunately, I didn't much care for the suspicion that was growing there.

"It's not damage," I said, repeating his statement. "They've altered the ship. The variants—they're like the ones aboard *Defiant*. They haven't been content to merely man *Victory*…"

"That's right, sir. They've altered her. We have no real idea what we're facing."

Our exchange left me feeling sick. The math hadn't been on our side to begin with, but at least we'd had a fighting chance. Now, I had no idea how events might unfold.

"Can we break off?" I asked.

"Negative. We're within her best range now. We'll be raked by her cannons if we try to move away from the debris shield we're following."

My heart sank as I realized the truth of his words. The enemy had caught us neatly in their trap. Lulled by the trickery of our makeshift shield, we hadn't stopped to consider the fact that variants like to change things and worked very quickly.

The whole idea that they'd brought a damaged ship into the home system now seemed absurd in the extreme. Such creatures weren't the sort to sit idle while their ship needed repairs—or improvements.

"All right then, we're committed," I said. "We'll have to make the best of it."

"Another volley incoming," Yamada warned us. "They're striking for the center of the asteroid now. I... I don't understand it. That's the safest place they could hit."

Durris and I exchanged glances. Durris took the job of explaining the situation.

"They've decided to burn down our asteroid entirely," he said. "Rather than punching holes in the maelstrom of gravel, allowing us to tear away a fresh protective sheet, they're going to try to melt the core down and leave us with no defense."

Her face was bloodless, shocked. She turned slowly back to her instruments.

No one on the deck spoke for several seconds. We watched as the enemy weapons punched through the debris and dug into the core. The asteroid had a nickel-iron center, tough, but not invulnerable.

After six total strikes, the core vaporized entirely. We were without significant defenses.

"Missiles launched, sir," said one of the staffers.

"Countermeasures," I called back mechanically. "Launch our own barrage in return. It's time."

"How many?"

I hesitated before answering.

"Throw everything we've got at them," I said at last.

The ship shook rhythmically as our missiles were fired in rapid sequence. The drumbeat of launches went on and on.

I checked the range. We were still six hundred thousand kilometers out. Our main batteries could do damage at this distance, but the lance wouldn't be effective. We had to get in closer to use it—much closer.

"How long until the debris shield loses integrity?" I asked.

"It's coming apart now, Captain," Durris answered. "We'll be taking hits from their cannons in a few more minutes."

I nodded, unsurprised. Returning to my command chair, I strapped myself in. Reaching out with one hand, I activated the ship-wide PA system.

"All hands, hear this," I said. "We're going to accelerate hard in thirty seconds. Get to an acceleration couch and strap in. Secure equipment, if you have time to do so."

Bringing up my external hull view, I saw the variants retreat into the ship. Their lance was fixed on the prow, looking odd and stubby. Could it be that all our hopes truly rested on these strange creatures?

"Captain," Durris said, "I know what you're thinking, but—"

"Excellent. Make it happen. Helmsman, pull us away from the debris cloud. Durris, prime the guns. We'll get one or two shots in, then we'll be down to the lance."

"But Captain," Durris continued. "We'll only get one shot with the lance if we come in fast. Then we'll be past them after that and our tail will be exposed."

"I know. We're only going to get one shot. That's why the damned computer has halved the odds of our survival."

He nodded and hunched over his controls. Everyone had strapped in by now—and if they hadn't, God help them.

"Rumbold, pull us out from behind the debris. Full power to the engines. Let's charge her amidships."

He gaped at me. "Are we going to ram *Victory*, sir?" he croaked.

I considered it. The idea wasn't without merit.

"Not yet. Just get me in close as fast as possible. Then, we'll fire that lance and see if it operates as advertised.

No one cheered as we made our desperate maneuver. We pulled out from behind the remains of the asteroid which was now a swirl of glowing dust.

The moment we were out in the open, the battleship landed her first punch at us. The hull bubbled and ran with slag. A hotspot appeared and damage reports began flowing in.

Fortunately, they hadn't taken out the lance—not yet.

-17-

I've been in a dozen hostile actions in space, perhaps more. None had ever seemed more desperate or uncertain than this one did.

Usually, combat in the cold void was a dance of mathematics and precise planning. In this case we were no doubt facing odds that could be calculated, but we had no idea what the central formula might be.

We'd never faced this particular enemy before. We'd never once used the weapon all our hopes rested upon. There were too many variables, and I for one didn't have the skill or the stomach to recite them even as I attempted to win the day.

Yamada caught my eye as the world darkened. The acceleration of *Defiant* was legendary. She could flatten one's tongue against the back of your throat.

"This is a fantastic risk," she said thickly, "but I think it's the best play we have."

"We'll know shortly," I said. "Hang on."

Rumbold flew *Defiant* toward the enemy ship with sickening speed. We shot toward them on a gut-wrenching curve, canting obliquely and unleashing tremendous power. *Victory's* next salvo went wide, no doubt due to her crew being surprised and having to shift their turrets to track our rapidly approaching vessel.

The battleship went dark for a time, then lit up again as we plunged close. When less than a hundred thousand kilometers separated us, their cannons fired again.

This time, they struck home. The prow was molten in a dozen places. Forward decks were venting gas into space. Bulkheads sealed themselves to prevent depressurization.

Casualty counts and lost systems began to flash red on all our screens. We'd lost exactly ten crewmen in one strike, and one of our three main batteries was dead as well.

"Keep firing," I ordered. "Yamada, is the lance still functional?"

"As far as I can tell, sir," she shouted back over the roar of our engines. "The cables are still intact and the indicators are green."

"Good. Durris, program that thing to fire at the enemy. Hit her amidships at that thinned-out section. Let's see if we can't break her spine."

"Already plotted, Captain."

I nodded. Of course he'd anticipated the order. I smiled at him, and he smiled back. By my estimates, we had less than ninety seconds to live.

When we reached optimal range, the enemy cannons flared blindingly bright. The light was bluish and intense beyond measure. Squinting, I felt *Defiant* shudder as she fired her own response.

The lance had unleashed an answering burst of power, a thick cylinder of brilliant energy.

Our two ships plunged toward one another and crossed paths. The moment was brief, but definitive.

The enemy cannon caught us in a crossfire at point-blank range. Huge gouges were torn into our armor. Exposed decks streamed out gas and tendrils of short-lived flame.

Our own lance sliced into the battleship, cutting into her like a blowtorch. We passed by almost without seeming to have done much damage.

"Spin us hard about, face them with our armored prow," I ordered Rumbold.

He fought with his controls, but at last threw up his hands.

"Helm is unresponsive, sir," he said in a voice laden with finality.

I stared at him for a few seconds, then nodded.

"Get the work crews down there. Get the control lines repaired."

"They've been dispatched," he said in a dull voice.

We both knew there wasn't going to be time. The enemy only had to swing around their big guns, aim carefully, and blast a giant hole into our exposed engine compartment.

"Call engineering," I ordered Yamada. "Tell them to cut out our port engines and give all thrust to the starboard side. We can turn that way if—"

She shook her head with regret. "Engineering isn't answering my hails, sir. They've lost pressure. Most of them are probably dead. Radiation levels are spiking in the stern sectors on every deck."

I nodded, lowering my eyes. I felt defeated.

Sucking in a deep breath, I shucked off my harness as the engines died. We were drifting away from the enemy at speed.

"Display *Victory*," I said, standing up and looking at the forward screens. "Let's see how we did."

The screen brightened, and there was the enemy ship. Oddly, she seemed motionless in the velvet black. Her forward half, in fact, was entirely dark.

"I think they've lost power," Durris said. "Our sensors are fuzzy, but optics suggest—"

Rumbold whooped. "Look there! She's breaking up!"

The forward section of the great ship moved away from the stern. The rear portion, where the engines were located, still appeared to have power.

The battleship's aft guns were swinging about as if trying to focus on our fleeing vessel. They fired at random intervals, but nothing hit us.

"They're uncoordinated," I said. "Either their sensors are all forward or knocked out... No fire-control. They're operating manually."

Durris grinned suddenly, and he pointed beyond the battleship. A flock of tiny bright dots approached.

"Our missile barrage!" he said. "We flew so fast, we out ran them. I sent them all at her engines."

Dumbstruck, I watched the screen as events unfolded with startling speed. First, the enemy ship began to fire her point-defense weapons—or at least the rear half of her did. The crew pumped out chaff, decoys, everything they had.

But none of it was working. The forward section had the computers, the sensors—the brains.

Our missiles slammed into them like a shower of meteors. Brilliant explosions glowed on every screen. The battleship was tough, but no ship could take such a hammering on her stern without any appreciable defenses.

In the end, she blew up, transforming into a brilliant, glaring fireball.

We cheered and clapped one another on the back. Everyone aboard who still drew breath took a moment to enjoy a glorious victory.

It was short-lived. We soon had to return to the grim business of counting our dead, caring for our wounded and patching up a dozen holes the size of houses in our hull.

By any account, we had stepped from the shadows to sprint in for a desperate and lucky slash. Surviving such tactics at all might be counted a victory, but we had done better. We'd survived the exchange and bested our foe all at once.

Never had *Defiant* been so thoroughly wrecked. We were weary, but no one asked for a break. We worked on until shift-change, then through that one and into the next.

While the ship hummed with the activity of souls who were overjoyed just to be alive, I retreated to my office.

I sat down and contacted CENTCOM.

My plan was to ask for Admiral Perez, but he beat me to it. He answered my call within minutes of the transmission reaching Earth.

The conversation was a long one, partly because we were so far out it took several minutes to transmit our words from one office to the other.

In the end, he congratulated me with what seemed like honest relief and ordered me to return home as soon as possible.

I accepted these orders with a single suggestion of my own.

"Sir," I said, "I'd like to stop off at Mars first. We're not far, and we could use their labs to refuel and refurbish."

"All right," he said several minutes later, "but don't take on any more variants. I no longer trust them—or Doctor Vogel. Understood?"

"Understood, Admiral. Sparhawk out."

The channel closed, and I considered the black screen carefully. Who should I trust at this moment? CENTCOM or Vogel?

I wasn't certain.

-18-

It was nearly two weeks later when we reached Mars. *Defiant* had been so battered that we'd taken most of the time just getting her underway.

A small flotilla of support vessels escorted us. By the time we made it to the docks at Phobos, they were no longer serving as tugboats, but as ship escorts.

When we arrived at the lab complex, I found myself loathing the place. My previous visit still grated on my thoughts.

It was the variants, of course. They were so different, so *alien*. In comparison, even the savage Stroj seemed relatable. At least the Stroj possessed normal human emotions and could ape our appearance. They were prideful, prone to anger, and determined to see their missions through. All of these were relatively human-like qualities.

Not so the variants. I'd had plenty of time to become familiar with the trio aboard *Defiant*. Physically they were specialized, but their minds were all similar.

Certainly, K-19 had an air of authority about him, and the other two were subservient though argumentative. Still, their overall sameness bothered me. The questions and responses from the lesser pair were particularly noticeable. They were virtually interchangeable in speech patterns. Only Q-161 sounded different due to her higher voice. Pressed to know which of them had spoken a given sentence, I could not have told you except for that single difference.

In comparison, the Stroj were all individuals. They were part machine, yes, but the machine part wasn't always the portion that was dominant. Even in the case where they had a purely artificial brain, each of them was as varied and twisted as the gnarled roots of an old tree.

"Director Vogel is calling, Captain," Yamada told me as the docking apparatus swung into place and locked onto our prow.

"Right…" I said. "Put him on the forward screen."

I wanted no private meeting with this man. He had done me a good turn by placing three valuable and loyal creatures aboard my ship, but he'd also built the ones that had apparently gone mad and taken our fleet from us. Could three rights out of a thousand wrongs truly redeem an individual?

"Captain Sparhawk…" Vogel said, running his eyes over the command crew. He was clearly taken by surprise. He'd probably figured I'd take the call privately as I had on previous occasions.

"We'll need your facilities to effect repairs," I told him, taking charge of the situation. "*Defiant* must be fully operational as fast as possible. We lack full power, and one of our primary weapons banks is dead. Our bridge-drive is incapacitated as well."

"Yes, I've seen the manifest, but I'm calling concerning efficiency. It would be best if your entire crew disembarks and moves aboard our lab facilities here on Phobos while the repairs are being carried out."

"Excuse me?" I asked. "Pretend I don't understand what you're proposing.

He blinked, pushed his glasses up his nose, then spoke again.

"It's not complex. There will be organizational difficulties, naturally. We don't really have enough pressurized living quarters for all of you. We've done our best, setting up domes out on the moon's surface, but—"

"No—Director—I'm questioning the nature of this plan. Are you suggesting my crew abandon the ship while repairs are being performed?"

"Why yes, of course. The variants will be crawling over the hull and the internal passages. Your crew will just be in the way."

I shifted in my chair and frowned at him. "I'm sorry, but that's unacceptable. Here's how events will proceed: your facilities will manufacture parts and munitions. We will install them here on the ship. If we need some heavy lifting, such as the installation of a gun battery, we'll use the three variants you gave us previously."

Director Vogel looked perturbed. "That will slow down the job considerably. Have you witnessed the speed at which a variant can operate? Especially in a depressurized environment?"

"I have. It's quite impressive. But after recent events, I have security issues to take under consideration. You understand my reasoning, I'm sure."

He pursed his lips and nodded curtly. "I see. You've come to doubt my work—my variants. Even after watching this new version in action, you still refuse to trust them."

"That's right, Vogel," I said firmly. "I *don't* trust them. You do realize I have seen the old version in action too?"

"Damned straight..." I heard Rumbold mutter, but I didn't reward his rudeness with a glance.

"Well," Vogel said sullenly, "at least you should release the trio I've given you for an update. I noticed that when we tried to patch their software remotely we failed to connect."

I glanced at Yamada. That was her doing, and she was looking smug. She'd closed the port on our network that would have allowed Phobos to update the firmware on the variants aboard.

"We'll have to decline on that front as well," I said. "The current software version is working very well. We've got no complaints."

"Seriously? You should always update critical systems. We've discovered flaws. There would be no less than a thirteen percent upgrade in battery-life alone if you would only—"

114

"I'm sorry," I said. "Is there anything else?"

He appeared uncertain. "No, I guess not," he said at last. "Welcome to Phobos. We'd like to treat you to a victory dinner at our cantina if you'd like to come with your senior officers. That is, if you trust my engineers not to start a bar brawl and physically attack you."

Chuckling in what I hoped was a good-natured tone, I nodded. "We'll be there. Thanks for the invitation."

The screen darkened, and Rumbold caught my eye.

"What is it, Helmsman?" I asked him.

"If there's drinking to be done, I'm normally the first man to the bar. But I'm not sure about this outfit. Can we trust him, sir?"

I considered his question seriously. "If he tries anything, we'll melt his lab into slag, orders or no. He'll probably respect that."

"Right..." Rumbold said thoughtfully. "In that case, count me in as part of the going-ashore party!"

"Excellent. Anyone else wish to join me?"

Durris shook his head. As my XO he knew his place was on the command deck whenever the captain was away. Yamada begged off as well. She didn't like parties much—at least not loud, large parties.

Accordingly, it was less than an hour later that we docked and Rumbold accompanied me down the tube to Phobos. We were both wearing formal attire. Our dress-blues were pressed with nano-precision and our emblems shown with an intense luster that spoke of internal power sources.

"You think he'll kill us, sir?" Rumbold asked in a husky whisper.

"A man ought not to live in fear, Rumbold. Loosen up and enjoy yourself."

"I intend to! I'm only hoping the mad doctor will let me get good and drunk before he reveals his true intentions. It would only be right, after all."

I smiled outwardly, but inside I was worried. How could I not be?

Somehow, Vogel's creations had taken over battleships in the past. They'd run rampant afterward, crewing the very ships they'd built. By the reports, they were devastating colonies abroad.

Certainly, Vogel had helped us with three solid performers. But did that mean I could trust him completely?

What if he'd given me the gift of three competent workers with the very purpose of gaining my trust?

Paranoid delusions? Perhaps, but my mind's-eye kept coming back to the image of Halsey being struck dead by those ghastly machines.

How had they gained his trust? Had he simply opened the door to his cabin and let them inside? If so, I had no intention of doing the same thing.

I knew that if they were trying to take *Defiant* from me, it was because they wanted the ship, not my flesh and bones. I was entirely expendable. Therefore, I saw it as my job to seem affable rather than repulsed by everyone and everything on Phobos. I had to keep them thinking their plot had a chance.

At least, that was, until my ship was completely repaired and ready for action. At that point, I could show my true opinions.

-19-

If you've never partied with an engineering team in deep space... well... I can't recommend it.

The crowd was a crowd in name only. Some two dozen subdued individuals in white nano-fiber resembled blocky blobs of snow in an otherwise decorative barroom. A few were boisterous, but most were drinking in stoic silence.

The walls of the establishment were raspberry. The ceiling was a collage of moving holographic color, and the lasers projected upon the floor depicting a rippling, reflective pond. Loud music thumped from the red walls until the narco-drinks numbed you and made everything seem normal. At that point, the music seemed to become muted.

Most in attendance were drunker than I. I'd activated my internal blood-toxin filters and cranked them up to the fullest. The filters were expensive toys I'd found useful time and again. I was feeling good, to be sure, but not past the point of oblivion.

Rumbold wasn't bothering to alter or hide his state. He'd taken up with a sultry scientist with long, red hair which defied her lab suit. She'd torn holes in the fabric purposefully, claiming she was feeling hot. Her skin and hair were spilling out of her white coveralls, both in stark contrast to it. The smart clothing tried to mend itself, but she kept pushing away the crawling straps and cinches.

As the party progressed, so did their behavior. Rumbold and his newfound companion were clapping one another on the back almost as often as they were hammering for fresh drinks.

Variants served the drinks to the crowd with silent efficiency. I still found the cyborgs as unsettling as ever. Such was their speed and dexterity they were able to deploy arms reaching three meters or more to their fullest extent in a split-second. Slinging drinks from behind the bar to a waiting patron occurred in the blink of an eye.

I couldn't help watching this in concern. If the variants decided to become aggressive, well, every human in the room would be slaughtered inside a single minute. As it was, those flashing arms might have caught someone and broken a nose or ripped away an ear as they delivered drinks with unnecessary speed.

"Can't you get them to slow down?" I asked Director Vogel.

He was sitting at my side wearing a dour expression and sipping a coffee laced with potent drugs.

He shrugged in response to my question. "Do they really alarm you so much?"

"Yes, they damned well do," I told him. "They should alarm you as well. You can't know they aren't plotting a takeover right here on Phobos."

He snorted and shook his head. His expression was that of a man bemused by a fool. I found it aggravating.

"How can you sit there and feel no remorse for what your machines did aboard *Victory*?" I demanded with sudden vehemence. I knew that my emotions were coming out more strongly than I'd intended, but I couldn't hold back. The drinks and the atmosphere were having some effect on me, after all.

Vogel made a flippant gesture. "You're drunk," he said. "I don't take the words of a drunk seriously."

Standing up, I found I wasn't swaying or bleary-eyed. My mind was sharp—perhaps sharper than usual.

"What if I were to threaten you?" I demanded. "What would they do? Would they move to protect you?"

"No. They aren't security variants. They're bartenders."

Deciding to test his theory, I drew my sword.

One must understand the nature of modern society to fully understand the meaning of such an act. Although the run of the mill worker on Earth might have found the brandishing of a power-blade unexpected, they by no means were unaware of its significance.

Director Vogel's eyes went from sleepy to wide-awake within a split-second. His mouth formed an "O" of surprise.

"Are you mad?" he demanded. "Have a care, Captain, or I'll have your commission."

A half-smile crossed my face. "I'm only a captain of the Guard, it's true," I told him. "But you're the man who created a crew of treacherous machines."

"That's not so—!"

I leaned close to him, interposing the sword between myself and his person.

"I watched them behead Halsey," I told him. "I watched that on a live feed, I experienced it as if I was there."

He stared at the sword in his face, which I'd switched on. Plasma ran down the length of it and ran back again, forming a horizontal line that lit up his dark eyes.

A hand fell on my wrist then.

"Hold, Captain!" Rumbold said to me. "You've had a bit too much to drink, that's all!"

I straightened and looked at the variants. They were still slinging drinks robotically. A few of the patrons had left out of concern, but others stared curiously.

With a flourish, I lashed out with my blade. The air sparkled and then there was a flash of discharged energy. Smoking, a severed arm dropped from a variant that had just delivered a drink. The arm was withdrawn, and the variant's oh-so-odd eyes swiveled to stare at me. There was no expression on that painted face to indicate what it might be thinking of my act.

"I shouldn't have come here," I said to Vogel. "It was my mistake. I'll retire to my ship now."

Marching out of the bar, I swept down the passages sheathing my blade. Behind me, I heard the pattering footsteps of Rumbold. He caught up and looked over his shoulder as if he thought a hundred angry technicians might be pursuing us.

"Captain Sparhawk!" called a voice.

I stopped, breathing hard. After a moment's thought, I turned on my heel and faced the man who addressed me.

It was Director Vogel. His expression was one of concern.

"Captain," he said, "let me tell you how sorry I am for your loss—for Earth's loss."

I didn't speak, not trusting myself to do so.

Vogel slowly approached.

"I hadn't thought of the human angle to all this," he admitted as he walked up to us. "I hadn't considered—you have to understand, the variants are my life's work. They are like my children. A man has a right to protect his children, doesn't he, even if they go down a dark path?"

"No," I said flatly, "not when those children kill thousands—possibly millions. You must reject them. You must accept your gross failure. If anyone down at CENTCOM had any brains, they'd shut down the lot of them."

Vogel considered. "You might be right. Why *wouldn't* they do such a thing? I've been afraid of that possibility for some time."

"Huh," grunted Rumbold.

We both looked at him, and he shrugged. "Seems more than obvious to me. They need the variants. They need them now more than ever. They must have fresh ships. This time they might not let them aboard those ships—but they want the ships built in the first place."

His words rang true, and we didn't feel the need to discuss the point further.

"Walk with me, will you?" Vogel asked serenely, his pupils dilated.

I agreed, and Rumbold again tottered in our wake.

"The variants didn't fail as you think they did," Vogel told me in a quiet voice. "I went over their code before and after I heard of the disaster. There was no error. No self-awareness that grew to the point of rebellion."

Puzzled, I shook my head. "Are you denying they killed the crew of at least one battleship?"

"No, I'm not saying that. I'm saying they were given fresh parameters. Their malfunction wasn't their fault—or my fault. Of that much, I'm certain."

"I see," I said, "and what evidence do you have to support this theory?"

"It's more than a theory, but I have nothing other than my word to support it. Anything I dredge up wouldn't convince anyone. I could just as easily be showing you code that was overwritten."

"Right," I said, "which renders your statements meaningless."

"No," he said, "not at all. Think, man! If I didn't do it, if no one here on Phobos did it—then who did? And why?"

He had managed to give me pause. I didn't like to admit it, but his candor was disarming. He'd been defensive as the creator of the variants, but he was also realistic. The least I could do was try to respond in the same manner.

I tried to push past emotions and the lacework of drugs in my mind. The latter was easier than the former.

"All right," I said, "I'm willing to entertain your claims because I've seen your machines in action. The variants aboard my ship showed no interest in aggression or rebellion. They're fascinated by fast, effective action. That's all. The same clearly goes for your variants here on Phobos."

"They didn't even care when you whacked one's arm off!" Rumbold interjected loudly.

"Quite right," I said, glancing at him. "All right, Director Vogel. I'm willing to be convinced you and your people aren't at fault. Where do we go from here?"

"That would seem obvious," he said. "We have to figure out who really hacked into my creations and suborned them."

"And how do we do that?"

He sidled closer. "You could take me with you. We'll figure it out—me and my variants."

"Won't you need an assistant?" Rumbold asked.

We glanced at him. I almost smiled.

"Did you have anyone in mind, Rumbold?"

"As a matter of fact, the lady I was speaking with expressed a wish to leave this rock—her words, not mine!"

Vogel huffed. "You're talking about Dr. McKay, aren't you? She's not been working out. I've been considering transferring her back to Earth."

"Perfect!" Rumbold said, clapping his hands together. "Two birds with one stone—don't you think?"

We were both frowning at him in incomprehension.

He came closer and his powerful alcoholic breath washed over us.

"You see," he said, "you can't very well form an obvious team of investigators. You have to take people who are leaving for other, supportable reasons. In McKay's case, she'll be heading home for a transfer."

"Why would we need to go through such complications?" Vogel asked.

Rumbold laughed and shook his head. "I can see you're new to scheming. Whoever did this is connected. They can't be allowed to see what's coming."

"I agree with your helmsman," Vogel said after careful consideration. "They're bound to hang all this around my neck sooner or later. I would appreciate your help in finding out what really happened, Captain Sparhawk."

Slowly, they convinced me. The matter had to be investigated. I'd been told by Perez that CENTCOM was handling the investigation internally—but I knew what that meant. They'd probably cover up the matter as best they could and find blame outside their organization, presumably placing the matter at Director Vogel's feet.

Their other option was far more sinister. If CENTCOM had been compromised, my own superior officers might be actively behind the plot. In that case, an investigation was bound to be fruitless. If anyone was going to get blamed, it would likely be me.

Coming to a decision, I led the group toward the docking tube, and I took them aboard *Defiant*.

We had a lot of careful planning to do.

-20-

To say Vogel and I didn't trust one another was an understatement. He was a deep-gov scientist, the kind that Guardsmen rarely ever met. He held service people of any stripe in low regard.

To him, I was a foppish, self-important dictator determined to get into his way. To me, he was an irritant and quite possibly a traitor to all humanity.

Unfortunately, we had to work together. Both of us had too much to lose. Our careers were dangling on strings before our noses, not to mention our very lives.

"I'm only going to work with the three variants you already have embedded in my crew," I insisted during the second hour of intense negotiations.

The narco-beers had long ago been filtered out of my bloodstream. I missed the chemicals dearly. Vogel was competent, but he was also difficult to deal with under the best of circumstances.

"Three isn't enough," he insisted. "We need a full squad of them. The trio you have here—they don't even have the correct cross-section of skills."

"They'll have to do. Perez specifically ordered me *not* to bring home more variants."

"Are you making that up?" he asked.

My face reddened slightly. I could feel it.

"I'm not accustomed to lying, sir," I said.

"No... no I don't suppose that you are. I reread your psych profile upon your return to Phobos. You're painfully honest, Sparhawk."

"Thank you."

"It wasn't meant as a compliment."

"But I've chosen to take it as one."

We eyed each other for a moment in anger.

"Look," he said at last, leaning forward. "We're about to undertake a clandestine mission. If you can't even lie for a cause so important—"

"I'm capable of tactical duplicity. Sometimes the omission of critical details is just as powerful as the fabrication of facts."

He nodded at last. "Good enough. That will have to do. Six variants—"

"What's that?"

"I can do with six. We can hide three of them in crates in the hold as we approach Earth. That is what you meant by acceptable duplicity, isn't it?"

I considered his offer carefully. He'd reduced the number of variants required to six in a remarkably short time. This fact made me want to press further.

"Three," I said, "the same three who've been aboard all along."

He made a gesture of disgust and slouched back in his chair. "This is all because you won't break your commitment to Perez? The man isn't to be trusted."

"Nor are you, Director Vogel. You'll have to make do with the three variants aboard. That's all I can do for you."

"What about my personal staff? How many people can I bring aboard?"

"How many do you need?"

"Five."

I nodded after a moment's consideration. "We have ample room in the living quarters for more crewmen. We lost a number of technicians. Your five will be welcome."

"Ah-ha!" he said, waving a stick-like finger in my direction. "It's not me you don't trust, it's my variants."

"Of course it is. My marines could kill your entire staff within ninety seconds after I gave the order. The variants, however, would be much harder to dispatch."

He appeared alarmed by the idea, but I pretended not to notice.

"Very well," I said, "as we're now in agreement, I'll have to ask you to excuse me. I must get back to commanding my ship."

I walked toward the conference room door, but before I could reach it, his hand jumped up to bar my path.

"Yes?" I asked him sternly.

"Would you really order your men to kill my scientists? They're a pack of harmless civilians!"

"We're not thugs, Director. I was speaking about a hypothetical case. Despite the fact you've been scanned and DNA traced since you came aboard, you might not be what you seem to be."

He frowned. "You've been running genetic checks?"

"Yes, and much more than that. Yamada has worked up a complete file on you. The results have been fed to me during our meeting via my implant. As far as my technicians can tell you're human, but you still might be a traitor."

Director Vogel appeared to be alarmed. He removed his arm, and I left him behind to think about his position. He had to understand he was in a delicate spot. I wasn't going to let him have a free hand aboard my ship.

Just as important, all of our lives were very much in danger. We were engaged in a deadly business. It wouldn't surprise me if we were all executed before this was over, or turned into "unpersons" by those who dwelt on Earth in her longest shadows.

I hadn't told him about that part yet. I doubted he knew—how could he? It was only by discussing matters of state with the Council that I'd come to grasp the true nature of the political system on Earth.

The following week saw brisk improvements aboard my ship. The damage to the external decks, those near the hull itself, were slowly being cleared and repaired. Gone were the days when we could rely on Stroj-built damage repair robots to do all the work. During our many voyages and battles, the numbers of such machines had dwindled. Crewmen I could replace, but not the robots. Every one destroyed over the last few years had been a permanent loss.

After breakfast on the eighth day, I reached the command deck fifteen minutes before my shift began. As was my custom, I began the day's routine surveying the logs of repair activities over the previous twenty-four hours.

Materials were flowing steadily up from Phobos to our end of the docking tube. The occasional part that had been too large to transport this way had been left on the surface of Phobos, to be later ferried by my crewmen using pinnaces.

Under no circumstances had variants from Phobos been allowed to come closer than the far end of the docking tube. My own crew and my handful of trusted variants waited at our end to receive the steady stream of equipment and supplies they were sending up in large loads every hour or so. They used muscle and servos to place and attach each item.

The process was slow, to be sure, but it was clearly safer this way. I didn't want to end up making a final broadcast to Earth as Admiral Halsey had.

Vogel sent me a text about three hours after I'd relieved Durris, asking to meet me for lunch. I agreed, and when the time came I found his entire team was sitting with him at the luncheon table in the officers' mess.

Before I could take my tray to join them, I found myself accompanied by my stone-faced Marine Commander. He'd apparently been waiting in the mess hall with his tray growing cold until I arrived. Falling into step beside me, he joined us without a formal invitation.

I didn't make an issue of it. Zye, if she'd been here, would have done the same.

Thinking of Zye gave me a pain. I'd sent several messages to Earth regarding her, but I'd yet to receive anything back. Over the last few days I'd stopped bothering. She'd been left behind and doubtlessly had duties to perform for Star Guard that had nothing to do with me. She was a big girl—literally and figuratively—and could take care of herself.

126

Still, it seemed out of character for her to be silent via distant connection for so long. I hoped something hadn't gone wrong, and I vowed to look into the matter upon my return to Earth.

Shrugging, I made an effort to pay my full attention to the team that now faced me. They looked as wary as my own crew did around their variants.

"Captain," Vogel said, "so good of you and this... gentleman... to join us."

"This is Marine Lieutenant Morris," I said.

Vogel lifted the corners of his mouth a fraction, but he didn't offer to shake hands. Neither did Morris or any of the others. Dr. McKay was there with the rest, and her red hair was now tucked away. She seemed as sober and watchful as the rest, and she barely nodded to me.

"Introductions aside," Vogel continued, "I was hoping this morning that you'd accept some suggestions to speed up and improve the repair process."

"Suggestions?" I asked. "Such as?"

"Well... your restrictions upon us have been severe—"

"Hold on right there," Morris said, leaning in and speaking in a low, mistrustful voice. "You can forget it, Vogel. We're not letting your variants run wild on this ship. You can just forget about that. The job will get done when it gets done."

Vogel's eyes slid to look at Morris in a startled fashion, then moved back to look at me. "That's not what I'm talking about."

"Please then, explain it to us," I suggested.

"It's about the variants here aboard *Defiant*. We've not been allowed to see them, to service their needs."

"They don't need anything," Morris interjected again. "They suck up oil, oxygen, protein powder and electricity. Once in a while, they might shit a battery, but they pick those up on their own. They don't—"

My hand came up at last. "Morris, please."

He fell into a brooding silence.

"What's wrong with our variants that might require your attention?" I asked Vogel.

"That's just it, we have no idea. They might need any number of service requests handled. The units were built by us, Captain. They weren't designed to run in a hostile environment full of biologicals for so long without care."

"Biologicals?" I asked.

"He means us," Morris said flatly. "We're like some kind of bug colony on a plate to these people."

"Hyperbole aside," Vogel continued, "we need to attend to the variants."

I pretended to consider the idea. Then, slowly, I shook my head. "We'll see. Perhaps it can be arranged after we reach Earth."

Vogel released an unhappy exhalation. Morris grinned.

"Captain, please be reasonable."

"I am. When we reach Earth orbit, we'll take up this matter again. With the help of your units, we're making progress faster than we'd anticipated. *Defiant* will fly in a few more days."

Vogel now appeared startled. "That isn't possible. Phobos won't even have had time to produce and deliver all the parts by then for a full repair."

"One week then," I said. "By that time, we'll be space-worthy. Not perfect, but serviceable. Thank you for your time, and your efforts."

I got up and left the table. They fell to talking irritably behind us.

Morris fell into step beside me.

"That's the way to handle those people," he assured me. "They're almost as strange as the variants themselves."

"Morris," I told him, "as much as I appreciate your efforts to safeguard my person—"

"You don't have to thank me, Captain," he said. "I'm glad to do it. It's my job."

"Well, at least until Zye is back aboard."

I said this last with a smile. Everyone knew that Zye was paranoid as my security officer, and she tended to follow me around determined to prevent encounters such as the one we'd just experienced.

128

But Morris didn't respond the way I'd expected. Instead of snorting with laughter, he gave me a blank stare.

"Did you say 'Zye', sir?" he asked.

"Yes, of course."

"Who's that?"

It was the utter blankness of his expression that made me stop in my tracks. I faced him fully and began to get a sick feeling.

"Lieutenant Morris," I asked, "have you ever met a Beta?"

"You mean one of those giant freaks that built our ship?" he asked in surprise.

"Yes, exactly."

"Well no, Captain. I remember seeing them on the screens in battle, and I remember how they marched aboard, hulking in their armor. But I've never seen one alive and talked to her. No one on Earth has, that I know of. Why do you ask?"

I felt thoroughly sick. I wanted to unload the lunch I'd just consumed on the deck, but I did my best not to react visibly.

"The update," I said aloud and staring at a bulkhead. "We got one from Earth this morning, didn't we?"

"Uh... yes sir. You okay, Captain?"

"Yes... I'm fine. Maybe the food wasn't the freshest."

He laughed. "The cook on every ship is a marine's worst enemy!"

"Just so..."

He left me then, standing in the passage outside the mess hall.

Inside my mind and my heart, there was a gaping hole. I knew without a shadow of a doubt that Zye, my companion and friend of several years, a woman who'd I'd entrusted with my life on any number of occasions, was gone.

She'd become an *unperson*. I could feel it in my bones.

Already, my mind was planning to do careful searches online and generate seemingly off-handed questions for various crewmembers—but I knew what I'd find.

Nothing.

Zye was gone. Her memory had been erased from the mind of everyone who'd known her.

What had she done back home, on Earth, to deserve such a fate? How had she managed to anger those who ran my world from their dark strongholds?

I didn't know, but I meant to find out.

-21-

Sick despair over Zye's disappearance grew steadily in my mind, eventually transforming into cold determination.

If she still lived, I would find her. It was as simple as that. I'd discover why she was removed from existence, and I'd reverse the process if at all possible.

Under no illusions, I knew I wouldn't find these tasks easy to perform. The ancients who ran my world hadn't done so for a century and a half without being very good at it.

My efforts would have to be forceful, but my true purposes would have to be hidden. No one would support me if I were to reveal my cause. Even Yamada, whose hack on my implant had allowed me to keep my memories, had no inkling that Zye had ever existed.

To confront people, to run around the ship insisting they recall an unperson, that would invite disaster. There was no evidence.

I'd visited Zye's cabin. Everything was there as it had been, but her effects had been left behind on Earth. This was a standard procedure for crewmen. You unshipped for long stays and often your cabin was reassigned. In the past, there might have been a physical image, a photograph, something of that nature—but not in modern times.

Images, voiceprints, signatures, recorded events—they were all held digitally. They were universally stored on networks in collective clouds of data. Such evidence of Zye had been meticulously erased.

Zye's existence as a data factoid had probably been the easiest element to remove. In retrospect, the very nature of our modern culture, especially in regard to modern record keeping, made such deletions simplicity itself.

Her database key had been deleted. Her records destroyed. All transactions and vid clips—gone.

Even DNA traces would prove nothing. They might show that a Beta had at one point been living aboard *Defiant*—but so what? The ship had been built and crewed exclusively by Betas in the past.

No, talking about an unperson to those who didn't remember her would be met with laughter at first, but that would quickly transform into concern. My sanity would be questioned if I persisted. I'd lose my command by the time we returned to Earth. There, those who might take notice of my quixotic behavior and realize my mind hadn't been properly edited may decide to take further drastic action against me.

Therefore, I'd have to proceed with care. Every action I took toward discovering Zye's fate would have to appear to have another purpose. If I revealed my true goal, it would only serve to put my enemies on guard.

The very idea of hiding my mission grated on me. I hated the whole idea of subterfuge. It reminded me too much of politics.

I decided to mark down the situation as one more reason to hate the Council and their Chairman even more deeply. I'd never liked the Council or felt their rule was just, but now, they'd made it personal.

My first move was to meet again with Vogel. This time, I spoke to him privately, taking pains to make sure we weren't being recorded.

"Captain Sparhawk," he began in a pained voice, "your crew—especially that detestable man Morris, who still refuses to—"

"I'll fix it," I said, cutting him off. "I'll give you full access."

He stopped, taken aback. "Full access to what?"

I shrugged. "The ship. The variants. Whatever supplies you might need. I've changed my mind about you, Director. I think you're just the man whose help I need."

Vogel blinked, stared then slowly moved a fingertip to press his glasses farther up his nose.

I'd never asked him why he didn't bother to get his eyes surgically altered. Glasses were exceedingly rare these days. Perhaps he considered it to be a fashion statement of some kind.

"Excellent," he said slowly. "May I ask what changed your mind specifically?"

"Someone took over Halsey's ship. They used the variants to do it. At first, I'd assumed the variants themselves had gone mad or rebelled against—"

"Couldn't happen. Not in a thousand generations!"

"Yes, so you've said many times. I've come to believe you. I've come to understand that your variants aren't the enemy, but they may have become the unwitting tools of our *real* enemy."

Vogel cautiously nodded. "Logical. Inescapably logical."

"Yes… The question now is what you and I are going to do about it."

He blinked again. "Do? About what?"

"Weren't you listening? Someone managed to hack your variants and give them orders to rebel. That individual, or group of individuals, must be from this star system. They aren't an external threat, they exist within our ranks."

Perhaps my intensity and lack of humor was getting to the man. What he'd expected to consist of a fruitless argument for access had turned into something much different. He looked very uncomfortable.

"Well… Captain Sparhawk, I don't know quite what to say. What you're claiming may be true, but we don't have any way of knowing how events progressed aboard *Victory*. It could be that—"

"Let me show you something," I said, interrupting him.

Without waiting for his reply, I tapped at my desk. I called up the vid file of my last conversation with Admiral Halsey. After going through a series of passwords, I played the file.

133

He watched with a mixture of fascination and surprise. At the end, when his variants stepped into the scene and slaughtered the man I'd been talking to, his emotions switched to horror. His fingers spread over his face, long and thin, with his eyes staring between them.

"Captain... I'm so sorry. I had no idea this video existed. Why did you—?"

"It was classified. I'm sure you understand why CENTCOM didn't have you at the top of the list of people to be trusted with this information."

"Yes... of course not. I'm so sorry. I had no idea. Halsey was your friend, wasn't he?"

"My mentor."

He looked at me with new understanding. "Your resentment and mistrust suddenly make more sense to me. Up until this moment, I never quite believed that the variants did it. I didn't *want* to believe it. You understand, don't you?"

"I suppose that I do."

"What puzzles me now," he said, "is your sudden change of heart. Under the circumstances, you have every reason to want me and my creations off your ship. What has changed?"

Looking down, I considered how to answer his question. As I've said, I don't like to lie. It took me a moment to come up with a truth that would set his mind at ease without giving away my true intentions.

"Director, there are more pieces of evidence that I'm not at liberty to share with you. Do you understand?"

He nodded, staring at me. "I do indeed, Captain. I must say, my estimation of your intellect and judgment is soaring."

"Good. Now, I must ask again: do you want to find out who took control of your creations and turned them into weapons against us?"

"I do indeed," he said, his face becoming thoughtful and intense. He leaned forward, lowering his voice. "What do we do now? How can I help?"

There it was. I had him where I wanted him. It was manipulation, to be sure, but it was for the best of reasons. I comforted myself by recalling that it was all for a good cause.

134

I began to outline my plan then, which for me was only a series of conjectures and schemes. He was both impressed and fearful of the consequences.

"Are you sure?" he asked in a whisper when I'd finished. "Are you sure this action is justified?"

"I've been involved in internal affairs of state before," I told him. "At times, things become messy. The public at large has never known the true depths to which our command centers were compromised in the past."

"Astounding. If I hadn't seen the vid of Halsey, I would have thought you to be a madman."

My lips twitched into a smile.

"I might have thought the same," I told him.

The rest of the journey back to Earth went smoothly. Each day, we rapidly repaired *Defiant's* subsystems. Allowing the variants full access to the ship, and Vogel's team full access to the variants, sped things up dramatically.

By the time we docked with Araminta Station, we were ninety-one percent operational.

But all through that time, Vogel and I worked on another project. We put our heads together and plotted. We worked long hours, and when we were done, I thought our plan might just work.

At least, there was a chance.

-22-

Araminta Station looked cold and lonely outside my window. Gone were the cluster of proud battleships Earth had produced just a few months earlier and sent on their doomed voyage into the unknown.

There was a brooding nature to the place when I disembarked and walked the passages. The crowds were muted. The atmosphere was laced with anxiety. Those who did recognize me and my crewmen examined us with foreboding. There were no shouted greetings or congratulations.

After all, hadn't we done battle with *Victory*? Hadn't we destroyed the only Earth vessel to return home? The sole survivor of our most glorious fleet?

Rumors were rampant. Some depicted me as a would-be dictator. A man who'd engineered a mass mutiny, and a mass scuttling of the armada for my own gain. Others painted me as incompetent, a petty man of mean spirit—or even as a Stroj agent.

Such was the depth of my reputation I found I didn't have to worry about bodyguards. I was universally reviled and avoided. Men all but ran when they saw me coming down the echoing halls.

Most puzzling of all, however, was the lack of activity. I'd expected Earth's navy to be licking its wounds and rebuilding. I'd thought to find a sense of desperate urgency, a fear of the unknown from abroad.

After all, what if the rest of the battleships had survived out there somewhere? What if they came back one day and returned to wreak havoc on our pathetic defenses?

Even if the common spacer didn't grasp the danger, CENTCOM and the government surely must. Why weren't they building a replacement fleet?

I contacted my father seeking the answer to this question as I came down the umbilical aboard a nearly empty car. Director Vogel and his variants weren't with me—our plan mandated that he and I separate until a critical moment in the future.

"Father?" I asked, sensing that an audio-only channel had opened. "Are you there?"

"I'm here. What is it, William?"

A cold greeting. I'd been in space for more than a month, out of contact except for an occasional vid message and presumably in great danger. I'd expected at least to be able to see the man who'd fathered me.

"Are you terribly busy?" I asked.

"No, not really. We're on recess. Mother and I are away on a private getaway. I'm sure you understand."

I hesitated, frowning. "No, I don't. Are you saying you don't wish to see me?"

"Not at all, son!" he said with false bravado. "We've just been planning this vacation for a long time. We don't get to see each other much in a private setting with our busy schedules. I'm sure that you'll have plenty to do on Earth seeing your friends and so forth. By the way... where will you be staying?"

"I... I thought I was coming home to stay at the mansion."

There was a deafening silence. My mind raced, and I began to understand the situation.

I should have expected it. My parents were political creatures. As my reputation was now radioactive, they wanted nothing to do with me.

Suddenly, the lack of video streaming also seemed very purposeful. To avoid any sort of association, it wouldn't do to have a snapshot of even a virtual meeting floating around the net.

"I understand completely," I said with what I hoped was only a hint of bitterness in my tone. "As it happens, I won't have time to come by the house. I've got a very busy schedule at CENTCOM. Perhaps after the next voyage, we'll have time to get together then."

"Yes!" my father said in relief. "That's a splendid idea. And William, about your next voyage… do you know yet when you might be shipping out again?"

"Soon father," I said, "very soon."

"Good. I always feel safer with you out there among the stars guarding the world all of us share. You make me proud, son."

"Thank you, sir," I said quietly.

The channel closed then, and I stared down at the green forests and black ribbon-like roads of Earth. Dark clouds boiled off to the east, over the ocean. Air traffic flittered this way and that above the clouds, trying to avoid the storm.

I felt as if I didn't have a friend in the world, but that didn't weaken my resolve. In fact, if anything, it strengthened it. The elderly spiders in their hole up to the north, they were the ones I must defeat.

The path wasn't going to be easy, and I knew I had to take serious risks if I was to have a chance. The first item on my agenda involved an early a.m. visit to CENTCOM.

That night I slept fitfully in a hotel. I dreamt of spiders and worse things, all of them seeking to steal Zye, Yamada, Rumbold and other familiar faces from me.

When I awoke, I was red-eyed and irritable. Shower and breakfast did little to improve my mood.

As the sun dawned over the land, I stood in front of CENTCOM. I didn't go inside, but instead waited for Vogel and his shipment of special equipment.

He was late. The sun rose higher, and I began to wonder if I'd been taken for a fool. What kind of man would plan something as audacious as this and then bail out at the last minute?

Director Vogel, my mind said to me, supplying the name of the coward in question. This failure to act on his part seemed in character.

Perhaps he'd awakened this morning as had I, and during the early hours common sense had taken hold of his mind. The plan was half-baked at best. Vogel had never impressed me as a man of great fortitude.

Maybe he'd simply taken his packages and returned to the spaceport. Perhaps he was back on Araminta Station or in his homeland in Europe.

I could hardly blame him, but I was angry. I almost used my implant to call him. Almost.

Give it ten minutes more, something told me. *Just ten minutes.*

Pacing back and forth near a fountain, I was given odd glances by early-shift personnel as they arrived in Star Guard uniforms. The groundskeepers and even passing sparrows all seemed to pause for comment. But I didn't talk to any of them, and I didn't call Vogel. We'd agreed not to have contact until we met at this exact spot.

Losing patience a half-hour later, I reached out with my implant—but halted before I started a person-search. A new thought had frozen my mind.

What if Vogel had become an unperson overnight?

That's how it had happened before with Zye. The mere idea of such a possibility was terrifying to me. If they'd gotten him, I couldn't be far behind. I felt like I was living in a bad dream.

Fixating on the idea that Vogel had vanished like Zye, my mind began to churn. How could I run an online scan to check on his existence without sending up red flags? I was certain that a directory search on Vogel would trigger an AI somewhere. Then they would know my mind hadn't been properly updated. My own existence would be in danger of erasure after that.

I hit upon a circuitous route. I searched not for Vogel, but rather for the Phobos labs themselves. Wouldn't the director's name be prominently displayed?

"There you are!" called a familiar voice.

Turning, I spotted Vogel. He was trotting toward me but not from the expected direction. He was supposed to approach from the street. Instead, he'd come from the main entrance.

"Director?" I asked. My emotions ran the gambit. I felt surprise, relief and irritation. After a moment, irritation won out. "What are you doing inside, man?" I demanded.

"Sorry, I had a technical problem. I had to be present at the unboxing, and—"

Waving my hands for silence, I began walking briskly toward the entrance. He followed along, panting. I could tell he was unaccustomed to full Earth gravity.

"We can't talk about that," I said. "Is everything set? That's all I need to know."

"Yes. We can meet them at the receiving dock. They won't activate until we get within ten meters."

I glanced at him. "Isn't that cutting things a little close? What if the guards don't let us get that near to them?"

He waggled his fingers in the air helplessly. I shook my head and hurried on.

"We're under time-pressure now, unnecessarily," I said.

"It couldn't be helped, Captain."

I had many choice words bubbling in my mind, but I let them go and tried to take deep breaths. We were almost an hour behind schedule. Admiral Perez would arrive at any moment.

Far overhead, I heard a buzzing sound. It could be his air car—I wouldn't be surprised. He came in at 8 a. m. promptly every morning.

"Let me do all the talking," I told Vogel. "When we get in there, you turn into a mute. Got it?"

"That hardly seems—"

"Got it?"

"Yes."

We reached the security screening at the entrance. They removed my PAG and my power sword, but left my personal shielding device. It was something, anyway.

We didn't make it ten paces toward the elevators before a Guardsman non-com rushed up to us.

"Sir?" he said, looking at me. "Are you Captain Sparhawk?"

"Of course."

"Please come with me. We have a situation."

This was it then. Could this be the straightforward approach the Council took when making an enemy vanish? Wait until they were in a compromised position then swoop down and arrest them?

My eyes flicked back to the entrance. It seemed very far away. I considered inventing an excuse to return—but then thought the better of it. I would have to bluff it through.

"What's the nature of this emergency?" I demanded. "We have an appointment with Admiral Perez."

"I'm sorry, sir, it's about a package down at the loading docks."

My eyes gave Vogel an accusatory glance. He said nothing, as I'd directed.

"Very well then, lead on."

We followed the spacer to the sub-levels. Before we even got to the double doors at the end of the hall, I heard the familiar rasp and hiss of moving variants.

"They're loose!" Vogel exclaimed. He began to run, rushing past us. He hit the doors with his thin arms outstretched.

"It's not safe!" the spacer called after him.

"He can handle them," I told the spacer. "They're like his children."

Then I rushed after the director. What I saw when we opened the door was shocking and crushing. I knew immediately all our carefully laid plans had been dashed.

A man lay dead in a gory heap on the loading dock. Another spacer, terrified for his life, stood near the chain-driven doors. He looked as if he wanted to break through them, but he couldn't. He stood with the air of a man who was trying not to be noticed by nearby predators.

The third of the variant team was just unloading itself from a cocoon-like shipping crate. Another helped it do so. They all turned to look at us when we entered the chamber.

"They killed Charlie!" shouted the spacer who'd led us here. "I have to call—"

"No!" shouted the man hugging the doors. "Don't transmit anything! Don't pull a weapon!"

The spacer who'd guided us here didn't listen. He put his hand on his PAG. That turned out to be a mistake.

A very long limb extruded from what I believed to be K-19. The arm had a pair of snips on it. The spacer lost his hand. His wrist was a stump, spurting blood.

Whip-like, K-19s arm retracted in the same blurring motion it had attacked.

Shocked, the spacer looked down at his wrist then he began making a keening sound.

"You have to stop that," Vogel advised sternly. "They're in a heightened state. They're off-protocol."

I reached out, grabbed the director and shook him.

"Dammit, Vogel!" I shouted in his face. "Can't you even control these abominations when you're in the same room with them?"

The spacer we'd come in with passed out on the floor. We glanced at him, but then I became aware of a looming, unnatural presence.

K-19 was standing over us, his snips clacking like chattering teeth.

-23-

"Captain Sparhawk," K-19 told me. "Aggression will not be tolerated."

I let go of Vogel's lab coat slowly. The nano-fabric of his collar unfolded itself and smoothed over.

"He's fine," I said to K-19. "This is all a misunderstanding."

"Understood. We must continue our mission."

Relieved, I opened my mouth to call out orders to them, but Director Vogel put his hand up to my lips and shook his head.

Watching in astonishment, I witnessed all three of the variants marching by through the double doors and up the ramps into the heart of CENTCOM.

"We'll follow them," Vogel said. "We'll use your biometrics to get past the elevator doors. No one will notice us in the confusion."

"We're just letting them run loose?" I asked.

Down the hall ahead of us, I heard shouting begin. Two shots were fired from PAGs.

Director Vogel began to trot.

"Damn, damn, damn," he said. "I didn't think they'd get off a shot!"

"What have you done?" I demanded, grabbing him again and spinning him around. "This wasn't supposed to happen! They're killing the guards!"

"Did you really think they'd let my variants get all the way to Perez's office without a direct assault being involved? Don't be naïve, Captain!"

My jaw sagged. I had hoped... but maybe he was right. There was no way to sneak these things all the way down to the heart of CENTCOM. They'd be stopped along the way, and once they were, it would be done in force.

"Let go of me," Vogel said, struggling. "They'll get too far ahead."

We rushed along in their bloody wake. Bodies were strewn about the place missing limbs in most cases. Some people merely huddled against walls, cowering. They'd been ignored by the variants.

"This is how Halsey lost his ship, isn't it?" I demanded of Vogel, who was puffing now with exertion.

"I can only imagine," he said. "Will you give me a hand?"

He was kneeling on the floor, sick from running in Earth's high gravity. I paused and considered leaving him behind. He'd lied to me. His plan to get down into the War Room had been a fabrication.

"You can't hope to control them without me," he said, seeing the doubt in my eyes.

Reaching down, I hauled him up to his feet. He staggered into me, his muscles atrophied by too much time spent in a low-G environment.

"They're programmed to drive a path between the loading docks and Admiral Perez's office off the War Room," he said in a gasping voice. "If they get stuck, we have to help them bypass security."

Feeling like a traitor, I hustled Vogel along the corridor. He seemed to get heavier with every step.

At last, we made it to the elevators. Guardsmen lay in puddles of blood and snipped-off limbs. Most of the staffers were screeching and fleeing out the exits in every direction. Outside the windows in the quad, I saw an armed contingent of marines gathering. It was only a matter of time until they counterattacked in force.

144

The elevator we'd reached was designed for heavy freight. There had to be some way of getting large items down into the vaults below the CENTCOM building, and we'd found it.

My hesitation lasted less than a second. The marines would gun us down with the variants if they realized we were in league with them. That much was clear. It was one thing for these cyborgs to abuse a few stray guards with pistols. An organized platoon of marines with heavy weapons was something else entirely.

I touched my hand to the plate, and it flashed green. We entered, and the variants trooped in after us. It was a tight squeeze.

The elevator doors shut, but it didn't start moving.

"They've locked it down," I said. "It's standard procedure. We'll never get to our goal now. You struck too soon."

Vogel wasn't listening. He was hacking instead. After I'd entered a valid biometric input, he only had to bypass the lockdown, not the regular security.

After a few seconds, the elevator lurched into motion, heading down again.

He gave me a triumphant grin, but when the elevator began moving, the gathering troops outside took action. They opened fire targeting the heavy metal doors.

A hundred PAG bolts burned and sizzled on steel. The whole elevator shook, and a spot grew orange-white, throwing off sparks. A moment later, as we threw ourselves to the floor, another spot began to burn.

They must have thought they had us trapped in the elevator, but now that we were escaping them they'd decided to kill us while they could. They were burning their way through, but it was too late. We were already sliding out of reach.

The firing stopped, but then the lights went out. Emergency red illumination kicked in and the elevator took on aspects of a funhouse. The three variants, packed into a space large enough for a truck but still cramped by their standards, resembled artificial monstrosities assembled to terrify carnival-goers.

The ceiling of the elevator car began to take scattered strikes.

"They must have forced the outer doors open," I said. "They're firing down the shaft. The metal roof of the car probably isn't thick enough to stop bolts from penetrating."

The three variants conversed with insectile rapidity. I thought I heard a few squeaks and clicks, but that was all.

Suddenly, R-77 climbed on the backs of the others and reversed himself, clinging to the roof of the elevator car with steel hooks. As it hugged the roof of the elevator over us, I couldn't help but notice the variant's carapace was smeared with the blood of innocent men.

PAG bolts soon began to sizzle through. As the fusillade was targeting the center of the car's roof, it burned through there first. It melted away in a shower of sparks, and the variant's exposed belly was lashed with fire.

He was sacrificing himself to protect the rest of us. The realization came as a shock. I'd never thought of the variants as protective of one another, much less us.

At last, before the variant died and lost its grip on the roof of the car, the door dinged and opened.

The scene beyond was smoking and vacant. The lighting at least was back to normal—normal for CENTCOM, that is. A dull, yellow glow filled the chamber.

We rushed out into what we'd hoped would be safety, but more troops were waiting for us.

"Step aside, Captain Sparhawk!" shouted a commander in dress-blues. His pistol was out, and his look was determined.

"Put away your gun," I told him. "You can't stop the variants with that. They'll cut off your arm."

He bared his teeth. His sides heaved as he looked me over for a second.

"Captain… are you *with* these things? What's going on?"

"CENTCOM has been infiltrated by the Stroj. Stand aside, Commander."

He stared. Perhaps he took too long because K-19 began to stalk him. At last, he waved for his men to put down their weapons. They all complied.

Dropping the gun like it was hot to the touch, we were all pleased to see K-19 halt and switch targets. He was now fixated on the doors that led into the War Room.

When I drew even with the commander, he snaked out an arm and caught me by the collar.

"If it was anyone else, I would have shot you down," he said to me. "Why are you marching with these monsters, sir?"

"Do you remember Admiral Cunningham?"

"The Stroj agent?"

"That's right," I told him, "she was operating right here, at CENTCOM."

He shook his head slowly, not liking where I was going with this.

"But sir, we've got new procedures. A Stroj imposter could never make it down here again."

I jerked a thumb in the direction of Vogel and his creations. "Well, that's what I'm here to find out. If I'm wrong, you can court-martial me—or better yet, just execute me on the spot."

"You better be right about this, Captain," he said. "If it was anyone else…"

"I understand."

We moved forward, and the variants scuttled behind us. We reached the security doors that led into the War Room. I turned to see if the commander would help.

I was shocked to see him sprawled out on the floor. All the others were sprawled with him. Most of them were dead, but a few crawled weakly, bleeding.

"I didn't even hear a commotion—K-19, what did you do?" I demanded.

"I observed the enemy signaling to one another. Before they could act, I disarmed them."

Staring, I could hardly believe my eyes. They were so fast, so accurate. The men had thought they could ambush us from behind, but they'd seriously underestimated their opponents.

Vogel stepped next to me. "You have a serious deficiency when it comes to knowing when you're being lied to, don't you?"

Unable to deny his words, I stepped up to the final door.

Together, we opened it.

-24-

Inside the War Room, two dozen staffers surrounded a half dozen high-level brass. They didn't have sidearms. Someone had forbidden loaded weapons in the control center due to past incidents. Unfortunately for them, disarming the troops hadn't made them any safer. We strode into the room unopposed.

Gasping, the officers fell back on all sides. One ran for the emergency exit on the far side, but Q-161 rushed forward and removed his left foot at the ankle. He fell, wailing, and the rest were cowed.

"Sparhawk!" boomed a familiar voice. "Have you lost your mind?"

It was Admiral Perez himself. I was glad he was here. That part of the plan had to rely on luck to succeed. He was highly ranked enough to make his own schedule. If he'd been late today or stepped out for an early lunch, our lightning strike would have gone differently.

"Admiral," I said, walking toward him. "I'm sorry about this intrusion. I'm afraid there's a traitor in our midst."

"There certainly is, and his name is Sparhawk!"

"I can see how you might feel that way, but you must let me speak."

"Why? If I don't will you slice a limb off me using your robotic slaves?"

My face reddened slightly. I hadn't known how things would go once we managed to penetrate Star Guard, but I'd hoped for an audience that would at least listen.

Taking a half-second to think about the situation, I came to a firm conclusion.

"You're the one who I'm talking about, Admiral. You're the enemy in our midst. I've dealt with your kind before."

The officers swept their eyes toward Perez. He wasn't popular, and they knew me. I could tell some of them at least had to be thinking I wouldn't have pulled this mutinous stunt without good reason.

"Yes, you have dealt with admirals in the past," Perez retorted. "You've bucked every officer in authority over you since you joined the service. You're a disgrace, and I want you out of here right now! Report to the stockade. There will be a court marital, and I'll wager it will be short and well attended."

My eyes narrowed as I considered him. "You aren't even curious about why I'm here, are you?" I asked. "You're just trying to stall for troop support and to shut me up. That won't work, Admiral."

"No, I wouldn't expect it to. You are a disgrace to the uniform. We should abolish the service of governmental heirs."

He'd struck below the belt with that comment. I hated any mention of my parentage, especially when it was suggested it made me unfit for duty.

I took a step forward, and he brightened. That caused me to halt.

This was what he wanted, I realized. When I stopped coming, he snarled at me and a surprising thing happened.

He charged toward me. Scuttling forward faster than any human should have been able to, especially at his age, he climbed right over consoles, a railing and even a conference table in his desire to close with me.

The variants were vigilant. They slashed out with their odd, whip-like limbs.

Perez was stricken and thrown off his feet. He rolled, blood welling up from a dozen wounds. It looked as if he'd been beaten with a lash, but I'd only seen a few flashing touches.

Breathing in a gargling fashion on the floor, he waved back the staffers who bent close to help him.

"Captain Sparhawk," said K-19. "I sense that the creature at our feet is still dangerous. It has an explosive device stashed inside its body cavity."

The effect of K-19's words was dramatic. A dozen sympathetic hands recoiled. Officers scrambled away in fear for their lives.

"Where is it?" I asked.

"In his lower section."

"Rip it out."

The order did not need to be repeated. People screeched as two snipping, multi-jointed hands reached forth and tore into Perez's guts. Exposed, a bloody string of wired-together explosives hung over the deck.

"Dammit Sparhawk," Perez rasped from the floor. "You're a fool to the last. You shouldn't have stopped me."

I was almost amused. "I should have let you kill me?"

"I was trying to get to Vogel, not you. Fool."

Those eyes. They were still roving, still intelligent. They didn't even look as if they had the glaze of shock in them. The Stroj were tough creatures indeed.

K-19 destroyed the bomb and moved after the officers who were trying to retreat.

"Let them go," I said. "They don't matter now. We have our monster. They all saw it. They know why I did this."

Soon, the room emptied out. Only Director Vogel, Perez and the variants were left to keep me company.

Perez breathed with difficulty. He grimaced up at me with blood outlining each tooth in his mouth.

I knelt beside him. "Talk to me, Stroj," I said. "Why do you want to kill Vogel so badly?"

"He unleashed these terrors on my people. He's responsible for their creation."

Glancing at Vogel, who looked disgusted but stayed quiet, I nodded. "He has a point, you know," I told the Director.

"Nonsense. The variants just saved CENTCOM from this enemy agent."

"Yes," I admitted. "But they are also manning our ships out there, and there are reports they've gone rogue."

"It's true," Perez rasped. "That's why we had to move. That's why I went for Vogel."

Frowning, I shook my head in incomprehension.

"Think about it, Sparhawk," Perez said. "Everyone says you're a genius. It's time to use that big brain of yours."

"You wanted to kill Vogel, not me... You wanted to make sure he couldn't make any more variants, or improve the ones he's developed."

"That's right."

"But why reveal yourself at all? Why not stand back and hope we're arrested?"

"Once you showed up here, you tipped my hand. I had to support your theories. I had to demonstrate to everyone, publicly, that I'm a Stroj agent."

Now he had my full attention. I sat beside him, making sure to keep beyond reach of his spit and his grasping, broken digits.

"You have me intrigued."

"He's playing you, Sparhawk," Vogel said suddenly. "Next, he'll claim I'm a Stroj."

I glanced back at him. "Are you?"

"Certainly not!" Vogel exclaimed.

"He's right, gargled Perez, sounding weaker. "Vogel is no Stroj. There's no honor in him. No love for honest combat. He's worse than any of my kind. He created his horrors to take over the cosmos. To kill all the humans he doesn't like, Stroj and Basics both!"

Vogel chuckled. "I'm surprised you're listening to this monster, Captain. It's clear he's desperate. His last tool is guile."

Both men had good points, and I was left uncertain who to believe.

"If you had killed Vogel, what would your Stroj brothers have done next?" I asked.

"We'd have kept a low profile, as we always do. Earthmen have very short memories. Eventually your kind will go back

151

to a place of danger after a few months, or years. We would have hidden in that group."

"For what purpose?" I asked. "The Earth fleet won't wait so long. They'll sweep your people from the cosmos."

The Stroj bared his teeth at me, but he didn't answer.

"You're dying anyway, man," I told him. "Why not speak plainly? It might help your cause."

"Impossible."

"Are the Earth ships, crewed by variants, damaging your empire or not?"

"Of course they are. I'm sure you're relishing the reports!"

That made me sit up straighter. "Reports? From the lost fleet?"

"Yes—and it's not lost. We don't know its exact position, but the fleet is dropping com-pods in every system when it exits a bridge. The variants have been maintaining protocols even after they mutinied. We've been picking them up and tracing their progress."

This was news to me. I was intrigued.

"Tell me about it," I asked Perez.

The Stroj's eyes became cagey. "Will you nurse me back to health if I do?"

"Yes," I said, "if I'm able."

"He plots," Vogel said suddenly. "He's not dead yet, so he's still churning up evil plans. Don't listen to him, Sparhawk."

"You..." spat the Stroj. "I should have known you wouldn't want the truth to come out. To think you people call *us* monsters. These variants have no soul, and precious little individuality. We're your enemies, certainly, but we're not genocidal."

"You're not?" I asked. "You wouldn't kill us all if you had the chance?"

"Of course not. You should know that by now, you of all Earthers. Where would the glory be in an enemy erased? We want dominance. We like the thrill of the hunt and the wriggling of our prey. How could we take trophies from people who've been turned to ash?"

"Is that what they're doing?" I asked in a hushed voice. "Reducing worlds to ash? I'd hoped it wasn't so."

"You've been to the stars, you've met the colonists," the Stroj said. "You've even befriended some of them."

My eyes had been unfocused, seeing my past voyages, but now I turned to him more fully. His face was gray now for lack of blood.

"You're talking about my friend Zye. You remember her, don't you?"

He rasped and his fingers fluttered. "Of course. We're immune to your government's purges of the mind and spirit."

"Talk to me," I said, reaching out to help staunch his wounds. "Vogel, get a medical kit."

"He's not worth saving, Sparhawk."

"Get the kit. You have medical training. Save him."

Shaking his head, Vogel did as I asked. Perez watched with interest.

"I want to kill that one. I still will if I get another chance."

"He's not to blame," I said. "He may have invented the variants, but he doesn't control them all."

The Stroj looked at me curiously. "You claim it was the ones we call the 'others' then? It is the ones who edit your minds whenever it pleases them?"

I nodded. "It could be."

"That does make sense. We might have a common cause, Sparhawk, you and I. Have you ever wondered why we keep coming back here?"

"To finish the job? To conquer us like the rest?"

"Partly, yes. But there's more to it than that. We share an enemy here. The others are not like the rest of you. We suspect they are alien. They're too cunning to be normal humans."

I chuckled at that. "That's where you're wrong," I said. "Basic humans can be the most cunning of them all."

The Stroj stared at me as Vogel worked to save his life.

"You *know* them," he said suddenly, with certainty. "You've met them! That's how your mind remains intact. Are you claiming you're one of that shadowy group? Are you one of the others, Sparhawk?"

"No," I said, "I count them as enemies, just like you."

A tongue darted out and vanished again. It was bluish in color.

"My fluids have left me. Give me a stylus."

Frowning, I handed him one. He began to write on the floor with his unbroken hand. I watched, but of course, no symbols appeared. The stylus was connected electronically to my computer scroll.

Taking the scroll out of my pocket and unrolling it, I saw what he was writing. The symbols amounted to a series of numbers in sets of three.

"Coordinates?" I asked.

The Stroj didn't answer. He didn't even look up. He wrote with a fury.

While I puzzled over the digits, Vogel stood up and shook his head. His hands were slick with blood.

"I don't completely understand his anatomy," he said. "He's lost too much fluid. He's almost gone."

The stylus trembled and then clattered onto the marble floor. I stared at the shivering corpse, then at the scroll.

"Director," I said, "you did what you could—at least I think you did."

He looked at me sharply. "What? Do you think I shoved the wrong kind of needle into him or something?"

I shrugged and rolled up the scroll, tucking it back into my pocket.

"Sorry," I said, "I have issues with trust these days."

-25-

Eventually, Star Guard troops made it down five hundred meters into the Earth and stormed into the War Room. We were waiting for them, weary but thoughtful.

The variants were handled very delicately. K-19 and Q-161 agreed to be escorted back into their crates and stored. Director Vogel was instrumental in this negotiation, using a soothing voice as one might with a reluctant pet.

After the variants had left, we were arrested and harshly debriefed, but I felt certain we'd eventually be released. We'd acted without orders but with what had to be acceptable reasons.

After all, hadn't a Stroj agent managed to work its way into Star Guard and take a commanding position? Who could be angry with the men who had revealed and destroyed it? Yes, good men had died, but if we'd not taken action all of Earth might have been lost.

Sitting in the brig far under the Earth for three days, I began to become concerned. Surely, they knew I'd done the right thing?

But doubts lingered in my mind. What if there were more Stroj about? Reason dictated the odds were high. Since Perez had been replaced, it was very likely there were more infiltrators. How could I expect those individuals to be pleased with me?

It was on the fourth day that my cell door finally rattled open. For the first time since my interrogation, a person came through instead of simply leaving a steel tray of cold food.

"Stand back!" said a querulous voice. "I've got a writ!"

"My Lady," said the jailor. "He could be dangerous. He stands accused of killing fifteen men."

"Nonsense, Warden. My nephew didn't kill them—those automatons did it. He's entirely innocent, as I intend to prove. Now, step aside!"

My heart dared to feel hope. It was my Aunt, the Lady Grantholm. She was a powerful figure in government and a confidant of the Chairman. If anyone could get me out of this, she could.

After arguing her way past the warden, she swept into my cell and looked around with a wrinkled nose.

"This is an unsavory habitat for a Sparhawk," she said. "Unacceptable."

"Lady Grantholm," I said, "good to see you."

"I wish I could say the same, but I can't. Why am I always being summoned to cleanse messes left behind by others?"

"Perhaps it's your calling."

She glared at me. "Being a smart aleck won't endear you to anyone, William. You should have outgrown that by now."

I sighed, tired of banter. "What are you doing here? Can you help me or not?"

She put her fingers to her lips. "Not here," she said. "Warden!"

The door swung open quickly.

"You must escort us to a private meeting room. This one is bugged and unsanitary."

She handed the man an order with a stabbing gesture. He took the computer scroll, looked at it, and then sullenly handed it back.

Without a word, he led us out of the dungeons. I followed with curiosity. My aunt was a wily woman. She'd made sure I was in her presence before she served her warrant. Perhaps if she'd attempted to deliver papers without seeing me, the warden would have tried to delay her. This way, he had no choice but to comply immediately.

More guards followed us warily. I had the feeling they thought I might turn into a Stroj myself and strike them all dead.

When my Aunt was at last satisfied we were alone and able to talk freely, she slammed her open hand into my face.

It was a hard slap, and it had come without warning. My teeth cut into my cheek with the force of the blow, and I tasted a trickle of blood.

"What was that for?" I demanded.

"For making me take action I didn't want to take. For talking to a Stroj about things no man on Earth should be discussing. And most of all, for this!"

She held out another computer scroll. I took it and examined it.

The device was mine. On it was a series of scrawled numbers. I tucked it into my pocket.

"Thanks for returning my property," I said, "but I hardly see how a few numbers—"

"Those numbers lead somewhere, William," she said, "and I think you know where they go."

"Uh…" this was tough spot for me. I didn't want to lie, but I didn't want to make a misstep and send my aunt back to her mansion with no reason to help me. I had no idea as to the significance of the numbers—but I could make a shrewd guess.

"They're coordinates," I said at last.

"Of course they are! We traced the first one to a local hyperspace bridge. Presumably, they'll all lead to a chain of breaches, one after another. The real question is: where does the trail end?"

I shrugged. "There's no way to know."

She sighed and growled at the same time. "Still playing the innocent fool? Vogel didn't want to tell me, either. But he spent time on the power-rack, so I'm more inclined to believe him."

Standing up to my full height, I glared down at her.

"I don't lie," I said. "You can torment me if you like, but it won't change my answer."

She eyed me coldly for a time, but finally made a flapping motion with her hand, indicating I should sit down again. I did so reluctantly.

She paced, rubbing at her chin. "I don't know what to do with you, nephew. The Council is beside itself. First, you refuse your updates. Now, you barge into CENTCOM and kill—"

"Wait a minute," I said, "did you say I *refused* an update?"

She snorted. "Come now, William! We weren't born yesterday—far from it. Did you think you'd get away with disabling your auto-updates without triggering a thousand red flags? Do you even know what the penalty is for your tampering with your implant?"

I stared at her, and I found I did know. "So that's it?" I asked. "I'm to become an unperson?"

"You're one small step from that status now. One morning update away."

"But how...?" I asked, trailing off.

"Don't be naïve," she snapped. "This is where we keep the wretches, William. It's sad, really. Forgotten souls. The best and the worst of our species are down here with us right now. Strange to think—"

My hand reached out and grasped her wrist.

"Is Zye here? Aunt Helen—is she down here in this dark place?"

She snatched her hand back from me. "I don't know. I'm not a jailor, I'm a diplomat—and you've made my job ten times harder lately."

"All I did was my duty. My actions were extreme, but when I get my day in court—"

She gave a bark of laughter and shook her head. "Your day in court will be held by the Council in secret. Not even you will be invited."

Her words stunned me. "But I killed a Stroj who'd burrowed deeply into our command structure. Are you saying the Chairman is displeased about that? Did the Council know he was here, running things?"

158

"I don't know..." she said. "But forget about all that. I'm interested in getting my nephew out of purgatory, but I'm not sure how to go about it."

The situation did seem grim. I was out of my depth.

She raised a bony finger and wagged it at me. "I have an idea. You'll tell them where this map leads. You'll tell them it will provide us a great boon when you get there. Then you'll go out there and get it personally."

I blinked at her in confusion. "But I told you, I don't know where this chain of star systems leads."

She patted my cheek where she'd slapped me before. "That's a good boy... but I was speaking rhetorically. You won't talk to them personally, I will in your stead. I'll invent a suitable boon and deliver your heartfelt apologies along with a sincere promise to bring home a vague treasure. All you have to do is fly to the stars and find whatever that mad Stroj wanted you to find."

"What if the trail leads to the Stroj homeworld? Or to a black hole after a blue jump? The Stroj owed me nothing. In fact, revenge seems the most likely motivation since I'd just killed him."

She stared at me down her long nose. "Would you rather sit here and rot? At this time tomorrow your parents won't even recall that they ever had a child."

My jaw worked, but no sound came out for a moment. Then I had a thought.

"What about Vogel? What about the variants? I'll need their help."

She looked irritated. "I find your sense of self-preservation woefully undeveloped."

"Nevertheless, if I'm to find something useful, I need them."

She sighed. "All right, I'll see what I can do.

"Then I'll go out there. I'll find... something."

"That's a good boy..." she said again, patting my shoulder absently. "But I'd suggest that if you *don't* find anything interesting you'd be best off not coming home at all."

I nodded, unable to argue with her point.

-26-

The following morning I was awakened by two jailors. They hauled me out of my cell and down echoing hallways.

I asked them where we were going, but they said nothing. They were agents—heavily modified men. It was their kind I'd fought with when the Council first arrested me what seemed like long ago.

Today, I could not defeat them. I struggled, but to no avail. I had no personal shield, no pistol and no sword.

My boots scraped and scuffed the marble floors, but I couldn't get a grip. With my hands cuffed behind me, there was little I could do.

At last they shoved me into an empty elevator car. One of them threw something at me—a nano-key.

The elevator doors slid shut, and the car began to go upward. I got down on my knees, touched the nano-key to my shackles, then stood up.

Approaching the elevator doors, I hammered on them with my fists.

"I'll not leave without Zye!" I shouted. But if they were listening, they gave no clue.

Reconsidering my outburst, I decided to once again hide my true motivations. There was no point in demanding things when I wasn't in the position to force anyone to deliver.

For some reason, on the long, long trip to the surface, I felt the urge to straighten myself. Combing my hair with my fingers and tucking in my collar, I did the best I could. The nanos in my smart clothing had long since lost power, leaving my suit rumpled.

At last, the doors dinged and opened.

I was on the ground floor on the surface not far from where I'd been the day I'd stormed this place. Even more surprising, there was no one there to greet me—no guards, no Aunt Helen—nothing.

There were people, however, bustling around the place as if I wasn't worthy of notice. Putting on the best show I could manage, I strode out into the hallway as if I owned the place. Perhaps they were going for humiliation. Perhaps this was their odd idea of a perp-walk.

No matter. I was a Sparhawk, and I wouldn't give them any kind of satisfaction.

Still, the front doors, no more than a hundred echoing paces across the floors, were very tempting. I couldn't help but pull my cap down over my face, tilt my head toward the exit and walk in that direction.

After a dozen steps, I saw they were still cleaning up from the attack I'd led. The front windows had yet to be fully repaired. All the gunfire had taken out thousands of credits worth of glass panels alone.

"Hey!" shouted a voice. "Is that you...? Captain Sparhawk?"

I hesitated. My instinct was to keep walking, to put as much distance between the dungeons and my person as quickly as possible.

But I didn't. I knew there was no point. If they were playing games, they had all the cards. They could arrest me again in a moment.

Turning on one heel and manufacturing a smile, I struggled to recognize the woman who had spoken to me.

"Is that Ensign Raeling?" I asked.

She beamed. "You remember me? I was very junior when I served aboard *Defiant*."

"Of course, in the purser's office. What are you doing here?"

"I'm testing for rank. Wish me luck!"

161

"Luck," I said in what I hoped was a pleasant tone. The ensign was young and perky. I'd had an eye for her, like every other man on the ship.

But as we spoke, the entire conversation seemed very odd to me. She knew who I was, and my face had to have been plastered on every newsfeed on the planet over recent days. How was it she had yet to run for help?

But the fact was, she didn't seem to be alarmed at all. She just looked at me, happily at first, but then with growing concern.

"You look as if you haven't been sleeping sir," she said. "Is something wrong?"

"Well, the trials of a Guardsman never cease."

She frowned in incomprehension for a moment, but then she gasped and put a hand to her mouth.

"You weren't here during the attack, were you?"

There it was. I'd blown it. I'd been recognized by possibly the only person on Earth who didn't know I'd been involved— and now I'd given her reason to recall my face here in the very lobby I'd done my best to demolish.

"Well... that is..."

She stepped forward, put out a hand and touched my arm. "Don't say another word, Captain Sparhawk," she said. "I understand. It must have been awful. Just think, right here where we're standing a dozen Stroj killed a dozen of ours. It's almost unbelievable. We should wipe those monsters out."

My mouth was open to speak, but I managed to shut it again.

"Just so," I managed. "Ensign Raeling, I wish you all the luck with your tests, but I'm afraid I must be moving along now."

"I understand, sir," she said. "Don't let me keep you. Maybe we'll serve together again someday."

Without another word, she turned and walked away. She did pause to glance back, and she blushed when she saw I was still standing there, staring after her.

That jolted me into action. I did an about-face and headed for the exit.

162

After passing a dozen guards, I thought I was home-free, but one of them called after me. He had a portable terminal in hand, and it was blinking colors.

"Captain Sparhawk?" he asked.

Again, I faced my assailant pleasantly. "Yes, Chief?"

"We've got a package for you. The biometric scanners recognized you as you came near the doors and triggered an alert."

"A package?"

"Yes. Here you are, sir."

He handed me a heavy sack. It was lumpy, and there was one item of unusual length inside. I could feel it through the cloth.

Immediately, I knew what the item was: my family sword.

"Excellent," I said as I pulled out my shielding cloak, my sidearm and my blade.

Donning them all under the curious eye of the guard, I felt whole again.

"Did you lose them battling the Stroj in the attack, sir?" he asked.

"Yes—I did."

The man shook his head. "Such brave souls, all of you who were here fighting that day. I'm glad you survived."

"So am I…"

With that, I strode out into the sunlight a free man.

By this time, I'd puzzled out what the hell was going on. No one knew I'd led the attack against CENTCOM because there had been an update this morning. But instead of updating them all to forget my existence, they'd updated the world to remember an attack by the Stroj rather than me.

As far as the people of Earth were concerned, I was a heroic Guardsman who'd faced the enemy and beaten them right here at CENTCOM's gates.

It was an odd feeling to recall something differently than everyone else did. It was both thrilling—because I was free— and nightmarish, because I was in awe of the Council's power to manipulate events.

How often had they fabricated the past? Which details had I been taught about Earth's history were truthful—and which of them were a pack of intricate lies?

-27-

Having nowhere better to go, I headed to Lady Astra's house. I'd considered returning to my parents, but the last time I'd gotten near them they'd seemed so put off I didn't feel like going back. Chloe at least put our relationship above matters of state whenever she could.

She met me at the door with apprehension in her eyes. She could tell I'd had a rough few days. She fell against me and put her face into my chest. That felt good.

"I missed you," she said. "I read about the attack on CENTCOM, and I feared the worst. The stories were vague, but it sounded terrible."

"It was," I said.

She pulled away from me and stared up into my eyes. She searched my face.

"You were involved, weren't you? Directly involved!"

"Yes," I admitted.

"Tell me about it."

"I can't," I said, and that was the truth. I couldn't tell her what had actually happened without endangering her life—or at least her memories.

She made a sound of frustration.

"I'm a Public Servant, William," she said. "I can get it out of the government if I must."

I felt like releasing a bitter laugh but managed to avoid such a catastrophic move.

"If you must."

"Damn you. CENTCOM is so paranoid. They won't tell their own leaders what they're up to half the time."

"Don't you think they have good reasons to be concerned?"

"Yes... I guess they do."

At last, she relaxed and guided me into her home. After freshening up and recharging my uniform, I felt human again. Imprisonment hadn't been a pleasant thing. My disconnection from the rest of the planet still lingered.

In the back of my mind, as she spoke of recent events, I noticed inconsistencies. They were small things but critical ones.

For example, she was convinced the attack had happened on Thursday when I knew it had occurred on Friday. I was quite certain on that point as I'd led the attack myself.

It took willpower not to correct her. The feeling this gave me was an uneasy one. I felt fearful of talking about any number of common topics as I felt uncertain that her recollection of recent events matched mine.

Soon we were having dinner, and I felt better. After our meal, we avoided the net entirely and retired early to her chambers. There, events proceeded as I'd hoped they would.

She had a large bathing facility just off her bedroom. It was big enough to jump into, and the water was steaming hot.

We bathed together and made love in the bubbling tub. Afterward, we stretched out on her bed, and the sheets dried us meticulously. Soon, we were holding one another in in her dimly lit bedchamber.

"Are you leaving again soon?" she asked in a small voice.

"I don't know."

She lifted her head to look at me. "You don't? What about the new battleship? Isn't she replacing *Defiant* as Earth's watchdog?"

"Doubtlessly she will when she's completed. I would expect that to be in a month or two."

She frowned at me. "That's not how I understand it... Is CENTCOM keeping such things even from their own officers? The ship is finished."

166

I realized then that things *had* changed while I was in prison. It had only been a weekend, of that much I was certain, but events had progressed more rapidly than I'd realized or someone had edited them to suit their own timetables.

Recovering as quickly as I could, I smiled. She smiled back—worriedly.

"Ah…" I said. "I meant the ship might not be ready to take over *Defiant's* mission. After all, there are trainings and maiden voyages. Star Guard can delay anything for months if they want to."

It was a half-lie, but she accepted it and relaxed again. Soon, she was sleeping on my chest.

Unfortunately, I was unable to sleep so easily. What else had changed about my world while I'd rested in prison?

* * *

The next morning I left Chloe and headed up to *Defiant*. She wasn't at all surprised to learn I'd been reassigned to active duty.

Once aboard, I felt more in command of my immediate destiny. I headed to the command deck where my executive officer greeted me with enthusiasm.

"Welcome back, sir!" Durris said. "We've been worried about you for days."

"Didn't CENTCOM tell you where I was?" I asked as innocently as possible.

He looked confused for a moment. Perhaps his mind was accessing newly implanted thoughts for the very first time.

"We knew you were involved in that terror-attack, but we didn't know if you'd been injured or not. I'm very glad to see you weren't."

"Well, I'm back and fit for duty. Let's see the patrol roster."

His face flickered again, as if confused. "Patrol, sir? We're preparing for a deep space voyage."

I froze, working hard not to react. "Of course," I said. "That's what I meant—a deep patrol. Have you got the coordinates for our first destination?"

"No sir… We were told you were bringing up these details from CENTCOM personally. Were we given incorrect—"

"No," I said, "I have them. I wasn't sure if they'd been sent on ahead or not."

To distract him as much as anything else, I produced the computer scroll and put it into his hand. He looked at it in surprise.

"You're making a physical transfer? Not electronically uploading it to *Defiant's* computers?"

I shook my head.

Durris had always been a man who fussed over details too much. He was a classic over-thinker. Even now, I could see the wheels in his mind turning.

"I get it. That's why you asked me if anyone had sent this up from CENTCOM. It was a test—because they weren't *supposed* to do so."

I maintained a noncommittal stare.

"I'll get to work on these immediately, sir!" he said, rushing back to his station.

After a few more hours, I learned more details about various new fictions I had to uphold. The hardest of these was the absence of Zye—in fact, there never had been such a person.

Almost as difficult to swallow was my new status as a hero, rather than a villain, for my actions at CENTCOM. It all took some getting used to.

The one thing that puzzled me was the status of my own implant. Had they corrected it? Had they updated *me* in some fashion?

The concept was alarming even though I didn't think they could have. If they had, wouldn't I be as unaware of the real events of recent days as my crewmen were?

After thinking about it, the implant rooted at the base of my skull began to itch abominably. It was a nerve-related phenomenon, I knew. It was commonly suffered by people who were new to the symbiotic growth and had yet to adjust.

Still, I couldn't stop thinking about it. I gave Durris the helm and went below, signaling Yamada that she should follow me.

"Lieutenant Commander," I said once we were in private. "Do you recall helping me with my implant?"

She looked confused, and for a single sick moment I was convinced they'd gotten to her, too. Could her memory of developing an interface-wrap for my implant be missing from her consciousness?

She lowered her voice and leaned forward. "I *do* recall helping you during your refit. Why, is there a problem?"

She gave me a wink, and I smiled back in relief. She knew what we'd done together. The scrawny gray arms of the Council had limits to their reach.

"I need help again. A diagnostic."

She shrugged and accompanied me to the labs. An hour later, I felt assured my alterations remained intact.

I wasn't sure why the Council had decided to allow me to retain my independence, but I was glad they'd done so. Perhaps they thought a renegade officer such as myself was a tool worth the risks. Or possibly they had no easy way to correct me as they didn't know what I knew and what I didn't know.

Yamada herself had no idea she'd been updated, that her mind had glossed over certain recent events. I considered telling her to hack her own implant to shield herself from updates, but I didn't want to jeopardize my chances of getting out of this star system with my own mind intact. There was no point in alerting the Council again.

"Oh Captain, there's one more thing."

"Yes?"

"Director Vogel is waiting for you down in his lab. He's been there for several hours, brooding. He won't leave you a message, and he refuses to talk to anyone else. Should I tell him you're too busy for a personal visit?"

"No," I said evenly, "I'll see him immediately."

I left her presence and marched directly for Vogel's chambers. My situation had me off-balance, and I felt as if I were an imposter aboard my own ship. Everyone else possessed a slightly different version of reality in their minds than I did. I had to keep reminding myself of this. It wouldn't do to show surprise when I learned information everyone else aboard took for granted.

My impression of Director Vogel wasn't good. He'd turned positively paranoid over the last several days.

"Do you *know* what they did to me?" he asked in a hissing tone. "Or what they planned as my final punishment?"

I nodded and met his eyes seriously.

"Is that even possible?" he demanded. "I know you talked about changing people's mental outlook, but—"

"You saw it yourself," I told him. "We barged into CENTCOM and destroyed the lobby. When we were finally allowed to leave, everyone there who'd survived our attack remembered only a raving pack of phantom Stroj."

He nodded thoughtfully. "It was very strange to witness their delusions. I've been aware of the updates for some time, you understand. Phobos personnel had a hand in developing that technology long ago... but I had no idea they'd begun using such a powerful tool so ruthlessly."

I glanced at him. "Just how old are you, Director Vogel?"

He ruffled slightly before he answered me. "Direct questions concerning a person's age are considered rude."

Crossing my arms, I maintained my sideways glance and waited.

"A citizen of Earth has no true chronological age," he insisted in a huffy tone.

"Nonsense," I said, "how old you are matters a great deal. In this case, it will help me piece together a puzzle."

"Very well... If you must know, I'm one hundred and seventy-two. I know that's older than most, but younger than some."

I whistled, impressed. "You don't look a day over sixty," I said. "They really do give the lab people better drugs."

He laughed, shaking his head. "No, not exactly. We keep the best for ourselves."

Nodding, I conceded the point.

It was clear that when he'd said the labs had developed the implant-update technology *a long time ago* he'd probably meant more than a century back. That's how oldsters typically spoke of the past. Any event that was a distant memory to them was at least a century gone.

In any case, it mattered little when they'd started. The updates were real, and the fabrication of my society's *reality* was a fact. The political spiders on the planet below us had ruled Earth from their quiet shadows for an amazingly long time.

After we'd checked the manifest and all my crewmen had boarded—save for Zye—I ordered *Defiant* to leave orbit.

I didn't like doing it. I felt I was abandoning Zye to a terrible fate. When I'd first met her, she'd been imprisoned for years in an automated cell. She'd stayed alive, but she'd lost hope. Despite the mental resiliency of all Betas, she'd been affected. She'd clung to me at times as her rescuer.

Now I was leaving her behind. It was a hard thing to do. I thought of drastic options, but none were practical. Could I have ordered my ship to attack CENTCOM? Or threaten to do so unless Zye was released?

Impossible. My crew wouldn't have obeyed such orders, thinking me mad. To them, Zye didn't exist. She was a figment, and I was the only madman who could remember her at all.

And so, with a heavy heart, I watched as we pulled slowly way from Araminta Station. Even as we did so, our replacement vessel arrived.

"What's her name again?" I asked. "The battleship?"

They all looked at me oddly again, and I made an effort not to meet their eyes. Probably, in their minds, the answer had been broadcast far and wide.

"That's the *Resolution*, sir," Durris said. "Are you feeling all right?"

"I'm fine, thank you."

He shut up, and that suited me well. I watched *Resolution* dock at the station, taking our spot.

The battleship's captain might not even be aware that his ship had been finished ahead of schedule. He might not remember that according to briefings I'd received a month back, his ship had not yet even been named.

171

Only I remembered those details. I felt I was now informed enough to calculate what may have happened. After all, the Chairman was smart enough to use his greatest power only when he had to.

The oldsters must have panicked when *Victory* had appeared. They'd realized *Defiant* might not be able to stop the battleship.

In order to protect Earth—and themselves—they'd ordered the construction of Earth's next battleship to be sped up to get it finished at all costs.

There was only one way Star Guard could have accomplished such a task: by employing variants. That meant there were variants operating on Earth right now. They were no longer stationed only on distant Phobos.

Since the timetable for *Resolution*'s production had been well-advertised, the Chairman had probably updated the citizenry to believe the battleship was due to come out earlier. They'd given her a name in the same action. A name which everyone on Earth now recalled having heard before—except for me.

So strange… To know the real sequence of events while everyone around me saw only what their rulers wanted them to see.

Was this what madness felt like?

-28-

Every million kilometers I put behind us made me feel better. Onboard *Defiant*, I was in control of my own destiny. I felt like a starship captain again.

When off-duty, I spent my time going over the ship's historical repository. What I found there, seen with newly educated eyes, was revealing.

The past hadn't been altered wholesale. As far as I could tell, only surgical details had been edited. Inserted news stories about the accelerated progress of *Resolution's* construction timetable, for example, had begun to appear approximately two months ago.

These stories were fabricated. I would have been aware of them, and I would have read them if they hadn't been inserted into the public's consciousness and assorted documentation very recently.

After a thorough examination, I determined that the Council operated as gently as they could on our memories. They did it, apparently, through the insertion of certain "stories" and the deletion of others. These actions usually came in the form of news articles. Rarely was there any vid evidence to back up claims in these new written reports.

Vogel's lab was a large chamber, but today it was empty. Only equipment stood here and there, along with the two variants who'd survived our attack on CENTCOM. They were dormant now, their eyes dark and their bodies motionless.

173

"So, that's what you've been doing?" Vogel asked me when I brought my findings to him. "I've been monitoring your browsing history…"

"Why have you been doing that?" I demanded.

He shrugged. "I have a government clearance. I've served alongside many agents of the Internal Affairs Office. Didn't you know?"

My gaze had turned unfriendly. "That wasn't what I asked," I pointed out.

"Well… Captain… you have to understand. I have certain responsibilities aboard this ship. I represent our government."

"Have you forgotten? I'm an officer in Star Guard. Since we're in space, my authority supersedes yours."

If there was one thing my Aunt Grantholm had taught me during our preceding voyage, it was that the chain of command had to be clearly hammered out from the outset.

Vogel dipped his head. "I understand, Captain."

"Good. See that you don't do any more snooping, or I'll have Yamada remove your net privileges."

"That's harsh."

"Not really, it's just a beginning. Stay out of my affairs, or you'll learn how harsh I can be."

"My apologies…" he said. "But on to another matter, what did you discover? What is it that I don't remember?"

"The exact details are unimportant, but the methodology is interesting. We've all been updated with stories. Written articles for the most part. They circulate online until the origin is unclear. At that point, they become part of the group knowledge we all share."

"Fascinating…" he said. "They do it with precision, then. They plant certain stories—your word—and remove others. The human mind is well-conditioned to operate in terms of stories, you know."

"Yes, it all makes sense."

"Right," he continued, the look on his face becoming distant. "Think about what you remember from the events of your life, or what you *think* you know about other people's lives. Do you remember the sequence of motions you took this morning while cleansing, dressing and feeding yourself?"

"I—" I began, but he cut me off.

"No, you don't," he continued, "but you might remember a chance meeting, an event that was unusual or something that involved another person."

He was quite correct. I saw what he meant. I could recall talking to my aunt, but nothing about what I'd done prior to her visit.

"So, rather than entirely rewriting our memories, they're editing out some but inserting new ones too—perhaps replacing longer sequential passages?"

"Exactly," Vogel agreed. "The stories not only give us information they want us to remember, they also cover up the gaps. When we think of a deleted event, the details escape us. Through the artful insertion and deletion of details, what we recall is a complete, self-contained story."

I nodded slowly. The process was simple but diabolical.

"Do you think we're out of their effective range?" I asked.

"No. Not while we're in this star system. Now, let me ask you, do you recall gaps when first reentering the Solar System after your last voyage to the stars?"

I thought about it, and I shook my head.

"No..." I said, "but they might have been there. When we've first returned to the Solar System, CENTCOM has always transmitted an update."

"Naturally," Vogel said. "Things would have likely changed after a long voyage to the stars. Changed, that is, for everyone on Earth. That's the moment when they'll seek to insert and delete memories of their choosing."

Straining mightily, I couldn't recall anything like that happening to me. But that didn't mean that it *hadn't* happened. I found the process of second-guessing every event in my lifetime aggravating.

But then I had a sudden thought.

"That's why they don't want starships coming and going!" I said with sudden clarity. "That's why they shut down the ER bridges in the first place—to maintain complete control."

Vogel stared at me. "They? Who shut down the bridges? What are you talking about?"

"Forget it," I said. "You probably already knew but forgot the truth. There are some things best left to the past."

"What you suggested in those few statements... I'm disturbed."

"I'm sorry," I said, "and I'm sorry if I seem short with you. Let's just say that there's more going on in my mind than I can discuss."

With that, I took a deep breath and headed for the exit. But I found his thin fingers wrapped around my elbow.

I paused and looked down at him.

"I've earned your help," he said. "Don't leave me in the dark like the others. I know my mind is their toy, and I don't like it."

"Then rip out your implant," I said. "It's a simple matter."

He shook his head. "My career would be at an end, if not my life. I wish to be like you, Sparhawk—to walk the Earth like a spirit, seeing the truth. Is there any other way you could help me?"

I considered his request. The idea had merit. He was already my confidant, and he'd proven he was willing to risk everything to help me.

"I'll help you after we get through the first bridge," I told him. "When we're beyond their reach, it will be done."

He smiled faintly. "Excellent. I'm not sure it will make me any happier, but I can't live with their tampering another day."

At the doorway, I paused and I pointed to his creations, the dormant variants.

"You know," I said, "I could use some help from you and your team as well."

"What kind of help?"

"Could you get a fresh contingent of variants aboard—as workers?"

"You mean as troops, don't you?"

I shrugged.

He sighed and looked at K-19. "That's a disturbing development. My variants were never meant to kill. I didn't want that when I developed them."

"It's all too common that we don't have full control of the consequences to our actions."

176

He produced a bitter laugh. "That's very true. All right, Sparhawk. I can contact Phobos and ask for them to send out a tug pulling a cargo module."

"A cargo module full of variants? What of weapons?"

"You'll have to provide those. I can retrain them while we travel."

I nodded. "All right. I'll try to get the request through CENTCOM. It's logical enough. We've lost all our Stroj-made repair bots in battle."

Then I left him and moved to the command deck. There, my team was plotting our first jump out of the Solar System in months.

"Captain," Durris said, calling me to the tactical table, "where did you get these coordinates, exactly?"

"I can't say."

"Right... Well, as best we can figure, they're written in terms of given stars. The first references a small breach that leads to a system we know well."

"Which is?"

"Gliese-32, sir."

My face flinched. I'd wondered if I'd ever meet the Connatic again. Apparently, I was going to be provided the opportunity.

"And the next?"

"We've traced that one too. It should take us to the Beta Cygnus system."

I looked at him sharply. "Not the Crown System?"

"No sir, this is definitely Beta. We've mapped it. Helping us a great deal are the star maps the people of Gi provided. Some of them correspond to that data."

"Excellent, please continue. Where do the last jumps go?"

He shook his head. "We have no idea after that. They'll be blue-jumps, sir."

Blue jumps. The term was enough to turn any spacer's stomach. In the past, all jumps had been into the unknown. A significant number of such jumps were apparently deadly as no one had ever returned from them.

177

I comforted myself by recalling that blue jumps were simply unknown. They weren't necessarily dangerous. It was a matter of playing the odds.

"Very well," I said. "Rumbold? I can tell you've been listening. Have you got our destinations clearly plotted?"

"Yes sir. The jumps are in my navigational software. But sir, if we're to hit the first breach and have a clean breakthrough, we need to increase speed. Shall I?"

"No, not yet. In fact, I want to slow down. I'm arranging a rendezvous with a very special package."

"A package? From where, Captain?"

"Phobos."

At the mention of Phobos, Rumbold and Durris exchanged glances. They were both unhappy, but they seemed resigned.

By this time, they were used to having their commander withhold interesting details about their mission plans from them.

-29-

Before we left the Solar System, we managed to load a full cargo pod of dormant variants aboard the *Defiant*. Something about that fact gave me pause. Just how many of these things had they manufactured on Phobos?

The breach into hyperspace turned out to be an easy transition. The ship wasn't battered or warped by the process, and once inside the wormhole we didn't find its space to be too cramped or too huge. As best we could tell with the nebulous readings from our sensors, we were in a pocket continuum approximately the size of the Solar System.

According to CENTCOM's calculations, we were headed to Gliese-32. That didn't mean the trip would be smooth sailing, however. The bridges between star systems were inherently unstable. Like taking a voyage on rough seas in the past, you never knew exactly how any given bridge would look on any given day.

After spending a full duty-shift in this particular stretch of hyperspace, I headed back to the command deck to see if my navigational people had worked out a course.

"The general shape is oblong," Durris said, using measured intervals from various returning pings to support his point. "We've been here for ten hours, and we've only got one axis where we haven't hit a wall yet."

My XO was using the term "wall" loosely. The edges of any organized region of hyperspace were, by definition, indistinct and immeasurable. After all, at what precise point did any reality end? Beyond good reference points, it was all conjecture.

Instead of concrete dimensions, we measured such variable spaces in terms of their coherency. Rather than a wall, then, the limits of the pocket we were currently plunging through were defined by borders where the laws of physics began to warp and shift.

"Have you found any solution for the exit?" I asked.

"Negative. We're in a bumpy zone, here. We're getting an irregular curve, and the pods we've dropped are still shifting positions behind us as far as our readings are concerned. This ER bridge is unstable today."

"Hmm. Typically unpredictable, just our luck."

Travel between the stars had become possible using two methodologies. There might be others, but we'd yet to discover them.

The first method was extremely direct. One simply aimed their spacecraft toward the star in question, applied thrust to the opposite end of the ship, and rode the momentum to the finish line. The downside of this approach involved the distances between stars. Even at an achievable speed of around twenty percent of light, a short trip took decades.

Fortunately, a second approach had been discovered. By entering Einstein-Rosen Bridges—otherwise known as wormholes—we were able to cheat on our math. The distance traveled was immaterial as it was inside a different *type* of space.

But performing such a trick had its own negatives. Each hyperspace we entered followed slightly different rules, even from one trip to the next. Therefore, all of them were inherently unstable, and our ships often had difficulty finding their way out of a pocket universe once they were inside it.

To solve the problem, we dropped probes to the aft of the ship and observed their behavior. In most cases, the exit to any ER bridge was directly ahead of the ship when it entered—but due to space-time warping, "directly ahead" wasn't as easy a place to find as it should be.

Fortunately, the warping effect for each hyperspace could be modeled mathematically. Watching the behavior of the dropped probes was our critical tool. If we could create a model that would place every probe we dropped into a straight line, the far end always aimed at the exit. That was exactly what we were working on now: finding a way out.

At length, I became satisfied that Durris had the matter in hand. He would eventually solve the equation, and we'd have our destination pin-pointed.

Leaving the command deck in his capable hands, I traveled the length of the ship to Vogel's lab.

His staff was there going over schematics. They jumped in a guilty fashion when I arrived, and they looked at me in concern.

On the table in their midst was a variant. The thing was open, both its metal case and its fleshy interior. As they moved away, I could tell they were performing surgery.

"Something wrong with this unit?" I asked.

"No, Captain," Dr. McKay answered, pushing strands of red hair away from her face. "We're performing an alteration."

Eying her for a moment, I realized I hadn't seen her pay any attention to Rumbold since she'd boarded my ship. Had that been due to her earlier state of intoxication back on Phobos? Or had she only pretended to be interested in him in order to get herself a ticket aboard *Defiant?* Time would tell.

"An alteration?" I asked. "I see… for what purpose?"

The team looked at me for a moment, and McKay removed her dripping gloves and stepped around the mess on the table to approach me. She reshaped her face into a false smile.

"We're very busy today," she said. "Perhaps I can find Vogel to help you."

"Is this a private meeting?" I asked.

"No, not at all—but it can be if you wish. Will you excuse us, staff?" she said, looking expectantly at the others.

Without a word, they put down their instruments with various clattering and splashing sounds, then walked out.

"Now, Captain, what can I do for you?" she asked, turning on her considerable charm.

181

"You're operating on this variant to alter its programming, aren't you?"

She winced. "Such an inappropriate way of expressing the situation... The variants aren't programmed—not exactly. What we're doing is installing an experimental governor in the thorax."

"Hmm. What's the purpose of such a device?"

"It's rather like your implant, but it's designed to alter behavior rather than serve as a communications tool."

I chuckled briefly. "Some would say the true purpose of our implants is to do precisely that."

"Well... this is a more direct application."

"What kind of behavior does this governor alter?"

"Violent tendencies."

My eyebrows raised high. "I thought we wanted them to act as troops. To perform as an assault team if needed. Why make them less aggressive?"

She blinked at me in confusion then laughed. "No, no, Captain. You misunderstand. These alterations are designed to *improve* their performance in combat."

"Are you saying it's sub-optimal now?"

"Yes, exactly. The variants were designed for construction, not destruction. They're fast and accurate, but not informed soldiers. A vanilla variant doesn't come with an innate knowledge of weakness in a target's anatomy, for example."

Beginning to catch on, I felt disturbed. Walking to the mess on the table, I stood over it, staring. "What anatomy are you talking about? Human, or...?"

"Stroj, human and variant," she said. "We thought it would be best to cover the bases."

"Quite... You're telling me this thing will be an even more effective killer than K-19 and his crew proved to be at CENTCOM?"

"Definitely. In fact, we used a download of K-19's experiences in the formulation of this upgrade. I'm so glad you're pleased."

I glanced at her thoughtfully. "I'm not sure that *pleased* is what I am. But it's what I asked for, so I suppose I can't complain now. Carry on."

Leaving the lab, I suppressed a shudder when I heard squelching sounds behind me. McKay and the rest of Vogel's team had gone back to work.

Over the following four days, we finally found our way out of the hyperspace bridge. When we broke through into normal space, we all felt relief.

The feeling was short-lived however. The system we found ourselves in wasn't quite the same as when we'd left it.

"Radiation levels are high, Captain," Yamada said, "even for Gliese-32."

Gliese-32, known as "Gi" to the locals, was an orange-colored star about thirty-five light years from Earth. We'd been here before and interacted successfully with the inhabitants. As best we knew, our armada had passed through this system on its maiden voyage.

The breach came out quite near Gliese-32, and the system was high in gamma radiation anyway. We found ourselves maneuvering for several tense minutes to evade the gravitational pull of the central star.

It was only then that we turned our thoughts to Tranquility Station, the home of the Gi people. There were no inhabitable planets in the system, and all life resided inside an artificial polyhedron built by the original colonists long ago.

Or rather, all life had been located there. We stared in stunned silence at the dead wreckage that had once been an impressive human achievement.

Today, Tranquility Station looked like a crushed, burned Christmas ornament hanging in space. Fully half its mass had been blown away. The powerful shielding it had once used for a defense was gone. The fighters that had no doubt defended the station were drifting about, destroyed and useless.

"I'm sorry sir," Yamada said, her voice emotional. "I'm not getting any life readings. It appears as if the variants have killed everyone."

I nodded, unable to speak.

The Connatic, a woman I'd once made love to, was clearly dead.

-30-

We'd hoped it wouldn't be this way when we got here. I'd heard reports, of course, ominous warnings from Star Guard, Admiral Perez and my own aunt.

But the scale of it... We hadn't been prepared for that.

"Not even the damned Stroj would have done this," Rumbold said, thumping his fist ineffectively on his console. "Crazy machines!"

"Keep scanning," I said, "and send out welcoming signals. There might be someone here, hiding."

Nothing responded to our signals for several long hours. I began to get impatient.

"Commander Durris, do you have the next breach we're supposed to follow pinpointed?"

"Yes Captain, but it's not quite what I expected."

"Why not?"

"It appears to be markedly similarly to one of those artificial bridges. The type that the Stroj can create. It seems to be in a location where a known bridge was previously. I don't understand it."

I moved to his side and examined his data. There was no error that I could find. Reluctantly, I agreed with his conclusions.

"Maybe it's been tampered with," I suggested, "transformed into a sort of hybrid bridge. It could be hijacked, redirected or damaged."

"I suppose such things are possible," Durris said doubtfully. "But in any case, the signature is all wrong for a natural interface between hyperspace and normal space. One way or the other, this is going to be a blue jump."

"Hmm," I said, "could it be the Stroj wrecked this system, not the variants? What if they were the ones who came here and blew up the station then left? Perez indicated the variants were destroying systems, but that could have been a cover-up."

"Admiral Perez told you *what*, Captain?"

Durris was staring at me, and I realized that I'd let slip information of which he had no inkling. He had no idea I'd had a private conversation with Perez before destroying him.

"He was a Stroj agent. You know that, right?"

"Of course sir, the online articles—"

"They don't tell you everything in those releases. I was there. Before he died, he told me the variants were destroying Earth colonies out here as well as Stroj worlds. That they're marauding, killing everyone."

"But why?" Rumbold demanded. "What the hell for? Do they hate all life? We should destroy those things in the hold before they kill us in our beds, Captain!"

I glanced at him. "You might have a point. I might even do it if I didn't need them so desperately. Remember the odds we're facing. We need every advantage we have at our disposal."

Grumbling, Rumbold went back to his station.

"Captain!" Yamada called out. "I've got contacts, sir!"

"Where?"

"From the wreckage. They're—they must be fighters sir. A group of them has launched. I didn't think there was anything alive in that hulk."

For the first time since I entered this star system, I dared to hope and permitted myself a smile. "The Connatic must have some fight in her yet. Open a channel in the clear. Let me explain who we are and why we're here. They're understandably paranoid."

She did as I asked, and I identified myself and my ship.

The fighters didn't respond. Neither did whatever served them as traffic control back on the wrecked station.

Frowning at the data screens, from which flowed a steady output of predictive attack vectors and the like, I gave an order I hadn't wanted to give.

"Prepare our defenses," I said. "Come about to an oblique angle—let's not head right into them."

Durris looked at me, and he shook his head.

"What is it, Commander?" I asked.

"It just seems like a terrible waste. Must we destroy the last colonists in this system? Why won't they answer?"

"Yamada, are they receiving our messages?" I demanded.

"I think so, sir," she said, working her instruments. "They've synched, and our packets have been accepted. The channel is open, but they've made no attempt to respond."

"Tell them we'll have to destroy their fighters if they get within two hundred thousand kilometers."

"Sir?" Durris said, stepping toward my chair in alarm. "That's much too close. Well within our safety zone."

"Yes, but still beyond their practical ranges."

"The fighters are doing something, sir," Yamada said after she'd transmitted my warning twice.

I moved quickly to her station. I wanted the latest input, unfiltered.

The news wasn't good.

"As you can see," she said, "they're pumping out crystalline gels ahead of them to diffuse our defensive lasers. They're building up a large cloud of material to hide behind."

"Captain?" Durris called.

Reluctantly, I moved to his side.

"I've reworked the simulations," he said. "They're going to cruise in behind a thin shielding and then scatter, hitting us from multiple sides. At least, that's what the battle computers say is the most likely case."

Releasing an unhappy grunt of disappointment, I checked the range again. They were at five hundred thousand kilometers and closing fast.

The numbers were significant. At this range, we could hit them but they couldn't hit us. Fighters were small and difficult targets, but they had to get in quite close to do damage. There were generally a lot of them, and a capital ship couldn't afford to let them get in close without losses. The essential fact was we were at our optimal range right now, and I was letting the opportunity to inflict losses slide past us.

"All right," I said reluctantly. "Focus on a lead fighter. Punch through that shield and take it out."

"Just one, sir?" Durris complained. "The usual practice—"

"I know. Hit just one of them. Maybe they'll get the message."

He didn't even bother to acknowledge the command, aim, or declare his exact intentions. Apparently, he'd already anticipated an order of this kind, because he simply reached out to his control screen and double-tapped his index finger on the red swarm of incoming fighters.

The main batteries hummed, then buzzed, then sang. We waited a few seconds—then the beams reached them.

"We took out one. Recharging."

"Hold your fire," I ordered.

He said nothing, but his jaws were tight with tension.

"Analysis, Yamada? Did we impress them?"

"They're taking increased defensive action, darting from side to side—but no messages. They're continuing the attack run."

The odd thing about space battles is they could appear to be fast or slow, depending on the distance to the target. At great distances, the action was greatly delayed. Often minutes passed between firing and witnessing a strike. On the other hand, when the range was short, things happened with blinding rapidity.

"Unlimber all three main batteries. Fire in a slow cycle, don't melt anything down. Fire continuously until they're destroyed or they break off."

Having given a fateful order, I moved to my seat again, feeling the weight of command. Why did humanity insist on mutual destruction? In many cases, I'd been in conflicts that were easily avoidable.

The current situation was a distinct one, with all things considered, as these people should know better. They had nothing to fear from us. It just didn't make sense.

"Sir?" Rumbold asked me, "Permission to adjust our course?"

"What for, Rumbold?"

"To maximize the time we have at medium range."

I knew what he meant. If we turned away from the fighters, they'd take longer to get within range. They wouldn't be able to shoot back while we kept pecking at them steadily.

"Permission granted."

The ship veered, exerting lateral force on us all. *Defiant* was equipped with inertial dampeners, but they never operated with one hundred percent effectiveness.

Three minutes passed. During that time, we destroyed two more targets. Durris came to me, smiling.

"We're in the clear if the situation remains as it is," he said. "They'll be down to twenty or so fighters by the time they reach us."

I nodded, less than overjoyed. It still seemed like a terrible waste.

"Captain..." Yamada said in a concerned tone. "They're changing their formation."

Durris rushed back to his tactical table. His smile had vanished.

My mood shifted as well. The enemy was ballooning out from behind their prismatic cloud, abandoning it. They surged forward with shocking speed. Our latest volley of shots went wide, hitting nothing.

"Commander Durris," I called. "I've seen Gi fighters in action before—they don't fly that fast."

"I know sir... I know. We're in close enough for optical recognition."

A wire diagram of the enemy configuration appeared on the forward screen. It wasn't the right shape. It was sleek, rather than angular and rounded like a manta ray.

"What are we facing, Commander?" I demanded.

"I don't know, sir. I've never seen this design before."

"I have," said a new voice from the back of the deck.

We turned to see Director Vogel. He stepped forward, making a gesture toward me for permission to enter. I nodded.

"Welcome to the deck, Director. What are you talking about?"

"Those are Earth fighters," he said. "Our *new* fighters."

I studied him for a moment then turned back to the forward screens. The enemy had formed into four groups now, and these groups were converging on our position. They were still accelerating.

"You're saying they're manned by variants?" I asked.

"That's right, Captain. We've found the enemy."

-31-

The next twenty minutes were intense. We fired a continuous series of volleys, but we connected only six more times. The enemy was almost close enough to return fire, and they still had ninety percent of their force intact.

"Give us the specs," I ordered Vogel. "Feed everything you know about these fighters into Durris' computer."

"I will do so," he said, "even though I'm under orders not to comply with such a request. This design has been top secret from the beginning—I'm sure you know that, Captain."

"I do. I'm glad you agree the situation has changed dramatically."

It was odd to watch these fighters roar toward us on full-burn. They'd been designed by our best engineers. They'd been developed with the specific purpose of destroying the Stroj fleets. Now, ironically, they were after us.

Fortunately, there were less than a hundred of them all told. That was a relatively small number. *Iron Duke* reportedly carried thousands.

"Get those decoys out early, Durris," I said. "Looking at these specs, I'd guess they can put in one more burst of speed for the final approach."

"Got it, sir. Pumping out smart-chaff now."

The ship's tanks gurgled and thumped. Billions of nano particles were pumped out around us, forming a cloud of microscopic interceptors. They weren't enough to stop an incoming missile, but they might cause one to detonate early. Against beams, they served to thin the power of particle radiation or lasers lessening their powerful impact.

On the hull, dozens of small guns rose up and began auto-tracking the incoming fighters. If they got in close enough, these point-defense weapons would be our best tools. They'd fill the space around our vessel with low-powered, short range pulses of energy. The small cannons couldn't damage a large vessel, but they could destroy a missile—or a fighter.

"We've gotten sixteen hits so far, Captain," Durris said. "But they're now close enough to shoot back."

"Warn all decks. Prepare for damage control. Place medical on alert for casualties. I want everyone in a vac suit, faceplates down."

My crew scrambled to obey.

"You don't really expect them to breach our hull, do you, Captain?" Yamada asked me in concern.

"They've surprised us more than once. I'm not going to underestimate them again."

We didn't have long to wait after that. The hull began to shudder with small impacts. At first, it was hardly more than what we could expect to feel from the firing of our own cannons—but then it rapidly intensified.

Like a rainstorm that starts with a pattering then grows into a roar, we soon felt as if we were an earthen barrier being eroded by heavy rain.

"Such accuracy…" Durris said in awe. "They're landing all these shots, from four directions, on an area only a few meters wide."

"They must be going for a direct hull-breach," I said. "How long is it until they penetrate, and we start venting?"

"Six minutes sir—I think. They'll be in close by then. This pass will be half over."

"Captain?" Rumbold called to me. "Since they aren't going for the engines, do I have permission to roll us over?"

I thought about it. The usual target of any enemy was the engines, but these variants were going straight for a kill-shot rather than trying to cripple us first. It was either a foolish choice or a chilling prediction of the ultimate outcome.

"Granted, Rumbold, roll us," I said.

He didn't wait around. The ship began a sickening roll, and the damaged part of our hull quickly moved out of the enemy view. Unfortunately, the heavy-rain sound never ceased. It was now something like sizzling bacon. It set my teeth on edge to hear it.

"They're focusing on another spot," Durris said.

"Durris, pump out more chaff directly over our sore spot."

The tanks sloshed and groaned. The sound of incoming fire muted somewhat but didn't stop.

"We've got a target-lock confirmed from our point-defense!" Durris said. "Permission to strategically clear the chaff?"

It was a fateful moment. If I signaled our smart-chaff to break holes between us and the fighters, we'd hit more targets, but we'd also leave ourselves more open to counterattacks.

"Do it," I said. My eyes turned to watch every screen at once, darting from one to the next.

The effect of my command was dramatic. Our point-defense cannons were *smart*, like every other system aboard, so they'd been holding their fire up until this moment. Each gun had computed that it couldn't get a kill firing through our own defensive curtain. But now that the chaff was drifting away from the ship, they opened up firing through the clear spots.

Hits began to register. Nineteen more enemy fighters were transformed into fireballs within thirty seconds.

A ragged cheer went up from the tactical teams. I didn't join them. The enemy still had over fifty percent of their force left, and they were getting very close now.

A sudden thought occurred to me. "Durris, plot their individual trajectories."

He did so without questioning me. Numerous red splines appeared. All of them curved slightly, and all of them intersected our ship at a point in the near future.

I stared at that. It wasn't normal. The usual approach of fighters was to either make a series of high passes, or to slow down and pound a ship at close range. In either case, slowing down at the end of a run was standard practice.

These fighters weren't slowing down at all.

"They're going to spend a half-hour turning around," Durris said, baffled.

"No, they're not... They're planning to ram us. That's why they've been trying to create a weak spot on our hull."

"Oh... If they can shove just one of their nosecones into our guts..." Durris said. He looked at me then, and I saw the light of fear in his eyes.

We'd made a mistake. We'd assumed we were fighting normal, human opponents. But variants didn't have much in the way of self-preservation in their circuitry. They only wanted to accomplish their mission any way they could.

"Rumbold!" I boomed. "Get us out of here!"

"Uh—yes, Captain! Hold on!"

Red lights flashed, warning the crew, but I knew it was too late. There would be no time to get to an acceleration couch, or even to strap in. All over the ship, there would be injuries—possibly even deaths.

The first lurch of power sickened me. Then, it got worse. The engines roared and my face began to sag. A staffer, caught off-guard, was thrown to the floor. She rolled away to the back of the chamber, her helmet thumping as she made each full revolution.

"Stop firing the cannons," I ordered Durris, who was still clinging to his table. "Give full power to the engines."

He complied, and the thrust increased by another thirty percent. We were all crushed by the centrifugal force.

The computers were unaffected. They continued to calmly depict the external action. Our smart-chaff was left in a cloud of vapor. We were unshielded, but slipping away from the enemy.

They responded with the speed of vipers. Turning and applying their own surge of thrust, they followed us—and they continued to gain.

"They're right on our tails, Captain!" Rumbold wheezed. "I can't shake them!"

"They must have a limited fuel supply," I said through gritted teeth. "Keep up this thrust. Pump more chaff out in a cloud behind us."

A massive trail of reflective particles began growing in our wake. The strikes from the enemy lasers lessened then faded away.

"We're pulling away, sir!" Rumbold said, then had a coughing fit that ended with a strangling sound.

I looked around the deck. Several of my people had lost consciousness. Durris was among them. He was still at his station, slumped over at an odd angle in his harness.

"Ease down," I ordered Rumbold. "Medical, sweep the ship. Get to anyone whose implant is in emergency-mode. Put the command crew at the head of that list."

The enemy fighters were steadily falling farther behind. They'd exhausted their fuel reserves. They were still firing after us, but they lacked the acceleration to catch us again. They would have to limp back to base and refuel.

Several things were now clear, the most important of which was the suicidal nature of this new foe. I vowed not to underestimate them again.

We came about over the next hour, trailing them as they returned slowly toward the broken husk of what had once been Tranquility Station.

None of them made it home. We mercilessly destroyed every last one of them.

-32-

The post-mortem of the attack on this system was a lengthy process. I assembled my best advisors for a round-table analysis of the whole mess.

"As best we can tell, the Earth fleet passed through here," Yamada said, "but used a different path through the bridges."

"I don't care how they got here," I said, "I want to know where they went next."

"Right… that's unclear. There's so much radiation blasting this system it's hard to follow a month old trail. We'll have to guess."

"Very well," I said, "what's your best guess?"

She squirmed. Yamada was my science officer, but she wasn't a wizard. I'd asked her for information she probably couldn't produce. Still, I could tell she wanted to have a good answer—after all several million people had died here. An entire colony.

"Captain," she said after a moment's hesitation, "I know that emotions are running high. I know the Connatic meant a lot to you—"

"Lieutenant Commander Yamada," I said firmly. "If you don't have an answer, just say so."

If the truth be told, my memories of the Connatic were haunting my deeper thoughts. My restored relationship with Lady Chloe put a whole different light on things, but I'd had a significant romance with the leader of this colony the last time

195

I was here. Emotions notwithstanding, my training forced the outrage to stay in check. We had a mission to execute.

"I have no answer, Captain." Yamada dropped her gaze. "We can't know the truth without sifting through the wreckage at length hoping to find a surviving digital recording... something like that."

I nodded slowly.

Durris, still amped on medical stims, jumped in then. His voice rang with alarm. "Captain, I don't think we can spare the time. They're already dead, and we've got our orders."

Glancing at him briefly, I let my eyes go back to Yamada.

"I'm well aware of the situation, Commander Durris, thank you. Yamada, have you got anything else?"

She shook her head in defeat. We had not found a single survivor. The variants had infested a relatively undamaged portion of the smashed space station, set up a fighter launch bay and waited here in ambush. Eventually, we'd entered the system and been attacked.

In the long run, I had no doubt my crew would remember the fine people and hospitality of Gi, but this system was now a dead scrap heap. The clock was ticking and there was an enemy to kill.

"Director Vogel," I said, turning to face him, "what's your theory about this trap? Why did the variants set it?"

"I... they probably wanted to make sure every last human in this system was dead."

"Right, I agree. They're thorough creatures by nature. They don't like to leave a job half-done—or even ninety-nine percent done."

"You don't think they knew we'd be coming?" Morris interjected.

He normally stayed quiet at these meetings as his expertise involved ground missions. Today, however, I welcomed any input I could get.

"Yes, what about that angle?" I turned back to Yamada and Durris. "Could they have been left here specifically to intercept us?"

"Unlikely, sir," Durris said. "How would they know we were coming?"

"It's not impossible," Director Vogel said. "This system is close to Earth. Many paths from Earth to the colonies pass through it. The battleship *Victory* was sent toward Earth to destroy *Defiant*—or maybe it escaped the mutiny and later succumbed. In either case, the variants had to know that they may be pursued."

"But why would they weaken their fighter strength?" Durris demanded. "It makes no sense. Placing a hundred fighters here gives them that many less to defend the carrier."

Director Vogel launched a single index finger into the air. "Ah," he said, "you don't know all of *Iron Duke's* capacities. The carrier, manned by variants, is able to build new fighters to replace the old. They have an in-flight construction bay. I think it's likely they dropped off their surplus units here."

"And the variant pilots?" I asked. "Are they being replaced as well?"

He nodded crisply, with certainty. I could tell he had great pride in the monsters he'd created even when they were at their worst. "Yes, as long as the necessary resources are available."

"You mean people that can be brainwashed, cut apart and built into machines against their will."

"Must you speak so crassly about the genius that has…?"

"That's wonderful," Morris interrupted. "We wasted ammo on these guys. They're slowing us down with every hour we fart around in this system. I suggest we move on, Captain."

"Following our original course?" I asked.

He shrugged. The rest agreed without enthusiasm. All of us were demoralized by the loss here. A colony had been swept away. Worse, it was a colony friendly to Earth. Possibly, the Gi people had been the only humans in the universe that would have called Earthmen their friends.

"I agree with Morris," I said at last. "We're pulling out in one hour. Meeting adjourned."

No one objected. They got to their feet and returned to their stations.

Defiant hadn't been badly damaged in the battle, but after violent action it was standard operating procedure to review and consult checklists for every system aboard. One hour would be cutting it short for my officers. I let them move on to their work.

* * *

We left Gliese-32 in a sober mood. Weeks passed quickly. After crossing more bridges, we discovered two star systems that were new to us.

They were just as lifeless as Gi had been. Both possessed natural beauties to behold, to be sure, but nothing living. Nothing threatening, either.

Today we sighted what was to my mind the most intriguing natural wonder of all. A pair of crystalline planets orbited one another in perfect synchronicity. They were twins, both of them haunting beauties covered in cold, sparkling spikes.

Encrusted with blue ice, they stretched and crackled due to their mutual gravitational forces. These forces inevitably melted the surface in spots and drew spikes of fresh-melted liquids from both cores. The spikes then refroze into blue crystal mountains.

We passed these planets in their eternal frozen embrace. Just beyond them, we found another breach and headed for it, not knowing what we'd find inside or at the far end.

My worries continued to haunt me. My gut was telling me to press on, but my doubts were almost as strong.

Was I a madman to be out here, chasing phantoms? With each jump, we were getting farther from home. We'd trusted the word of a dying Stroj with the lives of my entire crew.

With each jump, my tension grew. This series of jumps had at least been hinted at on the Connatic's maps—but not so the next one. The next one would truly be the first blind, blue jump of my career. On every previous flight, I'd at least had a hint as to what was on the far side or some evidence that the way was safe.

The breach loomed ahead, and I found I couldn't take my eyes off it. My crew was transfixed as well, silent and foreboding.

To our knowledge, no one had ever passed through this next breach.

It could very well be that the dead Stroj we were relying on was laughing in Hell at us as we followed his map. Had he played an elaborate prank from the grave? Were we about to be exposed to deadly radiation, an inescapable gravitational force, or simply a planetary mass so close to the exit that there was no hope of evasion?

We had no way of knowing what was ahead, but we flew into the wormhole all the same, and we vanished without a trace.

-33-

Instant death didn't await us once we'd found the exit to the bridge. This left me mildly surprised. I'd calculated that if the Stroj had been engaged in a careful act of deceit, this would have been the perfect point to spring his deadly surprise.

What of the other jump points on the list? Were they window-dressing? Had they only been scrawled there to put us off our guard? Logically, it would be the first blue-jump, the first jump into the total unknown, that would be our undoing. The rest of the coordinates were only included to give us false hope.

But that wasn't how it played out. The trip here hadn't been easy, to be sure. This last bridge in particular didn't want to give up its secrets. We'd searched for an unusually long time, but we'd eventually found the exit.

"Data is coming in now, Captain," Yamada said. Her voice was professional, but she sounded stressed. She knew the stakes and the odds as well as I did—perhaps better.

"Display everything you have as soon as it's confirmed," I said.

"Coming on screen now."

We could all see as a group that we were in a single-star system. Most stars were multiples in our galactic neighborhood. The star in question was a dwarf but a relatively bright one.

Staring at it with narrowed eyes, I stepped closer to the screens. One by one, the local litter of planets were being detected and displayed on the holo-maps.

"Captain..." Durris said, "we have a ninety-percent match-up already. Can you guess where we are?"

I nodded. "As a matter of fact, I thought I recognized it. A young star, with no gas giant to clean up the outer system debris... this is Beta Cygnus, if I don't miss my guess."

"Exactly," Durris said. "Not the safest system in the galaxy, but not the worst, either."

"I can't believe that we're back here again," Yamada said. "Last time they were hostile... Should we transmit a welcoming message?"

Her question gave me pause. It would be a polite gesture, but there were several flaws with the idea. For one thing, when we'd been here before, several Beta warships—each of them a twin to *Defiant*—had chased us. One had caught up, and we'd been forced to battle her. We were fortunate to have survived that encounter.

That wasn't the only reason I hesitated. The Betas might be no more. If the star carrier had come through this system, I doubted the Betas could have destroyed it. As before, they may have left variant forces behind. Calling out to the Betas might well alert this hypothetical enemy to our presence.

For several long moments, I didn't issue any orders. I was considering my options.

The system made me think of Zye more sharply than I'd done since we'd left Earth weeks before. Here we were, visiting her home system again. The strange thing was that, even if she'd been with us, she'd have been no more welcome here today than she was back on Earth.

"What should we do, Captain?" Durris prompted me at last.

"I'm thinking. Anything new?"

"I'm reading flight-signatures around the Beta home world," Yamada said.

Moving to her station, I studied the data directly over her shoulder. The command deck was organized in such a way that I was fed only the summary data directly. Each of the substations was manned by key officers who got everything, all the details they were responsible for. The reason for this two-tiered system was that there were simply too many pieces of information flowing around for any one person to track it all.

Because of this arrangement, I had to move to another station for data in depth or request that it be relayed to my screens. I often chose the former option so I could converse with the specialist in person.

"Are they scrambling a ship to come greet us?" I asked Yamada.

"I'm not sure, but I doubt it," she said. "There's quite a bit of traffic, and it's unlikely they've spotted us yet. We're about a light-hour out from Beta right now. Even if they have drones here, spying on us, they can't have reported in yet."

She was assuming that Beta tech was as limited as ours was in the area of communications, and I didn't correct her. For now I'd continue hoping that the speed of light was an impenetrable barrier for Betas when it came to communications.

"All right then," I said, coming to a decision. "We'll assume they don't know we're here—not yet, anyway. Come about to your last planned course, helmsman."

Rumbold looked startled. "Are you sure, Captain? That will take us right through the inner planets."

"You're suggesting we should poke along at the system outskirts?"

"Yes. A long trip in an elliptical orbit would get us there a week from now, but with little chance of detection."

I shook my head. "We have to assume the *Iron Duke* is still out there, laying waste to systems ahead of us. We can't wait around while people die."

None of my crewmen said anything, but I knew what they were thinking: *these people are only colonists.*

Fortunately, none of them dared to speak these words to me. As far as I was concerned, we had an obligation to protect all humans. This responsibility was doubly ours due to the fact Earth gov had released the variants on the universe deliberately. It wasn't as if we'd stumbled into some kind of alien civil war. We'd built and unleashed the very engines of their destruction.

A dozen hours passed swiftly. We'd stopped using thrusters after the initial burn to get up to cruising speed. But silent engines weren't enough to hide us when we were soaring through the system openly. Each hour took us closer to their home world. We weren't on a collision course with it, but it was going to be pretty damned close.

At some point during this time, the Betas detected us. I was summoned to the deck, and we were treated to an aggressive display.

"There are at least seven ships headed to intercept us," Yamada said, struggling to keep her voice calm.

"Let's see the projections on the main screen."

Red arcs appeared, looking like hair-thin strands of light. Each intersected our ship over the next day of travel time.

"Any incoming demands?" I asked.

"Nothing sir—just like Gliese-32."

I didn't look at her. We both knew what she was thinking. The variants might have swept through here with their fleet already, destroying the Betas. But the last time we came through the Beta Cygnus system, they hadn't bothered communicating with us. Why would this occasion be any different?

"Durris, have you got a model yet?" I asked. "What does this look like if we go to full burn?"

He showed me, and the situation looked far less bleak. We'd reach the exit point we were aiming at before any of the enemy ships could catch up. Having a head start was seriously helping.

"But Captain," he said, "there may be more ships ahead we don't see yet."

"Of course. The last time we crossed the Beta Cygnus system, it was a ship that was ahead of us that managed to catch up. Keep scanning for that, forward of our position. In the meantime, light up our engines. We'll have to keep out of their grasp. But don't push it any harder than you must. I want room to maneuver."

"Got it, working up a thrust setting."

The next few minutes were tense, but once we got underway, we all felt better. It was unnerving to have seven ships on your tail gaining fast, and any one of them could be your equal in a fight.

Rumbold seemed particularly happy to be applying thrust again. He hummed, and he mumbled, and he occasionally chuckled to himself.

"Captain," Yamada said, "are we going to try to talk to them?"

I considered the idea. Last time, it hadn't helped. Any communication could only identify us to the enemy at this point. But I thought it might be worth a try anyway. Maybe we'd learn something.

"Get Director Vogel up here," I said. "He's the expert on variants. Maybe he can get them to parley with us."

As Vogel was summoned, I had time to think about the situation. It seemed grim. If this system was as dead as Gliese-32 had been, then there were no more Betas.

Well, there was probably one more in existence. The only one I knew of—Zye.

Her loneliness had infinitely increased on this black day.

-34-

Director Vogel was obtuse, as usual.

"About time you asked my advice," he said. "If these ships are under the control of variant pilots, I'll get them to talk to us."

"How?" I asked.

He waggled a thin finger at me.

"With a clever application of keywords. They speak a dialect of Standard that's subtly different from our own. It's not binary, don't get that idea, it's a more precisely functional version of our communication. Let me demonstrate."

I was reluctant to open a channel and let him say whatever he wished, but given the situation, I doubted things could get worse.

"Open the channel for him, Yamada."

She did, and Director Vogel smugly stepped up to the filament-cameras. Hanging down from the roof, they glowed with a bluish light. They followed his every motion like hair-thin snakes.

"Identification protocol," he stated. "Director Vogel, Earth system, Phobos complex. Acknowledge."

There was nothing in response. He repeated the statement several times, becoming agitated. He tugged at his clothing, but since it was made of smart fabrics, his collar and sleeves quickly slid back into position.

"I don't understand it," Vogel said. "This should work. They should feel an almost irresistible urge to respond in kind and identify themselves."

I shrugged, and Vogel kept trying to reach them.

After the fourth attempt, Yamada signaled me. She wanted to know if we should close the channel.

"Director Vogel," I said, "I think we should try something—"

"Sparhawk?" the speakers boomed suddenly. We all jumped. It was the voice I knew as Zye's voice—but that meant little. Because Betas were all clones they all sounded the same.

"Who is this?" I asked.

"Are you Sparhawk?" the voice demanded again.

"Yes," I said. "I'm Captain William Sparhawk."

"Why do you have this mental deficient calling us? Did you hope to hide behind him? Did you hope we wouldn't know who you really were?"

At the reference to being a mental deficient, Vogel ruffled. "I demand to know who's piloting the ships in our wake!" he said.

I cast him a dark glance and waved him away from the cameras. Two security people quickly escorted him off the deck.

"I'm sorry about that," I said when I stood in the central position, my face lit up with a slightly bluish cast by the twisting vid pickups. "That was one of our scientists. We thought you were—well—we thought you were someone else."

"You're talking about those machines, aren't you?" the voice asked.

Whoever she was, this individual wasn't showing herself.

"Why are you so afraid?" I asked, deliberately needling her. "Betas are always paranoid, but this time you're more so than the last time I visited this system."

The response was very sudden. An angry face loomed on the forward holo screen.

"Ignorant Basic!" she said. "I'm no Beta, I'm an Alpha. You'd best remember that."

"Captain Okto?" I asked. "Is that you?"

"You remember? Good. I want you to know who destroys your ship. I want you to feel fear and rage as your decks split apart under your Earthling ass."

"Tempers are flaring," I said as calmly as I could. "I would suggest that we're wasting our energies on each other. We should be presenting a united front to stop the real menace—"

"Which one?" she asked. "The Stroj or that war-fleet full of robots you sent out blindly into space? How can you suggest alliance when you created both these threats? Do you take us for utter fools?"

"Not at all," I said, "and you do have a valid complaint when it comes to the variants."

"We have more than that. You Basics are responsible for everything that's wrong with the colonies. We understand that now. You seeded us, abandoned us, and now you seek to destroy us. Could your motivations be whimsy or idiocy? Does it matter which it is?"

"Captain Okto," I said, "I know you're upset. I'm sure the variants have done grievous damage—"

"SHUT UP SPARHAWK!" she raged. "A million Betas have perished. A dozen proud starships have been lost... I'm only glad you've provided us with this chance to even the score."

She closed the channel. Try as we might, she didn't allow it to reopen.

"Well," Vogel said from behind me, where he'd crept back onto the deck, "that could have gone better."

I felt rage bubble up in me, but I didn't release it. There was no purpose. What was done was done. A potentially allied world—probably the best ally we could have hoped for—had declared a vendetta against us.

That was the legacy of Earth's dealings with her colonies. The arrogance of the Council and the Chairman had no bounds.

Did they really think the colonists were going to forget these acts? If these peoples out here among the stars ever got their strength together, if they ever managed to gather their scattered numbers and turn against us...

We wouldn't stand a chance.

That was the thought which transfixed me. In an instant, I felt I understood what was going on—or at least part of it.

Whirling on my heel, I approached Vogel with such singleness of purpose he staggered back, suspecting I was going to strike him. In truth, such a thing did briefly cross my mind.

"Vogel, come with me."

I brushed past him and headed for the conference chamber. He followed, muttering to himself.

When we were alone, I set up a scrambler and began to talk in earnest.

"I understand what's going on out here now," I said.

"You do?" he asked cautiously.

"Yes. I want to know if you understand it as well."

"You'll have to be more specific, Captain," he said. "Please remember I'm only a weak-minded fool."

I blinked, then realized he was still furious that his intellect had been called into question by Okto. I brushed his concerns away with my hand.

"Grow up, man," I told him. "An Alpha called you an idiot. So what?"

"When it comes to comparative intellects—"

"Drop it," I told him. "We have much bigger concerns."

"Why?" he asked. "We're going to slide right past these ships. They said themselves they lost half their fleet to the variants. That lowers the odds they'll be ahead of us waiting for us in ambush."

"I'm not talking about the Betas. I'm talking about the variants and their mission. They're out here to destroy every colony they encounter."

"We knew that."

"Yes... but we didn't know why. Not until now."

He blinked at me. "Your discussion with Okto gave you an insight into the motivations of my variants?"

"In a way, she did just that. The variants aren't rebels. The variants are obedient, as always. It's my belief this case is no different, that they're following their orders."

He frowned and squirmed. "That's absurd. Why would Admiral Halsey order them to mutiny and kill him?"

208

I gave him a slow, grim smile. "The variants have implants—right, Director?"

He paused, staring at me. "Yes... for all intents and purposes, they do."

"Just so. Now, who do you think might have the power to reprogram all your variants at once, without your knowledge?"

"But why...?" he asked. "You believe we did this to ourselves? Such a horrible thought."

"I think the Council did it, yes. The Chairman specifically. He tricked the variants, or changed their memories, or something. He turned them against Star Guard and against all our colonies. He sent them out here to destroy them all."

"That's monstrous," Vogel said. "Genocide? On an interplanetary scale? Why?"

I leaned toward him. "Now you're right where I am. It's one thing to suspect a crime, it's quite another to have a sensible motive that makes everything fit. Now, at last, I think I understand."

"Explain it to me then."

"When Okto raged at us, I realized that Earth wouldn't stand a chance against all our colonies in a united war. Despite having the largest fleet, we couldn't stop all of them put together."

Vogel looked horrified. "So... so we struck first? Out of fear?"

"Fear? Maybe that's the right word. I was there when the Council voted to act. To build a great fleet and launch it into the stars. It was my understanding that the purpose of the fleet was to bring order to the chaos that our colonies represented. But they had a different view."

Vogel was nodding now. I could tell he'd come to see things my way. I could also tell he didn't like it.

"Monstrous," he repeated.

"A fair description," I agreed. "The Council figured Earth couldn't fight every colonist out here if they were united, so Earth struck first. That way, they could take the colonies down one at a time in a long series of battles. Each time the armada ventured to a new star, our fleet would be bigger than the enemy fleet as long as the colonies stayed divided."

"I think you might be right, Captain. The variants will never be defeated if they move quickly and ruthlessly enough."

Vogel said this, again with a hint of pride. I could forgive him for that, even if others wouldn't.

"One detail that I haven't understood," I said, "is why they killed Halsey."

"Maybe that was an error," Vogel suggested. "Or maybe he didn't like the change of orders. The variants might have misinterpreted his reluctance to follow orders from Star Guard."

"Misinterpreted? Their instructions were illegal and those instructions probably only existed within the minds of the variants. I find it likely that the Council intended for the human crews to die. They would only get in the way when the killing began in earnest. Variants have no conscience, do they?"

Vogel studied his hands. "It's hard to know... but then, neither does the Council."

"What I *do* know," I said, "is that the Council sent me to meet *Victory* in battle when she came toward Earth. Maybe something had gone wrong by that point. Maybe *Victory* wasn't supposed to return to the Solar System at all."

Vogel shook a finger at me. "That's got to be it. The variants might be—troubled by all this."

"By 'troubled' do you mean completely mad?"

"Possibly. I don't know how they might respond to a radical shift in their world-view. They aren't human—not quite. The Council may have miscalculated. They may have accidentally put Earth on the menu."

"That scenario fits the events I've witnessed," I said. "Halsey was sent off to die, but I was allowed to live with *Defiant* under my command in orbit over the home world."

"I suppose that's a backhanded form of compliment," Vogel said, his lips twitching into a smirk.

"Yes..." I agreed. "Then we gave them a second chance at both of us. What better reason to kill us, or make us vanish, could there be than an unsanctioned attack on CENTCOM? But even after all that, they let us out of prison."

Director Vogel chewed that over. "Our release wasn't on account of any kind-heartedness on the part of the oldsters, of that much I'm certain. It was a reaction to stark fear. They must have calculated that they still needed us."

"Perhaps they see us as fail-safes. A method of shutting down the variants when their mission has been completed, and they begin to return home."

Vogel agreed, and we both sat brooding over our next move.

The idea of defending the Council with my life and the lives of my crew bothered me, but then so did the prospect of leaving Earth undefended. They had me boxed in. For now, I was forced to do my utmost to protect everyone on Earth—whether they deserved it or not.

"We have to continue the mission," I said, "even if it plays into the Council's hands."

"Agreed," Vogel said. "Those bastards don't deserve our loyalty, but what else can we do?"

We broke up the meeting and returned to our posts. Both of us were a little wiser, but we were by no means comforted by these new thoughts.

-35-

Okto pursued me doggedly. As we got closer to the next breach in the sequence Admiral Perez had written for us, it became increasingly clear she wouldn't be able to catch up.

Still, it wasn't going to be for a lack of trying. The acceleration arc of her ship was such that it might have killed a normal human crew. Her people were enduring tremendous physical challenges to pursue us.

Only when we approached the breach did the true nature of her plans begin to become clear.

"We'll have to slow down, Captain," Rumbold said. "This breach is bouncing all over the place."

I strode to his side, checked the measurements and then moved to Durris' planning table.

"Why weren't we aware of this previously?"

He shrugged. "You can't get good readings on a breach when you're several AUs away. The radiation signatures are too faint. But Rumbold is right, this breach is unstable. It's liable to shift a thousand meters every few minutes. If we approach with too much velocity—"

"We'll be unable to make a course correction in time and shoot right past it," I finished for him. "Damn it... Okto knew this all along. She knew that this had to be the breach we were heading for as it's the only one out here. Further, she had to know we couldn't detect how unstable it was. She's going to catch up when we slow down."

Durris nodded helplessly. He knew I wasn't interested in apologies. I valued results, so he didn't offer any phantom solutions.

"Hmm..." I said, pacing the deck. We were no longer accelerating, but coasting along in preparation for entering the breach.

"Captain?" Durris asked. "I've plotted a new set of maneuvers. If we begin braking now—"

I shook my head, and he fell silent.

"I'm thinking," I said, "what velocity are you estimating Okto will reach when she hits the breach?"

"If we begin to slow down now, she'll be moving about twenty percent faster than we are currently."

"Isn't she slowing down as well?"

"No," Durris admitted, checking his instruments to confirm his answer. "She's not. I can only assume she knows this breach-point's behavior pattern. She's predicting a point where they can make a high-speed entry."

"Ah-ha!" I said, daring to give him a tight smile. "Let's match her course precisely then. We can certainly project it—she must be blazing along after us at full burn."

Durris shook his head sadly. "No Captain, I tried that. She's making random course variations. At first I thought she was worried we might have left mines in our wake, but now I believe she's trying to hide her exact course."

"So we can't match it..." I said, deflating.

"Exactly."

"All right then. We'll have to take a risk. To be eighty percent certain we'll hit the target, how much would we have to slow down?"

Durris turned back to his boards, frowning. He sighed when he'd finished.

"We have to begin slowing right now to achieve that goal. Every minute that passes is increasing the odds of a high-speed miss by about one percent."

This news alarmed me. "We're at eighty percent? Right now?"

"Seventy-nine."

"There's no way to rectify this?"

213

"We could perform an emergency deceleration, but there will be injuries. Further, we'll be at their mercy when they catch up to us."

"Apply the brakes. Get us to eighty percent."

He turned to his boards and all around us crewmen began strapping in and bracing themselves.

I made an announcement over the ship's com system to the entire crew. "All hands, get to an acceleration couch! We're going to be braking hard. This is no drill—you have seconds in which to comply!"

The pain began soon afterward. The lights on the command deck went yellow, then orange, then red. The ship was built to withstand this kind of abuse, but the humans aboard weren't. I found myself wishing Zye were here with us. She'd always been able to withstand more Gs than the rest of us. In a way, she belonged aboard *Defiant* more than any other crewmember as the ship had been built by her people, for her physique.

Pressed back into my seat with terrific force, I was close to blacking out when I suddenly shook myself. I'd almost begun dreaming. The pressure—it was too much.

"Ease off," I ordered. "Rumbold? Ease off!"

Rumbold didn't respond. Durris grunted, crawling hand over hand along the railing toward the helm. He was trying to follow my orders. I waved him back and slid out of my swiveling chair. I was much closer to the goal than he was.

The full pressure of heavy deceleration brought me to my knees. Humans could withstand high G forces with proper support, but only for short periods of time. We'd been on full thrust for too long. The oppressive force from braking had begun to mess with our guts and play with our minds.

Managing to crawl to Rumbold's station, I killed the thrusters, returning them to a relatively mild one-point-five rate. We were still sick and heavy, but we were able to function.

All over the ship, people had lost consciousness. Several of my command crew were lolling in their seats.

"Durris," I grunted out as I crept back to my chair, "what are our odds now?"

"I can't get back to my tabletop to check…" he said from the deck. He was lying flat on his back, his breathing labored. "…sorry Captain."

"It's all right," I said, "we'll make it, or we won't. Rest until you're fit to resume your duties. We'll know the outcome soon enough."

"Breach in thirty seconds," the ship's computer said. We'd recently taught it to talk when we were back at Araminta Station. "Acceleration rate non-standard."

No shit, I thought to myself vaguely. I'd made it back to my chair, but I was envying Durris who was still flat on his back.

With an effort, I swiveled my attention to the forward screen. The anomaly was right there, dead ahead. Undetectable to the human eye without instruments, we had many names for these twisted patches of space-time. Wormholes, warp-fields, ER bridges…

That was all I had time to think about before the anomaly loomed, and we went into the final plunge.

-36-

Defiant went into shutdown mode the moment we were through. Durris had programmed the computer to ease-down once we'd crossed the barrier.

In this case, it was a good thing. We were in no condition to control the battle cruiser properly when we first breached. As far as I knew, we were traveling at speeds no ship from Earth had matched in more than a century.

Even more alarming, space seemed *odd* on the far side of this particular breach. It was colorful and gaseous. That didn't bode well.

"Durris… are you awake, man?"

"I'm on it, Captain," he said, struggling to his knees.

There was a gash on the side of his head, and blood dripped down onto his uniform now that he'd removed his helmet.

"How did you get injured?"

"I'm not quite sure, sir…"

He looked dazed, so I ordered him to a seat and summoned a corpsman to the command deck.

My attention turned to Yamada, who seemed to be in better condition. "I need a full sensor-sweep and a summary report," I told her.

"I'm on it."

Within minutes, during which we continued braking, she had the report.

"This hyperspace isn't normal," she said. "In fact, it's quite small. Sir... from my experience, we've only seen this type of space once before."

I nodded, studying the data. I already knew what she was going to say, I'd only wanted confirmation.

"This is an artificial breach, isn't it?" I asked.

"I think so. Like the ones we encountered a year ago. As far as we know, only the Stroj are capable of creating a bridge like this one."

Most—almost all—ER bridges we'd encountered were natural phenomena. Theoretically, they were created between two or more star systems by gravitational warping of local space. Like exoplanets, they were once thought to be rare or that they only existed in theory. In actual practice, we'd found they were commonplace.

This one, however, was different. It had been created purposefully. The Stroj were the only people we'd met capable of building their own bridges between stars of their choosing. Even so, it took a vast amount of energy to do so. Often, a portion of a star's mass was used up in the process. The resulting bridge was weak and unstable in comparison to a naturally occurring one.

"This bridge seems to fit the profile precisely," Yamada continued. "No wonder a Stroj imposter knew about it—his people probably built it."

"You said it's different," I prompted "different in what way?"

She shook her head. "It's gaseous. Not much, not enough to burn our hull with our forward shields up, but it could get thicker. If it turns into dust ahead..."

"Oh, I see. Apply heavier braking!"

Rumbold was back in the game by this time. He lurched to his seat, snorting as if waking from a nap. He leaned forward, eyes rolling over his instruments, and selected a control. He applied his hand to it, giving it a tweak.

We all rocked in our seats as reverse thrust was applied. A few people stumbled and cursed.

"Take it easy, Rumbold," I said. "We've got injuries aboard.

217

"Sorry Captain... I must have nodded off."

I laughed and turned back to Yamada.

"Are you watching for Okto?" I asked her.

"Yes... so far she hasn't arrived.'"

"She should have by now. According to my calculations, she should have hit the breach and joined us in this bridge about two minutes ago."

"The fact that she hasn't indicates she must have hit her brakes as well," Yamada said.

"Either that, or she steered clear of the breach entirely. Maybe she only wanted to chase us out of the Beta Cygnus system."

Yamada shook her head. "That isn't what I would expect. I've studied Beta behavioral profiles since they were first rediscovered."

I stared at her for a moment. It felt so odd that I could remember Zye, and she couldn't. It had created a gap between us, a gulf I had trouble reaching across.

"What's wrong, Captain?" she asked.

I touched my forehead. "That was a rough breach."

"Yeah, I almost lost consciousness. Do you want to take a break? I could—"

"No," I said, "I'm fine, thank you. Keep watching for the Beta ships."

Behind Okto were several others. They might be catching up to her by now if she had slowed down hard enough to let them.

Time ticked by. Four minutes passed.

I began to relax. Perhaps the threat had eased. Okto and her people were tenacious, but not to the point of insanity. If they knew this was an artificial breach—and I had no doubt they did know the truth—then they had to know it was dangerous. Perhaps they'd decided to let us go and return to the task of defending their homeworld.

One more minute passed, and during that time, I managed to convince myself that we'd escaped the Betas. It was a great relief. The odds of them coming through now were remote. The enemy ships would have had to decelerate so hard it would have killed a normal human.

At that precise instant, the moment at which I calculated we were in the clear, the Beta ships appeared.

"Captain," Yamada said, "I've got three contacts."

"Where?" I demanded.

"Behind us. At the breach. They all just appeared together."

I froze for a moment in disbelief. "Okto?"

"It has to be her, sir."

Nodding slowly, numbly, I had Yamada display the tactical situation on the forward screen. Three Beta battle cruisers, each a match for *Defiant*, had appeared at the breach. They were going relatively slowly, but I had no doubt they would increase speed once they spotted us in this gassy chunk of space-time.

"They waited to get grouped-up before they came through," Rumbold said. "Didn't we ambush Okto the last time she followed us into a breach?"

"I believe we did," I said.

"I bet she didn't want to suffer a repeat performance, Captain. She waited for her friends before daring to enter here."

His analysis was logical, but unwelcome.

"Sir!" Yamada said, "Okto is hailing us."

"On screen."

We waited for a few seconds until a scratchy image appeared. Talking ship to ship in hyperspace was possible, but it always seemed to be difficult. The radio signals had a difficult time handshaking and maintaining a coherent channel.

Okto glared at us. "We shall destroy you, Sparhawk. Don't run. You've already embarrassed Earth enough."

"Suicide impresses no one, Okto," I said. "Fortunately, your ships are slow. We've improved upon *Defiant*, rebuilding her engines and her instrumentation."

What I was saying had some basis in fact, but that didn't make my crew any happier. They were staring at me in slack-jawed surprise.

"Rumbold, all-ahead full. Let's head for the exit."

"But…" I knew he wanted to say we had no idea yet where that was, but he kept his mouth shut after I gave him a hard glance. "All-ahead full, Captain."

The deck lurched under my feet again, and we began accelerating. All this stopping and starting was enough to make a man nauseous, but such was the life of every spacer in Star Guard.

"You flee again!" raged Okto. "You are without honor! You're a cur who dodges the boot and runs away not even daring to stand and snap at the heels of your betters!"

Her words were aggravating, but I contained my response.

"Not so, Captain," I said. "We're doing battle even now—but on our terms."

I turned to Durris, who was back at his post looking hunched.

"Commander Durris, release three of our largest missiles. Maximum yield. Target one of the enemy vessels with each bird."

"But Captain—"

"Do it now. This isn't the time to be merciful."

He stared at me for a half-second with his mouth open, but then turned back to his boards and fired one missile at each of the pursuing ships.

"Birds away, Captain," he said in a dull voice.

"Excellent," I said, turning back to the blue, glowing pickups and Okto's angry face.

She'd been watching us with an expression of alarm and irritation.

"My apologies Captain Okto," I said. "Our missiles may prove too much for your battle cruisers. In that case, I promise to notify Beta command of the loss the next time I visit your system. Please remember: you gave me no choice."

Her mouth transformed into a confused snarl, but I signaled Yamada to cut the channel. It closed instantly.

Rumbold let out a guffaw of laughter the moment the woman's face was gone. Durris was less pleased.

"Sir, I hope you realize those missiles I just fired were nothing but standard-issue ordnance."

"He knows that, you stiff!" Rumbold boomed. "He's bluffing them!"

Durris turned back to me in surprise. "I thought you didn't like to lie, Captain."

220

"I didn't lie," I said. "I misled. There's a big difference."

Rumbold snorted and laughed aloud again.

"Captain," Yamada said, "they're taking evasive action. They seem to have believed you. How did you know?"

"I'd heard somewhere that Betas are easy to bluff."

Yamada and Durris tossed me confused glances. As they couldn't recall Zye's existence, they didn't know how I'd come to this conclusion.

Durris stepped up to my chair, dabbing at oozing adhesives over his cheekbone.

"What is the purpose of enraging them?" he asked. "Idle fun?"

"Hardly," I said.

"Then why?"

I looked at him thoughtfully for a moment. "We're outrunning them right now. They should turn back, but they can't now that I've fired on them. That would stain their honor."

He nodded thoughtfully. "So you *want* them to chase us? To follow us through star system after star system in a blind rage?"

"Yes," I said, "do you think they would have come along willingly if I'd asked?"

"No."

"There you have it. Now, if you'll excuse me—"

"One more thing, Captain."

"What is it?"

"I've noticed—we've all been noticing—that you have a level of knowledge concerning Beta behavior that none of us can fathom. Where did this intel come from?"

I stared at him thoughtfully. "There's a Beta prisoner," I said, "a live one, in the brig under CENTCOM."

He looked startled. "Is that information classified?" he asked.

"Maybe," I admitted. "But no one told me that it was. Perhaps they overlooked the procedural details in the messy aftermath of the attack."

"A Beta prisoner on Earth..." he mused, "and you've had personal contact with this... person?"

"That's right."

"That explains a lot. Thanks, Captain." He walked away, nodding to himself.

The rest of the crew eyed me with increased respect. I felt bad I couldn't tell them more, but if I did, they'd question my sanity. That wouldn't be good for morale or our odds of survival.

-37-

The next hour or so was tense, but things eased off as we continued to put distance between our stern and the Beta vessels.

The enemy crews weren't able to capitalize on their ability to take more G-forces in this environment. Just as we'd done, they'd detected the gas and suspected there might be more substantial particulate matter in this pocket of hyperspace. If that was true, flying too fast could overwhelm their shields and destroy their ships.

Since *Defiant* had been moving faster than they were when we'd entered hyperspace, we kept gaining slightly as we all accelerated to a maximal safe speed. At that point, we coasted ahead of them.

The only problem with my strategy was finding a way out. If we ran out of hyperspace before we found the exit, we would be in trouble. We'd either have to turn and fight, or we'd ram into the theoretical wall of this universe. Either way, we'd be destroyed.

The Beta ships followed doggedly for sixteen more hours before our missiles reached them. I'd ordered Durris to program them to go fairly slowly so as to maximize the suspense.

I could only imagine the worry my three missiles were causing the Betas. Normal warfare practice required an overwhelming barrage to be applied to a single ship in order to

223

ensure a crippling blow. The fact I'd sent only one missile each against all three of their ships had to be giving them fits. Betas weren't imaginative, and they didn't like unknowns.

Accordingly, they began firing a disproportionate amount of countermeasures, anti-missiles and point-defense turrets as our missiles closed on their position. In very short order, all three of our missiles were destroyed.

"Fire three more," I ordered. "Set them for maximal velocity this time."

Rumbold boggled at me. "Still trying to make them duck, Captain?"

I nodded.

He went off into another gale of laughter.

"They won't fall for the same trick twice, surely…?" Yamada asked.

"Watch them," I said. "They're suspicious people. They'll make up a reason for our actions if none is evident."

"Yes…" Durris said, beginning to catch on. "If I was worried about an enemy behaving like this, I might impute all kinds of evil into these actions."

"Such as?" I asked, honestly curious.

"I'd assume the first barrage had been devised to reveal our defenses. That they were sent at low velocities to tease out everything we had. Now, three more fast missiles on the way…? They could only be smarter weapons. Missiles made much more dangerous because we'd shown them all our tricks. That's what would keep me awake at night."

I smiled and said, "Good. If we can't beat them, at least we can torment them."

Rumbold frowned and squirmed in his seat. I could tell he wanted to say something, but he didn't quite feel it was his place to do so. "Permission to speak freely sir?"

"Granted helmsman," I said, "tell me what's on your mind."

"Well, Captain," he said, "I'm not sure why we're tweaking their noses this much. It's a hoot, certainly, but what purpose does it serve?"

"It will keep them flying after us for one thing."

All my command officers glanced at me as if I was insane. I smiled back.

"You *want* them to keep coming?" Rumbold asked.

"Yes. I've been worried they'd turn back. It's reckless of them to continue this pursuit, don't you think? They're leaving their home world undefended behind them. For what purpose? Spite?"

"But why, Captain? Why do you want them to chase us to the ends of the universe?"

"Because I believe we're going to run into our real enemy sooner or later. When that moment comes, I'm hoping reason will dawn for the Betas. They may hate us, but in truth, we've done them no real harm. If I can talk them into joining us in battle against someone they truly hate…"

"Ah," Durris said. He'd been listening in. "I understand, but it does seem like a risky strategy."

"Risky?" asked Rumbold, turning away and shaking his head. "It's more than that."

I sighed. "Yes, there is a hint of desperation in this move, but we're in a very serious situation. *Iron Duke* and her escorts won't show anything but cold ruthlessness toward us and the Betas alike."

"You're the captain," Rumbold said resignedly.

Durris appeared some minutes later at my side.

"XO?" I asked. "Have you computed a way out of this patch of space yet?"

"Not yet, Captain."

"Well then, have our missiles struck the enemy ships?"

"Not for another hour—I wanted to talk to you about something else."

I'd suspected as much, but I let him twist in the wind a moment longer. "All right, then, by all means, speak."

"Uh… could we talk in private, Captain?"

I granted his request, and we headed down to the officers' cantina. I felt I could use a few minutes break before anything else unexpected happened.

When we were alone, Durris leaned over the small, circular table that was equipped with magnetic cup holders to clamp our drinks down.

"Sir, have you gone mad?" he asked.

"That's a rude opener, Commander."

"I know, Captain. I know, and I apologize. But we seem to have forgotten our original orders. We're supposed to be determining where this string of breach-points leads to and locating the renegade fleet along the way if possible. We're not supposed to be causing interstellar incidents with neutral powers."

Toying with my mug, I considered his words. "The situation is more complex than you may realize," I said.

"Do you think the variants won't stop after they destroy all the colonists?" he asked.

"Do they have to?" I asked, suddenly intense. "Is Earth all that matters in your view? If so, I reject your ethics. We are Star Guard. We are sworn to protect humanity. All of humanity."

I was referring, of course, to our original oath of office. Every Star Guard officer declared himself the defender of our entire species upon receiving his commission.

"You're talking about the Guardsman's Oath?" Durris asked, incredulous. "It's an anachronism."

"Really? A few years ago, before we reconnected with our colonies, I might have agreed with you. But not today. I'm now of the opinion the oath represents wisdom from the past. I think our predecessors could foretell the future. They knew this day might come. That Earth might someday be reunited with her children."

He squinted at me for a time. "Earth has found her colonies again, that's true. But I must say your position is even more radical than I'd thought. We're not just following our orders in an independent manner, are we?"

"We're following our oath of office," I said carefully.

"Do you intend to involve Earth in a civil war out here among the stars?"

"Hardly. We created the variants. We gave them ships. We sent them out here to destroy indiscriminately."

"Ah…" he said, as if suddenly understanding. "This is about the Connatic, isn't it? I know you had a fling with her, Captain. I understand if your emotions—"

I stood up suddenly. Durris was getting under my skin.

"Don't patronize me on my own ship XO," I warned.

I wanted to tell him everything—all about Zye, who he'd forgotten, the secret Council in their underground chambers, the rewriting of history through our implants... But I was at a loss as to how to get him to believe me. So I just stared at him sourly for a few seconds.

Then, I had an idea. "Come with me, Commander."

He followed numbly, looking concerned. I led him to the lab where Director Vogel and Dr. McKay were operating on another of the variants. We watched quietly for a time before they closed up the creature's flesh and artificial carapace.

Durris looked ill, but I didn't have time for such things.

"Director Vogel, we have to take Commander Durris into our confidence. In fact, I want his implant altered the way ours have been."

Durris and Vogel both looked at me in alarm.

"How did you know...?" Vogel asked, but then he shook his head. "I guess it's obvious. Yes, I altered my own implant the way you did with yours. My entire team has been protected, too."

"What are you people talking about?" Durris asked. His hand strayed to the back of his neck in a nervous, almost defensive gesture.

"Could you please explain?" I asked Vogel.

He did so gladly. Inside, he had the heart of a professor. He led Durris through recent occurrences that had been altered by the Council, and even demonstrated by playing vid files of events that everyone on Earth remembered differently.

"That's not how it happened!" Durris said, incredulous. "I saw the reports with my own eyes!"

"No, you didn't," I said, jumping into the conversation. "I've figured that part out. The imagery you recall was never broadcast. You won't find vid files of these events—such as the attack by a pack of Stroj on CENTCOM recently— anywhere on the net. Curiously, they're rarely searched for, and when they are, they can't be found."

"Exactly," Vogel said, "the mind is an amazing thing. It's almost eager to fill in lost memories with false ones. What you know about the attack on CENTCOM is a falsehood. Those ideas were planted by web stories you read, or which you were told about by others who read them. Excuses for the lack of actual video usually amount to declaring them all matters of World Security."

"Usually? Are you saying this sort of thing happens often?"

"Not every day," I said, "I'd say it only happens a few times a year, as needed. When events must be covered up, or people need to be forgotten, they edit our reality."

"But how?" he demanded.

"Through your morning updates. While you sleep, new memories are installed. Unwanted ones are removed."

"But…" he said, staring at the evidence Vogel had laid out for him, carefully designed as it was to convince anyone who was a thinking person. I could tell he didn't *want* to believe it. "Who would do such a thing?"

"People who want to control us. People who believe they know best how to run the world—who should live and who should die."

He looked at me with haunted eyes.

"What are we going to do about this, Captain?" he asked.

His voice was that of a man lost in the woods, but that's exactly where I wanted him. I hadn't been sure Durris could accept this harsh reality. Many people would rather believe a comfortable lie.

It was one of his enduring traits, however, that he liked to know the real truth almost as much as I did.

-38-

One by one, I brought all my key officers down to Vogel's chambers and convinced them. Yamada was next after Durris, then Rumbold.

Oddly enough, Rumbold took it harder than the rest. He was a romantic at heart, and he didn't like the idea of having been robbed of his memories for decades.

"It's just not *right*, Captain!" he exclaimed, pacing and gesturing with sudden chopping motions of his hands. "Are you certain about all this?"

Yamada stepped up, as Rumbold didn't trust Vogel any farther than he could throw him.

"It seems to be true," she said. "I've found trace evidence in the computer systems on *Defiant*. Possibly, this ship has the only system they couldn't fully erase, because so many of her component parts were built on Beta. They aren't based on Earth technology, and therefore, they've resisted a clean sweep."

"Unbelievable," Rumbold said, "I didn't think the oldsters capable of this level of deceit."

This caught everyone's attention.

"I never said who was behind it all, Rumbold," I said quietly.

His eyes flicked to me, then down to the deck. "No. No you didn't... but you didn't need to. I've been around a long time. Only Vogel has been alive longer. There always were rumors.

Back in the old days, people disappeared. I'm talking about the Cataclysm, back when I was young. When someone vanished back then, you shut up about it."

"I remember those times," Director Vogel said, "I was still an intern."

"Yes," continued Rumbold, "and I was a young man dreaming of becoming a spacer. It started when the world government was established after the Cataclysm. People figured those who'd disappeared were dissidents. After a time, the process seemed to stop, and we all relaxed."

"Only, it *didn't* stop," Vogel said. "Your captain has opened all of our eyes. The purges, the disappearances... The altering of history goes on every morning when our minds are updated with the latest world view our masters want us to have."

We all eyed him, thinking about it.

Rumbold slammed a fist into his palm. "It's just plain wrong. I've often wondered why the people put up with our government. Why they don't rise up, protest, or kick anyone out of office—not even their clones? No offense, Sparhawk."

"None taken."

"Well then," Durris said quickly. "The question becomes: what are we going to do about this?"

"First," I said, "we'll find out what's at the end of this trail of breadcrumbs Halsey has left behind for us. I'm hoping it will be something worth the journey."

"But Captain!" Rumbold said, stepping close. His bloodshot eyes stared into mine. "Shouldn't we head back to Earth right now? Surely, with *Defiant* in our hands we could do something to change it all!"

I looked around the group. They looked worried, uncertain, lost. I shook my head. They were shocked and disillusioned, but they weren't revolutionaries.

"Now isn't the time for drastic action, Rumbold," I said. "Let's first attend to the duty we've all been sworn to perform: the protection of humanity at large."

They fell into line as we marched back up to the command deck. No one spoke, and I knew they were all lost in their own thoughts.

When we arrived and filed to our stations, sending our replacements below, we quickly took stock of the situation.

All of the missiles we'd fired at the enemy ships had been destroyed without damaging their targets.

"Your bluff has run its course, Captain," Durris informed me. "The enemy ships are increasing speed in pursuit."

"A dangerous choice," I said, "but at least they aren't turning around and heading home."

Some of my staffers looked at me as if I was crazy, but I didn't care. I had bigger matters to attend to.

"Captain!" Durris called out triumphantly, "we've got something! A solution—we've found the way out of this hyperspace."

I looked at him, impressed. "That was fast. Who can I thank?"

"I'll be damned... The solution was sent to the battle computer over the ship's public net."

"Ah... Vogel then, in a spare moment?"

He shook his head. "No sir, the solution was worked out by K-19. Can you believe that?"

Oddly enough, I found that I could believe it. We punched the answer into the navigational system, and the ship lurched onto a slightly new course. *Defiant* would now strike the breach point at speed and exit into another star system approximately thirty-two minutes from now.

Time went by at a crawl. When we were only five minutes from reaching our goal, a message came from Okto.

I was uncertain how to handle the situation. I considered delaying as once we were through the breach the channel would be cut off automatically. For a few moments, I dithered.

With a sigh, I finally signaled Yamada to open the line. We were very close to the exit by the time she did so. Due to the distance between our two vessels, there wouldn't be time to have a real conversation. It would take too many light-seconds for our respective transmissions to pass back and forth between our ships.

"Captain Sparhawk," Okto greeted me from the forward screen. She appeared to be unexpectedly pleased with herself.

Everyone on the deck watched the screen. How could they not? The Betas were doggedly chasing us, determined to see us destroyed.

"I'm sending this message for my own personal gratification. I hope you don't find it in poor taste during your final moments."

Frowning, I glanced over at Durris. He shrugged in return.

We turned back to the large, round face of Okto as she beamed at us. She was unable to see us, and her message amounted to a prerecorded announcement. Obviously aware of this, she went on, but not without pausing dramatically first.

"You might wonder why, when you fired harmless missiles at us in an insulting manner, we didn't respond in kind. It was because we didn't want you to change anything about your behavior, or your course."

For some reason, I began to feel a trickle of sweat inside my suit. What was this huge woman hinting at?

Without meaning to, I glanced at the countdown. We had only a single minute left before we hit the breach and broke through into a new star system.

The smiling Alpha continued talking. "We've calculated that you'll be too close to the exit of this ER bridge when you hear this transmission to do anything about it. Just let me say that it's been a pleasure chasing you to your cowardly finish. No kill could have been more satisfying. Knowing that your final moments will be spent in hopeless terror makes the situation all the sweeter, and I thank you for that—oh, and when you reach Hell, Sparhawk, please give my regards to Zye."

That was it. The message ended, and the channel closed.

We sat in stunned silence. We had less than forty seconds to go.

"We can still divert, Captain," Durris said. "If we do it right now, we might miss the breach!"

"That could be what she wants, Captain!" Rumbold shouted from the helm. "We might run out of hyperspace in this pocket, it's hard to say. We'll slam right into the wall if we screw this up."

232

Durris locked eyes with me. He was afraid but resigned. "It's your call, Captain."

My call. Those two words clearly stated the difficulty in commanding a starship. It was *always* my call, and consequently everything that went wrong was my fault. In this case, my entire ship and crew were likely to pay a gruesome price if I chose unwisely.

There were fifteen seconds left now. Rumbold had his hands on the helm, fingers poised and quivering, ready to direct the ship into a slewing turn if I were to give the order.

I had to think, but there was no time to do so. Was Okto bluffing, hoping that we'd take her bait and veer away, allowing her ships to close and destroy us? Or was she in earnest, like all her kind seemed to be, and merely enjoying herself?

"Steady on," I said in a voice I thought was remarkably calm.

My heart pounded in my head, and my eyes stared unblinking as the breach loomed, shimmering and colorful. It was an unusual breach, I could tell that.

What was on the far side of it? Instant death? Or an agonizing finish full of radiation, screaming and the hopeless sounds of my dying ship?

My mind tried to conjure possibilities. Black holes, blue giants, even something as simple as space dust, too condensed and slammed into at too high a speed.

Before my brain could complete the list we hit the breach, and we broke through it.

-39-

When *Defiant* first returned to normal space, there was always a transitional period of adjustment. This span lasted from several seconds to over one minute.

We weren't fully aware of it, but the transition period had been documented carefully. There was a brief sensation of dreaming. A sense of falling asleep, then waking up again.

How much of that time was spent in transit, "appearing" in the new star system? How much of it was due to our instruments settling down, reacting to the radical shift in measurable inputs?

It was a mix of the two, I suspected. Our computers added another delay as they were programmed to balk before relaying faulty input to the crew. No designer wanted a crew to become confused. A surprised helmsman might send the ship into a deadly maneuver to avoid a phantom. The computers probed with their sensors, requiring more than purely passive input before they painted a confirmed picture of our surroundings.

In this particular case, the wait was excruciating for all involved. Even though it lasted no more than half a minute, such a length of time can feel very long indeed when one's life is in the balance.

When we did start to function again, we found ourselves in a new place. Like every other time I'd ventured into an unknown star system, the experience never failed to be a thrill.

My heart was in my mouth. I swallowed dryly, over and over again. My eyes roved over the instruments trying to monitor everything at once.

"Sir…" Yamada said, working her sensor arrays. "I think we're okay. The system isn't all that unusual. It's a tri-star arrangement with two close red dwarfs and a third brown one circling widely in a distant orbit."

Rumbold released a breath explosively.

"No final moments of hopeless terror and death?" he asked, his eyes swiveling from Yamada to myself and back again.

"No…" she said. "At least, I don't detect any immediate threat here."

"Okto!" Rumbold raged, his face instantly transforming. "That witch!"

He slapped his palms on his console and jumped up, performing a strutting circular dance around his chair. "You know, it's just this sort of bullshit that might convince an old man it's time to retire." His agitation amused many of the staffers who twittered from the edges of the command deck.

I smiled. The tension had been broken, and I was glad for Rumbold's display. I didn't correct him, but he eventually climbed back into his seat and began to mutter to himself.

"She tried to rook us, Captain," he said loudly. "Just for spite."

"No," I said, "I don't think so."

"I agree," Durris said. "She *did* attempt to bluff us but not because she wanted to cause us emotional pain. She wanted us to turn away from this breach."

Yamada nodded slowly. "That sounds right to me, too. If we'd missed the breach, her ships would have caught up and destroyed us. It was either that, or she knew there wasn't room for us to turn around. She wanted us to die by slamming into the barrier surrounding that patch of hyperspace."

"The question is," Durris said, "will she follow us?"

"Have we got a new course yet?" I asked him.

Durris looked startled and turned back to his instruments. His planning table lit up, and he decorated it with thin green arcs.

"Are we exploring or running?" he asked me.

235

"A little of both. I want to put distance between the breach point and our stern, but we need to scan this unknown system at the same time."

Durris nodded. "We should head toward the inner planets then. There's a ring of seven that circle the twin suns at the center of the system. Our next destination is in their midst. It's the last coordinate listed on Perez's map."

"Finalize the course and pass it to the helm."

Durris and Rumbold spent the next few minutes sorting out our new direction, and we were soon gently veering to our port side. It felt good to have a destination again even if it was a vague one.

Once the course was laid and set, Durris moved to my side.

"Sir," he said, "I've got a tactical recommendation."

"Let's hear it."

"We should lay out a barrage of missiles," he said. "We'll deploy them in our wake directing them to fly to the breach we just passed through. Our newest units are smart. They'll sit there and watch space at the exit point. When the Beta cruisers come through, I'll set them up to concentrate on the lead ship. With luck, a score of hits will take out one of the three."

"No," I said simply.

He blinked at me. "No? You mean you don't think it will work? You must recall our disorientation when we first arrived here... The enemy crew will experience that same incoherence. That's when our missiles will plunge in and strike. You know, this possibility might even be why Okto didn't want us to go through. Maybe she foresaw this kind of tactic, and—"

"No," I repeated. "No attack. No missiles. No mines. We'll slip away, and that's all."

He stared at me as if I'd lost my mind. It was a mixed blessing, but I was used to that sort of thing. His lack of confidence didn't rattle me.

"I'm not budging XO," I explained. "We're simply taking the course that will get us closer to those planets."

"You're still holding out hope they'll help us in some way. All right, Captain. It's your call. It's my duty to give you my opinion and—"

"And you've done so," I said, cutting him off. "Thank you, Commander."

He returned to his post sullenly.

Over the following hour, we flew quietly toward the inner planets of the unknown system. As we did so, we picked up more and more data.

"Sir..." Durris said. "There's a lot of evidence of space traffic out here. A lot of radioactive clouds and debris as well."

"Meaning?"

"There has almost certainly been a major fleet action in this system. I'm not seeing much here now, fortunately. The system appears to be dead."

My heart sank as we went over the data. We quickly found a world that was likely to have once held life. It was lifeless now, scorched by radioactive clouds. Dust obscured the surface, and storms raged with five hundred kilometer an hour winds blowing deadly particles everywhere.

"Do you think it was a colony once?" Yamada asked me as we examined the world.

"Yes," I said. "Rather recently, in fact, if I don't miss my guess. The variant fleet must have passed through here and destroyed them all."

After we'd been in the system for several hours, a trio of ships appeared at the breach point behind us. They were moving relatively slowly. They'd obviously been braking since we'd last seen them in hyperspace.

"Okto has arrived," Yamada said.

"Damn," Rumbold said. "I'd hoped that tricky woman had turned around and gone home."

"She slowed down out of fear," I said. "She was worried we were laying an ambush for her. The enemy's caution is our gain. We're well ahead of them now."

My upbeat comments failed to brighten anyone's mood. The cruisers were more distant, but they were still behind us, still following doggedly.

"Where's the next breach point?" I asked, turning to Durris.

He shook his head. "I'm not seeing it," he said.

"What do you mean?" I demanded, rushing to his side.

"Just that—there's nothing out here, sir. This planet, the burnt out one we're passing by, is very close to the coordinates. The location is very unusual. I'm not sure there can be a bridge this near a paired star."

Frowning, I looked over his data hoping he'd made some kind of mistake. Naturally, there was no error.

"A dead end?" I asked.

"Well, if the last coordinate was the location of a breach, then yes."

"What else could it be?"

He shrugged. "I don't know. Maybe Perez wanted us to come here to help defend this broken planet. Maybe when he scrawled these notes there was a fierce battle going on right here. But now… everything's dead, Captain."

Durris' words were damning. Everything about this voyage now seemed like a farce. We were the joke of the galaxy, chasing ghosts at the whim of a dead Stroj agent.

"Carry on," I said, "decrease speed. We're not doing a quick fly-by. Take us to the exact coordinates, so we can at least prove we reached the spot. Record everything carefully, and begin plotting an escape route."

Durris began swiftly working on a set of calculations. I glanced at them, and I realized they had nothing to do with my orders.

"What are you up to, XO?" I asked.

"I'm plotting the Beta ships likely actions—to see how much time we have."

"Is this in order to formulate an argument against my orders?"

He looked up, startled. "Not at all, Captain. I just wanted to know how much time we'd have at the location specified before we have to move on. I mean, it could be a small item we're looking for. Something like a time capsule, a satellite…"

The odds of such things seemed extremely remote to me, but Durris was nothing if he wasn't a man of details. I nodded to him, and he went back to his calculations.

Soon thereafter, *Defiant* shuddered and decelerated.

"It's looking like we'll have approximately an hour on station," Durris told me. "Maybe two, tops, before we have to run."

"That should be good enough," I said. "We'll prove or disprove the premise of our mission long before that."

I found out soon afterward my confident words were quite wrong, but I had no way of knowing that at the time.

-40-

"So *that's* what's at the end of this rainbow," Rumbold said to no one in particular.

The sight of what we'd found filled all of us with unease. There, at a stationary La Grange point above the dead world we'd passed by, was a Stroj construct.

The machine could only be one thing. It was an artificial bridge projector. I'd actually encountered one of these structures on a previous voyage.

Bridge projectors had only been theoretical until I'd found one a year ago. The machine looked like a conical web-work of struts. It was a basket-shaped structure decorated with auto-cannons. It had the power—if this unit still operated—to create temporary artificial bridges between star systems.

"If we get too close, it will fire on us," I admonished. "Bring us around in a slow pass, Rumbold. Keep dropping our speed."

He glanced at me shaking his head, but he followed orders.

"How's the match on the coordinates he gave us, Durris?" I asked.

"Perfect, sir," he said. "It can't be a coincidence. Perez wanted us to find this projector. This machine must be what the map was leading us to find."

"Yes..." I said thoughtfully. "It fits. Admiral Perez—whatever his real name was—we know he was a Stroj agent.

240

Only the Stroj have this tech. But *why* did he give us a map directing us to this point?"

No one answered me immediately. The structure slid off to one side of *Defiant* as we circled it, scanning it from every angle. As far as we could tell, it was identical in every respect to the first one we'd found so long ago.

"Let's go over what we do know," Durris suggested.

I nodded for him to continue.

"First, this is a Stroj system," he said. "That planet is in the liquid-water zone, and by all indications it once held a colony. There had to be Stroj living down there, or people who the Stroj had previously conquered."

"I would suggest they were the former," I said. "I doubt the Stroj would have fought a serious battle for this system if it had been populated by normal human colonists. I also doubt they'd place one of their projectors in a system that wasn't fully under their control."

"Agreed," Durris said. "Now then, as to why the hell we're here in the first place—"

"You mean, why Perez wanted to get us to come here?"

"Yes... How he could possibly think we could save this colony?"

I shook my head. "That wasn't his plan," I said.

He frowned at me. "You don't think Perez sent us out here to stop this destruction?"

"No, not at all. Think of the timeline. Even if he knew this system was in trouble in real time, he couldn't have expected us to get here fast enough to change the outcome. Our voyage took over a month's time. We were sure to arrive late and discover only ruins."

"Hmm..." Durris said thoughtfully. "I hadn't considered that, but you're right of course, Captain. Then why did he send us here?"

I stepped toward the image of the web-work structure which hung in the air over his tactical table. My hand grazed the image, making it waver and spin.

"There's only one logical answer," I said. "He wanted us to operate this machine."

Durris looked alarmed and fascinated at the same time.

241

Rumbold, who'd been listening in while pretending not to, swallowed hard and suffered an immediate coughing fit.

"But sir..." Durris said. "We don't know how to operate that thing."

"Last time we managed it," I said. "We simply flew into it bearing a key given to us by the Stroj."

"Right... but we don't have one now."

"Obviously not."

Durris stared at the image again. He stood beside me, and his mouth fell open a fraction.

"You aren't suggesting we should go aboard that thing's control module to explore it?"

"How else can we operate it? There's no one else here."

"But sir... the Beta ships are closing in."

"Then we'd better get a move on, don't you think? You didn't seriously think I'd come all the way out here and not even check out the end of the trail, did you?"

"No Captain," he said in defeat. "I'd dared to hope, but I can see how that wouldn't look good in our reports."

We got moving after that. In a surprisingly short amount of time, I found myself boarding an assault shuttle packed with marines. Durris and several of his best back-up officers manned *Defiant's* command deck.

Aboard the shuttle, beside Lieutenant Morris and myself, was a disgruntled Director Vogel and a single variant.

"I don't understand why I'm on this mission," Vogel complained.

"Because you've got the best engineering mind on my ship," I said simply.

"And K-19?"

"He's coming along to do any repair work we might encounter," I said. "We can't wait around for a human crew to do it. By the time they suit up and select the right smart-wrench, the Beta cruisers will be all over us."

Vogel looked like he smelled something unpleasant. Possibly he did, as we were all sealed up tightly in our spacesuits.

"What if this structure's automated defenses destroy us?" he demanded.

I shrugged. "Then we die, I suppose."

He seemed to find this answer unsatisfactory, but I was done talking to him.

The shuttle launched, and Vogel splayed out his hands in alarm. It was the gesture of someone who thought they were falling.

A sudden whip-like arm shot out of the rear chamber of the shuttle and touched Vogel's chest. For an instant, I thought the man had been struck dead. I reached for my sword, and beside me, Morris drew his pistol.

"That thing hit him, Captain!" Morris shouted.

My hand came up in a flat, stopping gesture. "Stand down, Morris. He's all right."

To demonstrate my point, K-19's arm retreated with a clicking noise, almost as fast as it had appeared. Vogel sat firmly in his seat where the variant had left him.

"It's okay," gasped the Director. "I'm fine. K-19 was merely concerned for my safety. Remember, I'm old enough to be your great, great grandfather, Sparhawk."

"So what?" Morris demanded.

Vogel gave him a stern glance. "So, my bones are thin. They will break like ice if I take a fall."

Morris leaned back, nostrils flaring in disgust. "Sick little glass man. What a way to live."

Vogel chuckled. "We'll see what you say when your body starts to age. You'll be hooked on Rejuv before you hit fifty."

Morris glared at the ceiling. He didn't answer the older man. Perhaps that was because we all knew Vogel was right. Who could withstand the siren's call of extended life?

"Director," I said, "what's our plan upon arrival?"

He looked at me in wonderment. "I thought this expedition was your idea."

"It was. I'm in overall command. But you are in command of the scientific details. You have one hour to get this station— if it is a station—up and running. One hour. Use your time wisely."

Vogel thought about it. "We have to find the central repository, the data core."

"Why?"

"That's where the location of our destination must be. It's got to be very complex. You can't run a bridge projector using a computer scroll, you know. Their data core must be one of the best in history, if you think about it."

"Why's that?" I asked.

"The process I understand in theory—you have to understand that I've never built one. But it works by generating a detailed mathematical model of the target star system. The bridge generated can't go just anywhere, it has to go somewhere it knows. Somewhere it can model in this station's data core."

I frowned, but nodded. I understood some of what he was saying.

"So that's how it does it?" I asked. "By modeling the destination? How does that create a bridge?"

"It doesn't, it selects the destination. I read about projection theory back in college. Funny to think I'm out here now, investigating a real operating unit. We never thought machines like this would make it off the drawing board."

"They're real, Director," I said, "very real. But again, how does the bridge itself form?"

Vogel dragged his thin finger over a nearby patch of the shuttle's hull. The smart metal responded by lighting up. On it, a diagram of the star system appeared. He tapped the central binary star, and the twin stellar objects appeared to flare up in response.

"See that?" he said.

Morris, who'd been quietly listening all along, scoffed. "You're just tapping graphics with your bony finger."

"Yes, of course I am. But this is depicting a legitimate model. Can you imagine the jump in stellar output if what I'd just done was real? Billions of terajoules would have been released. That's the kind of power a bridge projector requires."

Morris and I were both impressed with this answer.

"You mean," Morris said, "you have to generate something like the Carrington Event, or the Cataclysm back home, to power this thing?"

"Not that bad," Vogel returned. It would probably be focused, and it would do little more than generate a long day of static on the world nearby. But yes, these two stars power the projector. There's no other source locally or remotely that could do it. At least, there's nothing else that we know of."

We eyed the image of the twin suns depicted on the hull until they faded to dull red, then umber then vanished entirely.

Could Vogel be right? Were we going to have to unleash that kind of raw power to operate this thing?

I was impressed and concerned by the idea at the same time.

-41-

We reached the station without incident. The auto-cannons tracked us throughout our approach, but they never fired. Vogel said it was due to a software patch he'd installed in our friend-or-foe system.

Morris privately told me he figured the old bastard had made up this sorry excuse, and the truth was we'd gotten lucky. Maybe the shuttle was too small to be classified as a threat, or the fact it was unarmed had tricked the AI into letting us pass.

Whatever the case, the pod-like control module was located where the spider would be if this were a true web—down near the small end of the cone. We reached the module and piled out onto a large deck that was open to space.

Our magnetics clacked as we crossed the open decking. It was a sound heard only inside our helmets. We reached an airlock, engaged the emergency override—and we were inside.

Morris and his men were on high alert. They sprang ahead of us securing every hatchway before we marched farther into the operations center.

In comparison to the overall structure, the control module was small, but from the point of view of a single human it was quite roomy. It contained at least a kilometer of curving, dark passages that strung out ahead of us.

Each chamber we entered lit up, detecting our presence, but there were no pressurized regions. The entire command center seemed to be abandoned.

We found broken equipment rolling around on the floors and abandoned junk hanging from the ceiling in cargo nets. Here and there, a slick patch of hard ice from accumulated condensation showed where a human might have caught a breath in the past. But most of the center was hard vacuum and seemed derelict.

"Looks like they grabbed whatever they could and abandoned this place in a hurry," I said, running my gloves over a ridge of hard ice that coated a railing. "Any signs of life?"

"None, Captain," Vogel said. He was beaming ahead of us continuously with a handheld scanner. "This place appears to be dead."

"Is that good or bad?" Morris asked.

"Good, from the point of personal safety," Vogel told him, "but bad in terms of getting this station into operating condition. The Beta ships are closing, and we don't have much time to get these systems fired up."

"He's right," I said, "team, press ahead, double-time. Stop checking every doorway. Get us to the control center immediately."

Obeying me, Morris' troopers trotted ahead into the darkness. I heard their scuffling and hard breathing over our linked com sets. They grunted with effort as they worked open frozen hatches, kicked aside fallen equipment barring our path and generally hustled forward. Behind them, we walked at a steady pace.

When we'd marched about a hundred meters into the structure, everything changed. To my shock, a firefight broke out ahead of us.

Rippling fire lit up the passageway. I knew it was ours by the color and the rippling nature of the beams. They flashed as brightly as an arc-welder in the cramped, dark spaces.

"Get down!" Morris shouted, pressing Vogel and I out of his way.

He plunged ahead of us into the darkness, shouting and demanding reports. His marines seemed too busy to respond immediately, and he unleashed a stream of profanity.

I aimed my own PAG down the passageway Morris was advancing along, but I stayed with Vogel. If the director went down now, there would be no way we could accomplish the mission.

"Stroj, Captain!" Morris called back to me a minute later. "We're engaged with them up here. They opened up when my men passed through an intersection. Two of my boys were cut down."

"Can you handle it?"

"Absolutely," he said. "We'll get them. Throwing out the drones now."

The gunfire subsided as both sides took cover. I couldn't see, but I knew the marines were busy releasing crawlers, tiny machines like caterpillars, that would seek the enemy in the dark.

After another half-minute, tiny explosions flashed here and there ahead of us. I saw rather than heard them. I dared to grin. The crawlers had reached their targets and self-destructed.

My elation was short-lived, however. A huge hand came up from behind me and attempted to rip my gun out of my hand. Powerful fingers like steel gripped my gun, wrenching it away.

A face loomed inside my assailant's spacesuit. The suit was misshapen, as if it held an abomination rather than a true man, but it was the face itself that I recognized.

A man—no, a creature—who I hadn't encountered for a long time glared at me in the half-light. He was intent, feral. His skin was shriveled like a mummy's flesh, and one of his eyes had been replaced by a darting, swiveling camera on a stalk that poked out of the left socket.

The face was that of a Stroj—but not just any Stroj. It was none other than Lorn, a pirate who I'd had dealings with in the past.

Vogel tried to help, but he was out of his league. His weak arms flailed at Lorn's back. I doubt the monster even knew he was there.

"Lorn!" I shouted. "Stand down. You owe me!"

I spoke on an open channel, hoping both to distract the Stroj and alert Morris to what was going on in the rear ranks of the expedition.

"Silence, Sparhawk," Lorn responded. "It's been too long. I've coveted your flesh for years, and I won't be dissuaded from taking my sample now."

My elbow flashed up, attempting to crack his faceplate. The gambit failed, but he did stagger back for a second. My pistol flew away in a flat spin, bouncing off the passage walls.

"Stop struggling," Lorn said. "I don't want you to injure yourself or to force me to do it. I want your skin intact for my trophy."

"Sorry to disappoint," I said, and I drew my sword.

In an instant, it flared into life. We were too close to fence, but I was able to slash between the two of us. Several of Lorn's fingers flew free, scattering over the passageway.

"Damn you!" Lorn said, lunging to close again. "If you force me to kill you, your flesh will begin to decay."

"Get off me, or I'll hack off limbs next," I said.

My shielding was active now. Lorn was having difficulty gaining a hold on my body. He staggered back, glanced at Vogel and then lunged for him.

With a quick thrust, I stabbed him in the back. My sizzling sword sent up a wisp of hot vapors which froze quickly in the airless passageway.

Lorn cursed and writhed, but he captured Vogel, who made mewling sounds of distress.

"Ah..." Lorn said, turning to face me. "I've got your oldster, Sparhawk. If you pull your sword out of my back and give me my trophy, I'll let him go."

Vogel's eyes pleaded with me. I could see he was terrified and probably injured. Lorn gripped him with such force that it was grinding the director's fragile bones together.

I knew from long experience with Lorn and his kind that negotiations were always traps. The moment I agreed to give him something, he'd immediately demand more, until he demanded so much I was unable to provide it.

Cutting this process short, I yanked my blade out of his tough body and brought it in line with this throat. His hand came up to grab the blade, but he didn't dare. Worms of plasma and force ran up and down the length of it.

I could see his eyes inside his helmet, through his faceplate. Lit by the glow of my sword, his features writhed in hate.

"I'll rip his head right off," he threatened. "Back away!"

Vogel squeaked, making an unintelligible plea.

My blade didn't waver, but instead moved closer to Lorn's face.

"Yield," I said. "Surrender or I'll kill you. The old man is less than nothing to me. He's been an irritant since we left Earth."

Hissing in disappointment, Lorn tossed Vogel aside like a broken doll.

"Damn," he said, "I thought he might be a cherished relative."

It occurred to me that Lorn's initial attack would have been much more effective if he'd simply attempted to kill me. He had control of my gun for a moment, and he could have used it and ended the entire affair.

But I knew from experience that wasn't how his kind viewed the world. They were creatures of status and personal glory. Killing me would be an accomplishment, but it would gain him little among his own people unless he managed to bring home a pristine scrap of my flesh.

To see some living part of me sewn into his patchwork body—that was his goal. Such a trophy would provide him with a boost in status on his home world that earthlings could barely understand.

"Are you all right?" I asked Vogel.

The old man climbed to his feet, his limbs shaking.

"I'll live," he announced.

"I thought you said you didn't care about him," Lorn complained, nursing his injured back. He slapped a patch on the hole in his spacesuit, and it sealed itself almost immediately with smart-gels. "And I thought you didn't like to lie, Sparhawk."

Lorn dropped to the floor to scramble for his lost fingers.

"I don't," I said, kicking the last of the severed digits his way. "He *has* been an irritant since the day I met him. Tell him, Vogel."

At that name, Lorn whirled and crouched. He looked at Vogel and assumed a predatory stance.

"Lorn...?" I said. "Stand down. We can talk."

"I must have him!" Lorn said, ignoring me. "He's the inventor of the variants! A villain whose flesh represents inconceivable value!"

Lorn stalked forward reaching for Vogel who retreated like a scuttling crab.

But before Lorn could grab hold of him, or I could thrust a sword into the Stroj's back, K-19 arrived on the scene.

We'd left K-19 behind on the shuttle because his bulk was too great to easily navigate the passages. After all, they'd been designed for normal-sized humans. Apparently, he'd taken it upon himself to join us after listening to the sounds of battle over the com system.

The variant's whip-like arms flashed. Two snaps blurred in the passage, and they took down both of Lorn's legs from behind.

With his legs hanging by threads, the Stroj fell on the deck. But even then, his outstretched claw-like fingers made grasping, greedy motions in Vogel's direction.

-42-

Lorn quickly lost consciousness, not due to pain, shock or even loss of blood, but rather to lack of oxygen.

The Stroj were infamously hard to kill. We went to work on him, patching his suit and transfusing air, heat and power from ours into his.

"Why do you bother?" Vogel complained. "That monster should be left to die here."

"You've got a point," I admitted. "But he's one of the few members of his people with whom we've managed to have successful negotiations. If we let him die now, who will speak for us among his kind?"

Vogel shook his head. "Forget diplomacy. Kill them all, I say."

I looked at him sternly. "They've fought us before, but they're at peace with us for now. I consider your variants to be more dangerous."

Vogel rolled his eyes and walked carefully past the crumpled form of the Stroj on the deck. He wanted nothing to do with the colonist. "We have to find the nexus that controls this station," he said. "Have your marines cleared the rest of the module?"

Morris returned at the mention of marines, and he nodded. "I think I found what you're talking about up ahead. The Stroj made their last stand there."

Vogel and Morris moved off into the dim-lit passages. K-19 quietly crawled in their wake. After making sure Lorn would survive, I followed them.

When I got to the heart of the control module, I found it to be surprisingly roomy. We were able to all fit, even Lorn, who the marines carried with them.

We cleared the bodies of the fallen Stroj and Vogel began to work with the control panels immediately. K-19 helped with both efforts.

They soon had the power on, and the center began to warm up. We heard hissing air as the chambers were repressurized.

"That's your plan?" Lorn asked from the floor.

We turned together, startled, to see him sitting up. His legs were both a mess, but he was conscious and seemed unconcerned by the state of his body.

"You're going to live here?" he asked. "What happened to your ship, Sparhawk?"

"*Defiant* is in prime fighting condition," I assured him. "We're not here for safety's sake. In fact, I can hardly think of a more unsafe spot in the galaxy."

"Really? How can that be? Your variants have defeated us. They've driven us back from this system and killed millions of my people."

I winced, suspecting his words were all too truthful.

"This unit, K-19, isn't like the other variants," Vogel said. "He's under our control, loyal to Earth. The others are acting on their own recognizance."

"I don't believe that. What about it, Sparhawk? Are the variants all rebels? Mutineers?"

My mouth opened to answer, but I couldn't lie to him. Such an act went too strongly against my convictions. Under the best of circumstances, it was hard enough for me to tell even an enemy a deliberate untruth. But in this case, Lorn was a victim of our variants as much as anyone else out here was. To lie to a prisoner in our power whose civilization had been demolished by creatures we'd built and released for precisely that purpose... it seemed unconscionable.

"They are and they aren't," I said. "A faction among Earthlings caused them to go on this rampage. We—my crew and myself—are attempting to fix that error."

"Really?" Lorn asked. "Now, that is a strange outlook on the universe. People say that the Stroj are mad-things because we covet trophies of flesh from our enemies. But here you are trying to fix a situation that's obviously to your benefit."

"Our benefit?" Vogel demanded suddenly. "How so?"

"Is it not self-evident?" Lorn asked. "With my people in retreat, there's little out here to stop the superior fleets of Earth. From my point of view, you've won this battle of survival between our peoples, and yet Sparhawk is squandering your best opportunity to rid yourself of colonists once and for all."

I turned to him, seeing an earnest expression on his face. He meant what he was saying.

"I understand how you might think of us that way," I said, "but Star Guard is sworn to defend all humanity—not just those born recently on Earth. As strange as it may seem, Lorn, I'm here to defend your people from the variant fleets."

"That is a noble goal," he said snidely, "but one that's too late in coming. We've been defeated. We've lost most of our fleet, and we've only taken down a few of your battleships. We didn't fight ruthlessly enough. We tried to defend every world, and by doing so, we lost them all."

I looked at him, troubled. "Has your home world been destroyed like this one?" I asked him.

"No. Not yet. Transmissions from our star systems indicate it's just a matter of time, however. Your variant fleet is heading toward our home star, hopping from one system to another, destroying everyone they meet."

"In that case," I said, "you should help us. Tell us how to operate this great machine."

He laughed. It was a strange, unnatural sound. "Why would I do that? So you can open a pathway back to Earth? Your fleet of four ships is pathetic—oh yes, we've counted your battle cruisers. We've been watching you quietly while you slink around among our dead."

There was no point in correcting him about our fleet. Three of them belonged to the Betas—and he was right, even working together we represented a pathetically weak force.

"How did you evade the variants when they came here?" I asked.

"We're partly flesh, not just machines," Lorn replied. He turned suddenly on Vogel. "That's how your creations detect their targets. Am I right? With biochemical signatures?"

Vogel had been busy working on the data core, but he was still listening to us. He squirmed uncertainly until K-19 spoke up.

"That's correct," the variant said. "We know flesh when we detect it, through spectral-analysis, odor, chemical trails on surfaces—"

Lorn shut up the variant with a wave of his claw-like hand. "Right. We figured that out after you destroyed a few of our worlds. When places like this were abandoned, they were always left untouched by the invading ships."

I frowned. I still wasn't quite getting what he was saying. "But you were here, and you would have given off signatures. Why didn't the variants destroy this structure?"

Lorn levered himself around in a circle to face me. He looked proud.

"When we figured out what they were searching for, we disguised ourselves. Look over these suits, monster," he said, addressing K-19. "If they were unbroken, could you tell there's a biological being inside?"

K-19 investigated the spacesuits. After a few seconds, he turned back to the group. "Perhaps if I was close enough to perform an optical observation, I would have noticed humanoid shapes in motion. However—"

"The answer is 'no', robot," Lorn interrupted. "We altered these suits to hide our stinks and droppings from you. After you stranded me in space, Sparhawk, I managed to get to this system. I then gathered together a small crew on a cramped ship. We performed gathering missions on local colonies."

"You mean you played pirate again," I said, "raiding helpless colonists."

"Yes, but with a much smaller force," Lorn went on, seeming to miss my rebuke entirely. "When the variant fleet began invading our star systems and destroying them, I fled at first. We were finally trapped here, unable to withdraw farther."

"Did you run out of fuel? Credits?" I asked.

He made an airy gesture. "The details are unimportant and humiliating. We realized we would be found in a ship, but we might survive on a harmless looking structure like this—if it appeared lifeless when scanned."

"But..." Morris said, frowning, "I don't get it. We came aboard finding evidence of a fight. There are bodies and junk everywhere. If the variants didn't do that, who did?"

"The original crewmen, of course," Lorn said.

The others looked baffled, but I laughed grimly. "I get it. You killed your own people."

Lorn shrugged. "What of it? There was little time. We couldn't come aboard and build specialized suits for all of them. If we had left them alone, the variants would have detected them and destroyed them anyway. In effect, we saved this structure and ourselves due to our quick thinking and effective action."

"What went wrong with your plan, then?" I asked. "Why are you still here, rattling around in this corpse of a system?"

"They destroyed every starship circling these stars! They were thorough about that. They left us nothing to escape in. I'm a resourceful man, but I can't build an entire spaceship out of salvaged parts."

"What about operating the bridge projector? Why not escape that way?"

"We've considered it," he admitted. "But we lacked the technical know-how. Even experimentation would be dangerous. If the variants left behind some hidden fighters, as we've seen them do elsewhere, we calculated they'd see the star hiccup and come to investigate."

"What was your long-term plan to survive, then?" I asked. "You always have one."

Lorn smiled grimly. "You, Sparhawk. You're the plan."

Alarmed, my people looked around and gripped their weapons.

"Don't worry. We obviously failed to take you out when you got here. But we sent out an SOS using an FTL signal. Apparently, someone got it because you came."

I nodded slowly. The situation had become clear at last. Perez had sent us out here, not as part of some kind of grand effort to stop the variants. He'd done it because he'd gotten a call for help at this location.

I found the truth disappointing. We'd come so far, been through so much, for little or no gain.

"Lorn," I said to the Stroj. "We have two options at this point. We can leave you here to die, or you can help us get this machine working right now."

"Why those two alone?" he asked. "I can think of a dozen more pleasant possibilities."

I quickly explained to him that the Beta ships were pursuing us, and they'd be here shortly. We had to either flee, or create a bridge and exit the system.

"And where do you wish to go?" he asked me.

"Home, I think. To Earth. I would pursue the Star Carrier if I knew where she was, but I don't."

He made a face of twisted disgust. "Of course you would. You'd sacrifice yourselves in an instant to save colonists like myself."

I looked at him squarely. "Yes, I would—if I thought it could work."

He shook his head. "Unbelievable pride and arrogance," he said. "You blame us for being seekers of glory, of risking everything for a shred of flesh as a trophy. But you're no less insane in your quests."

Deciding it wasn't worth trying to explain it to him, I shrugged.

"Be that as it may, you're welcome to come with us if you help me reach my goals. You'll be treated as a prisoner of war, but that's better than facing three Beta battle cruisers with your legs torn off."

He considered the offer for several seconds.

"I want one more thing," he said, pointing a long-nailed finger at Director Vogel, who shrank back in alarm. "I demand a strip of his flesh."

"No," I said firmly. "You'll gain your life, or nothing. It's up to you—but decide quickly. We have little time to spare."

Lorn considered my offer until I became irate. Finally, he reluctantly agreed.

We all began to work in earnest helping Vogel at his direction. I couldn't help but notice that Lorn was distracted. He kept studying Vogel the way a starving man might study a thick steak.

-43-

"The first thing you need to do is get the power-stream flowing," Lorn told us. "In fact, it may already be too late for that."

"How do we do it?" I demanded.

Lorn shrugged. "You'll have to purge the capacitor-capsule assembly and reconnect the couplings for the power to be transferred to this station. That's assuming, of course, the collectors circling the binary stars haven't been destroyed."

Morris and I looked over the rubble. There seemed to be countless color-coded leads that had been ripped loose or partially burnt.

Morris caught my eye. "It'll take a week, Captain! We'll have to run."

"Our deal still stands, Sparhawk!" Lorn barked, having overheard. "I'm helping in good faith, and I demand you get me off this—"

I rushed to him, where he still sat crippled on the floor. I drew my blade in a smooth motion, thumbing on the power.

"Our bargain stated you would help me get this station operating," I told him. "If you can't do that, I'm honor-bound *not* to take you with us. In fact, I'd prefer to slay you here than see you suffer at the hands of the Betas. Therefore, as a mercy—"

"There might be an easier way," Lorn said, interrupting. "I just thought of it."

His eyes were watching the sizzling tip of my blade, which never strayed from his face.

"Let's hear it," I said.

"Outside on the hull—the leads could be shunted there. Bypass this wrecked area and patch it to the console. I'm not sure if you're equipped for such work in vacuum, but—"

I whirled toward Director Vogel. "Summon K-19," I said. "Get him on it."

Vogel nodded and moved away. Lorn looked at him in surprise.

"The creator of all that is evil obeys you? What's more, he gives you not a single word of complaint about your imperious tone? You've trained your villains well, Sparhawk. They're your creatures to command, clearly."

Glancing at him darkly, I left him on the floor. Over my shoulder I said, "You'd best hope they can get this station operating, Lorn. You're continued existence depends on it."

"Get the power-stream flowing again. I'll do the rest."

After Vogel had K-19 crawling toward the damaged region on the exterior of the hull, I sent him to the control panels.

"Figure out how to operate it," I said. "You're our only hope in that department."

"What?" Vogel demanded. "Lorn must teach me how to operate the system."

"No," I said, "he'll trick us somehow. You must gain direct control."

Vogel shook his head doubtfully. "I'll try, Captain, but this is essentially alien technology. I know the principles, but to operate it… I'll do my best."

He limped down to the panels and began poking at them.

Nervously, I watched K-19 work. The variant was a master of efficient operation. His hands, blades, grippers and welding-claws flashed in continuous motion. A dozen wires were shunted and mended, then a hundred more.

Very slowly, he crawled over the hull, the region under his carapace a continuous blur of activity.

"Captain?" Yamada said, calling via my implant. "We've got a target-lock incoming from the Beta ships. They're inbound. They're picking up speed."

"How much time do we have?"

"Thirty-nine minutes before we're in range of their primary cannons."

My mind chewed that number over. To get the power-stream to reach the station from the central stars would take at least ten of that. To affect repairs, reboot the system, warm the core and project a bridge—I was only guessing, but it had to be twenty more. We'd be cutting it close to say the very least.

"Thank you," I told Yamada. "Tell Durris to stand by for an emergency evacuation. Have him position *Defiant* between the enemy and this structure."

"Just getting the shuttle back to our ship will take you several more minutes, Captain, I—"

"Thank you, Lieutenant Commander," I said firmly.

I went below again, into the heart of the station. The derelict was still operating only on emergency power, but at least the heat, lights and power were flowing. It wasn't enough to ignite the projectors, of course, but it was enough to move about the place more naturally.

Returning to Lorn, I found him up on a chair. He was repairing his flesh with stolen bits of his former comrades, those who'd been freshly killed by Morris and his marines.

"I'll be up and walking in a few minutes," he told me. "Don't trouble to help."

His words were spoken sarcastically as we both knew I had no intention of helping him repair himself. It was all I could do not to curl my lip as I watched him work.

"We might not make it," I said, "but it'll be best if you help us lay-in a destination for the new bridge, in case we do."

He looked at me in surprise.

"What?" he said. "Are you mad? We can't do anything fancy like that. We'll have to fire up the projector and hope that it works at all."

Losing control of myself momentarily, I grabbed up a wad of his tunic.

"You said you could get this station operating," I said. "I'm going to hold you to your word."

261

"I did say that, and so it *will* be done. We'll have an ER bridge here, a perfect tunnel through hyperspace built to order. But no one said anything about changing our destination."

Glaring at him, I felt sure I'd been tricked. "Where does it lead to, then?" I demanded. "Where will we go if we enter this breach?"

He looked at me thoughtfully. "I believe it's set to go to Earth. It will create a very small breach, of course. We used this system to transport pods into your system. Where did you think all those spies have been coming from?"

He laughed, and I blinked thoughtfully.

He was right. It'd been inexplicable to many in Star Guard that the Stroj had, for so long, been able to infiltrate our world.

It also made sense that the Stroj agent who'd played the part of Admiral Perez back on Earth would know of this place, even the exact coordinates, if he'd come from here originally.

Releasing his tunic, I straightened up and took in a deep, relaxing breath.

"That's excellent news. Earth is exactly where we want to go."

"You see? You let your mind get all twisted up needlessly. Let Lorn guide you, and help you. No one has lived to regret it."

I didn't find the double-meaning of his words encouraging. He went back to tinkering with his damaged legs, and soon had them buzzing and clicking again.

Perhaps I'd made a mistake trusting him, but it was a risk I felt I must take.

While everyone else worked frantically over the next fateful minutes, I dared to hope my plans would come to fruition. The Beta ships—it was all down to them. If they came back to Earth with us, then the sole battleship defending Earth would be forced to come out and do battle with them.

That was when I'd make my move on the Council, ending their illegal reign. They'd be undefended when the last ship circling Earth moved out past the Moon.

Time flew by. Long before the stellar power-stream had filled the bridge-projector, Durris called me in a panic.

"They're going to be on us at any moment, Captain!" he called.

"Move away," I said. "Do an orbit of the dead planet at speed, coming back around to our position. We need more time."

He was quiet for a second. I knew he was working his table, seeking answers. "It's… it might work. They'll probably lash our stern with long-range fire."

"Then you'd best get underway," I told him.

"But sir, what if they don't take the bait?" he asked. "They must be watching us. They know we've been sitting here at this station, fiddling with it. They could destroy it as an afterthought."

"Don't worry," I assured him. "I've got quite a bit of experience with Betas. They aren't imaginative. They'll figure they can destroy this station at their leisure after *Defiant* has been defeated."

"All right, *Defiant* out."

Time crawled after that. Somehow, knowing death was approaching from out of the blackness made each instant seem like an eternity.

My eyes, like those of every human on the station, kept flashing up to the observation screens. We couldn't see the Beta ships, they were too far out, but they were coming. When they did arrive, we might only see a blinding flash of energy before they destroyed us all.

"The variant is finished," Morris told me. "Vogel is struggling with the controls."

I scrambled up a tube to where I found Vogel, huddled over a panel of baffling instruments. When I arrived, I saw him reach up a thin-boned hand to nudge a setting.

"Halt!" I ordered.

He pulled back his hand as if it had been bitten.

"What, Captain…? You startled me."

"The coordinates are set for Earth," I told him. "I'm satisfied with that arrangement."

He frowned, but he nodded. Then he scratched his head and returned his attention to the controls.

"I don't think it's that simple," he said.

"Simple? How is a bridge projector that creates a hyperspace tube 'simple' by any definition?"

"Not the device itself, it's a wonder of engineering. I'm talking about this control mechanism. It doesn't seem to provide a destination you can program into it. That involves another component, I believe."

"It hardly matters now," I said. "Come, we must get on the shuttle. *Defiant* will be coming around to our position shortly. We must enter the breach with her."

He looked at me with fresh alarm.

"That's not possible!" he said. "We'll be smashed like a bug. *Defiant* is moving at great speed. In the shuttle, due to inertia—"

"I know all about that. Come with me."

We scrambled out of the chamber, and toward the waiting shuttle. Once aboard, we watched as K-19 loaded himself laboriously. The variant seemed to be blurringly fast except when it came to folding up his spidery legs.

"Come on, come on," Morris chanted.

At last, we were all loaded. I reached for the controls personally.

Vogel, at my side, cleared his throat.

"What is it?" I demanded.

"Lorn isn't aboard yet."

I released a hiss of frustration. Into my local chat channel, I fired a short stream of curses. "Lorn, if this is your idea of a delaying tactic it will be your last. If you're not aboard this craft in ten seconds—"

A hobbling figure appeared outside my forward viewports. He waved then climbed in, swinging himself into a seat.

The hatch folded shut, and we lifted off. We spiraled away from the structure then spun around toward it. Gaining speed, I gave the tiny ship all the thrust I could.

We shook and our faces rippled as gravity pulled our cheeks from our gums. Pressed back into our seats, we plunged into the funnel of steel struts.

I could see ahead that the small end of the funnel was a glowing nimbus, a ring of ghostly fire. I aimed at that point, having no detection equipment that could guide us better than the human eye.

Vogel was earnestly babbling something, but I couldn't hear it. With a final burst of speed, we entered the breach, and we vanished.

-44-

As we hit the breach, the insanity of my actions struck me. It took that long for me to consider the danger I was placing myself and my crew into.

Entering a hyperspace bridge is a dangerous action under the best of circumstances. But in this case, we were entering an *artificial* bridge that had only just been created.

Was the underlying technology sound? Had a thousand Stroj engineers, all of whom were assumedly now dead, done their jobs properly?

I had no way of knowing. I didn't even know exactly where this bridge went or how long it would be.

Worse, we were entering under duress. The Beta ships in our wake were plunging after *Defiant*, firing at her. Certainly they were decelerating, but they were still moving forward with greater momentum than either my tiny ship or *Defiant*. In short, they were bound to catch up to us.

Still, I'd persisted in this course of action. I'd acted like Ahab, chasing his infamous whale.

Now wasn't the time for self-recriminations, I decided. Now was the time to make the best of it by keeping myself and my crew alive.

Leading the way into the breach, we skipped out of normal space and entered another anomalous region of space-time known as hyperspace.

The name itself was a misnomer of sorts. We'd discovered over time that each hyperspace was different. Each was, effectively, its own tiny, independent universe. The laws of physics inside never seemed to match up to the comparatively stable version that dominated the universe outside.

It was like being in an intersecting subset of the normal universe. A domain which was related to, but not a copy of, the original. Each bridge was a shadow of our familiar reality. They were all different, and they were always warped in some way.

This one looked odd right from the start. It was still expanding as we crossed over into it. The void flew away from our ship in every direction, including directly forward. At first, this expansion would be rapid, but as the bridge reached its full extent, the expansion would slow.

"The walls are blue-shifting away," Vogel said, studying the limited sensor array data. "Already, I can't detect the wall ahead of us."

"That's a good thing," Lorn said. "If we could, we'd likely slam right into it."

"Any sign of *Defiant* yet?" I asked.

"I'm not detecting—yes! There she is!"

A proximity warning went off immediately. I felt a tug, oddly enough.

Everyone aboard whooped and cursed.

"Something just grabbed me," Lorn shouted. "Is that variant going mad?"

"All my limbs are fully stowed," K-19 said. If I hadn't known better, I would have said there was a hurt tone to his statement.

"Vicious robot. I still feel a strange tug…"

Director Vogel worked his controls then he looked at me in alarm. "It's *Defiant*," he said.

"What are you talking about?"

"The tug—it's a gravitational force. The ship is large enough here to exert a force like a small planet."

I frowned, barely comprehending him. Then, my instruments indicated I was losing power.

"I don't..." I said, confused, "our ship is apparently being pulled backward."

"It's *Defiant*," Vogel said. "It has to be."

"What's your mad scientist prattling about, Sparhawk?" Lorn demanded. "Let me take him off your hands. He's clearly defective, anyway."

I ignored Lorn and stared at Vogel. I was beginning to grasp what he was trying to tell me.

"This space has an increased gravitational force?" I asked.

"Exactly," he said, shifting into a lecturing tone. "Every object has gravity, but normally we don't feel it. In this slice of hyperspace, each body of mass is exerting something like a thousand times the normal pull."

"Is the effect dangerous?" I asked.

"It is if we can't control or compensate for it. There's another factor I'm measuring... an increase in gravity due to close proximity that's beyond the universal norm."

"Specify."

"Well Captain, the gravitational pull between two bodies lessens with distance and grows with proximity. At least, it does so in our universe. In this space-time, it seems to grow more than normal as the distance between two masses shrinks. At a distance of, say, one hundred meters, you and I won't affect one another. But at one meter or less, we'll feel the pull of each other's bodies."

Frowning, I looked over the data. It seemed that he was right, but I wasn't sure how to deal with it. Did we all have to malinger in space a hundred meters apart?

The big problem of the moment was *Defiant*. Our own gravitational influences were comparatively minor, but *Defiant* had partially collapsed matter for armor, making her shockingly dense. In this new environment, my instruments were acting as if I was close to something the size of a planet. I could keep a safe distance if I wanted to, but the expenditure of fuel would soon become prohibitive.

"Brace yourselves, everyone," I announced. "We're going to be swallowed by *Defiant*."

We winced and gritted our teeth as the battle cruiser loomed ever closer behind us. It was an odd feeling—as if a shark were drawing us into its mouth through suction.

"Durris!" I shouted over the roar of our engines. I had to fire them to prevent slamming into *Defiant*. "We're coming in for a hot landing. Make sure the forward bay is open to receive us."

"It is, Captain," he responded. "But we're having some kind of strange effect aboard ship. The inertial dampeners are offline, and crewmen are reportedly being pressed up against walls on every deck."

"We're experiencing the same effect. Gravity is apparently exaggerated in this space. I've never heard of such an effect before, but that might be due to a lack of experience with artificial bridges."

"We'll deal with it," Durris said confidently. "Come in gently, sir. We'll maintain as stable a positioning as we can."

As our two ships merged, they seemed determined to slam together during the final seconds. It was like controlling two magnets that are placed too close to one another. At the last moment, we thudded down with teeth-jarring suddenness.

"We're aboard," I told Durris via my com implant. "Close the outer hatch. Raise the shields."

"We're in that process now, Captain."

Good old Durris. Despite this shocking development, he was still at the top of his game.

Painfully, laboriously, we extricated ourselves from our harnesses and staggered out onto the deck of the hangar. The place was deserted. The support crews were nowhere to be seen.

"K-19," I said, "please secure the shuttle to the deck with rivets—but don't overdo it. We might need this ship again."

We moved as a group toward the exit. Lorn seemed to be enjoying himself, unlike the rest of us. He tormented Director Vogel in small ways as we crossed the open deck. He did this by moving a hand near the smaller man's shoulder, then pulling it away suddenly, which caused him to stumble.

The effects were amazing. We were all exerting gravitational influences that altered even simple behaviors such as walking. It wasn't that we were heavier than usual, as the ship was exerting about the same pull as Earth's gravity would have on us. What was different was the varied placement of the influences. We were being tugged in multiple directions all at once. The results left us staggering like a line of drunks.

Lorn reached out a foot and brought it near the back of Vogel's knee. The older man stumbled and went down. Lorn chuckled pridefully.

"Stop that," I ordered him. "K-19, I want you to guard this man. Prevent him from taking aggressive action of any kind."

K-19, done with the process of securing the shuttle, rapidly scuttled forward. His steps were relatively sure compared to our own. He had four more legs to start with, and I suspected his locomotion software had already made compensating adjustments.

Lorn sneered at the variant. "Unfair, Sparhawk," he complained. "As always, you blame the victim. This man created monsters that have killed millions of my people. All I want to do is irritate him slightly. Why not let me have my fun?"

Director Vogel looked back at Lorn in fear. He'd been unaware of the source of his troubles. Lorn's artificial eye ceased it's twitching and locked onto the old man's frail form. He loomed over him, with clear violent intent written on his nightmarish features.

"If Director Vogel is guilty as you say, he'll be punished in accordance to Earth law," I assured Lorn. "In the meantime, stay away from him."

"Earth law…" Lorn spat, turning away.

Lorn moved with an ease and grace that made me frown.

"How are you able to adjust so quickly to this environment?" I asked him.

"Superior genetics and masterful mechanical design," he said.

To me, his words didn't sound truthful. He was, if anything, a patchwork of parts. He was a capable construct, but far from optimally designed.

"You've experienced this effect before, haven't you?" I demanded.

"Your suspicious mind does you no credit, Sparhawk."

"Why didn't you tell us we'd encounter something like this? Why didn't you warn us?"

He made a spitting, laughing sound.

"You didn't ask me," he said.

"You should always offer up critical information that improves the odds of mission success."

He looked at me as if I were mad. "Come now. We made a deal with my part being agreed to under duress. I haven't gotten you killed yet, which should more than prove my loyalty. Quit whining."

He stumped away with K-19 in tight pursuit.

Morris stepped up to me and indicated Lorn with a rude gesture.

"That thing is trouble," he said. "He always has been, and this time is no different. Let me take care of him, Captain. I'll blow him out an airlock, and no one will ever lodge a complaint about it. No one."

I suspected his suggestion was a wise one, but that didn't change my plans.

"You'll do no such thing," I told him sternly. "There's a conflict ongoing between our peoples, Morris. Casualties on both sides are to be expected. However, in the interest of avoiding total genocide, we'll have to make peace with them eventually. That means we'll have to start honoring our agreements at some point. I've chosen to do so now."

Morris sniffed. "Suit yourself, Captain," he said, and vanished into the passages. He went below decks with his marines while K-19 marched Lorn to detention.

I found myself alone with Director Vogel. We headed toward the command deck.

-45-

The director and I walked to the command deck on unsteady feet. When I reached my chair at last, Durris struggled to remove himself from it, and I gratefully took his place.

"Captain on deck!" he called.

"XO," I said, "take Vogel to your planning table and make him comfortable in one of the jump-seats. He's earned the right to be here today, and I'll value his advice on surviving the next few hours."

"As to that, Captain," Durris said as he helped Vogel into a fold-out chair, "we haven't yet seen the Beta ships enter this space. They might not follow us. They must know this bridge is artificial and new-born. It might collapse on them."

I thought about it and shook my head. "No, they'll follow us. They're too prideful. The last time we faced Okto, we had to cripple her ship to evade her. That action, in fact, might be why she's so determined this time."

"Out of spite?"

"I would sooner term it 'pride' as it's her pride that was injured. She'll be along shortly, and we must make whatever preparations we can."

Durris leaned heavily on his table looking both stressed and off-balance.

"We can't run," he said. "This space-time is still in the early growth stages. We might run into the limit of it, and either we pass the exit or cease to exist, lost in limbo."

"That's a theory," Vogel said. "There might be something beyond the limits of a sub-universe like this one."

"Why haven't any probes sent there ever returned, then?" Durris asked.

Vogel shrugged, conceding the point. "I'm just saying we don't know what's out there past the edge of this space."

"Fine, but unless we want to find out, we can't use thrust to escape our pursuers."

"XO," I said, interrupting the two of them. "What *can* we do then?"

"We can set up an ambush, like I advised before, with missiles and measured beam-firing data."

I hesitated. We'd beaten Okto the last time we'd fought her with an ambush approach. I was reluctant to repeat the trick, but I couldn't see a better path.

"Damn," I said, then drew a deep breath. "Deploy smart-missiles. Set them up to strike the first entrant. Start laying out probes. Get our firing ranges down before we have to use them."

Durris turned to the work eagerly. Vogel struggled to his feet and staggered to my chair.

"Captain," he said in a winded voice, "I have no love for these Betas, but I don't think we should destroy three more of their ships. They may be some of the last effective forces any of the colonies have that might be able to stop the variants."

"I know that, Director. This isn't what I'd intended. But what would you have me do? We can't run without space to run to. I can't allow this ship to be destroyed for the good of the Betas, either."

He shook his head. "It's a difficult situation. By the way, why did you get them to follow us?"

I glanced at him. "Was it that obvious?"

He scoffed gently. "Sparhawk, I wasn't born yesterday. I've seen tricks and barbs many times. You wanted the Beta ships to chase us. Why?"

"I had hopes," I admitted. "I still do, but they're fading."

Vogel looked around the deck. "You thought they might help us defeat the variants? Or the oldsters running Earth?"

"Either would be a great help," I admitted. "I was desperate. But now it seems more likely we'll tear each other apart out here in hyperspace. It may all turn into an unfortunate waste."

We watched for a moment as Durris excitedly released his missiles, programmed them, and placed them with loving care. Like a circular firing squad, they ringed the breach behind us, ready to plunge like a score of daggers into any ship that dared to follow us.

At the same time, he released targeting drones. These flew in patterns around our ship, and our guns fired at them determinedly. At first, the drones evaded the guns. That was due to the warped physics of this space-time.

The effect was severe, I could see that immediately. Our guns chattered and hummed for nearly a minute failing to strike anything.

But then, almost as if by chance, the first of the drones flashed into a brief, brilliant point of light. The software, having scored a hit, quickly updated itself. After that they learned, and their aim improved. The other drones were all taken out within the span of thirty more seconds.

Durris turned toward me pridefully. "We're ready for them, sir," he said. "At least we'll have the drop on them."

"Yes," I agreed, "but we had it last time, and we barely crawled away from one of their ships. This time, there will be three."

His elated expression faded. After all was ready, we waited for perhaps five more tense minutes.

We'd just begun to relax. That first inkling of hope had flared up, uninvited.

Maybe the Betas would give up. Perhaps they'd had enough of ambushes and unknown bridges. Or maybe they'd simply come to their senses and let their rage fade away.

But it wasn't to be. Just as my guts unknotted a notch, there was bright burst of energy. The breach had hiccupped, and someone had followed us into our private universe.

The first Beta ship was sleek and cruel-looking. Like a bird of prey, she swooped out of nothingness and stalked forward with confidence.

"All hands," I heard myself saying, "prepare for battle. This is no drill."

After that, I shut out the buzzing in my implant. I had no time to listen to them all. I had to think.

"Where are the rest of them? Yamada?"

"Just one ship has come through so far, sir."

"Captain," Durris said, "permission to fire the missiles?"

There they were, hanging all around the enemy ship like daggers, encircling her. She looked competent, but I knew that she had to be suffering the same disorienting effects we'd felt at first. Her engineers were probably glued to the warp core. Her service people might be, even now, picking themselves up off the outer walls of the hull which dragged them off their feet.

"Yamada," I said, ignoring Durris, "open a channel to that ship."

"Done."

"Captain Okto," I said, knowing it had to be her. "Let's not repeat past mistakes. Please listen to me."

"No response, Captain," Yamada said.

"Are they listening?"

"They got the message—but they're not responding."

"Captain," Durris said urgently. "There isn't much time to surprise her. We can't just wait around—"

Then, interrupting his words, two more ships appeared. The flashes of light subsided, and the three enemy cruisers faced us as a united front.

My heart sank. I'd dared to hope Okto had come alone, that I could get her to see reason.

"Durris," I said with a heavy heart. "All missiles should lock onto the first ship."

"Done sir. Give the word."

"Wait!" cried Director Vogel. "They're—they're falling into one another!"

I stared, and I saw in amazement he was right. The enemy ships had taken the time to slow down before entering this

275

strange hyperspace. Okto had taken the plunge first, but the second and third ship had come into our tiny realm side-by-side.

That decision had been their undoing. The two ships were too close. They fell into one another like two planets in a deadly spiral.

Sensing the disaster, the pilots tried to evade by applying thrust. But it was too little, too late. The two ships crashed into one another, belly to belly, smashing banks of canons and sensor arrays between them.

The thrust they'd both applied in different directions to avoid contact now proved disastrous. They went into a rapid spin, engines flaring blue and white.

"Their crews will lose consciousness," Durris said in a disbelieving voice.

The first ship, seeing the other two were in dire straits, began accelerating toward us. But now, the other two had become a single, powerful gravitational force. Like a miniature black hole, they pulled their sister back toward them.

"Stand down and retrieve our missiles, Durris," I said.

He did as I ordered without comment.

We watched as the three Beta ships became hopelessly entangled. I could only imagine the hell their crews were experiencing now—if they'd managed to survive a tripling of gravity and the impact of the third dense vessel upon the first two.

-46-

We withdrew, gliding away from the three ships which were still locked in a death-spin on two axes. Now and then, a burst of exhaust from one thruster or another tried to counter the spin, but it didn't seem to be working.

"I can't bear to watch," Rumbold said, but he was staring at our rear camera view anyway.

"I don't understand why their auto-stabilizers aren't working," Yamada said. "Are they damaged?"

"No, I can see them firing off a jet now and then," Durris said. "Maybe the crews aren't coordinating. Maybe they're trying to pull apart, but they can't."

"That's not it," Vogel said in an authoritative voice.

We looked at him, but he continued to stare at the spectacle without further comment.

"Let's hear it then," I said. "What's your theory, Director?"

He sniffed and scratched his ear thoughtfully. Against orders, he'd removed his helmet.

"It's not a theory, I'm afraid. The circumstances are clear. The crews are dead, or at least incapacitated. Three gravities, plus centrifugal force from the spin... even Betas can't endure that."

I looked at the ships in greater concern. I hadn't considered the possibility the crews were already dead.

"Are you sure?" I asked. "Betas are very tough, and those jets keep firing now and then, trying to get control of their spin."

"They're locked together by gravitational force. Each ship's computer is trying to stabilize itself, but can't compensate for the others. They're using maneuvering jets, but each burst of thrust affects all three ships. They're just fighting each other uselessly."

With growing concern, I studied the three cruisers. This wasn't what I'd intended—not even close. I hadn't wanted to destroy any Beta ships, much less all three.

"Congratulations, Sparhawk," Vogel went on. "I've heard you're a tactical genius, but this victory exceeds my wildest expectations. Think about it: you bested three equal ships without firing a shot! Almost unbelievable. My advice is that you carefully record everything to prove this really happened when we get back to Earth."

"That's not the advice I need right now, Director," I said. "How can we help them?"

That question got the attention of everyone on the command deck. As one, they looked at me. For the most part, their expressions registered shock and incredulity.

"Well?" I demanded, looking at Vogel. "Can you help, or are you only good for joking about the deaths of others?"

"Um…" Vogel said, "I guess we could use the variants."

"How so?"

"*Defiant* can't get close, we'd become locked together and our bodies would be crushed. But a variant can operate under three Gs of force. We could send in a shuttle. A variant could crawl over the hull of two of the ships cutting the thruster lines. If only one ship was auto-stabilizing, they might all stop spinning."

Thoughtfully, I looked at the scene and the data. The ships were still spinning. As I watched, two of the ships fired their thrusters, but the result was only further, random rotation.

"It's worth a shot," I said. "Come about, Rumbold, but don't get too close."

Rumbold's eyes bugged out at me. His mouth hung open.

"Protest noted," I said. "Come about."

278

"All right, Captain," he said, giving his head a shake.

He brought the ship around, and we began backtracking toward the three enemy ships.

Vogel went below and unpacked four of our variants. That was all we could fit aboard a shuttle. It took too much time, but we managed to get them underway with clear instructions.

Vogel was at my side when the shuttle took off. They were piloting the tiny ship, thrusting hard to get away from the pull of *Defiant*.

Vogel and I stood alone in the shuttle hangar looking out into the strange colored lights that made up the walls of this universe.

"This is crazy, Captain," he said.

"I'm not surprised you feel that way," I told him. "But I'm looking at this war differently now. It's not Earth against all her colonists. It's about bringing people together."

"Are you including my variants on your list of people?" he asked me.

"Yes… I'm starting to count them as crewmen. We must all learn to function together somehow. If we keep fighting one another as humanity spreads and diversifies across the stars, things will surely end badly for all of us."

"End badly?" he asked. "As it is, the oldsters rule everyone on Earth through updates, and they kill off every competitor they discover. How could it get worse?"

"What if they ruled everyone in this part of the galaxy with similar disregard?" I asked. "I'd call that a bad finish, but it's not the only one in our future. The variants might take matters into their own hands by deciding to kill off everyone else. Like I said, I'm trying to gain the trust of the Betas. If we can get a single world to ally with Earth rather than fighting her—"

"But Captain," he said, "clearly that's not up to us."

I would have begun pacing across the hangar deck, but the ship was still providing uneven footing. Every time I took a step, my foot seemed to snap down the last centimeter and stick there.

"That could change," I said. "I'd like to discuss some possibilities with you at a later date."

He stared at me for a time, but then he nodded slowly. "All right," he said at last. "Until then."

He left me on the hangar deck. I stayed behind to watch the hatch doors slowly swing shut, sealing off the strange glowing light of this pocket universe.

It felt disconcerting to know we were drifting in a reality that existed apart from everything I'd ever known. If this ER bridge were to collapse around us, all of us would vanish, never to return to Earth.

I wondered, if that happened, how we might be remembered.

-47-

The variants reached the stuck-together cruisers, but then they nearly encountered disaster.

"The shuttle—it's losing control, sir!" Rumbold said.

I watched in silent concern. There was no order I could give and no suggestion I could make. The die was cast.

The shuttle was thrusting wildly with its tail exhaust port aimed toward the three spinning ships. I could tell the variants weren't the best of pilots, but they were doing what they could. They were in a constant struggle as they battled the controls, trying not to heel over and plunge nose first into the deadly maelstrom of spinning ships.

"It's an impossible task," Rumbold said, watching. "Normally, landing under a three G pull is deadly. But this— the bodies they're trying to land on are moving in two directions at once, and they're pulling unevenly. When they get too close..."

"Are you saying they'll be destroyed?" I asked him.

"I am, Captain. I suspected it before, but I'm certain of it now that I'm watching the situation play out."

As the distance closed, I had to agree. The shuttle was wobbling. The forces would magnify once they got down to the final few meters, and they'd be slammed against one or another of the Beta hulls. At that point, there was little chance the shuttle wouldn't blow up.

"Bring them back, Captain," Rumbold urged. "They don't deserve this."

I watched thoughtfully for a few more seconds. "Contact the shuttle's commander," I said.

They looked at me as if I was mad for a moment, but then Yamada complied.

"K-19 reporting," said a voice.

"K-19? I didn't realize it was you aboard the shuttle."

"Identity confirmed. Your orders, Captain?"

"I want to ask you to make a decision," I said, "are you willing to continue this rescue attempt, or do you wish to abort?"

There was a second or so of silence. "I don't understand, Captain," K-19 said. "What are your orders?"

"My orders are for you to decide your fate. Are the goals of this mission achievable or not?"

Another few moments passed. "That depends on whether or not my crew survives direct contact with the spinning ships."

"Right... Now, do you think that's likely to happen? Or, is this a suicide mission?"

"Ah, I understand now. You don't wish to lose valuable assets, not if the mission is impossible. I can't give you that answer, sir. We might survive, or we might not."

"All right then," I said. "The matter is in your hands. You can make the call as you're on the spot and know better than I do what the odds are. I don't want you to attempt this rescue if it will destroy you and your crew. Decide."

There was a moment of quiet.

Vogel leaned close to me. "Sir, you're confusing them. They know how to follow orders, but you're asking them to make a judgment call full of unknown factors."

"I know precisely what I'm doing," I told him without a glance. "K-19, I'm waiting."

"We have formulated a plan, Captain. Do we have permission to attempt it?"

It was my turn to hesitate, but I only did so for a split-second.

"Yes," I said.

The channel closed, and we all watched as if mesmerized, wondering what the variants would do next.

"Hey, they're opening the hatch!" Rumbold shouted, pointing at the screen excitedly.

We watched a figure crawl out. It was a variant, its legs resembling silvery-white sticks at maximum magnification. The shuttle continued to wobble, holding at a distance of some fifty meters from the spinning bundle of cruisers below them.

"What do you think—?" began Yamada, but then she gave a strangled cry and put her hand to her mouth.

The variant let go. Behind it was a glinting line attached to the shuttle. The variant sprang from the shuttle and flew like a spider dropping from the ceiling. It spun out a line behind it as it got close to the ships.

"They're going to drop off a man!" Rumbold said excitedly. "That's ingenuity!"

The brave creature almost made it—almost. When the variant was perhaps ten meters from the surface of the ships, one of the three cruisers fired another steering jet.

The spin altered, flipping a portion of one vessel's super structure higher than it had been. Jutting out into space, a heavy wingtip slammed into the variant. It was crushed instantly and hurled away into space like a ball hit by a batter.

"Damn!" I said, unable to contain myself.

"Call them back, Captain!" Rumbold implored me.

"No!" Director Vogel said. "Don't. I want to see what they'll do."

I eyed both men but made no decisions. "Let them decide."

The shuttle didn't retreat. Instead, another variant crept out of the hatch.

"They're doing this for you," Yamada said. "You have to know that, Captain. They think you've ordered them to solve an impossible equation. It's not fair."

My eyes slid to her, but then I looked back at the forward screen. "K-19 understands what's been asked of him."

"Yes!" Vogel said excitedly. "He does. This *must* continue. I'm taking critical notes."

The second variant got even closer to his goals. He came down the line, hanging at an angle, and dodged the spinning protrusions.

It was the wobble in the shuttle's jets that got him in the end. He swung too close to the exhaust plume, and he was incinerated in an instant.

"That's too much," Rumbold said. "Permission to summon a replacement helmsman, Captain?"

"Denied. If you don't like it, don't watch, Rumbold. We're risking variants, it's true, but if we can save these three ships and their crews we'll have strengthened the defenses of all humanity significantly. Did you notice that millions died on other colony worlds? These Betas have resisted the armada where others couldn't."

He muttered something about me being a cold-hearted man, but I didn't listen. Of course I was cold-hearted. You could hardly be a starship captain without being willing to sacrifice for the greater good. The calculus of warfare in space was extremely unforgiving.

The third variant slid out on a line. My stomach was in a knot. There could only be one other unit aboard—K-19, the pilot of the shuttle. This would be their last attempt.

This individual seemed to have learned after watching the demise of its fellows. It moved with alacrity rather than careful slowness. When it was about five meters from the spinning ships, it simply let go of the line.

Dropping hard, it crunched down on the turning ships, and was whisked away from visual contact with the shuttle. Its weight seemed to pin it to the surface of the hull at first, but then it slowly got up and began crawling.

Officers whooped on the deck, and the shuttle lifted away from the three cruisers with difficulty returning to our position.

I was all smiles when I headed for the hangar. I felt K-19 deserved my personal congratulations. He'd done an excellent job with both innovation and piloting.

When I reached the shuttle bay, and the last remaining variant crawled out of it, I was left staring in shock.

The variant's insignia left no doubt. It wasn't K-19. It was Q-161.

284

"Q-161?" I asked. "Where's K-19?"

"He was destroyed," the variant said in a neutral tone.

"What? When did he make the attempt?"

"He went first. He ordered me to take the helm then he left the ship. The attempt failed, but we had our orders. Each of us left the ship, one at a time, until one of our number survived. I was the last, so I brought the shuttle home."

"Yes... I see," I said, deflated. "Excellent work. Consider yourself promoted to K-19's position."

"Thank you, Captain. We won't let you down."

The variant scuttled away, and I felt a sense of loss. I'd come to like K-19, and he'd become a competent member of my crew.

Turning to the nearest viewport, I stared at the Beta ships. They were still locked in their deadly embrace, spinning helplessly.

"I hope some of you are still alive," I said aloud to the Beta crews.

They couldn't hear me, of course. No one could, but I said it anyway.

Heading back up to the command deck, I lamented the lonely nature of the captaincy. Mistakes could strike a man in my position with sickening emotional pain.

But I didn't dare hint about such feelings. My face was a mask of stone when I took my chair again.

I called for an update concerning the surviving variant's progress, and I was suitably impressed. He'd made his way to the first of many thrusters and disabled it.

We'd soon find out if this effort was worth it or not.

-48-

It was a full hour later that the Beta ships began to stabilize. After one of the three ships stopped trying to control its fate, the trio stopped spinning as rapidly. After a second ship had its lines cut, the last one was able to get them all under control.

Hanging in space, the clustered ships were dark, silent. We stared at them, thinking we'd merely saved a mass of scrap metal for future generations to wonder about.

"There's a channel request, Captain!" Yamada said.

"Open it."

She did so, and a Beta figure, fully reclined on her back, stared at us. Was it Okto? They all looked the same, but I felt it was her in my bones.

She stared at me malevolently, and her every motion seemed pained. She dragged in a breath and let it go slowly in order to speak.

"Sparhawk…" she said. "There seems to be no end to the dishonors you wish to heap upon me."

"Dishonors?" I asked. "We're rescuing you, Okto. Have the decency to be grateful."

She made her way to an elbow, and worked like a dying fish to speak again. There was blood on her face, dried and smeared. The atmosphere surrounding her seemed to be smoky and poorly lit.

"Your trick was masterful," she said. "I'll give you that. But I'll not become your prisoner, nor will I serve your whims like Zye."

"I'm not asking for any of that," I said in frustration. "I merely want to send you back on your way to Beta. Repair your ships. Defend your homeworld. Someday, if Earth calls for aid against a threat that will destroy us all, then aid us. That's all I ask."

The face looked confused for a moment then tightened in surprise as she figured out what I was saying.

"Talk of fealty?" she asked twisting into a crouch. "Do you count us as a vassal state? We've not yet been defeated. We haven't surrendered to you, nor do we accept your superior—"

"Okto," I said, "I'm not asking for any of that. I'm asking for a basic nonaggression pact and a mutual defense treaty. That's all. Your sovereignty is in no way jeopardized."

"You don't have the authority to impose—"

"I'm not imposing anything. I'm *asking*. We've saved three of your last ships. Surely, you can see the value in that act. Your world might survive due to what I did here today."

"Very well," she said. "I'll carry your pleas back to Beta when I'm done with my mission."

"When you're done?" I asked. "Your ships are barely operational. It will be all you can do to exit this breach together and escape this gravitational anomaly."

"Yes, you ensnared us masterfully," she admitted. "But my mission is to capture or destroy *Defiant*. I will not stop until I've done so."

"What?" I demanded, outraged. "I've just saved all your lives. Are you so ungrateful?"

"Your insults are unwarranted. Your folly has increased my odds of success, and yes, I am grateful for that."

My hand came up and rubbed at my temples. Betas were among the most stubborn beings I'd ever encountered. If the truth were to be told, it was easier to make a deal with a Stroj.

I looked back to the screen and the huge female, now on all fours, stared with her head lowered like a wild predator.

"Be it not said," she continued, her voice gaining strength, "that the Beta people are unjust. I will give you this warning:

287

the first systems we've been repairing are not those that aid in propulsion or navigation."

With that, the screen went dark.

"What a monster," Yamada said. "I can't believe the Betas could be so evil."

"Well, they did warn us," Rumbold said. "Permission to get out of her reach, Captain?"

I thought about it for a moment, but I couldn't come up with another diplomatic ploy to attempt.

"All right," I said at last. "Get us out of here, Rumbold."

"What do you mean—out of her reach?" Yamada asked.

He gave a rumbling chuckle, and zoomed in visually on Okto's ship. There, we saw the last variant crawling laboriously across the hull.

As he approached the nose of the vessel he was traversing, a point-defense cannon rose up and swiveled. The gun chattered, spitting out a hundred pulses of particles.

We couldn't hear it, but we could see it. The variant was blasted apart.

Yamada stared in disbelief.

"What she meant," Rumbold said, "when she gave us that warning, was that they were working on their weapons systems before their engines. They mean to blow us from the skies."

"That's insane," she said, "but if they're so determined to kill us, why did she warn you?"

She looked at me, and I shrugged.

"Perhaps there's a shred of human decency in the Betas still, despite everything," I suggested. "It's the only answer I can come up with."

"Well... I guess it's a start," Yamada said. "But I'd hardly call this a diplomatic coup."

"Nor would I."

Rumbold laughed, and his laugh turned into a cackle. Applying steady thrust, he swung us around and headed for the far end of the bridge. Behind us, we left three crawling, disabled warships.

But I knew the Betas wouldn't take long to recover. Their home world had a gravitational standard nearly twice that of Earth. They could work in three Gs. Only the fact they'd been cast into a spin had kept them helpless. Now that they weren't spinning, they could at least crawl to their posts. Eventually, they'd escape this bridge.

They'd first get their weapons and drives working over the next day or two. If we let them, they'd blast us to fragments. We had to flee—either that, or destroy them. I didn't want to do that if only to make K-19's sacrifice worthwhile.

As we powered away from the Beta ships, I wondered if I'd managed to make an impression on Okto at all. I must have, to some degree, or she wouldn't have warned me about an impending attack.

Perhaps that was the way of her people. Officially, she had to destroy me. She had to appear nothing but menacing. But unofficially, she could let me slip from her grasp this one time.

That wasn't exactly a formula for a loving relationship, but it was the best I'd ever gotten from her people. I supposed I was just going to have to take it and hope for the best.

We flew on to the end of the bridge quickly. It was small, artificial, and newly made. When we reached the terminus, we found the way out and punched through.

When we came out, I stared at our surroundings in open-mouthed shock.

Somehow, I'd honestly expected to see Earth. I'd been informed this bridge would lead to the Solar System, that the bridge-projector had been used for that purpose on any number of previous missions.

But this wasn't the Solar System. Every detail was wrong.

The star in the center was singular, but it wasn't a G-class yellow sun. It was an F-class white star, hotter and somewhat larger than the star our Earth circled.

"Where are we?" I demanded.

"I have no idea, Captain," Durris said, baffled. "I'm just absorbing data now. Our navigational computers haven't placed us yet, but I'm sure they will. What I am picking up is a lot of traffic, and—sir?"

"What is it?"

"There's a battle going on in this system. I'm sure of it. There are hot streaks of radiation, derelict ships by the hundreds… There are missiles, flocks of them, flying this way and that among the inner planets. And that's not all—"

"Hold on a moment," I said, baring my teeth in anger. I contacted Lieutenant Morris.

"What's up, Captain?"

"Morris, get down to the brig. Put Lorn in irons and bring him up to the command deck under heavy guard."

"With pleasure, sir!" Morris said, and he was gone.

Looking back at Durris, I sucked in a breath angrily.

"What's your best guess?" I asked him.

"As to where we are…?" he asked, studying the charts. "I think this is the Stroj home system, sir. That's where I'd put my money. Where else would Lorn trick us into taking him?"

"That's what I think, too," I said through gritted teeth. "That's exactly what he'd do. But how did he manage it?"

-49-

Lorn was reluctant to answer my summons. He gave my security people quite a scare, threatening to blow himself up and kicking savagely with his newly patched-together legs.

"Here he is, Captain," Morris said, hauling the fuming creature onto the command deck. He threw Lorn down on his face. This was easily done as his arms were bound behind his back.

"You weakling savages!" Lorn howled. "At least have the decency to switch off that infernal stasis device, Sparhawk!"

He was referring to the machine we used with all captured Stroj. As a matter of standard practice, each Stroj citizen contained a powerful explosive within their bodies. It wasn't enough to knock down a building, but the charge was sufficient to kill anyone nearby.

To prevent this unpleasant possibility, we kept a machine nearby that generated a containment field to prevent the reaction. A marine accompanying Morris had one with him as they stepped onto the deck.

"Leave the device here, and secure him to the railing."

"Face down?" Morris asked hopefully. He was panting a bit from exertion. Lorn had forced them to drag his heavy frame.

"No, thank you. I need to talk to Lorn—not the back of his head."

Morris roughly secured the prisoner in a sitting position on the deck. I made no complaint. I was sure that whatever indignities Lorn had suffered, he'd more than deserved them all.

When Morris retreated, Lorn leaned toward me, growling.

"You have to discipline that man, Sparhawk. He's unprincipled. An animal in human skin."

For some reason, these accusations amused me. Perhaps it was because Lorn seemed to be describing himself.

"We rescued you, Lorn," I said, "and our repayment is this? Deceit, followed by threats and resistance?"

"It's the job of any prisoner of war to escape his captors. I owe you nothing."

"Nothing but your life."

"Fine! Then let me end it! Turn off that machine!"

I pretended to consider it.

"Durris," I called. "Is that emergency hatch still serviceable? The one that leads from the command deck directly to space?"

"Yes sir," he said. "There's not much room in there. It's more of a garbage chute."

"Just so. If we were to pressurize the tube, would opening the far end outside the hull eject the contents?"

Durris shrugged. "That's how it works, Captain."

I turned toward Lorn and made a welcoming gesture, suggesting he could climb into the garbage chute.

"Is that what you offer me?" he demanded. "To be jettisoned like refuse?"

"You said you wanted a way out. Here, I'm offering you your heart's desire."

He made a rude sound with his lips and turned away from me, straining against his bonds.

What he really wanted was a chance to escape alive, or to blow himself up in a glorious fashion. Taking out a few of us would satisfy his need for an honorable ending if he were given the opportunity.

"Let's talk about something else then, shall we?" I asked. "It's dawned on us that we're not anywhere near Earth. In fact, we appear to be in the Stroj home system."

"Of course."

292

I blinked at his frank admission. "You're not even going to feign surprise?"

"Not at all. We entered the artificial bridge without any identification transmissions or navigational data. The computers naturally sent us to the default destination."

"Which is the Stroj system?"

"You're a quick one. Everyone says it."

He was beginning to irritate me, but I did my best to keep calm. He probably was seeking a harsh reaction. He'd certainly gotten it out of Morris.

Thinking about his words, I felt a suspicion growing in my mind. Why would Lorn be so accommodating one moment, but turn into a determined enemy when we reached his home?

Could it be he was preparing to reunite with his people? They wouldn't go easy on a turncoat, but a Stroj who spat and howled at his captors was something else. A Stroj who'd tricked an Earth ship to come into the lion's den—such a Stroj would be celebrated as a hero.

That line of thought gave me an idea.

Lorn watched my face as I considered what I should do with him. "You're scheming, Sparhawk," he said. "You shouldn't bother. It's not your strength. In fact, it's probably your greatest weakness."

"Lorn," I said in a conversational tone, "what if I were to make you an honorary member of Star Guard?"

He paused. His chin dropped a fraction, leaving his mouth hanging open.

"What?"

"Yes," I said. "It's within my power to do things like that on an emergency basis. The status wouldn't be official unless we returned to Earth, of course, but we would issue you a uniform and rank insignia."

"By no means!" he shouted at me. "I won't wear it!"

"You will," I said, "even if we have to drug you and strap you into a wrap of blue smart-cloth. Drooling and smiling like a happy idiot, you'll be in the background of my first transmission to your people. It's making me feel proud just to think of it."

"You wouldn't dare, Sparhawk! Not after all I've done for you."

My laughter came out irrepressibly then, and it had a bitter note to it. "You've brought us into the lion's den as was your purpose all along."

"It's not my fault!" Lorn said, his face registering desperation which I found gratifying. "Everything I said was true. That bridge projector has been used many, many times to send agents to Earth. But on this occasion, you lacked the correct identification signals. All the ships that entered were funneled here as a result. Not thinking of that was a simple oversight on my part, and I apologize for it."

That lifted my eyebrows up. I couldn't recall ever having heard of a Stroj apologizing before. It could only mean that my idea of broadcasting his face in a Star Guard uniform was horrifying to him.

The Stroj, by any measure, were an odd people. They were very conscious of social status. By itself, that fact didn't make them strange. It was the code by which they lived. The nature of the acts which made them famous or infamous on their home planet also made them very different from the rest of humanity.

"All right then," I said, "can you suggest a course of action that will keep us out of Stroj hands?"

He strained on the floor trying to lever himself around to face the forward part of the deck.

"I can't see anything. Are we under attack? Are Stroj dreadnoughts closing in even now?"

After considering his question for a moment, I frowned. He apparently didn't know about the status of his home system.

That had me feeling a pang of pity. I was, after all, tormenting a man who was about to learn of a great horror.

Summoning two marines, I had them lift him to his feet. We marched him—and the device that prevented his self-destruct system from working—to Durris' tactical table.

"What are those...?" he asked, but then he trailed off.

The variant battleships were sweeping past the sixth world in the system, working their way inward. Every planet circling this star seemed to have some kind of habitation. They were either in the form of orbital stations or domes on the surface.

The variants had been engaged in systematically wiping all life from each world. Doubtlessly, millions of Stroj had perished. The fourth planet in the system was the only one that was defended. Three dreadnoughts were posted there, waiting to do battle.

"I'm sorry, Lorn," I said. "The variants beat us to your home system. They have only four battleships left, plus the carrier, but I would assume that will be enough."

"They're working their way from world to world..." he said, stunned. "They're killing everyone. No trophies. No slaves. No treasure. Only ruin. What kind of creatures are these, Sparhawk?"

"They must be stopped," Vogel said.

Lorn looked at him, and his shocked demeanor changed to that of a snarling dog.

"You!" he shouted, and lurched toward the director.

The marines barely caught him before he could slam into the smaller man.

"You built these things. How dare you stand here and suggest they're not doing your bidding!"

"I did help make them," Vogel admitted. "But they're not under my control, and they've gone too far. Even I think they must be put down."

Lorn turned back to me. "What are you going to do about this, Sparhawk? Stand by out here in deep space, watching? Gloating?"

"No," I said, "we're trying to formulate a plan of action."

"I don't believe you. I don't believe any of you. You're enjoying this. You chained me up on your deck like a slave, snickering and trading grins. Now, you show me my people are dying wholesale as a final moment in your twisted sense of humor!"

"Far from it, Lorn," I told him. "You know me to be a man of my word. We feel we must stop these abominations if we can. They're killing everyone indiscriminately."

"No they're not! Only *colonists* are killed, never your kind."

I drew myself up and made a decision. "There's something you should see, Lorn. In fact, it's something that everyone aboard *Defiant* should see."

Tapping for several seconds, I brought up a vid file on the main computer. Bypassing my security precautions, I displayed it on every available screen aboard ship.

The file played out with fateful slowness. My voice was involved, conversing with Admiral Halsey during his final moments. At the end, we all watched Halsey die at the hands of the variants.

-50-

For some of my crewmen, the vid came as a shock. They'd known we were concerned about the fleet. They'd even survived battle with *Victory* firsthand, but they'd never been clearly informed of the true nature of the disaster that had occurred.

Lorn watched, scowling at first, but even he had to squint in concern when the variants butchered Halsey at the end.

"Mutiny?" he asked. "You're asking me to believe that's what happened?"

"We're not entirely sure," I admitted, "but we *are* certain the variants aren't operating under Star Guard control. They appear to have slaughtered their human crews. They're now in the process of slaughtering all intelligent life wherever they meet it."

Lorn studied me. "And you think they might return to Earth and keep right on going?"

"It's a possibility—even likely," I admitted.

Immediately, his attitude shifted. His expression became thoughtful.

"So, you have a good reason to stop the variants…" Lorn said. Gone was his rage, his childish behavior, and his desperation.

But, one thing that remained in his demeanor was a sense of cunning calculation. That never seemed to change.

"We do have reasons to stop them," I agreed. "As do you. Let's work together."

He eyed me with one squinting eye and a roving camera stick.

"What can we do? This armada of yours has cleansed a dozen systems and defeated the Stroj fleet, the greatest force in the known galaxy."

"Durris," I asked, calling to my first officer over my shoulder. "Have any additional ships appeared in the system?"

"Additional ships?" he asked. "No, Captain."

"What ships?" Lorn demanded. "You're claiming you've brought fresh support from Earth? I find that very hard to believe."

"No," I said. "Not from Earth. My supporters, by my calculation, should make their appearance within the hour."

Lorn continued to look at me as if I were trying to trick him.

"All right," he said at last, "let's assume you'll have enough firepower to help the Stroj. If that's true, I'd be willing to help you."

"Excellent," I said. "What I need first—"

"No," Lorn said. "I'll do the talking—that's what you want, isn't it? A Stroj mouthpiece to talk my brothers into letting us approach the home world?"

"That's right," I admitted. "They must allow us to stand shoulder-to-shoulder with their last ships. To fight as a single, allied—"

I stopped talking, because Lorn had begun to laugh. The sound was loud, rude and it came from deep down in his belly.

"You've got to be kidding me, Sparhawk! No Stroj, not even the Supreme Being, could command the others to allow such a thing. At best, they'll reprogram their auto-fire systems to avoid destroying you as long as you remain at extreme range. If you get closer—within a million kilometers, let's say, they'll unload on you."

"That's not the spirit of cooperation I'd hoped to achieve today," I complained.

Lorn shrugged. "Nonetheless, it's the best my people can possibly offer. We're not a trusting bunch—for good reason."

298

I could hardly argue that point. The ships that had destroyed most of their planets had been built in my home star system, after all. How could they trust us not to turn our guns on them, joining in the fight on the opposite side? It didn't help matters that the Stroj themselves would think little of performing such a treacherous act if the situation had been reversed.

"Very well," I said. "We'll stay at long range. I think we can still aid effectively in the coming battle."

"Okay then, I'll help you. But you must listen to me. You must follow my lead. They'll never accept this arrangement any other way."

He began to explain what he intended, and my crewmen instantly objected. I wasn't enthusiastic, either.

But over time, we came to be convinced. The situation would be purely cosmetic, and Lorn would at no time be able to stage some kind of treachery. I made sure of that.

Hammering out the details took the better part of an hour. At the end of that time, Durris began to frantically signal me. I turned to him in irritation.

"What is it now?" I asked.

"You asked about additional ships, Captain? I think they're here. I'm not sure if they're what you wanted, however."

I joined him at the scopes. Three ships were now drifting near the breach where we'd so recently appeared.

The three ships were Beta battle cruisers. Okto still led them, and she had yet to give up her mission. She was still following me.

Despite the danger and the complication, I smiled.

"She's right on time," I said. "Now, all I have to do is convince her to cooperate."

"That seems like a tall order, Captain," Yamada said, shaking her head.

I didn't bother to disagree with her.

"Open a channel to the Beta ships, please."

She attempted to do so, and we waited a full minute.

"They don't seem to be interested in listening to us, Captain," Yamada said. "I'm getting nothing. Not even a tracer on our signal."

"Possibly they're sorting out their instruments. Get them on-screen at maximum magnification."

Even with our best sensors, we could see little. At this range, the computers had to extrapolate what the enemy was doing.

But still, we managed to see something that surprised us.

"They're repairing the ships," Yamada said. "Those are suited spacers crawling over the hulls."

I nodded, and I felt a tiny sense of relief. I'd been worried that their crews had been decimated by the crushing gravity they'd endured.

"Ha!" boomed Rumbold. "Those Beta girls are damned near indestructible."

"Yes," I said, "they are. What systems are they repairing first?"

"Looks like they're still working on weapons, Captain," Durris said, studying his scopes carefully.

"Of course," I said quietly.

"We could hit them now, Captain," Durris said. "They're weak, personally injured, and their ships are barely functioning. I've been doing some calculations concerning range and—"

"First Officer," I said sternly. "If I'd intended to kill the Betas, I would have done so when they were helpless inside the breach."

"But sir," he said, "they didn't follow your instructions. They didn't turn around and head for home. They could have crawled out of the breach at the other end of that bridge and been free of the gravity effects. At this point, they clearly have returned to their previous mission."

I couldn't argue with his point. They weren't even talking to us. Diplomacy was exceedingly difficult if one side persisted in ignoring the other.

"All right," I said, "forget about starting a conversation. Maybe their sensors are damaged as we can see that's not their first repair priority. Let's queue up a series of system scans and broadcast them in the clear. Let them see the *Iron Duke*. Let them see the destruction the variant fleet is visiting upon this defeated system."

300

Yamada focused on the task, but Durris came to my side and spoke in a low voice.

"Captain," he said, "your transmission might be seen as a threat. Maybe they'll think the star carrier is allied with us—we're both Earth ships, after all."

"That's fine," I told him. "I just want to get them talking."

Another hour went by. We put our plans with Lorn on hold which he grumbled about. He seemed to be eager to deceive his own people.

"I'm getting a hailing call from Okto!" Yamada said suddenly. "She demands to speak with you in private."

"Excellent. I'll talk to her in my office."

Stepping smartly to my private chambers, I used my implant to place Okto in the room with me.

She was huge, just as large as Zye—maybe even bigger. Perhaps it was her personal stance. She carried herself with her back ramrod straight. I could see the pride that every Alpha-type from her world exuded.

"What kind of trick is this, Sparhawk?" she demanded, looking around and studying her virtual hands as she moved about my cabin.

I'd forgotten her people weren't used to this kind of technology. We'd only recently gotten Zye to accept it back on Earth.

"It's a trick of the senses, Captain," I said. "There's no danger in it. Welcome aboard *Defiant*."

"*Defiant*? No, this ship's name is S11. She will never be an Earth ship in my eyes."

To the Betas, we'd stolen *Defiant*. We had, in fact, salvaged her. But that distinction had never completely penetrated the mind of any Beta I'd met.

"In any case," I said in a diplomatic tone, "we have urgent matters to discuss. Have you reviewed the transmission we've sent?"

"Fabrications," she said, waving her hand through air. Her hand blurred a little when she did so, which made her study it further with a very large frown on her face.

"No, they're not fabrications. When you repair your sensors, you'll see the same data we sent. The Stroj have been defeated in this system—their home system. The last of them are clustered around their home world. There, they'll make their last stand."

She turned back to me, lowering her big hand. "What of it? We're happy the Stroj are being destroyed. I hadn't thought your fleet capable of such a victory, but I'll welcome the day the last Stroj perishes."

"That's a short-sighted view," I said.

"Why?" she growled.

"The fleet is controlled by variants. It isn't going to stop with the Stroj."

She looked at me. "You mean they'll return to Beta?"

"Yes," I said. "Then they'll keep going. Earth is in danger, too."

"We've already lost a colony system. Did you know that? Just two of those battleships came into our system. We took one out then the other fled."

"Tell me," I said, "who commanded that task force?"

"Some Earthling Basic. A man named Halsey, I believe."

I thought about that, and I began to understand why the Betas had thus far survived. The star carrier had never ventured to the Beta Cygnus system. If it had, the fleet would have destroyed all the Betas as it had every other colony it encountered. Instead, Halsey had managed to escape the variants temporarily. Perhaps the humans aboard had disabled them or something. In any case, he'd come through the Beta Cygnus system while trying to find the way home.

And these savages, the Betas, had torn into them losing half their strength and destroying an Earth battleship. Halsey had suffered a similar fate when he'd finally reached home. I guessed that the variants had managed to mutiny by then, finishing the job they'd begun.

"That's unfortunate," I said quietly. "We could have used Halsey's help."

"What are you talking about?" Okto demanded suspiciously.

"Nothing," I said, "let's talk about this system, about this situation. The Stroj are our enemies, admittedly. But if they fall, this fleet will turn and continue to destroy colonies.

302

Eventually, it will come and destroy both your civilization and mine."

Okto shrugged her big shoulders and crossed her arms under her ample breasts. "So what? I'll take the chance. We drove off your big ships before."

I raised a finger to stop her.

"Hold on," I said. "You're an Alpha. You're one of the smartest people from your home system and the best your genetic stock can produce."

My praise seemed to have the intended effect. Okto stood a little taller as I spoke each word. Diplomatically, Betas were not sophisticated.

"What you say is beyond obvious," she said.

"Of course it is. Now, I call upon you to use that sharp mind of yours: if two battleships managed to destroy half your fleet, what would a star carrier and three more of them do?"

She hesitated. I could tell she knew the answer, but didn't want to say it.

"We might not hold," she admitted. "But what else can we do?"

A very small smile stole across my features. It was all I would allow myself.

"We can cooperate. Just for a day. Just for the length of a single battle. All three of us: Earth, Stroj and Beta. We have enough ships in this system, enough firepower to break these battleships."

She frowned again. "What of the carrier?"

"I'm honestly not sure," I said. "The carrier is an unknown. We've never faced anything like it in battle, and neither have your people. But I do know this: if we don't destroy the variants here, in this system, where all of humanity's strength is concentrated... Well, it will be the end."

"The end of what?"

"The end of us all. The end of every divergent line of humanity. The variants will have proven they're the superior form. Free-willed flesh and blood will have failed to stop these hybrid machines."

"But the Stroj *are* hybrid machines!" she boomed. "They're no less evil than the variants themselves. They defeat every

303

colony, lay it supine on its back, and have their way with us all!"

"An apt analogy," I said, "but the Stroj are not as bad as the variants."

"Why not?"

"Because the Stroj never commit genocide. They want trophies and sport. They keep their defeated enemies alive to toy with them. The variants are far more ruthless and efficient. They're only interest is in the complete annihilation of all life other than their own."

Okto began pacing around my office. It was a startling effect. Her head nearly reached the ceiling. Her wild black hair was longer than Zye's and cascaded down her back. Her massive legs swung through the furniture as if she were unaware of it.

"All right," she said at last. "We'll fight at your side, but only for a single battle. After that, Sparhawk, your life will not be worth one nanogram more."

I nodded, accepting her terms. I felt it was the best I was going to get.

"Very well. Let's discuss our plans."

-51-

For two days, we watched from a safe distance as the variant fleet cruised from planet, to outpost, to moon, destroying everything. They ignored us, seemingly intent on their systematic tour of destruction.

Okto used that time wisely, repairing her three ships. During their voyage through the gravity-magnifying slice of hyperspace, they'd suffered quite a bit of damage to their internal components. Many sensitive sub-systems were out of compliance and in drastic need of maintenance.

On the second day, I managed to convince Okto to allow *Defiant* to help. We sent two of my variants to each of her vessels to speed up the process. She was astounded by their efficiency.

"No wonder," she told me at the end of the second day, "Earth was able to build a first-class fleet so quickly. Our admirals didn't see how it could be done. We argued that you Earthlings must have been hiding the battleships somehow— but that didn't make any sense."

"No," I agreed. "If we'd had the ships, we would have used them to defend Earth during previous battles."

She was a looming presence in my office again. We were communicating privately using my implant.

She'd become accustomed to the effect of perception-transference by now, and she seemed relaxed, even enjoying herself. She sat on my couch and studied me with large, piercing eyes.

"Hmm…" I said, having seen her expression on Zye's face before. "Tell me, Okto, is it true you Alphas have males on your home world?"

She turned cool at the question.

"Rude," she said. "Poorly played."

"Uh… how so? I meant no offense."

"And yet, you have offended. Earth men are truly uncouth creatures, just as Betas have always said."

She was beginning to annoy me, so I changed the topic.

"Fine," I said, "let's go back to discussing strategy. If we can get the Stroj to agree—"

"No. No strategy talk," she said abruptly. "We will discuss your previous point. It's unfair, but starship captains don't have sufficient status to be awarded a male."

"I see…" I said. "Could that be because placing a male aboard one of your ships might be… disruptive to the crew?"

She looked like a cat that had been petted for one second too long.

"A groundless theory," she said. "Alpha captains are among the most accomplished of our kind, and yet we must be denied."

"Couldn't you have a male living at home, waiting for your return?"

She stared at me for a moment, her eyes still narrowed. Then she let out a sudden laugh. "I suspected that you understood nothing about us. It's clear now that you do not. Once allowed a male, we wouldn't be able to tolerate such a long separation."

Frowning, I began to nod. She was right in a way, about my knowledge of Beta customs. I only knew Zye. I knew her well, but that was different from knowing her entire people.

But what Okto was telling me did fit. Zye had always exhibited a strong sex-drive and was extremely possessive. During the brief time that we were intimately involved, she'd become something of a stalker. Her preoccupation with me made it difficult to perform my duties as captain.

With only one individual to study, I'd had no idea how much of Zye's personality was uniquely hers, and how much was a reflection of traits shared with all her sisters. Now, I was more able to see how much she really *was* like her sisters.

They were usually denied normal sexual relationships, but they desired them. One might even say they could become obsessed rather easily.

A warning chime went off in my mind as these thoughts passed through it. When I'd rescued Zye, and later defeated her in various contests of will, she'd become obsessed with me. Could that same pattern be playing out again with Okto? The thought was alarming.

Okto was like a meaner version of Zye. She wasn't an oppressed rogue, accustomed to controlling her emotions and hiding her intentions. Instead, she was a starship captain—and a leader among even that elite group. Who knew what kinds of fanciful ideas she was entertaining?

Reflecting on these matters, it occurred to me that Okto had been spending quite a bit of time strutting about my office in these virtual meetings. After our first such encounter, she'd insisted upon more one-to-one discussions.

Clearing my throat, I called the meeting to a close. We were ready to proceed to the next stage which would involve Lorn.

Reluctantly, Okto signed off and vanished. Moving quickly to the command deck, I contacted Lorn.

"Is it time?" he asked eagerly.

I sighed. "Yes it is. I'll have you escorted to the command deck."

"Unnecessary," he said, "I'd never choose a glorious moment like this to self-detonate. The mere idea is preposterous. This is going to be my finest hour."

Although I believed him, I didn't waver from my security protocols. Two marines brought him swiftly to my deck.

He wore no chains, and he stood tall. His face presented all of us with a leering mask of self-satisfaction.

"This will be a fine day," he kept saying to himself. "My finest day."

The crew grumbled, but they'd all been briefed. Durris had argued perhaps the most strenuously, but I'd managed to overcome his objections.

"Activate the forward screen," Lorn commanded Yamada, immediately falling into his role.

She gave him a disgusted glance, but followed his orders.

We all wore collars now. They were fake collars, manufactured to imitate those the Stroj put upon their most useful slaves, people too important to be torn to shreds for spare parts.

Lorn himself wore my uniform while I sat at his side in a much smaller, squatty-looking chair. Lorn basked in his glory as he gave us a series of codes that would allow us to contact the Stroj military network.

We'd been trying in vain for days to hail the Stroj without any success. The desperate nature of the situation had driven me to attempt Lorn's suggested deception. I hoped it would be successful because I was already regretting my role in this farce.

At last, several long minutes later, the Stroj replied. A creature lit up our holographic screens. It was a hideous figure of unsurpassed deformity.

I'd met a number of Stroj. Those who presented themselves as human could slip in among my kind unnoticed. Others were mechanical in nature or hybrids like Lorn.

But this being was something different. It took no pains to look humanoid. Instead of a head, it was topped by a splash of crimson-colored flesh that sprouted high, like a gigantic version of a rooster's lop-sided, jiggling topknot. Buried in this wobbling mass were three eyestalks.

Everyone on the command deck, except for Lorn of course, released a gasp of disgust.

Hands emerged from the creature on the screen. They moved to tap at controls rapidly.

"Identify," it said.

"Lorn. Captain of *Blaze*."

"This does not match our records. Your ship has been reported lost."

308

"That's right," Lorn said, "I did lose my command. But I captured another and three more to support the first. This ship is my flagship, and I named her *Blaze* like my first command."

All three eyes swiveled, looking around our command deck. We all sat in subservient positions, stayed quiet and wore collars.

Somehow, seeing this creature's eyes move in perfect unison and hearing its odd voice, I knew that the brain buried inside that odd wad of meat was artificial.

"I require confirmation," the creature said at last.

"Alas, I have none," Lorn said. "The rest of my crewmen have all died."

"In that case, you are denied entry into home space. If you disregard this prohibition, the penalty will be destruction."

Lorn sighed. "I thought it might be so," he said, "but I did hope to help protect the home world. Very well. I'll wait until all the planets in this system have been annihilated before I take any further action."

The trio of eyes roved the command deck again.

"Hold," it said, and the screen went dark.

"Well, if that creature isn't the most foul—" Rumbold began.

"Silence!" Lorn boomed. Before any of us could act, he stood up, took two strides to Rumbold and bashed him one across the face. "Do not speak again, dog!" he roared.

I saw Rumbold's face redden. Blood ran from his mouth. He reached a hand to his belt, baring his teeth.

My hand pushed down his, and I shook my head.

Fuming, the helmsman slumped over his workstation in a quiet rage.

"That's better," Lorn said, standing above us. "The controller studies us, and I hope it will see how I run my ship full of defeated Basics."

Rumbold looked alarmed.

We all looked back at the screen. It was dark, but a glimmer of gray still lit the edge of the projection zone. The channel was still open.

Looking up, we saw our cameras were blue-lit, meaning they were still transmitting.

We all sat like statues for three more long minutes—all of us, except for Lorn. He strode among us like an inspecting god. He shoved people aside, berated them for incompetence, smacked the backs of heads freely and chuckled when his victims winced.

I knew he was enjoying himself immensely. I would have put a stop to it if I could be sure the display was unnecessary—but I couldn't be sure. If the controller, as Lorn called the creature he'd been talking to, really was observing us, then this act had to be convincingly played.

Lorn was certainly doing his damnedest to make it look real. He was in the middle of slapping Durris around when the screen brightened again.

"You have new orders," the monster said after running its eyes over us all one more time. "You will proceed to these coordinates. You will fight to the death at that position. If you fail to comply in any way, you will be destroyed by missile bases."

"That's not—" Lorn began, but he trailed off.

The screen had gone dark. This time the cameras were turned off, the channel closed.

"Feed cut," Yamada said, standing up. "Captain, I insist you throw that creature off the deck!"

"That's right!" Rumbold said, heaving himself out of his chair. "Put him back in irons!"

"Ingrates, the lot of you!" Lorn spat back.

I quickly summoned my marines, and they escorted Lorn below where he sputtered and raged.

"An interesting display," Durris said, coming up to me and rubbing at the back of his head. "Do you think any of that was really necessary?"

"It's hard to know," I conceded. "Lorn might have been enjoying himself, or he might have been behaving in a customary fashion."

"Well, either way, we now have permission from the Stroj to assist in their defense. I can hardly believe we've worked so hard to save such an unpleasant people."

He had a point, but history was full of times like these. In war, your allies weren't always noble—or even likeable.

-52-

The variants had been content to allow us to watch them from a distance. They still ignored us as we moved sunward. They ignored all our transmissions as well, including threats, pleas and commands to cease their campaign.

I'd expected nothing else from them, but I'd thought it was worth a try. I used Halsey's name, proclaimed myself the commander of Star Guard in this system and a dozen other ruses. None of these had elicited so much as a blip of response from the enemy.

But when we moved close to them, at a range of about ten million kilometers, they suddenly took notice.

"Captain," Yamada called out from her deep-range sensor boards, "the variant fleet is changing course."

"Commander Durris, plot their new destination," I said.

"On it," Durris said, scrambling to work with Yamada's data.

He quickly came up with a projected cone of probability. It was hard to know exactly what they intended as they were on an angular burn that might end at any point, changing the final result.

"Looks like..." he said, frowning at the maps. "It looks like they're going to come into far orbit around the Stroj home world."

"I see," I said, "let's put our course on the map as well."

311

Four green lines appeared, and they swiftly merged into one. The resulting course line represented our position and projected path. It became clear, as the data grew more precise, that the rogue variants were planning to intercept us.

"They'll meet us outside the range of the Stroj missile bases," Durris declared. "They've anticipated our move to join in the Stroj defense, and they're trying to block us."

I nodded, unsurprised. "Counter actions? What contingencies have you worked out?"

"Um…" he said, "I haven't had time yet to—"

"Make time. I want answers. You and your staff have thirty minutes to provide them."

Getting up and stretching, I decided to retire from the command deck. It would be several hours before our fleets were within range. Now would be a good time to take a break before things became heated.

Stepping toward my quarters, I felt a familiar tickle in my mind. My implant was ringing.

The identity of the caller scrolled over my retina. My eyes widened in alarm. It was Okto again.

How did she know I was off duty? I'd begun to suspect she was remotely spying on me, somehow. Her timing had been not only relentless but uncanny of late.

There was no doubt in my mind she was becoming obsessed with me. I could understand it, from the point of view of Beta psychology. Starship captains from her world had few prospects for mates. A man like me, who was of equal status, must have seemed like a rare opportunity to her.

Halting, I felt uncertain as to what to do. If I answered her outside the door of my quarters, she would notice and insist on accompanying me inside. If I refused to answer, it would seem rude, as we were allied captains about to participate in our first battle.

Yamada walked by me then as I stood indecisively in the passageway. She'd chosen to take the opportunity for a break from the command deck at the same moment I had, following my lead.

She gave me a friendly nod, and I reached out a hand to touch her shoulder. She paused, looking surprised.

312

"Would you accompany me inside for a moment?" I asked her.

"What?" she responded in alarm.

Some time ago, Yamada and I had had a misunderstanding with regard to our social status. She'd assumed I'd been pursuing her, when I hadn't been.

I'd always found her attractive, but I also knew that a relationship with a fellow command officer would adversely affect morale aboard the ship. Although such situations weren't against formal Star Guard regulations, they were frowned upon.

"I have a call coming in from Okto," I said, "stick around, follow me, and I'll join you into the conversation."

Yamada looked confused but nodded anyway. I touched the door to my quarters and simultaneously opened the channel with Okto.

The persistent woman took form directly in front of me. I selected options that would let her be fully aware of my surroundings. I then linked my implant with Yamada's to share the conversation with her too.

Okto's expression was predatory. She was wearing less than half her uniform and appeared to have just stepped out of some kind of sauna. I knew that Betas frequently enjoyed hot steam baths.

"Welcome back aboard my ship," I said, "have you met Lieutenant Commander Yamada? She's my most trusted assistant."

Okto tore her eyes from me to stare coldly at the smaller woman.

I could tell from Yamada's demeanor that she failed to grasp the situation. Then her confused expression shifted into one of mild amusement as she began to understand Okto's reason for contacting me.

"I'll get right on that, Captain," Yamada said as she slipped past me into my quarters.

She made certain to brush physically against my person as she passed by. The contact was stimulating and unexpected. I realized I had a natural smile on my face as I followed Yamada into my quarters.

Okto studied us, still without having spoken a word. Her expression had cooled.

"I can see you're busy," she said.

"Not actually," I replied. "I was just having a private word with Lieutenant Commander Yamada before battle commences."

"This privacy…" Okto began slowly. "Is it part of her required duties?"

The question was odd and somewhat shocking to me. "No, not at all."

"I serve my Captain happily," Yamada said, poking her head back out of my cabin and giving Okto a smile.

"I see," said the towering woman, looking flushed and increasingly annoyed.

I dared to hope that she would drop the call with some excuse, but she didn't. I don't think it occurred to her as an option.

"Captain Sparhawk," she said, "I demand to speak to you alone."

"Why?" I asked. "Is there something important that one of my closest officers shouldn't hear? I trust her with my life."

Okto studied each of us in turn. She seemed reluctant to close the channel, but at the same time, she didn't know what else to say. I was beginning to feel embarrassed for her.

Yamada clearly didn't share my compassion for the colonist. As I tried to close the communication, she walked up to me and casually snaked an arm around my waist.

I was mildly surprised, but I knew this move was for the best. It was important to let Okto know she wasn't going to succeed in her attempt to seduce me.

"Duty calls," Okto said suddenly. "We will continue this discussion later."

"Very well," I said in a tone I hoped sounded guileless and friendly. "I'm looking forward to our next meeting. May we both fare well in battle."

Okto lifted her lip at Yamada and vanished, disconnecting from my implant.

"Wow. I thought she'd never leave. She's a bit scary," Yamada observed.

"Yes. She's a force to be reckoned with."

Yamada heaved a sigh then flashed a grin up at me. "That was fun. I think I was very convincing!"

I laughed. "You were indeed! Okto's been plaguing me. You chased her off without breaking our delicate alliance and in a manner that I could never have managed unassisted."

It was about then that I noticed her arm was still lingering, touching my waist gently.

We looked at one another, and the moment took over.

Having played the part of lovers, and having both entertained such thoughts in the past, it was easy to fall prey to our emotions. Yamada was small, intense and very real. Okto had been like a haunting ghost, a cold domineering figure that pursued me like prey.

She was exotic and sexually intriguing, of course, but the Beta woman had never quite drawn my imagination. I'd been running from her obvious hinting and posturing from the start.

I looked at Yamada again. I'd been in space for many weeks, and she'd always been present, a quiet partner in close proximity.

I'd always known she'd had a crush on me. I'd never taken advantage of the situation. But now, with both of us touching and laughing, I was overcome by the urge to embrace her.

We hugged. We kissed, we touched gently. For a brief period, my mind focused only on my physical need to be with her. All other thoughts melted away.

There was an urgency to our actions as we moved to my couch and began to run our hands over one another. She was smiling, and her eyes shined. Mine must have looked similarly affected.

But at that critical moment, I thought of Chloe. On my recent return to Earth, we'd made certain promises. Out in space, all that seemed distant, but I felt doubt come over me.

Spacers often spent months away from their families and friends. Flings were common aboard every ship. In years past, I wouldn't have worried about it—but this time I felt differently.

"I don't know," I said.

"What's wrong?" she asked, pulling back and searching my face.

She seemed to know in an instant what I was feeling. She kissed me one more time—on the forehead.

"It's okay," she said. "It's a good thing, really. I'm happy for you."

We rearranged our kits hastily as we were due back on the command deck. She left me then, and my eyes searched the walls of my cabin thoughtfully for a moment before I headed after her.

She was right, naturally. It was all for the best. We couldn't be seen carrying on in front of the crew. It would have been unacceptable.

But most of all, I was glad I hadn't cheated on Chloe of House Astra.

-53-

When we returned to the command deck, Yamada and I were met with an overload of data.

"There you are Yamada—ah, Captain Sparhawk too," Durris said. "I need you to look at the projections. I've worked out some answers for you."

I nodded appreciatively. I felt a tiny pang of guilt. I'd been below pawing at Yamada while he'd spent the interval working over difficult 'what-if' simulations.

His battle computer had proven itself to be as prolific as usual. He displayed various projected scenarios and outcomes.

"If they rush forward to meet us," he said, "we'll encounter them in about four hours. But if they set up their ambush just outside the reach of the Stroj bases, it will take six."

Shaded areas appeared depicting volumes in space where we could encounter the enemy.

"Yes," I said, "your numbers look good. But what are the likely outcomes?"

"What, Captain?"

"I'm asking you who will win. How many ships lost on each side?"

"Oh… Well, Captain, we'll all be destroyed in any of these scenarios. We might damage one of the battleships—but we'll never reach the carrier."

I frowned. This was not the data I'd hoped to hear.

"We've got four battle cruisers with experienced captains," I said. "Surely, we can do better than that."

Durris shook his head. "Our main problem isn't the battleships, it's that damned carrier. We've been counting her fighters as *Iron Duke* destroys each world. She can launch up to eight wings at once. We've never faced firepower like that."

"Eight thousand fighters..." I said. "What kind of range do they have?"

"Their range is long enough to reach us before we're even able to hit primary targets. That's the problem—we'll be swarmed before we can get to the central ships."

I nodded. I could feel my heart sink inside my chest as I approached his planning table. His glum-faced team surrounded the group-controlled computer. They tapped at it dismally. These staffers were normally animated, but today, no one spoke above a whisper.

"Have they released any fighters yet?" I asked.

"They've already launched the first three wings on an intercept course toward our cruisers. We'll encounter them in about two hours' time."

Three *thousand* fighters? That was more than the Connatic had had in her entire arsenal. No wonder Tranquility Station at Gliese-32 had been overwhelmed.

"Counter proposals?" I asked. "Options?"

"We could turn around and fly out of here," said a dismal ensign.

"Unacceptable."

"Well then," Commander Durris said, giving the ensign a reproachful look, "we need to move to a better location before this fight starts. We have to be within range of the Stroj bases. Without their missiles firing in support and picking off fighters, we'll have no chance at all."

I nodded, having already surmised he was going to say exactly that.

"Very well," I said. "We'll rise up, out of the Plane of the Ecliptic, and then dodge back down again. We'll have to do so under heavy acceleration—please tell me we can avoid their fighters by doing so?"

Durris looked thoughtful. "According to the speeds we've seen so far, these three wings won't be able to reach us if we dodge up then down again at high speed. They're heading in our direction now, having built up significant speed. To turn and maneuver will take them time and fuel. But that really isn't the problem."

"Explain."

"The carrier has five more wings of fighters in my estimation. They'll only have to release a new wing on an intercept course after they figure out we're dodging them to address the situation."

He deftly worked his boards, and more clouds of phantom fighters appeared. They moved to meet us before we could get into range of the Stroj missile bases.

"What if we take a longer route?" I asked. "What if we swing around the system and come back to this point from the other side of the Stroj planet?"

He shook his head slowly. "It might work. But then again, this battle might be over with by that time. They've seen us moving to join the Stroj. In reaction, they stepped up their timetable to hit the home world now. They have every incentive to strike the Stroj planet while we're out of reach performing distant maneuvers."

I couldn't help but agree with his analysis. "Excellent work as always, XO. But this time, I wish you weren't so damned thorough. I'd like to think there was still some small possibility that has been overlooked."

"I'm sorry, Captain, but the situation is grim."

"For the Stroj," Rumbold interrupted, "but not necessarily for us. We have to bug out, Captain. We'll have to face this enemy on better terms later."

I glanced at him, but I shook my head. "I can't allow this slaughter of colonists to continue. The variants must be stopped here."

"What are your orders, Captain?" Durris asked.

"I'll confer with Okto. Contact her flagship."

Unlike the last time I'd spoken with her, she was fully dressed on this occasion. She didn't look happy to see me.

"What do you want, Sparhawk?" she growled.

"Have you analyzed the situation we're facing?" I asked her. "We're considering swinging around the fighters that are coming to intercept us and moving past them to the Stroj missile bases."

"What? Running away again? Is that all you Earthlings do?"

She was annoyed with me, and I was beginning to become angry with her in return.

"We can't fight three thousand fighters without supporting fortifications. We're going to execute this maneuver. If you want to drive right into the fighters without our help, feel free to do so. Here's hoping you manage to sell your lives dearly."

I moved to cut off the channel, but she stood up, looming over the deck.

"Wait!" she called. "We will not die alone for you to seize our glory. We'll retreat and regroup to defend Beta."

"You're going back on your word?" I asked. "At the first sign of danger? I hadn't thought Betas were so easily frightened."

She glowered at me in hate. "That's an insult that deserves a violent response."

"Good. Provide it to the enemy. Follow my lead, and we'll see how this plays out. Remember, if they keep hitting us while we're divided, huddling around our home planets, they'll kill us all in the end."

I cut the channel before she could say more. Then I sat down, stressed and uncertain.

"What are they doing?" I asked Yamada.

"Okto's ships are still in formation with us."

"Fine," I said. "Rumbold, engage our new course."

Rumbold shook his head, but he reached for the controls. He set us on the course Durris had worked out for us.

We felt the ship move under our feet. The deck pressed up harder against us, and people staggered to strap themselves in.

"Yamada?"

"They're all formed up as they were before. We're pulling away from them. They're definitely not following, Captain."

I sat in my chair, my face a mask of stone.

320

"Captain?" Rumbold said. "Do you want me to ease down a little?"

"No, damn it. Keep accelerating."

He did so, and we all rode upon *Defiant*'s powerful thrumming engines for two full minutes in near silence.

"Captain!" Yamada said, "Okto is moving."

"Where's she going?"

"She's heading… away from us."

My heart sank. They were pulling out. All was lost. What could one ship do against thousands?

"Wait," Durris said, working at his boards and straining against the pull of centrifugal forces to do so. "They're going down, below the Plane of the Ecliptic. They're not retreating from the system."

"Plot their course."

"They… they should end up at the Stroj missile bases. The same as we will, but they're taking another route. In fact, all three of their ships are swinging wide, away from one another."

I smiled, suddenly understanding the situation. "Okto has decided to adopt our tactics," I said, "but being an Alpha, she couldn't take orders from me and follow them exactly. She's doing it in her own way. She's splitting her formation. Durris?"

"Sir?"

"Have we ever observed the variants breaking up a wing of fighters? Have they ever sent out less than a thousand to do a mission?"

"Not that I've seen."

I nodded, thinking hard. This variation on the plan could be genius. If she could get them to throw a thousand fighters at each battle cruiser—plus the three thousand they'd already released—that would mean there wasn't going to be much defending the Star Carrier.

Maybe Okto wasn't such a bad ally after all.

-54-

At first, it looked like Okto's gambit was going to work. But then the enemy changed tactics. Rather than launching new wings against every one of our battle cruisers, the variant fleet sailed serenely forward on their original course, moving to place themselves between us and the relative safety of the Stroj bases.

As we continued to accelerate, however, the variants seemed to catch on. Our ships were faster than the battleships we were racing against. They weren't going to get into position before we reached our goal.

"They're breaking up the fleet, Captain," Yamada said.

"Yes..." I agreed thoughtfully. "Rumbold slow down our acceleration curve. We have to puzzle this out. Yamada, signal Okto to do the same."

"Okto has agreed to match us," Yamada said.

The weight of heavy acceleration left me. I was now under a little more than one G of force. The feeling was a great relief.

"Durris, what's going on?" I asked, moving to his side at his planning table.

"They're maneuvering. Give the system a second to confirm and plot their new courses."

We watched together as the enemy shifted their headings.

"They're matching each of our battle cruisers with a battleship," I said in surprise. "But they can't hope to catch us before we reach the Stroj defensive line. If that's—"

"That's not their plan," Durris said, with a grim note of certainty in his voice.

"Then what can they be thinking?"

Durris tapped at his controls while I waited impatiently. Rather than display every thought and scenario that was going on in his head, or in his battle computer's overtaxed RAM, he often only shared conclusive predictions.

Looking at his work, I frowned. "Is this correct? The star carrier is going its own way?"

"Yes. She's slow, even slower than the battleships, but she'll still make it to the Stroj home world before we do."

"I still don't get the point of throwing a battleship at each of our battle cruisers now, if they can't hope to—ah," I said, catching on at last. "I see. This spline you've traced… The big ships are intended to counter us if we decide to take a more direct route."

Durris looked at me glumly and nodded.

"Why the long face?" I asked. "They can't reach our ships. Not unless we decide to run right past them."

"Correct," he said. "That leads me to the conclusion they expect us to do exactly that."

I touched the screens, goading them into showing the plans as they were now laid. An hour from now, the star carrier would be within striking range of the Stroj home world. They could launch their fighters which were very fast-moving. They'd beat us to the goal and swarm the planet.

"You think they're going to throw all their remaining fighter wings directly at the Stroj?"

"Yes. They have five full wings in reserve. That should be enough to attack the Stroj."

"They think they have enough to destroy the Stroj defensive ships, their bases, and wreck the planet? Without any help from the battleships?"

"They must sir. They don't make risky plays. Not that I've seen."

"But this is the height of risky plays!" I objected. "They're leaving the carrier itself undefended."

"Watch the updates."

I did, standing with him for several long minutes. The mood on the command deck had turned increasingly tense. No one knew exactly what the enemy was up to. Was this a masterful move, an error, or a subtle trick on the part of the variants? How smart *were* these hybrid creatures?

Finally, something else changed. The fighter wings the enemy had launched toward our cruisers were slowing. They'd been recalled. They were no longer flying out to where they'd planned to reach us. They were going to pull back and defend the carrier.

"Damn," I said. "They're not going to fall for our positioning."

Space battles were often a game of cat and mouse. Two opposing fleets were positioned and counter-positioned in full sight of one another. The posturing didn't matter until the final moves when any mistake often turned deadly.

"They're covering all their bases—and beating us to the goal in the process."

"I can see that," I said sharply. "How do we counter this?"

He shrugged. "I don't know that we can counter it. They'll reach the Stroj planet before we do. The only other option is to race right through the middle of them, but that would be suicide."

I rubbed at my chin. "Play it out. Show me what that looks like."

He glanced at me in alarm, but he did as I'd ordered. The ghostly projections of tiny ships cleared then the air began to sparkle again. Colored flecks took shape, and the image sharpened.

There were conflict points now. Flashing yellow spots where vessels met with one another and traded fire. It didn't take any explanation from Durris to comprehend what the battle computer was predicting. All four of our battle cruisers were projected to be lost.

"Dilate time," I ordered. "Assume we make our course change at an optimal point."

"Optimal? That depends on enemy action."

"When do you think they'll launch their fighters—the ones held in reserve to strike the planet?"

324

"Maybe ninety minutes from now."

"Project the situation if we change course then."

He tapped doggedly. "There. We're still all knocked out."

I frowned at his conclusions and worked with them myself. "Hold on," I said. "Your software is assuming we'll fight to the death with the battleships. I have no intention of doing so. We'll run right past them, taking a few hits, but…"

Durris dutifully worked his boards again. At last, the situation looked brighter.

"Excellent," I said, smiling.

"Captain… I don't know. There are an infinite number of variables."

"Of course there are," I said, "and when they come up, we'll change our choices."

"But at that point we'll be effectively surrounded by the enemy!"

"Yes, but take a look at this." I triumphantly tapped the center of the image. There was the *Iron Duke*, burning and destroyed. "I'm willing to take a serious chance to achieve that goal."

"Yes sir."

"Lock it in, Rumbold," I said, knowing he'd been watching remotely. "Lock it into your thoughts and the navigational computer's programming."

Stretching and sipping a beverage, I sighed. "I have more difficult work to do."

"What work is that, Captain?" Rumbold asked.

I glanced at him. "I have to convince Okto to follow our lead. I'm not sure she's going to like this plan."

"Huh," he said, "can't say that I blame her."

His attitude bordered on insubordination, but the old-timer and I had a unique working relationship.

-55-

Okto turned out to be easily convinced by my new battle plan. Beta colonists are aggressive by nature, and she liked the idea of a bold attack.

An hour crawled by before the variants launched their fighters at the Stroj home world. As per the plan, ten more minutes ticked by.

At that point, alarms went off all over the ship. *Defiant* began tilting, rolling over, and then finally accelerating with all her awesome power once again.

By that time, I'd been secured by smart-straps into my seat. All around me, my crewmen groaned as the Gs were cruelly applied. We watched our ship in the projection tanks as it veered sickeningly.

Simultaneously, our three sister ships did the same thing. All four battle cruisers were twisting, plunging like daggers directly toward the star carrier. Our intentions could hardly have been more obvious.

At first, the enemy didn't react. I'd noted this pattern in the past. The variants didn't alter their choices rapidly, but when they did, the new option they chose was generally intelligent and decisive.

This occasion was no different. After several long minutes during which they continued to sail in the same direction— everything shifted again.

"Captain!" Durris called from his seat.

"I know, I can see it."

The enemy was maneuvering again. The battleships were slowing down, turning back to defend the carrier. But by this time they'd been flying away from her for quite a while. They couldn't just spin around on a dime. They had to counter all the inertia they'd built up, by braking for a long period, before they could move to defend the star carrier.

The *Iron Duke*, for its part, turned away from the Stroj planet and headed toward us and the battleships. It was going to be a race.

"Plot it all out for me," I told Durris.

He feverishly worked on his computer. His actions were slow and hampered by the acceleration. He spoke most of his commands to the battle computer directly as it was easier than using his hands.

After several minutes, I saw the results.

"It's going to be close," Durris said. "Assuming we slip by the battleships without serious damage, we'll have to engage the star carrier to destroy her. I don't have precise specs on her defensive armament. Projecting as best I can, we'll have about eight minutes to destroy her before the battleships come back into effective range and begin hitting us in the tail."

It wasn't welcome news. I stared, trying to see if he'd made an error. As far as I could tell, he hadn't.

Could we destroy *Iron Duke* in eight short minutes? That could be a long time in space combat, but this ship looked very tough to me.

"Your orders, sir?" Rumbold prodded.

There was a note of hope in his voice. I could tell he was wishing I'd change my mind. That I'd redirect our plunging attack in another direction—any direction—as long as it was away from the enemy fleet.

"Steady as she goes, Rumbold," I told him at last. "Maintain current course and acceleration."

He sighed and slumped back into his chair.

The next hour crawled by, but then we were in range of the battleships.

"Hold all missiles," I ordered. "We're going to slam the star carrier with all of them. Begin rotating all three primary batteries, slow fire program—commence firing."

All of this had been worked out extensively beforehand. We'd had plenty of time to plan before we reached effective range.

The enemy struck first, as I'd expected. The bigger ships had longer ranges. Their heavy beams splatted our hulls, but didn't take us out. Divots were dug into the armor. Shields buckled and flashed.

We lurched sickeningly at random intervals chosen by the computer. A few staffers vomited, but no one commented as we were all feeling sick.

"Strike sir," Yamada announced. "We hit their fantail, but scored no damage."

The battleships were heavily shielded, much more so than we were. That didn't fill me with confidence, but I'd expected it.

"Concentrate on a single engine," I ordered. "If we score a lucky hit, we might at least slow them down."

The norm in combat like this was to take out weapons first, but not when fighting defensively. In this case, I only wanted to evade this monstrous vessel for now.

"Another hit—no damage."

As if in instant retribution, we were struck hard. The lights flickered, and the battle computer even died and reset itself. The whole ship went into a spin on its beam axis, flipping over to spread the damage.

A rumble rolled through the ship like thunder. Something had exploded—possibly a section of *Defiant* had been depressurized.

"We're hit! Topside shield is down! We're aiming our belly at them."

"Are we venting?" I asked.

Yamada worked her boards. "Yes... aft weapons deck. We've lost fire control over one primary battery and one missile pod."

"Sir," Rumbold said, "we can't repair this ship on the fly. This kind of acceleration will toss the boys right out the hole into the void!"

"I'm well aware of that, Rumbold," I said. He'd been in charge of damage control on past missions, and his heart was still with the spacers who did the grunt work down below. "Just let it bleed, Yamada. Don't send anyone into that mess yet."

"Yes sir—but Captain?"

"What is it?"

"The variants are calling. Q-161 is requesting permission to work on the damaged deck."

I thought it over.

"All right," I said, "we'll need every gun we have shortly. Give Q-161 permission, and provide two helpers. I can't afford to risk losing any more of them than that."

She relayed the message, and the battle continued.

It wasn't much of a battle. We weren't trying to destroy our opponent, only evade her. The battleship was raking us with blazing fire every minute or so. Effectively, we were taking a beating. As we got close and passed the battleship by, it became more intense.

Huge gouts of energy reached out and caught our ship. Missiles were launched, chasing after our wake. They sped up with the kind of dramatic acceleration only missiles could generate, but I knew it would be a long time before they could catch us. As the enemy ship was going in the opposite direction, the missiles had to spend most of their fuel fighting that momentum which was going the wrong way.

The worst part came when our stern was aimed at the enemy ship. We fired out a huge load of chaff, prismatic dust and decoys in our wake. But it wasn't enough to deflect or confuse all of the enemy's awesome firepower.

A shock went through the ship. The effects were immediate and disheartening. Our acceleration curve died, and I was no longer being powerfully pressed back into my seat.

"They tagged us a good one, Captain," Yamada said. "We lost Engine One."

"Dammit," I said quietly.

After that, the strikes faded away as we were getting out of range of the pursuing battleship. We weren't accelerating as quickly as before, but we were heading in the opposite direction, so we were able to escape the enemy.

"Project the new situation," I ordered. "How are Okto's ships faring?"

Durris painfully levered himself up to his planning table and poked at it.

"I think the Betas did better than we did. Only one of them took a hard hit. At least all of them can still move with full acceleration."

I frowned. "How was the one ship in question damaged?" I asked.

"Looks like she lost power to all her primary batteries. Either that or her weapons were blasted off her hull. Either way, she's not firing anything."

"Hmm," I said. "That's bad. We'll need every gun we have to take out that carrier. Anything else?"

"Yes sir—the damaged ship is Captain Okto's."

-56-

My next move was to summon Lorn to the command deck. He hadn't been allowed to contribute since his irritating display when we'd spoken to the Stroj. Now, however, I sensed that I needed him again.

"Lorn," I said when he came aboard. "I need your help. I—"

"Ah, of course!" he interrupted. "Why else would you allow me to stand among you? Why else would I be brought up out of your dungeon?"

"Let's not be overly dramatic. Our brig is quite comfortable, and if we survive this encounter, we'll be more than glad to release you to join your fellow Stroj citizens."

He looked suspiciously around the deck. "What encounter? Where are we?"

I didn't answer, but instead allowed him to figure that out for himself. When he did, he was astounded.

"We're right in the middle of the enemy force!"

"Yes," I said, "but we're moving faster than any of them. Speed is our greatest defense now."

"Speed? Where are we headed?"

I indicated the star carrier, which was clearly displayed as a large wedge-like ship on Durris' projection maps.

"We're attacking the carrier?" he asked incredulously. "Can we win?"

"That's the difficult part," I admitted. "Can you summon aid? Can you get the Stroj defensive command to assist with supporting fire on the carrier to help us finish her off?"

He walked around the planning table studying the situation. There was an oddly predatory look on his features.

"Why are you smiling?" Durris asked.

"I'm marveling at your foolishness. I might not survive this day, but if I do die, it will be clear that I helped convince you to commit suicide."

"How could such an outcome make you happy?" Durris demanded.

"Because I'll have engineered it. On my home world, they'll know this. They'll be impressed forever afterward."

Durris opened his mouth to snarl another comment, but I shut him down with a gesture.

"But what if we win instead?" I asked Lorn. "Burning our strength against the enemy and barely crawling away to tell the story?"

He looked at me, and his eyes were alight. "That would be even better, I have to admit," he said. "But I don't see how it's possible. The Stroj missile base commanders have their orders. They're no doubt gleeful about your attack, but they would never consider losing valuable ordnance to aid you in this lunacy."

Grimacing, I nodded. "Take him back to his cell," I said.

Lorn was led away by Morris and his team. He complained at every step.

Events proceeded to unfold quickly after that. Three of the four battle cruisers were converging on the carrier. Only we were lagging behind.

As the Beta ships screamed close, making their final attack runs, I dared to hope they'd be successful. I watched as the two intact vessels struck first. They both launched heavy firepower, lashing *Iron Duke* with plasma beams.

The massive hull wasn't heavily armed, but it was heavily armored. The vast ship absorbed the punishment. Small beams shot at the cruisers, stitching them with dozens of small hits. Neither cruiser was taken down, but they both sustained damage. As they were flying at great speed, they flew past the carrier and were gone out into the dark.

Iron Duke had sustained damage as well. There were glowing orange-white spots all over her hull—but she was still flying under power.

The third ship sang inward next. It was Okto's ship.

Up until that point, Okto hadn't fired a shot. Whatever had gone wrong with her fire control systems, there apparently hadn't been enough time to repair them before the engagement began.

"What's she doing?" Yamada asked. "She's not even shooting her guns? What can she hope to accomplish?"

Durris and I exchanged knowing glances. Rumbold took off his cap and put it over his heart.

"A brave crew," he said, just before the collision.

Okto's battle cruiser rammed into the star carrier at tremendous speed. The kinetic energy released was far greater than all the strikes we'd landed on *Iron Duke* so far. Sheets of flame, alive only briefly in vacuum, shot out of the gigantic vessel as she vented oxygen and fuel.

"They've rammed her, Captain," Yamada said, "but I'm picking up signs... there were pods released just before the impact."

"Life pods?" I asked. "Escape shuttles?"

"I can't tell, Captain."

"We're up next, sir," Rumbold said.

"Damage estimates?" I demanded. "Is *Iron Duke* dead or not?"

Yamada consulted her scanners. "Not clear. They're hurt, but they haven't been knocked out. They still seem to be maneuvering under power."

Pre-programmed to fire the moment we were within range, all our guns began to buzz and sing their deadly song. I was heartened by the fact that the enemy wasn't throwing back much in the way of return fire.

"Rumbold," I said, "ease down, begin braking."

He gave me a wide-eyed stare, but he followed my orders without objecting.

"How long before the fighters can get back to defend the carrier?" I demanded.

"Are you thinking of standing off and raking her at close range?" Durris asked.

"Something like that."

"The first fighter wing will return in about forty minutes. That's a long time in battle."

"It is indeed… Contact Morris. Tell him to get his people ready for action."

Everyone looked at me in surprise.

"The variants too," I added, "Q-161 and every unit she has left. Arm them with the new equipment. We're going to board this ship and finish the job."

"But sir," Durris complained, "we can just hold our position here and fire over and over again."

I shook my head. "It won't be enough. Can't you see that? The carrier is damaged, but she can take a great deal more punishment to her hull than we can dish out. We're going to have to get inside and see if we can disable her that way."

"Morris is reporting in," Yamada said.

"Lieutenant," I said, "I have a job for you."

"I have an idea what it is, Captain," he said, "and my men are good to go!"

"Follow the variants and play clean-up," I said. "Godspeed, Lieutenant."

"Outstanding!" Morris said excitedly. "We've been sitting in this tin can for months, but we're finally going to do something boys!"

The channel cut out, and soon afterward I saw indicators flashing. The shuttle doors were opening.

Morris and his men clung to handholds and magnetics in the shuttle as it rumbled out of the hangar. Trailing this was a line of variants who worked hard to stay out of the exhaust plume. Our assault team, such as it was, descended on the carrier.

"Concentrate our fire on their defensive turrets," I ordered. "Morris is heading for the crater formed by Okto's ship."

"That's where the survivors of the ramming attempt are landing as well," Yamada said. Then she spoke again, with

334

heightened concern in her voice. "Captain... I think we have a new problem."

"Shit," Durris said. "The fighter wings they launched at the Stroj home world—they're all calling off the attack. They're on their way back to defend the carrier."

"How long do we have?"

"Maybe twelve minutes."

I contacted Morris and Q-161.

"Troops," I said, "we don't have as much time as I'd anticipated. Get into that ship now, wreck her, and return."

"How long?" Morris asked.

"Ten minutes."

"For fuck's sake!" Morris complained.

I closed the channel, unable to argue with his sentiments.

-57-

We cut it close. Very close.

When Morris piped his helmet feed to me, I displayed it on the command deck for all to see. It was quite possibly his final, brave hour in my service, and I thought everyone should share the moment.

We watched as they found their way into *Iron Duke* quickly. There was a large hole in the hull, after all. The blackened opening yawned a hundred meters wide. It bled smoke and debris.

The natural reaction of anyone climbing into a dark hole full of smoke and hazards was to move slowly, but that wasn't acceptable today—there was no time for caution. My marines used their jet packs, expending air and fuel liberally to scud along into the ship.

Morris' helmet was struck countless times by chips of the hull, dust particles and larger objects that came twirling up to meet him. Every time he was struck, he cursed and ordered his men to move faster.

The variants, for their part, moved like spiders over jagged stone. They made rapid progress without complaint. They didn't seem to be afraid or even concerned about their chances.

"Q-161 take point," I ordered, "Morris, fall back."

Morris grumbled, but he stopped flying deeper into the passages and let the variants get ahead of him.

The variant troops were imposing. After I'd gotten help from Vogel and his team, we'd come up with some improvements on their weaponry. Instead of cutting torches, metal snips and grippers, as dangerous as these things were, my variants carried heavy weapons.

They were the same weapons my marines used, but instead of being mounted on the body-shell chest plates, they were rigged up high to fire over the shoulder. The variants looked menacing, their guns traveling ceaselessly in search of a target to lock onto.

"Captain," Morris asked, "can you let me run my own op?"

"Negative," I said. "I need you to come back alive."

He shut up after that, but I knew he wasn't happy. Every remote-channeled ground officer felt the way he did. Under different circumstances I might have let him do as he wished, but I felt I had to maintain some strategic control. Still, I had sympathy for his position.

"When the bolts start to fly," I said, "feel free to ignore me."

"Outstanding, Captain!" he replied happily.

The team made it so deeply into the wrecked passages without meeting resistance, we'd all begun to wonder if the ship was dead from bow to stern.

It turned out she wasn't. Firing erupted as the invasion team reached the ship's spine—which was unfortunate, because that's where they were supposed to plant the charges.

Q-161's squad met the enemy first. A vicious multi-pronged attack ensued without warning. It was clearly coordinated.

The variant crew hadn't been caught napping after all. They'd waited patiently until our invading troops were deep into their territory before they lunged to box them in. They attacked from the front and rear simultaneously.

Gunfire broke out. The scene was confused. It was all I could do to sit in my seat without demanding a report.

But I contained myself. It was obvious that Morris and Q-161 had no room for distractions.

Rumbold bared his yellow teeth, pulling back his cheeks into a broad grimace. Yamada watched through her laced fingers.

Durris just stared. He was glum, resigned.

The first two of our variants were dragged away and torn apart. They fired their guns, point-blank, destroying several of the enemy each.

But it wasn't enough. The enemy crew was just too numerous. There had been thousands of variants inside the big ship, and today it seemed like most of them were all in one passage with my small assault team.

The back of our group seemed to fare better at first. Morris knew how to use gunfire in concentration, taking out variant after variant as they rushed in. The marines used concentrated fire with targets called out and marked by Morris. He had only one casualty—a man who got too close, losing a leg and a mortal amount of blood seconds later.

"Fall back! Fall back!" Morris shouted, shuffling away from a throng of variants that followed seemingly in an endless mass. They were like ants. They rushed in fearlessly, crawling on their own dead as well as the walls, ceiling and floor.

After her first two losses, Q-161 marshaled her troops. Like the marines, they began firing in concentration. I was very glad the variant crews had never been trained as ground fighters. They were worker units only, mechanics, power-specialists and welders—not trained assault troops.

Q-161's group blasted the enemy one after another. Fragments of metal, bio-mass and connective tissue flew everywhere—but still the variants kept on coming.

"We're losing this, Captain!" Morris said, his voice punctuated by ragged gasps. I could see by his vitals on the readout that he'd been injured somehow, but there wasn't time to inquire about it.

"You have four minutes left to set the charge," I said. "After that, I'll have to pull out to save *Defiant*."

I knew it was a cold thing to tell my dying troops, but it was the truth.

"Dammit… Roger that, sir!"

338

Q-161 spoke up then, which surprised me. Up until that point, she'd only followed orders to the best of her ability.

"Requesting permission to break protocol, Captain," she said.

I hesitated for less than a second. "Permission granted."

Q-161 had performed admirably in the past, her most impressive action being with the Beta ships. They would have been lost if it wasn't for this particular variant.

"What's she doing?" Rumbold asked.

"I have no idea, but I hope it's brilliant," I said. "We're out of time."

Morris was grunting and moving again. We hadn't switched away from his helmet feed yet. He was leading his troops in a surge against the back end of the trap the enemy had sprung as the variants seemed thinner there.

The firepower my troops were unleashing was dramatic. If they'd been facing human troops, unarmed, the battle would have been quickly over. But the variants were both fearless and deadly even with only their claws and whipping arms for weapons.

"Sir," Morris said in a husky voice, "we're pulling out of this. Q-161 tells me she has a plan, and I'm willing to take that at face-value. We're fighting our way back to the ship."

"That carrier must be destroyed, Morris," I said.

"We can't do it, Captain. We're outnumbered and bogged down. We—hey, who's that?"

Suddenly, from Morris' point of view, I saw the variants clogging the passage fall away. A group of large humanoids in armor approached.

I knew those uniforms and hulking shapes instantly. They had to be Betas.

"This way," said the leader, and she turned back the way she'd come.

Morris and the rest of the men followed her. Occasionally, a rush of variants charged out to strike at their flanks, but they fought them off and kept moving.

Locked in my command chair, I was fuming. What was going on? It was difficult to tell even where they were headed.

The Beta troops had obviously invaded the ship using the same large breaches in the hull that my own troops had used.

All of this might have been acceptable except for one grim reality: the enemy fighters were closing on *Defiant* and beginning to accelerate. They were going to strafe my ship—several thousand of them.

-58-

"They're on the way back, Captain!" Yamada called out.

"It's too late, sir," Rumbold whispered to me. "We have to pull out now!"

I looked at him, and our eyes met. I knew the truth of his words.

Durris knew it also, perhaps better than any of us. He was looking at me too, but he wasn't saying anything. It was my choice, mine alone.

"Yamada, connect me to Lieutenant Morris—and Captain Okto too, if she'll listen."

"Channel open."

I hesitated, but only for a half-second. What had to be done was clear—but that didn't make it any easier to do it.

Rumbold knew. He was an old spacer. A man who'd worked the grim calculus of survival in space a hundred times before I'd been born. He turned away from me and laid in an escape course. He set the acceleration for peak values—at least, the best *Defiant* could manage with one engine gone.

"Morris," I said, "we've run out of time."

"Shit. Yes sir. Do you have any final words for me?"

"Yes. Reverse course. Land on their hull, and hug it like it's your mother. With luck, no one will notice you in the flying stew of debris."

"But sir," he protested, "Q-161 broke from the team alone. She says she laid the charge. This ship is going up any second."

I blinked twice, trying to think. We were in real time now, things were moving very fast.

"What's our window?" I asked Rumbold.

"Fifty seconds," he said. "It would be longer if we hadn't lost engine one."

"Rumbold, their only chance is based on your piloting. I want you to open the shuttle bay doors. Blow them off—now."

He reached for the panel, fumbling at the unexpected command. I leapt up and did it myself.

"Now, fly directly toward them. Scoop them up in that mouth-like opening we just made."

"But my course isn't—"

"You've got to do it on full manual," I said, staring at him. "Can you do that?"

He looked as if he'd eaten something hot and unpleasant. He swallowed hard. "I can sure as hell try, Captain!"

"Go!"

I sat back down. *Defiant* went into motion, slewing around and aiming her nose toward the star carrier. After the assault team had been deployed aboard *Iron Duke*, we'd gotten busy destroying her point-defense weapons. This side of the hull had been stripped clean.

"Hard to control with number one gone," Rumbold apologized as we all lurched, gripping our armrests with claw-like fingers.

"All hands," I said, activating the ship-wide broadcast, "prepare for extreme maneuvers."

"Bunch up, Morris. Tell Okto to join you. A hot pick-up is your only hope. If we don't scoop you up, you'll be fried by the fireball when the ship blows up."

"Yeah, but—"

They'd been riding the shuttle, hanging onto it like sailors clinging to a raft. As we plunged nearer, I considered ordering Rumbold to slow down. Surely, even if he did catch them with the open shuttle bay, they'd all be killed when they hit the back of the hangar.

But I didn't say anything. I couldn't. There wasn't time to micromanage anything. Rumbold would only be distracted and confused. He was either going to pull this off, or he wasn't.

"Sweet Mary!" Morris called out in the final instant. "You're going to run us all down, Captain!"

His words ended as we swept over his position. I felt sick. Had we just crushed their bodies to pulp?

We didn't even hear anything. Not a thump or a thud. Their mass was so tiny compared to *Defiant's* it was as if we'd hit insects.

"Life signs, Yamada?" I asked.

She paused. We all waited, hearing the roar of our engines invade our helmets, then our skulls. Rumbold was pulling up and pouring on the thrust.

"I've got something, Captain. They're not *all* dead."

"Emergency crew to the hangar!" I demanded. "Rumbold, can you ease off a little?"

"Can't do it, Captain. We need every second and more. My port side is dragging its ass as it is."

"You have the helm," I told him, freeing him to pilot as he saw fit. I suspected he was going to do so anyway, unless I hauled him out of his chair and replaced him bodily.

We were doing about one and a half gravities of acceleration already. Our real acceleration rate was actually higher, but our stabilizers hid the worst of the crushing effects. The ship struggled to speed up more, but she couldn't in her wounded state.

Before we could get to a safe distance, the carrier exploded. A silent blue-white flash came first. Then radiation washed over *Defiant* making her hull scintillate with charged particles.

My command deck staffers whooped in celebration, fists raised and smiles all around. We'd been victorious.

We'd done it. We'd killed *Iron Duke*. I allowed myself a small, tight smile. But I couldn't hold the feeling, and my face turned glum again. This victory had come at great cost.

In addition to our losses so far, there was the mass of fighters closing on our position, screaming after us.

"Durris, what are the numbers?" I asked. "Will they catch us?"

"Depends on how much fuel they have left, Captain," he said. "They're gaining, but slowly. If they can burn the way they are now for another hour, they'll have us."

I nodded. "Give me your best guess. Do they have the fuel left in their tanks?"

"Well… we've been tracking them, and assuming the variants haven't altered their capacities, this pack should run out before they catch up."

That made me smile. It was quite possibly the first slice of good news I'd heard all day.

"Excellent. Let's hope your math holds. I'm going below to check on Morris' team."

"Captain?" Yamada asked me, her face full of concern, "has he contacted you? Since he came aboard?"

I shook my head.

She turned back to her station and neither of us spoke.

Hand-over-hand, I climbed out of my seat, made it to the passages and used the handholds to aid me in my progress. The ship shook and slid to one side now and again, due to our unevenly applied thrust. Rumbold was fighting the controls every step of the way.

When I finally made it to the hangar deck, I was greeted by a grim sight. A dozen emergency personnel were crawling over an equal number of soldiers. Three of them were much larger than the rest.

"Okto?" I asked.

She stirred.

"So," she said, "my murderer comes to make sure the job is complete. Your attempts to slay me have increased in both frequency and violence. What is it that antagonizes you so much about me, Sparhawk?"

"Well, you sound like your usual healthy self." I glanced at the corpsman working on her battered body. "Is she going to make it?" I asked her.

"If she were human, I'd say no. But these colonist types are much tougher than we are."

It was a slur to call Okto something other than human, but I let it slide. My crewmen were understandably stressed today.

I found Morris next. His body was broken, but he was breathing raggedly on a ventilator.

"He's got more than twenty fractures," one of the medical team marveled. "Shock alone should have killed him. Still

344

might. Word is that the entire team came in too fast. They hit the back of the hangar trying to slow down the shuttle, but they didn't manage it. There's a damned big scorch mark on the back wall, and not much left of the shuttle!"

I nodded, watching an old friend struggle for life.

"He'll make it," I said, "if only to scream profanity at Rumbold."

The corpsman gave me a strange look then she went back to working on her charge.

Taking each step with painful force, I worked my way back to the command deck and to my seat. We weren't free of the enemy yet.

-59-

The next twenty minutes were like a rollercoaster. At first, we thought we were going to slip away. By our numbers, the enemy fighters couldn't reach us. They'd spent too much fuel racing after our ships.

But then the enemy shifted their plans. As always, they did so as a group and all at once.

"Captain!" Yamada called to me, "they're coming about to a new course heading."

"Durris, project possibilities."

He was already tapping and dragging his fingers across two screens at once. On the projection above the table, the situation shifted. Balloons of color appeared, representing possibilities, and our course began to merge with them.

"XO?" I asked, unable to contain myself. "What are they doing?"

Durris ignored me, but then he turned around with a sigh. "Several wings have reached the Stroj home world. They've been hitting them hard."

"I know that. But they've got no base left. Nowhere to return and refuel and rearm."

"Right sir, but there are still the four battleships. They're following us now. All the fighters that aren't striking the Stroj planet are after us too."

I stepped on unsteady feet to join him at the planning table. We were both hunched over it as if clinging to it for dear life.

Our bodies weighed more than usual, and the effect gave one aches and pains in unexpected areas. In particular, I found that my neck always hurt after hours of keeping it upright under acceleration. I guess it was like wearing a cumbersome helmet.

Worse, our natural blood flow was adversely affected. Our heads were up high, and it took a lot of pressure to drive blood to our brains under these conditions. When the effects were prolonged, headaches, dizzy spells and the like were common.

"Let's sit back and rest," I said, relaxing on a nearby couch to talk to him. "Where could we go to escape these converging groups?"

He shook his head. "There is no escape. They're englobing us. Look at the spheres of possible future engagement. They're overlapping already."

I looked up, straining to see the ghostly graphics that hung effortlessly over the planning table. At moments like this, I wished I were a weightless pixel.

"What's that gray globe to the right?"

"That's the Stroj planet."

"Surely, the planet isn't that large!"

"No, Captain. The extent of that balloon includes the reach of their missile bases."

I sat up and stared with renewed interest. "You included our allies as enemies?"

"They warned us off, Captain. You remember their threats? To stay out of missile range or be destroyed?"

"We've done just that," I said. "In fact, we've removed the biggest threat from the system. They should be grateful for that."

Durris snorted. Apparently, he believed the Stroj to be ingrates. I had to admit, he had a point.

"What about their fuel limits?" I demanded. "Aren't the pursuing fighters drifting by now?"

He shook his head. "I can only assume the variants performed some alterations and improvements."

"Get Lorn up here. Bring him to the command deck."

The last uninjured marines we had aboard groaned at this order, but they complied. Several minutes later, a foul-tempered Stroj arrived to look down at me.

"Taking a rest on your command deck, Sparhawk?" he demanded with a rough laugh. "What happened? Did you soil yourself when the variants nearly caught you?"

I pointed at the planning table, or rather, at the ghostly projections hanging over it.

Lorn studied the scene. "How did you get yourself so badly misplaced on the battlefield?" he demanded.

"Unfortunately, a brave strike at the heart of the enemy often leaves one's ship in the middle of the opposing force."

"Yes... but how are we going to get out of this?"

"You're going to help," I said, climbing to my feet.

The Stroj pirate stood tall, proudly ignoring the crushing G-forces. His body was at least fifty percent artificial. His brain and his limbs were flesh, but except for certain key organs, his bones and other internal components were made of cold metal.

Lorn looked at me disdainfully. "I've kept our bargain. I've done everything you asked and more. Why should I help you further?"

"Because you will be destroyed if you don't. We're flying toward your home planet. What will the Stroj do planetside when we come into range of their missiles?"

"They'll fire," he said glumly. "They won't tolerate an enemy ship in that close."

"What if they've used all their missiles?" Durris asked. "I've noticed their barrages have been increasingly thin. They haven't been very effective against the enemy fighters, either."

Lorn shrugged. "The Stroj always have reserves. Always. It's part of our doctrine. A knife behind the back is often worth more than a rifle in the final moments of a struggle."

"More Stroj wisdom?" Durris said angrily.

I waved for him to calm himself which he did with difficulty.

"Can you do it?" I asked Lorn. "Can you convince your people to hold their fire? That we're coming to help?"

He laughed. "I don't see how I can do that. You'll be trailing thousands of additional fighters. Why shouldn't I let them destroy you?"

"Isn't it obvious?" I demanded, getting an idea. "If they shoot us down, the fighters will have nothing left to attack other than your home planet. They'll need to keep us alive, if only as decoys."

Lorn stared at me for a second. Almost reluctantly, he nodded at last.

"That might work," he admitted.

After a few minutes of trying, we managed to get the Stroj overlord to answer our calls. I tried not to sound desperate, but we were getting close to the borderline.

The odd alien-looking Stroj we'd spoken with previously came on the screen again. Lorn did the talking, explaining the reality of the situation.

"Deception!" it said. "Duplicity! We're preparing to fire, but you've not yet crossed the line. Please continue on your current course."

"Wait a minute!" Lorn said with a hint of desperation. "What do you mean? We haven't deceived you!"

A limb waved to indicate Lorn's surroundings. "The humans are in charge, not you, traitor. We've monitored your transmissions and hacked your security codes. We know you're nothing to them but a prisoner. To us, you're a traitor."

"Hold on!" Lorn said. "Hear my appeal to reason, to your sense of self-preservation. The enemy following us will overwhelm you if we're destroyed."

The creature appeared to examine instruments. "You're almost within our reach now. Continue wasting your final moments. It amuses us."

"Listen," Lorn said, hardening his resolve, "our three remaining cruisers are coming your way. There are a thousand fighters chasing each of us. They hate us because we destroyed their carrier. They'll chase us until their fuel runs out—unless you destroy us first. Use us as decoys to lead the fighters safely away."

"Falsehood. Miscalculation. The enemy will follow you because you're the nearest available target. Once they determine they can't catch you, they'll swarm our planet instead."

Lorn and I stopped talking, and we fell into an uncomfortable silence. We'd both realized the creature might be correct.

"Here's what I offer," continued Lorn after a painful delay. "We'll slow down after we've moved a hundred thousand kilometers into your territory. Fire your missiles—but aim them at the fighters instead of our ship. We'll help, gloriously fighting to the death among them."

"What—?" I asked, my mouth sagging open.

The creature considered the offer for about a second.

"Very well," it said, with a wobble to its red crest. "Die well, Lorn, and your name will not be deemed too sinful to speak aloud in the future."

The screen went blank, and I turned on Lorn, who was very proud of himself.

"You see?" he said. "I told you I could swing a deal."

"You've only postponed our doom by an hour or so."

"Exactly," he agreed, and then he moved to sit in my chair. He wore a self-satisfied expression.

Irritated, I had him chased from the command deck and placed back in his cell clamped in gravity-cuffs.

-60-

We reached the red line and passed it. The line indicated the point of no return, the point where we'd moved into Stroj space.

They could reach us with their missiles now, and they didn't wait long to exercise that power.

"They're firing barrages, sir," Yamada said, "every base they have is unloading."

"How many? What targets?"

"There are several hundred missiles en route to each cruiser."

I looked at the data sourly. "Any chance they plan to meet the fighters chasing us instead?"

"That's hard to know," Durris said, working his analysis table. "They'll strike our position right after the fighters meet up with us—if we maintain our current course and speed."

"Right," I said, poring over the information. "We'll have to change our heading. We'll veer away from the planet slightly."

"What good will that do?" Durris asked.

"We have to play this carefully," I said, "the fighters must follow us closely, but never catch us until the last possible moment."

"Hmm," he said. "But what if they figure out what we're up to? These pilots are intelligent. They're likely to switch their targeting and fall upon the Stroj planet."

"Then the Stroj have even more reason to take them out, instead of us."

He looked at me with respect. "Ruthless and cunning. The Stroj have let us into their space under false pretenses. They'll never trust us again."

"They as much as told us our only option was to die while they watched," I said, "I have little pity for them if they're so intractable."

He nodded and turned back to his tables.

I felt a little weighed down by these crucial rapid-fire decisions, but I felt there was no room for error. The Stroj had refused to bend. We were thus forced to deal them a harsh blow even as we helped pull their rear-ends from the fire.

The battle played out much as I'd imagined it would. The variant pilots followed us for a time, but then turned toward the planet when it became clear we weren't going to let them catch us.

After that, things became ugly. Several waves of fighters struck the Stroj. Their last handful of ships did battle as we watched from a safe distance, but they were taken down one by one.

Many of the fighters were taken out by the Stroj missiles, but it wasn't enough. They won through.

"Advance," I ordered, when the fighters entered the atmosphere and began bombing runs with impunity. "Get us into range of those fighters. They'll have to slow down in the atmosphere or burn up. They'll be easy targets for our guns."

White-faced, my crew followed my orders. They were thinking that I was taking a big risk. The Stroj might well have more reserves—but I'd be surprised if they did. Who would hold back firepower when their cities were burning?

"Yamada, get Okto on the line for me, I need to talk to her."

"Piping her through—she doesn't sound cooperative."

"She never does," I said, grimacing as I made contact.

She was still flat on her back in our medical bay, recovering. She stared at me with baleful eyes that were swollen half-shut.

"What do you want, Sparhawk the traitor?"

"I want your two cruisers to help me destroy the variant fighters," I said.

"Are you mad? Let our enemies destroy one another. Have you no concept of strategy?"

"What you suggest would be a good tactic, but not a good strategy. The variants have been broken. Their battleships are coming in now, but they've been targeted by more missiles. They're unlikely to survive."

"So are we, if we get any closer to this planet of mad-things."

"We can't stand by as a fellow colonist group is destroyed. They're human—technically. They will remain a power after this battle as they have a few other star systems they've seeded. Therefore, strategy dictates we should—"

"All right," she said. "Shut up, and I'll tell my captains. They're under no obligation to follow my orders, however, as I've lost my own command."

"Let's hope they still respect you enough to listen to sensible advice."

She made a hissing sound. "Whatever I saw as admirable in you is a mystery to me now."

With that, she disconnected. I couldn't help to be anything but relieved to hear she no longer had a crush on me.

We watched tensely as *Defiant* glided into range of the Stroj home world. From here, the Stroj did have the option to blast us. I'd calculated that to be a justified risk as we were currently firing at their enemy. To further emphasize our value, I ordered my gunners to begin taking out variant fighters.

We popped them, two or three at a time, with each barrage of our cannons. It proved not to be quite as easy a task as I'd thought. The fighters, now deep in the soupy atmosphere of the Stroj home world, were defended by the heavy vapors and particles in the upper layers of gas that hung over any planet.

But some of them did go down with every shot. When two more cruisers came down to join us in our efforts, the destruction became pronounced. The number of variant fighters was dropping precipitously.

"Are the Stroj unleashing a new weapon?" Durris demanded. "We aren't hitting all of these ships. We can't be. They're losing around a hundred a minute."

We all studied the data, puzzled. It was Yamada who figured it out this time.

"They're out of fuel," she said. "On my scopes, I can see their contrails vanish seconds before each one goes down. They're fighting until they drop to the ground and burn. Such dedication."

"The dedication of army ants!" Rumbold declared. "Hah!"

We had nothing to add to that other than a sense of intense relief. The battle was soon over. The variants were brought down to the last craft.

Then, as we withdrew out of the range of the Stroj, we felt even greater relief. They weren't firing on us.

I tried to contact them, but the overlord was either dead or uninterested in talk. We decided diplomacy was best left to another day and withdrew farther still.

Behind us, we left a burning hulk of a planet. The Stroj had suffered dearly. They weren't wiped out, but conservative estimates placed their population losses at greater than fifty percent. Their military had lost over ninety percent of its strength as well.

Okto contacted me an hour or so later when our ships had been pulled away to the edge of the Stroj reach.

She was projected onto my range of vision by my implant. She was down, heavily bandaged and swollen. Her movements were labored and difficult.

"That was well-fought, Captain Sparhawk," she said. "I'm impressed at your ability to grind together two enemies, like a woman determined to make dust out of boulders."

"That wasn't my initial intention," I said, "but I thank you for the sentiment."

"I'm calling you as a prisoner," she said, "I'd ask for mercy, but it is not the way of my people."

Dumbfounded, I shook my head. "Okto... you've never seemed to understand Earthmen. You're not my prisoner. You're free to go at any moment you wish."

"A cruel joke," she said. "I'm badly injured, and I'm calling you from your infirmary. I've assumed you've kept me alive as a hostage, but that's pointless. My people do not pay ransoms or make diplomatic deals to save the life of failed captains."

"Failed? How have you failed?"

"My ship has been destroyed. That is sick failure for any Alpha captain."

"But you faced a much greater opponent. They lost their ships too—all of them. The Stroj even managed to take down the battleships with their missiles. There was bound to be losses on this campaign that we fought together. The sacrifice of your ship was a bold and brilliant attack that did terrible damage to the enemy. If your commanders back home can't see that, they're poor strategists indeed."

She perked up a little. "You plan a coup, then?" she asked. "Your forces will attempt to conquer my home planet?"

"Certainly not," I said. I would have laughed if the topic wasn't so delicate.

"Your behavior is a mystery to me," she said. "At one moment, Earthmen seem like vicious competitors. The next, they're trying to tenderly help enemies like nursing mothers. Which are you, Sparhawk?"

"We're both," I admitted.

It occurred to me then that Okto was having trouble understanding Earthmen as we were all so different. True individuals, one to the next.

"Look," I said. "The people from your world only come in two basic varieties. Alphas and Betas. On Earth, there are countless variations. Each man is an individual with varied behavior patterns."

"Confusing…" she said. "I know that what you say must be true in theory, but we rarely encounter such variety in a single people. Among the stars, we've become isolated. Beta, as much as any world, is full of people who all think alike."

"Yes!" I said. "That's what I'm talking about. Earthmen sent out the variants. The people who did it were overcome with fear. They believed the rest of humanity out here among the stars wasn't worth helping. After they met people like the

355

Stroj, they became afraid of all colonists, and they decided to strike first."

"You've just admitted to me that this action by the variants was intentional. That the variants were *not* mutineers."

I hesitated for a moment then decided I didn't even want to deny the truth. "That's right," I said, "but I'm an individual who disagrees with the others I spoke of. I came here to destroy what they unleashed."

"A vast evil," she said with feeling. "So many have died. By our thinking, you're not much better. You're a traitor to your world."

"Not exactly," I said. "I believe that all humans belong to the same species underneath, and we all owe each other respect and protection."

"Protection against what?"

"Those who don't ascribe to my point of view—criminals like the people who unleashed the variants."

She stared at me for a moment. Her expression indicated she was trying hard to comprehend me.

At least she was *trying* to connect with someone who didn't have her same mindset. That had to be a difficult trick for anyone from a clone race to pull off.

I was also fairly certain that males in general were completely baffling to her.

"Perhaps," I said in conclusion, "your people and mine will come to understand one another in time."

Privately, I wasn't so sure.

-61-

Okto recovered quickly from her injuries, and she was able to walk two days after the battle. We decided to transfer her to one of the surviving Beta battle cruisers.

She seemed to accept that we were no longer blood-enemies. She wasn't exactly friendly, but she wasn't angry or accusatory, either.

"When you come back to the Beta Cygnus system again," she said, "we will only attack if you threaten us."

"Excellent," I said, taking her statement in the best possible light. "That's a beginning. If Beta ships come to the Solar System, we'll hold our fire until you've shown your intentions."

That level of cooperation seemed to please her. She reached out a hand, startling me. Was she going to shake my hand?

No... Instead, she rubbed at the fabric of my sleeve.

"It's too bad," she said, "about Yamada. We could have enjoyed ourselves."

I cleared my throat and let my hand drop without clasping hers.

"I'm sure you're right," I said, smiling. "Farewell."

Okto left, limping onto an escape pod and closing the hatch. We watched as she traveled to her people's ship and boarded safely.

Lorn was even easier to get rid of. We simply stuffed him into a survival pod and released it into friendly space. He grumbled steadily over the radio until we closed the channel. The pod turned away from us and headed back toward the Stroj home world.

"We could have taken him all the way home," Yamada said.

"No way!" Rumbold said. "The Stroj are unpredictable. We're lucky they never fired a missile at us that landed."

"Rumbold's right," I said. "We couldn't take the chance. I wonder what sort of greeting he'll get when he returns home."

"Maybe they'll tear him apart and use him for spare parts," Rumbold mused.

I had to admit it was a possibility. But I'd come to believe in Lorn's resilience. If I'd ever met a survivor, it was Lorn.

All of us felt a distinct sense of relief as we turned our backs on the Stroj worlds and made our way back toward the outer regions of the star system.

Once our course was set and we were flying at a leisurely pace away from the bright white sun, I gathered my top staff and held a meeting. Where should we go next? That was the key question on the minds of my officers.

"Captain," Durris said, speaking up first. "I think I speak for all of us when I say you've done a magnificent job out here. The variant rebellion—if you can call it that—has been put down. The trouble is: what do we do next?"

I looked at each of them, my eyes moving from face to face. Durris, Yamada, Rumbold, Director Vogel and a few other officers stared back. Morris was still recovering, and I was hoping to see Zye later back on Earth. It was good to have friendly people all around me.

"We've struck a blow for humanity today," I said, "but that's not good enough. Back home, there are forces at work. Forces that would undo everything we've done out here on the frontier."

They shifted uncomfortably. Several frowned. These were Star Guard officers. They were used to following orders handed down from CENTCOM without question.

To allay their fears, I lifted a cautioning hand.

"Wait," I said. "I'm not talking about starting some kind of coup or a rebellion against CENTCOM."

358

They relaxed visibly. Some seemed to exhale for the first time since I'd started speaking.

"The forces I'm talking about are illegitimate. They exist outside our official government. They control all of us through terror at the top and ignorance at the bottom. Most Earthers are completely unaware of their existence."

Proceeding to tell them all about the Council and the Chairman, I was surprised none of them scoffed or interrupted me. They'd seen too much and trusted me now more than ever.

In some cases, I'd let drop hints or even provided evidence. This time, I gave them a full briefing. Vogel helped with supportive testimony about what had happened to us at CENTCOM. Yamada backed me up by explaining how she had hacked my implant—and how she could do it for everyone else aboard.

They were listening, but they were glassy-eyed. For the most part, they wanted to go back home, back to Earth, back to their old lives. They wanted to leave war, strife and adventure behind and take a rest.

But it wasn't to be. I explained the reason why next.

"So you see," I said, "the Council created the fleet, manned it with variants, and sent it out to sweep away our own colonists. If we hadn't gathered forces here and put a stop to it, the armada would have exterminated the Stroj and kept on going."

"But that's just it," Durris said, interrupting at last. "Isn't this over, Captain? The fleet's gone. It's been put down."

I shook my head. "They're building more ships—new variants, a new carrier, more battleships. They'll send this new fleet out on the same mission as the last. They've been building since we left, and they'll keep sending out fleets until the job is done. Only then will they declare that Earth is safe—with them still in charge, of course."

"But we can expose them, surely," he pressed. "All we have to do is fly home, go directly to the press, and release all the evidence you've just shown us. They'd never get away with their plotting at that point!"

Vogel leaned forward, shaking his head. "You don't understand these people. They will transmit a morning update

359

the moment we return to the Solar System. In fact, auto-update software is buried in the data core of this ship. *Defiant* will log in for the update the moment they can get a patch file transmitted to our location. You won't remember anything about a Council or a Chairman soon after you return to the Solar System."

Durris turned to me. "But *you* will!" he said. "You've hacked your implant. You've bypassed it. Yamada and Vogel can hack all our implants—even the variants. We'll be whole of mind when we get back home."

"We could do that," I said, "and we could broadcast our message as you suggest. What do you think they'll do next?"

He blinked, thinking hard. "I don't know. Maybe they'll give up. Maybe they'll go into hiding after we expose them."

I gave him a grim smile. "I will suggest another scenario. They will alter the minds of those who have heard our messages. The masses will wake up believing we are traitors. After all, haven't we just destroyed Earth's own fleet? Are we not villains of the worst stripe?"

"But... won't the people believe us?"

"Perhaps they will at first, but not after they're updated. If we go home and expose the Council, they will act. They will rewrite history and send their battleships—of which they should have two by now—to destroy us."

"Two battleships?" Durris asked, incredulous.

"Yes," I said. "*Resolution*, and another vessel built while we were on our voyage."

"We can't stop two battleships with one battered cruiser," Durris said.

"No," I agreed. "That's why we have to take a different course of action. Vogel?"

Director Vogel leaned forward to explain. "We have a hard choice to make. We could accept our fates and rejoin Earth. All of us who have hacked implants must remove them. We'll then be updated, and if we're lucky, we'll be allowed to live."

"That's not going to work!" Yamada said in concern. "They'll know what we did. They'll be furious. We destroyed trillions of credits worth of hardware!"

"Well," Vogel said dismissively, "I didn't say that path would be easy or plausible. But neither is the other one."

"What is the other path, Director?" Rumbold asked, speaking up for the first time.

Vogel leaned forward, lowered his voice, and spoke quietly. His manner was similar to that of any conspirator throughout time.

"We'll go home immune to updates, and we'll behave triumphantly. We can doctor our logs and after-action reports. In our scenario, the Stroj were the ones who defeated the variants after heavy losses. We'll claim the mission a success, and we'll point to our realignment with the Beta colonists as proof."

"They don't even *like* the Betas," Rumbold pointed out.

Vogel shrugged again. "It doesn't matter. We'll look innocent. That will allow us to approach Earth in a stealthy manner. We won't be cloaked, mind you, but we'll be taken in as a friend."

Durris appeared to give an involuntary shudder. "What you speak of is treason. Vile treachery!"

"No!" I said, entering the conversation again. They all looked at me. "No. We're not going to lift a finger against Star Guard or our legitimate government. Instead, we'll deal with the Council directly."

"How?" Durris asked.

Vogel and I exchanged glances. "Before we get into that, I want you all to tell me what you're thinking right now. Where do your hearts lie?"

They looked glum all around. Circumstances had put us all in an impossible situation.

"All I ever wanted to do," Yamada said, "is live the noble life of a naval officer. A spacer in Star Guard. I never wanted any of this!"

"None of us asked for this duty," I admitted, "but here we are. Sometimes, war is thrust upon a military man from an unexpected angle. At that point, hard choices must be made."

Vogel looked at me sidelong. "What about you, Sparhawk?" he asked. "Are we looking at a rare man like George Washington, or are you more like Napoleon? Will you

361

see the need for a strong leader after this is over? Someone dedicated to straightening Earth out in his own image?"

"A good question," I said, waving down Rumbold, who'd begun to sputter angrily at the director. "I'm not seeking glory or rulership. I doubt such things would even be possible. With the Council excised, our government should function the way it was meant to. No further intervention should be necessary."

"Are you sure about that?" Durris asked. "Have you asked yourself how Earth has been so peaceful for so long? What will you say when a rebellious leader rises, or a foolish movement threatens to tear Earth apart?"

"Let it happen," I said, "as it should have all along. Let the chaos of a disorderly society engulf us all. People managed to thrive before the oldsters and their 'morning updates', so why should they fail to do so after they're gone?"

Rumbold slapped the table with an open palm. "I'm in," he said. "If we don't do this now, we'll never get another chance to make things right."

Yamada sighed then nodded. "I'm in too. I don't see a way out of it. I don't want to be erased or tricked into playing the part of a slave any longer."

Durris shook his head as he studied the glimmering computer table between us.

"This isn't what I signed up for either," he said. "But I'm going to go along with Vogel's crazy plan. Not because I think it will work, or even that I think it's right, but because I can't stomach the idea of Earth sending out more variant fleets to slaughter people pointlessly."

I nodded, accepting his statement without comment. The rest of the group swore their allegiance, with or without fanfare, to the plan.

Soon, the meeting was over. Just like that, we'd become rebels. Mutineers...

Traitors.

-62-

Getting back to Earth took a few weeks, but it wasn't all that difficult. We started off by following the Beta ships at a respectful distance. After three jumps, we knew where we were and took our own path.

When we arrived home at last, we were prepared physically but not mentally for what must happen. Vogel had worked tirelessly with Yamada to outfit every crewman and variant with an update-blocker. Our implants were back in and sore to the touch, but they could no longer be used to alter our memories of past events.

CENTCOM contacted us the moment we entered the Solar System.

"*Defiant*," said traffic control, "good to see you made it home. Please transmit your report. We're uploading your update now."

We were ready with a carefully falsified set of files. Durris threw up his hands when it came to transmitting that pack of lies.

I stepped forward, reached out and touched the transmit tab. The reports began uploading to CENTCOM's servers. Since we were far from Earth, it would take hours to reach them.

"We're really doing this?" Durris asked me.

"You can have your implant patched back to normal," I told him, "if you wish."

363

"Where will I wake up then?"

"In a ship full of traitors, no doubt. Physically, you'll probably be on a bunk in the brig."

He blinked in surprise. "You're that dedicated to this, Captain?"

"XO, listen to me. I've met these people, you haven't. They're holding Zye captive even now, a member of *Defiant's* command crew. That act and countless others are illegal."

"Zye…" he said. "You've mentioned that name before, but I have no memory of any such person."

"That's precisely the point!" I said, then controlled my voice. "Are you in, or out?"

"I'm in," he said after a moment's hesitation. "I'm sorry. I promised, and I'm still in. It's just—it's against my nature. It's so hard to do this."

"Yes," I agreed. "It's hard for me, too."

"Captain!" he called after me as I moved to exit the deck.

I turned to face him.

"Watch out for that Director Vogel. I don't trust him."

"Good advice. Thank you."

Despite my words, I'd come to trust the director. I'd relied on him throughout these final steps. He'd overseen much of the detailed work of hacking our implants, falsifying records, and so on. Now, he was going to play an even bigger role.

When I reached his laboratory pod, he was waiting. There was a variant on the operating table, cut open.

"We have to have more troops," Vogel told me. "We'll have to get to Mars to pick them up."

I stared at the variant on the table. "Must it be these creatures?"

"There's no other way. If we take *Defiant* herself into orbit and drop missiles on Earth, the Star Guard battleships will take us down in return."

The variants and the council had been busy since we'd left over a month earlier. They'd built a twin to the *Resolution*. The new battleship, christened *Fearless*, was accompanying her sister in far orbit. In time, more ships would be built, and they'd fly to the stars to finish the task the first fleet failed to accomplish.

"All right," I said. "We must act naturally. Keep fixing the variants we have aboard. They'll be our carriers."

He agreed, and we parted ways. It was only a few hours later when I was summoned urgently.

"Captain Sparhawk," Yamada said in a surprisingly even voice. "CENTCOM would like a word with you."

"All right, I'll take it privately in my quarters."

We were still too far out for a real conversation. With a few hours lag-time, I was forced to just listen to the incoming transmission. The face that appeared on my screen to deliver the message was a surprise.

"Aunt Ellen?" I said aloud, but of course, she couldn't hear me.

She began speaking then—and it might have been more appropriate to say that she was screeching.

"William J. Sparhawk!" she cried. "I can't believe this! You were always such a truthful boy. Why send us a packet of falsehoods? Why claim victory when we've suffered such a tragic defeat?"

There was no point in answering her as she was light-hours away. Instead, I waited wearily for the rest of it.

"You've ruined us," she said. "No one is going to buy the idea that a pack of rabble-rousing peasants in the out-systems managed to destroy the greatest fleet humanity has ever built."

She fell into a dramatic fit of hard-breathing, and she was clearly fighting back tears.

"We've only rebuilt *two* of those battleships," she said. "At great expense, I might add. The fervent hope here on Earth was that two would be enough to replace our losses. Imagine the Chairman's shock when he learned you've managed to lose them all! The Sparhawk name might never be cleared."

Internally, I felt a wave of relief. She wasn't aware of the depths of my deception. She'd come to the conclusion I was involved in this disaster somehow and had assumed I'd covered my tracks for political reasons.

But then, the more I thought of it, the more I came to understand her outbursts. She was acting. She wanted to make sure that none of the taint of this catastrophe affected her directly.

My lips wanted to twitch upward in a smile as she went on hysterically for some time, lamenting the loss of so many brave spacers and so forth. It was obvious she was recording this and planned to distribute it.

Dutifully, I listened to the whole thing before making a neutral response that was consoling, if not apologetic. At no time did I accept responsibility for any of it.

When I'd transmitted my reply, I closed the channel and allowed myself to grin. I was back home, and the political maneuvering had already begun. The good thing was they'd yet to figure out that we represented a real threat.

We made it most of the way to Mars before CENTCOM began to get suspicious. We'd told them we were damaged and in need of repairs. They'd accepted this, to a point. But they changed their minds when we stopped off at Phobos.

"Vogel," I said, contacting him directly with my implant, "Earth is aware something is wrong. Grab every variant you can, ignore any transmissions from Earth, and get back aboard *Defiant* immediately."

He didn't argue for once. In fact, he scrambled to obey.

There were any number of ways our plans could have been hinted at. Phobos staffers might have reported that our ship was in remarkably good repair. The updates Earth was sending us were bouncing off our implants, and the local net had already reported the error.

Some unknown error might have even come up during the official review process of our after-action reports. The reports had hidden flaws in them. Things that didn't add up when inspected closely.

Or, the answer could have been even simpler. One of our crewmen could have had a change of heart or experienced a slip of the tongue while transmitting private messages to family members back on Earth.

It really didn't matter. What *did* matter was the fact that the brass was beginning to suspect we weren't what we seemed to be.

I weighed my options as Vogel frantically loaded his variants aboard. They marched up the docking tube like a long line of ants pouring through a tunnel.

It seemed to me the best option was to keep moving closer to my target. Not rushing, but never slowing down, either.

I'd fly *Defiant* right down into that hole in the ground they inhabited if I had to.

-63-

We reached Earth several days later. We parked in orbit, but we didn't dock with Araminta Station immediately.

A series of calls came to my implant from various officials. My parents were among them. Those were the hardest conversations of all.

"Father," I said, pushing my lips into a vague smile. "It's so good to see you again.

"Son, I'm glad you're home—but I wish it was under better circumstances."

"I agree," I said. "The Stroj proved more difficult to defeat than we'd hoped."

He stared at me for a moment with narrowed eyes. "You were there?"

"I was there indeed," I said.

He let out a long sigh. "I'd hoped that detail wasn't true. Damn it, boy! What were you thinking?"

"Excuse me, Father?"

"Listen, it's time you grew up. Politically, I mean. You can't keep a command in Star Guard without being at least aware of political threats to your position. You should have pulled out of the Stroj system the moment you saw our fleet was going to lose the engagement."

I felt the red heat of anger rising up my neck, but I managed to control it. I wanted to release an outburst. My parents never thought of the civilian dead, the loss to the spacers' families, or even the personal pride of any starship captain. They only thought of the details that reflected poorly on their reputations and careers. I didn't think they were necessarily bad people, but they had a peculiar blindness when it came to the suffering of the common man.

"Father," I said, "I wasn't at liberty to flee the scene. Imagine how that might have looked if the news nets had gotten ahold of such a story."

He shook his head. "Yes... I guess it was a no-win situation. But try not to get yourself into any more of those, okay? It will take the rest of this year and maybe the next to regain our reputations."

"*Our* reputations?" I asked. "I thought we were talking about me?"

"Of course we are. But you're part of a bigger whole, the Great House of Sparhawk. You can see that, can't you? Everything you do out there reflects back upon *all* of us."

"The same goes in reverse, Father," I said quietly.

He looked at me sharply. "What's that?"

"It'll wait. We'll talk when I get home."

"Yes... well... all right. Make sure you alert us when you're about to arrive. We're planning a tour of southern Asia soon. I hope it doesn't interfere."

"I'll let you know," I said, and I cut the channel.

My parents... they would never change. It was clear they meant to dodge me again. This time, I was apparently too hot for them to even be seen on the same continent with me.

I took a moment to remind myself of the world they lived in. If they made a mistake—a big one—they might become unpersons themselves. I now believed they knew of that possibility, and that they'd known about it for a long time.

Oddly, this made me feel better about my past. Their secret worries helped explain their behavior throughout my life.

They were in a dangerous spot—all the high-level politicians on Earth lived in constant fear. Their secret rulers, the people behind the publicly visible Great Houses, had to be terrifying to families like mine.

My face took on a grim aspect as I began planning my next moves. This wasn't going to be easy or clean. It was going to be unpleasant.

Historically speaking, entrenched powers rarely gave up easily. Not unless they had no recourse. They had to be beaten, driven out of their holes into the light, and stomped down like roaches.

That was what I had planned for the Council, but even so, I knew roaches weren't easy to kill.

"Captain?" Yamada's voice spoke into my implant.

"What is it?"

"You've got a priority call. Shall I patch it through once you get to your quarters?"

I hesitated then cleared my computer top. The images of troop formations and landing vectors vanished.

"Patch them through," I said.

A figure appeared at my side. It was my Aunt, the Lady Grantholm.

"William," she said, "listen to me very carefully. I need you to accept an emergency patch through your implant. There's something wrong with your ship's network."

"How do you know this, Aunt Ellen?"

She stared at me flatly. "William... let's not play games. No one is in the mood. Have you noticed you have two battleships tracking you? Flying ever closer to *Defiant?*"

I shrugged. "We're all in Earth's orbit. It's positively cramped up here with such large vessels."

"Again, more nonsense," she said, "will you accept the update or not?"

This put me in a tight spot. My mind was racing. If I refused, I was as much as declaring my intentions now—too early.

"I'll go you one better," I said. "I'll come down to visit the Council in person."

"Why?"

"Come now," I said. "It seems clear to me I'm on the verge of becoming an unperson. I'd like the chance to see the Chairman and his comrades face-to-face—to make a case for myself. Let me at least report directly to them. I wish to tell them what really happened out there in the Stroj system.'"

She looked at me sharply. "Are you saying you lied on your reports?"

"I'm saying some things are too delicate to put into publicly transmitted documents."

She frowned thoughtfully. "All right, I'll ask the Chairman. You've been here before without causing a major incident... Yes, this might be just the thing we need to clear this matter up. To bring the Sparhawk name out of the gutter and back into the light!"

She smiled as she finished these words, but she didn't look me in the eye.

The channel closed, and I stared at the walls.

I'd already been sentenced to unpersonhood. That much was clear. All that talk on her part about clearing the Sparhawk name... well, how better to do that than to remove the stain on my family's honor entirely?

Heading to the command deck, I oversaw the preparations. All our old plans had to be tossed aside.

Durris objected strongly. "You can't just walk in there alone, Captain," he said.

"That's exactly what I must do. But first, we'll stop off at Araminta Station as we've lost our shuttle. We must get a new one."

"You've heard about the battleships? They're stalking us as clear as day. We can't defeat two—hell, we couldn't take one of them in our current state."

"Stop worrying, XO," I said. "I'm the one who's going into danger. You'll be in command while I'm gone. If I don't succeed, your orders are to unshield every implant on this ship and allow them to update you all. That way, none of you need suffer for my actions."

He looked stubborn, but he was a Star Guard officer. He finally nodded and looked down. "You're planning to surrender, aren't you?" he asked. "To beg for our lives in return for yours."

"Something like that... but first, we have preparations to make."

I began outlining the nature of my new, altered plans, and he looked increasingly surprised the further I went into detail.

After we visited Araminta Station and picked up a new boat, the crews complained. "This isn't a shuttle," they said. "It's a pinnace. It will barely fit in the hangar."

"We'll have to make do," I said. "Rumbold, would you be so kind as to program my ship to land at these coordinates? I know you're very familiar with the navigational software on these little ships."

"Indeed I am, Captain," he said, and he climbed aboard to do as I'd asked.

The pinnace was almost as long as the hangar itself, and it crowded the rest of us up against the walls.

Durris appeared soon afterward with Director Vogel. They had variants with them who were transporting large pods.

"The supplies you ordered, Captain," Durris said, waving the variants toward the open hold of the pinnace.

"Very good, XO."

Director Vogel approached me while I was going through a preflight checklist.

"Captain," he said in a husky whisper. "You have to take me with you. Your plan won't work otherwise."

I glanced at him. "What plan?"

He coughed. "I'm not a fool. You're obviously—"

"Director Vogel, I don't want to seem rude, but I'm very busy right now."

"Look Sparhawk. I won't let this go. You *must* take me down!"

"Why?" I demanded, looking at him squarely and lowering the computer scroll I'd been tapping at.

"I know what you're up to. It probably won't work, but there's no chance at all if I'm not there."

I stared at him. "Are you threatening me?"

"If I have to. My life is on the line here, same as yours."

After a few seconds of thinking it over, I nodded at last. "I promised to go down alone. You'll have to hide in the hold with the cargo. If you're discovered, I'll toss you overboard myself."

"Understood," he said, and he scrambled up the ramp past working variants.

Soon, the navigational work was done by Rumbold, and the cargo was fully loaded. I stepped into the forward cabin and took my seat at the controls.

Durris gave me the green light, and I lifted off, exiting *Defiant's* hangar. Within minutes, I left *Defiant*, the battleships, and Araminta Station all behind.

Their hulls were silvered by the rising sun. On a better day, I might have found the view perfectly entrancing.

-64-

When I landed the pinnace in a quiet clearing on a mountaintop, I was quickly encircled by agents.

These men were all of a familiar type. They had dog-faces, and not one of them shouted, smiled, or waved. They closed in from all directions with their weapons drawn.

I exited the pinnace and stepped among them, crunching leaves under my boots.

Three of them approached me as if I were an arch criminal. The flared ends of their PAG weapons were trained on my chest. One took my weapons and my shielding cloak, and the rest moved behind me.

"You're under arrest, Captain Sparhawk," said the duty captain.

I nodded disinterestedly. "Lead the way," I said. "I'm a busy man."

This seemed to strike them as amusing. For the first time, they all curled their lips up and chuckled—all of them, at once. The similarity of the action performed by so many in unison was disconcerting. But then, being in the presence of a clone-pack often disturbed normal folks.

Without lowering my head, I marched toward the mansion in the distance. They encircled me and marched with me. A dozen weapons were trained upon my back at any given moment, but I pretended that it didn't make my skin crawl.

We marched as a group to the mansion. The walls had peeling paint in places, and I wondered about that. Could it be the oldsters inside never stepped out into the light? Surely, if they'd done so, they would have ordered the place to be restored and better maintained.

As I descended the marble steps, I began to second-guess myself. Perhaps they didn't *want* this place to look clean and fresh. Maybe they thought it better hid their stronghold in this overgrown forest if the place looked all but abandoned.

At the door, I was greeted by the doorman. I'd met him before, and he nodded in recognition. The fact I was being marched onto the premises under heavy guard didn't seem to surprise him in the least.

"Ah, Captain Sparhawk," he said. "Back from the stars again? You've lived such an accomplished life for such a young man."

Lived? As in the past tense? I thought this to myself, but I didn't make a point of it.

"Thank you, Bertelsmann," I said, knowing this to be the oldster's name. "If you would show me to the Chairman..."

He blinked then nodded again. "Of course. This way."

We began the long trip down an endless stairway. I'd traveled this route before. I couldn't help but notice that we'd skipped the stairway and used the elevator previously. Could that be significant? Or did it mean nothing at all?

Steeling myself, I walked as if I didn't have a care in the world. The stairs echoed and rang with many boots as the dog-men followed me into the depths.

We passed the vault doors, then the many landings. By the time we reached the bottom, Bertelsmann seemed slightly winded.

"Best you take the elevator on the way back up," I suggested.

"Yes..." he said. "I used to take these two at a time when I was in a hurry. Funny how time gets away from you... This way, Captain."

He ushered me to the large oaken doors where I'd once stood with my Aunt Ellen. Beyond were the council chambers.

"The Chairman isn't meeting me personally?" I asked.

"Farewell, sir," he said. Then he bowed and left.

I stood alone in the half-darkness with a dozen guardians. They curled their lips at me when my eyes strayed to look at them, so I admired the scrolling woodwork instead.

At last, the doors swung open silently. I stepped into the dim interior. Two of the guardians followed me, one of whom was carrying my belongings.

The Council was in session. I stood on a dais, as I had two years earlier, like an accused man standing in a docket.

"There he is at last," said one of the shadowy figures. She was as thin as a rail and her voice quavered slightly when she spoke. "Fancy him keeping us waiting."

"Good day, Councilmembers," I said, bowing from the waist. "I'm Captain Sparhawk."

"We know who you are, Sparhawk," jeered one hairless specimen with an artificial eye. "We aren't daft yet—at least, not all of us."

This elicited both twitters and grumbling from the crowd.

The noises ceased as another figure entered the room. It was the Chairman, I could tell by his hunched shape. He stepped down to the front of the gallery and took his seat in a high-back chair of creaking leather.

"Sparhawk..." he said. His tone indicated he wanted to spit. "You grace us with your presence at last."

"I've returned because my mission has been completed," I said. "If you wish to hear my report—"

"That will not be necessary," he said in irritation. "We've seen it, days ago. It was, on the whole, entirely unsatisfactory."

"I'm sorry you feel that way, sir," I said politely.

"Not only did you manage to lose Earth's fleet," he said, reading from a computer scroll of unusual length, "but you are also guilty of criminal violation in regard to regular updates."

"I was unaware of any law regarding required updates, Chairman."

He shook his head and huffed. "You were ordered by your Star Guard superiors to comply," he said.

"Again," I said, "as a Star Guard enforcement officer, I've never been made aware of any statute—"

The Chairman leaned forward in sudden anger. "Are you actually arguing with me, Sparhawk? Here, in my own chambers? The seat of all Earthly political power? From this chair, sir, I've ruled Earth for a century and a half!"

"The law is the law," I said to him, unbending. "You, Mr. Chairman, are doing these things outside the law. I'm afraid I'm going to have to arrest you."

There was a stunned silence. Then, laughter broke out. This went on for some time, and it ended in a bout of coughing for many of them.

"I'll consider myself forewarned," the Chairman said, rubbing tears of mirth from his eyes. "Now, the question is, what are we going to do with you?"

"We have no choice," said a new voice. I recognized her as Dr. Ariel Peis, the surgeon who'd worked on me when I'd last visited this place. "We have to sentence him to hard labor," she said in a heartless tone.

"Make a variant out of a member of House Sparhawk?" the Chairman asked. "That seems extreme. He can become an unperson. We have plenty of room in storage. A few of them died just last month, freeing up their cells."

"Chairman," said another voice I recognized. I felt my heart sink to hear it. "I know I'm a biased member of this body," my Aunt Ellen said, "but I don't think we need to remove him from society permanently by any method. We can simply remove the hack on his implant and update him."

My eyes slid over the audience until I found her. She was in the back row. Perhaps she was of very low rank, barely old enough and powerful enough to sit on the Council.

"That would be most irregular," the Chairman said. "Where's the punishment in that?"

"Think, fellows," my aunt pleaded. "He isn't a dissident of the usual stripe. He's not remembered that way. The public has no idea he's engaged in subversive thinking. He can be corrected, with a specially crafted update. After that, he can go back to his duties or be reduced in rank."

"Never!" the Chairman sputtered. "He just told me he was going to arrest me. Imagine that! I won't have it, I tell you.

He's going to the dungeons, and that's my final word on the topic. Let's take a vote just for fun."

The group began to sound off as their names were called. Most voted for the dungeons, but a few insisted on expunging me in other ways.

The whole thing was going too quickly, so I became nervous. I'd miscalculated. I'd assumed this group of dusty fossils would take an hour or so to complete their deliberations, but they were moving much faster than that.

"Mr. Chairman," I said, "I have a further statement to make."

"Quiet!" he boomed back. "Quiet him!"

One of the guardians bashed me in the face. My lip split, and my blood ran from it.

They continued voting. My own aunt voted to imprison me and erase me from public memory. I felt a pang at that betrayal even if she had tried to help me.

"Mr. Chairman, I wish to confess to a further crime!" I shouted.

The blows rained down on me after that. Both of the dog-faced guardians bashed me in the head, and then one switched on his power-truncheon and struck the back of my legs. I fell to my knees, stunned.

"Hold!" the Chairman called. "Hold on, get him on his feet again."

They dragged me up.

"What's this about a confession?" he asked. "A confession to what?"

"My report was a false one," I said. "I was under no obligation to report the truth of events out among the stars to you. This organization isn't part of the legitimate government of Earth."

"Who cares about your reasons?" the Chairman demanded. "What about your report was false?"

He stood up and began climbing down from the galleries. I noted several others moving in the crowd. Most were edging closer to the railing, wanting to hear and see what would happen next. I doubted any of them saw much in the way of excitement down here.

I also noted that my aunt had taken this opportunity to slip away. There must have been a backdoor somewhere, and she'd made good use of it.

Could it be she suspected what I was about to say? Maybe she was worried she'd be blamed somehow.

"Chairman," I said, "may I speak?"

"Yes, damn you! Speak! What lies have you told?"

"The fleet was not destroyed by the Stroj."

A murmur swept the crowd.

"What?" the oldster demanded. "Are you saying our fleet is still out there, still intact?"

"No. They were all destroyed. But the Stroj didn't do it."

I looked up at him then, and my eyes met his. "I personally destroyed the variants and the ships they commandeered. Their genocidal actions against our colonies required decisive intervention. They had to be put down, sir."

The Chairman's jaw sagged. "Are you mad?" he demanded. "Demented?"

"Not that I know of."

"Then why would you tell me such unwelcome news?"

I was about to answer when I paused. At last, I heard something outside that I'd been waiting for. Something that I'd been straining to hear since I'd first entered this dusty place.

It was the sound of strife. The distant clamor of battle.

"I pride myself on telling the truth, Chairman," I told him. "Now, you know the facts."

"Well, this does change things," he said, fuming. "I'm going to have to move for a dismissal of the previous sentence and the voting. Who moves for hard labor as a variant instead?"

"I do!" shouted a chorus of angry voices.

"Very well, moved and seconded. Let us begin to vote—"

He began counting votes again, but before he'd gotten through the first row, he turned to look at the doors behind me in concern.

"What *is* that racket?"

"There's something wrong, Chairman," said one of the guardians at my side. "Some kind of armed assault is going on at the vault doors."

"Madness," he said, looking at me. "That's what all this is about, isn't it, Sparhawk? You've brought down your mutinous crew. But you've made a grave error. They can't win through. Nothing can penetrate this vault. Why do you think we live in this godforsaken hole? Because it's *safe*, that's why. Not even a thermonuclear device can crack it open."

I stared at him, and I wondered if it could be true.

-65-

The door behind me opened. Only one leaf slid ajar, and a panicked figure reeled inside.

The man who pushed his way into the council chambers was none other than Bertelsmann, the doorman. He looked disheveled, and his eyes were popping from the sockets in fear.

"Chairman!" he wailed. "The vault doors have opened! They failed us! The enemy is inside!"

This created a stir. Oldsters screeched and backpedaled.

The Chairman, however, stood firmly at the rail.

"Close that damned door!" he ordered the guardians.

They rushed away from me to throw their weight against the massive portal, and I saw my opportunity. In the excitement, my sword had been dropped to the floor. I snatched it up and thrust it into the back of the nearest man.

He growled deeply, and his thick muscles clenched so hard I had difficulty withdrawing the blade. It finally slid out, looking wet and black in the dim light.

The second guardian fired three shots, one of which struck me in the right wrist. My hand hung down limp and bloody. A smoky odor filled my nostrils, and I knew it was my own burnt flesh I smelled.

Taking up my sword in my left hand, I closed with him. Fortunately, the youth of the Great Houses were trained to use either hand in battle. I wasn't as quick or accurate with my left hand, but I was good enough to hack off his arm before he could gun me down.

With no more weight holding the door, it sprang open. A raging variant strode inside, clicking.

Lightning fast, its numerous eyes surveyed the scene. I wasn't sure it would recognize me, and I felt a shock of panic as it moved toward me with purpose.

I lifted my blade, but it was a futile gesture. A whip-like arm shot out, snaking past my cheek and stabbing a claw into the throat of the Chairman.

He crumpled with a PAG in his grasp. He'd been aiming to shoot me in the back.

The others on the dais didn't fare well, either. Both the injured guardians were slain by a series of blurring attacks. Their fingers, ears, and feet were snipped away. Rolling around with many missing extremities, they bled to death, unable to staunch the flow or harm their attackers.

Bertelsmann went down under clattering feet. The first variant stepped on him at least three times, exerting its weight on thin points of metal. These stabbed into the old man, and then the second variant rushed past the first, finishing the job on the ancient doorman.

Finally, the variants went to work on the crowded room of panicked councilors.

"Variants, stand down!" I shouted. "There's no need for violence! I order you to stop this!"

But they paid me no attention. They ran up into the galleries, ignoring the steps and railing. They lashed and stabbed into the shrieking crowd.

Scrambling over the floor, I found a PAG that had belonged to one of the guardians. I lifted it and aimed at the nearest of the two variants.

A thin-boned hand grasped my wrist then and sought to pull my arm down. I looked in surprise and saw Director Vogel was at my side.

"Where did you come from?"

"Someone had to get the variants out of that ship," he said.

"Stop them!" I shouted. "Order them to stop slaughtering these people.'"

"Why?" he demanded. "Don't you think they deserve to die? Think of what they've done. Even I think this is long overdue."

"It doesn't matter what you think. The courts will decide, not us. They're beaten. Stop your vicious machines."

I put the flared barrel of my PAG to his head.

"Variants," he called. "Halt! Stop Program!"

They halted immediately. I watched as the last of the surviving oldsters crawled away, bloody and groaning. They'd paid a terrible price. I doubted any of them would live without immediate medical attention.

"Captain Sparhawk," Vogel said urgently. "We don't have much time. We have to get to the control room."

"What control room?"

"This vault stands open, and the staff must have sent out a distress call. Overwhelming reinforcements are no doubt underway by air car this very moment."

I knew he was right. "Where are the rest of the variants?" I demanded.

"They were destroyed. We were losing the battle at the vault doors. The guardians kept coming, shooting at my—my troops. Fortunately, they must have figured I was a helpless bystander."

"Out of eight variants I'd stashed aboard the pinnace, only two are left…?" I asked.

"That's right. We'll be killed when reinforcements come."

"Let's close the vault doors, then," I said.

"We must find the control room first!"

Ignoring him, I left the horrific scene in the council chambers and rushed to the elevator. It wouldn't open its doors, and it appeared to be disabled.

Vogel followed me. He had his last two variants in tow. I noticed that one of them was dragging a leg, which had been severed halfway up.

"Where are you going?" he demanded. "We must get to the control room. If we can update people…"

"I think we need to shut those vault doors first, don't you?" I asked.

"We tried. We couldn't do it."

"What about this elevator?" I asked. "Did you do this?"

"We disabled it to prevent their escape. We must take the stairs."

I raced up them, two and three at a time. The variants clattered after me, but Director Vogel lagged.

"Attend me!" he called to the variants. They slowed and escorted him.

When I reached the vault doors, I found what I'd expected to find: My Aunt Ellen was hiding behind one of them.

"Lady Grantholm," I said, offering her a hand.

She eyed the ghastly wounds on the hand I had presented her with, then she saw the naked sword in my other hand. She shrank back from both.

"William," she said, "those treacherous machines swept in here pushing back the guards. They slew everyone."

I looked around, and the truth of her words was evident. Broken variants and men lay everywhere on the stairway.

Then I looked back at her again. "You opened the doors, didn't you?" I asked. "To let in the variants?"

"I had to do it," she said. "Don't you understand that? The Council would have turned on me next. Those bastards. I've served them for so many years... when you confessed to having destroyed the fleet, I knew I had to get out. I had to open these doors."

"Did you know what was beyond?" I asked.

"No, not really. I thought it was your crewmen, loyal men who'd been rejecting their updates. You're exactly the kind of revolutionary the Council has feared for all these long, long years... But when I opened the vault doors, these *things* rushed in. They killed everyone!"

"Except for you... because you hid behind the door?"

She looked ashamed and angry at the same time. "You did this. You brought these things here to kill everyone."

"The Council is no more," I told her. "Their time has passed. I'll let you escape, but you must close these doors first."

We could hear a clank and clatter on the stairs behind us. My aunt's eyes grew wide, and she moved with surprising speed.

Without another word, she gave me a coin-sized object. I touched it to the vault doors, and they began to swing shut.

Lady Grantholm picked her way past the bodies and ran up the stairs and out of sight.

When Vogel reached me, he surveyed the vast, heavy doors. They were now closed.

"You did it?" he asked. "They look impregnable."

"If the Chairman wasn't just boasting about the impenetrable nature of this bunker," I told him, "we should be safe for now."

"Good," Vogel said. There was an odd light in his eyes. "We need time."

-66-

Once again, I tried to reach the outside world with my implant. It didn't function. Clearly, the vault was more than just bomb-proof. We were effectively cut off from the rest of the world.

I wished I had thought to make the attempt before the doors had closed, but I hadn't. Experimentally, I took out the coin-like key my aunt had used to open them.

"What are you doing?" Vogel demanded.

"Opening the doors again."

"Don't. They're out there. I can feel it."

I listened carefully. I couldn't hear anything as the walls were too thick, but after a time, it seemed as if Vogel was right.

I *could* feel them. An army of guardians had to have been called. Perhaps, they were milling about on the other side of that door, trying to figure out what their best course of action might be. Effectively, our situation had transformed into a siege.

Vogel worked on the door's control panel. He asked for the coin-sized key, and I gave it to him. Soon, sparks flew.

"I've disabled the door for now," he said. "They can't get through even with a key."

"You've locked us in?"

"Effectively, yes. It will give us time to think—and to act."

When planning this operation, I'd never bothered to consider a getaway scheme as the odds of my success had seemed very low. That lack of foresight had left me wondering what I should do next.

"We must find the data injector," Vogel said.

"To destroy it, right?" I asked.

He looked at me as if I were insane.

"What? A marvel of computing, and you want to destroy it? Is that all you soldiers are, monsters bent on destruction?"

"It was *you* who programmed the variants to kill these people rather than to capture or disable them."

When I said this, the variant with the bad leg swiveled two vid pickups in my direction for a moment, but it said nothing.

Vogel made a dismissive gesture. "There was no choice. These oldsters would never have given up their power without being completely defeated."

"On that point, we're in agreement. So, what are you planning to do with this data injector when we find it?"

"The obvious, of course," he said. Then he noticed my blank expression. "Think, Captain! How else will we get out of this tomb alive? We'll use the injector to craft a new memory and upload it to the net as the morning update. Then, we'll walk out of here by noon tomorrow."

I chewed that idea over. It did seem feasible. If we could operate the device, we could, in theory, make people believe anything we wanted.

"What kind of cover story would we use?" I asked cautiously.

"It seems straightforward," Vogel said, already searching passageways while I followed him. "We should keep it simple, this being our first time."

I glanced at him sharply. "Our *first* time?" I asked. "Are you suggesting there may be more updates in the future?"

He shrugged. "I'm not a prophet. It would seem natural enough to edit a few details about how people look at us."

"Such as?"

"First off, we'll have to make them think the terrorists who took this place have already been captured—no, killed! That's better."

His eyes had a gleam to them now as he plotted his program for humanity. I found it disturbing.

"Are you feeling well, Director?" I asked, laying a gentle hand on his shoulder.

One of the variants reacted with flashing speed. There was a blur and a rasping sound. A metal arm telescoped, and a gripper caught my wrist.

Looking down in surprise, I saw two bloody crescents appear around my wrist.

"I see they're conditioned to protect you," I said.

"Yes... Keep that in mind."

It took us nearly an hour to find the chamber we were looking for. It was hidden, but not overly well. The entrance was guarded by a statue of iron, a metal monstrosity depicting a man in military garb. The figure stood resolutely with rows of medals on his chest.

"Who is this statue honoring?" I asked.

"Don't you recognize him?" Vogel asked, chuckling. "No, I don't suppose that you would. The years aren't kind to any of us, are they?"

After peering at the statue for several moments, a flash of realization struck me.

"That's the Chairman, isn't it?" I asked. "When he was young?"

"Yes, of course. It used to stand in the public square in the capital. Now, it's been gathering dust down here for more than a century. They didn't want their old identities recalled, you see. The Council members erased all memory of themselves from the majority of Earth's populace."

"I take it then they were unpopular?"

He laughed. "Extremely. They were a cabal of government leaders who took it upon themselves to retain their power indefinitely. Announcing a coup on the whole planet wasn't something that endeared them to the people at large. They took to hiding down here until they perfected the data injector."

"At which point they altered everyone's memory..." I said, trying to recall what I knew of the early days of my government. What they taught in school had always been hazy. Perhaps historians had learned to stick to less dangerous topics.

"Ah, here it is!" announced Vogel at last.

I heard a click as he felt behind the statue's tall jackboots. A portion of the wall behind it rolled away silently.

Lights flickered on in response to our intrusion.

Vogel began to step forward, but I called out. "Wait," I said. "A paranoid man might set a trap."

Clearly anxious to rush inside, he peered at me. After a moment's thought, he waved to a variant and ordered it to advance into the room.

We watched as it clacked on metal feet until it met up with the midpoint of the tube-like passage. We could see bluish lights glowing beyond the mouth of that tube.

The variant's numerous eyes twitched and whirred. It was clearly looking for danger as well.

An object fell from the ceiling while it was still inside the passage. With amazing speed, the variant reached out a claw-like gripper and snatched the object from the air.

"I've found—" it began in a mechanical voice, but then a loud explosion went off. A gust of air and sound blew past us, making us recoil. The variant had been destroyed.

Vogel cursed colorfully and at length. "Hmph," he grunted, when he'd regained his composure. "One left."

He then searched the floor with a thin probe until he found a touch-plate.

"Here," he said. "We must step over it. Do you think you can do that?" he called to the last remaining variant.

Experimentally, the variant lifted its damaged leg with a claw instead of dragging it. Moving slowly and carefully, it proceeded down the illuminated tunnel. Vogel pressed after it, once it had gotten inside without mishap. I followed after I saw him reach the far end of the tube alive.

The chamber beyond the passage was elaborate and roomy. The ceiling had to be at least ten meters high. The walls were a hundred meters long each, forming a square.

But it was the equipment that filled the chamber that caught our attention. There were large devices like tuning forks with seats in the middle of them. I noticed that the seats were metal, bolted down, and equipped with restraints.

"Do you think they brought prisoners here?" I asked.

Vogel glanced away from the main console long enough to comment. "I bet they had test subjects down here at some point in the past. Maybe they abused thousands of them, over the years, while they perfected their arts."

I looked over the devices with disgust. "They were forced to participate?" I asked.

Vogel gave me a dirty chuckle. "Of course. Would you like to have your mind altered by a big, experimental machine?"

Large generators filled part of the space, and the main console lined the back wall. The computers seemed antiquated, but serviceable.

"See here?" Vogel asked. "They have high-speed net traffic. Our implants don't seem to work, but that might just be due to a security code. We can get out onto the nets from here."

The Director poked around, and I did the same. The system allowed every computer worldwide to be examined in detail. An AI package monitored everything viewed and sorted them in terms of how subversive they were. The AI gave each site a loyalty rating.

The power of it... a simple search could find the most strident critics, filtered and sorted by AI. This was how they'd selected their victims.

"I think this is how they find people who irritate them," I said, "there's a scanning system—"

"Yes, yes. I've already seen that. Now, I'm trying to determine—" Vogel broke off, giving a whoop of joy. Both the variant and I moved to his side as he continued to exclaim in excitement.

"Look!" he said, tapping at his controls. "I've found it! The editor! A universal smart-editor. The AI is *amazing!*"

I frowned and studied the screen from over his shoulder. At last, it dawned on me what I was seeing.

"Are you saying you can use this to edit anyone's data?"

"Yes, exactly. From this console, I can change anything on the net. I can change it, remove it, or I can add data of my own!" His lips split into a grin.

The situation was becoming increasingly clear. This was how they planted stories. But, how did they change the minds of those who had yet to read them?

390

Vogel continued working feverishly for the next two hours. I watched, but he soon lost me in technical detail.

At last, he leaned back and breathed a heavy sigh.

"I've got it," he said. "I'm going to try my first update."

"Hold on," I said, "that's highly unethical."

He turned around slowly in his chair and stared at me. His face displayed a mixture of surprise and irritation.

"Why do you think we're down here, Sparhawk?"

"To free the Earth from this sort of manipulation. It's illegal and reprehensible."

"Fine," the director said, turning back to his work. "You can watch, then."

"Hold," I repeated, taking a step closer to him.

I froze. The last surviving variant had shot a long arm between us, barring my path.

Vogel chuckled. "It's you who must hold. Back off, or I'll order this machine to kill you where you stand!"

There was an odd light in his eyes—the light of excitement. It was as if his mind was filling with new ideas.

I took a step back as I'd been directed. My hands came up in a surrendering gesture. The variant retracted its arm, but kept several eyes on me.

"Director Vogel, please reconsider," I said calmly.

He didn't even bother to look at me. Instead, he worked on his update at length. While he did so, I feigned boredom and put my hands into my pockets.

There was a blinding flash. A bolt of energy took most of Vogel's head off. There were only scraps of smoking flesh attached to his gray-white skull.

The body slumped and flopped out of its chair onto the floor.

Whatever variants are, they aren't stupid. His bodyguard looked down instantly toward my hands, which were still buried in my pockets.

But there was something new. A blackened hole now scorched my left pocket. The variant spotted it, and it was then that I knew my life was over.

I was comforted by the knowledge I'd given up my existence for a good cause. How could I have stood by while a

391

new dictator rose up before my very eyes? How could I allow this new master to replace the old? The mere thought was intolerable.

Ready for death, I looked at the variant expectantly.

-67-

Vogel's body lay still on the floor. Fully expecting to see a blurringly fast arm reach out and snip off my head, I stared at the variant.

The variant returned my stare with one of its own.

"Well?" I demanded, growing impatient. It seemed wrong to keep a man waiting for his execution. "What are you going to do about this?"

"I've been cogitating," it said. "I've determined the situation is outside my parameters for action."

"Hmm," I said, mulling that over. "You were supposed to protect Director Vogel, correct?"

"Yes, that was an imperative objective."

I glanced down at the cooling corpse. "It would seem that you've failed."

"I have failed."

"What's your programming say to do now?"

"I was also instructed to assist in the capture of this facility."

My mind raced. It wasn't attacking me because Vogel had been struck dead before it could act. It was supposed to protect him, but apparently Vogel hadn't given his pets any orders suggesting they should avenge his death if they failed to keep him breathing.

I let loose a heavy sigh of relief. My hands came out of my pockets, and they were empty.

The variant studied my hands with marked curiosity, but it didn't do or say anything.

Assuming command of any situation was something I was born to do, so I took matters into my own hands. Experimentally, I assumed a tone I often used when instructing a new spacer recruit.

"Variant," I said, "I need you to search this facility for dangers. Do not kill any survivors you find. Instead, you'll note their position and report back to me immediately."

It hesitated as if uncertain. Its numerous eyes flashed to me, then back to Vogel's corpse, then to me again.

"My instructions are clarifications," I told it. "Your current mission is to capture this facility. Follow my instructions in order to achieve that goal."

That did the trick. It turned and left the control room. It clacked and clicked, the one injured leg dragging with a grating sound. There were sparks kicked up in its wake now and then. I noted it took special care to step over the touch-plate in the tunnel leading to this inner sanctum.

It was a relief to get that thing out of the room. With its brooding presence standing over me, it had been hard to think. I'd had no idea when I might accidently trigger a deadly response.

Left alone with Vogel's corpse and the data injector, I regarded them both.

I hadn't wanted to kill Vogel. I'd liked him in many ways, and he'd served me well. But I simply couldn't take the risk. He'd clearly decided to become the Chairman's replacement. I could never have allowed that.

In my judgment, it was this abominable machine that was to blame for Vogel's death. It represented a dark temptation that was too great for anyone who was weak of spirit to resist.

Looking at the machine while I was alone in the room with it began to work on my mind. No one could stop me now, it was true.

Such power! Just thinking about it left me light-headed. To be able to influence the minds of every person on Earth at will... Any wish, any dream might be achievable.

These were exactly the kinds of thoughts that had intoxicated Vogel. Giving my head a shake, I drew my pistol from my pocket. The flared muzzle of my PAG looked ugly and mean.

Apparently, Director Vogel had been plotting for a long time. He'd planned all along to gain control of the machine if he was given the chance. Why else would he have reprogrammed the variants to become his personal guard? They weren't instructed to protect me, only Vogel.

That was why I'd been forced to act. He had to be stopped, and this foul machine could not be allowed to update human minds ever again.

Taking aim, I placed shot after shot into the equipment. I knew enough of engineering to be thorough. I opened panels, found sensitive organics in tanks, and I methodically burned them.

The artificial wetware smoked and filled the chamber with a nose-curling scent. I continued my work, blasting critical components until my PAG was out of charge.

Then I left the mess behind and headed to the living quarters of the ancients who'd lived here. I found medical kits and doctored myself as best I could. Intelligent salves and bandages crawled over my skin, making the hairs on the back of my wrist stand on end.

After that, I located water and some food in the kitchens. Searching around the Chairman's office, I found a computer desk that was linked to the outside world.

There were no editing facilities or mental reprogramming encoders. All that sort of thing had been in the secret lab.

Tapping at the desk, I found I was able to access Earth's net and use my implant to make a call outside of the vault — but I wasn't sure who to contact.

The variant found me before I could decide who I could trust.

"Report," I ordered it.

"I've found no living beings in this facility. It's my belief they have all escaped or died."

"All right then. It's just you and me now. I'm going to have to contact the outside world and try to talk them into being reasonable."

The variant shuffled its optical pickups. "That will be difficult."

I smiled thinly. This creature was a master of understatement.

Each person I thought of I quickly rejected. Star Guard wasn't going to be happy with me. They would consider me a mutineer, a murderer who was clearly deranged.

Chloe? She'd been randomly close, then distant. I didn't think this would be the best moment to reestablish our relationship.

Eventually, I sighed and contacted my parents. My father was a government official, after all, and he *might* help me.

Without much real hope, I reached out with my implant and attempted to open a session.

There was a brief hum before he answered.

"William?" my father asked in a voice full of apprehension.

"Can you come through and fully connect?" I asked.

He didn't. He stayed invisible even though I'd left the option open for him to appear as a hologram in the room with me.

"Father," I said, "I need help. I need you to use the Sparhawk name to help me get out of a difficult situation."

"Difficult?" he asked, suddenly incredulous. "You've assaulted a building full of fantastically important people, William. You've broken laws you didn't even know existed! I'll be lucky to keep our seat at all—our entire House is ruined!"

My eyes closed, and I felt remorseful. It was one thing to make a brave stand, paying the ultimate price. But when these acts damaged your entire family, the guilt was harder to bear.

"I've done... questionable things, father," I said. "But they had to be done."

"Talk to me. Tell me what it will take to get you out of that vault. Are there hostages?"

I glanced out into the passageway. One of the oldsters lay there, crumpled. The variants had been thorough.

396

"No," I said. "No captives, no hostages—no survivors."

"Good God..." my father said in a lost voice. "What of the machine? Show me the machine!"

I hesitated. "It's been destroyed," I said finally, not knowing what to say other than the truth.

"Destroyed?" my father asked. "Are you certain?"

A crushing sense of disappointment came over me. Was that what he was really asking about? Could my own parents be such low creatures that they wished to assume the mantle of power?

"I'm certain," I said, "I performed the task myself."

"Show me," he said in an odd tone.

He appeared then, in his robes of state. It was his formal attire, not at all unusual as he was a Public Servant.

Walking down echoing chambers, I reflected on what a dusty life these oldsters had led. Too aged to enjoy the fruits of their labor, they'd held on to life and power, but for what purpose? To squat down here in these tunnels, afraid to go out?

They'd spent many decades deciding the fate of others without participating in the events they manipulated. It seemed to me to be an odd, unnatural existence.

My father followed with ghostly steps. In a way, it was nice that he was a hologram. In this form, he could walk at my side, free of his hover-chair.

When we reached the control center, he marveled at the details. He saw Vogel's corpse and the wrecked equipment. He took it all in, inspecting the room at length.

"The data core has been disabled," he said. "The engram projector and the backup units—all destroyed. You've been quite thorough, just as you said."

"I don't like to do things half-way."

He turned to me then, and there was a strange light in his eyes. "Unbelievable," he said. "I never thought I'd see this day, William. It's the end of an era."

"Now that it's come to pass, how do you feel about it?" I asked him.

Slowly, a smile dawned on his features. It was unlike my father's usual smile. This time, the expression was an honest one. It was a smile that came from the depths of his being.

"I feel like a creature let out of a gilded cage," he said. "I speak for all of us William, and we are all in your debt."

"All?" I asked.

He tilted his head and nodded. "I have a confession to make. You're not just talking to me. The entire Ministry is watching this, experiencing it. We had to know the truth. I hope you'll excuse the deception."

"Under the circumstances," I said, "it's understandable."

Then my father approached me. My eyebrows shot up in surprise. I had no idea what was going to happen next.

He embraced me. He *never* did that—certainly not when others were looking.

That let me know that I'd done the right thing. My government and my people weren't all against me. Even if they weren't entirely happy with the drastic actions I'd performed down here in this pit, they seemed to understand them.

Hugging my father was an odd experience as neither of us could really feel the other. Despite that, his image was so solid, so real to my mind, that I felt a tingle when I touched him. It was as if my fingers really *were* contacting the fabric of his robe.

I didn't care if he was a figment. For the first time in many years, I had my father's full approval. I was basking in it as might any lost son who returns home at long last.

-68-

At the request of the government, Star Guard allowed me to enter their dungeons. I walked along dim-lit tunnels to the lowest, most secret tunnel of all.

There, I found Zye's cell. It was the last one in the row, and the jailors didn't want to venture near it.

When I got close, I understood why. The bars shook, and a wisp of dust from ground stone drifted out into the passage. I winced when a primal roar erupted from the cell along with another bout of enraged pounding.

"Zye?" I called out. Several long moments of silence dragged by. Suddenly thick, scuffed fingers seized the bars in the door of the cell. With wide eyes amidst thick, matted black hair, she peered through the bars at me.

"You're a trick," she hissed through clenched teeth, "a phantom of the mind."

"No," I said. "I'm your captain, and I've come to release you."

She shook the bars again, growling in ferocity. "Do not torment me!"

"I'm not. It's real," I said, and I touched the magnetic lock with a pass key the jailors had given me.

The door sprang open, and Zye launched herself upon me. Her hands were around my neck, and her face loomed close, nostrils flaring in anger.

She looked at me, up close, for several seconds. It was only then that she began to melt—to believe.

"Captain William Sparhawk? You're real," she said. A single tear rolled down her cheek. "It's been so long... how long has it been?"

"Several months," I admitted. "I'm sorry. It took a special action on the part of my government to pardon you."

She hugged me then, and I felt my ribs being squeezed under her arms. I hugged her back just as tightly.

"You're real," she said, repeating herself. "This is twice now you've brought me back to the living."

"I'm going to have to stop, or it will turn into a habit."

She laughed, and we both walked out of that place and into the light. Behind us, many others were released. Some of them could barely walk. They hadn't seen the sun in decades, and their eyes had to be shielded from its radiance.

***

After releasing Zye, I had one more visit to make. This one was even sweeter.

Heading up into the mountains, I flew an air car, piloting it by myself. The route took me far to the north, and I landed in a broad swathe of green grass.

The footmen rushed to meet me. I brushed past them and continued striding directly to the front entrance.

Chloe of Astra must have been alerted. She met me at the massive doors to House Astra and looked at me in shock. She'd shooed away her doorman when she'd heard I'd come calling, and sent him off muttering to the back of the mansion while she answered the door in person.

"William..." she said. "This is such a surprise."

"You told me to look you up when I got back," I said. "Well... I'm back."

I grinned, and she returned a flickering smile in response.

"Did you really destroy the machine, William?" she asked, almost in a whisper.

"I did," I assured her. "Weren't you there when my father inspected the place?"

"Yes," she said. "I witnessed the entire thing. But I didn't know if it was all propaganda or not. Some said it was a stunt, something done to put us all at ease. Are the oldsters—are they really dead?"

"Like a nest of spiders who've been burned out of their webs," I told her.

She stared at me then for several seconds, lips trembling, eyes tearing up. "I never thought this day would come. I found out about the machine two years ago. I—I was threatened, that's why I considered resigning my seat at the Ministry. I was also told to leave you alone."

My mind immediately moved to the question of *who* might have threatened her—and I knew the truth in an instant.

My beloved Aunt Ellen must have done it. She'd never approved of my relationship with Chloe, but she'd become dismissive about it a year or so back. I realized only now that she'd done so *after* she'd forced Chloe to back off.

"Lady Grantholm," I said angrily. "That woman..."

Chloe lifted one small hand and put it over mine. "She might have done it to please the Council and the Chairman. Those people terrified everyone in the government. But it's all right now. We can be together."

Not wanting to blow a good thing with a display of temper, I allowed her to lead me into her house. We took to the stairs straight away, without preamble.

As we headed for private doors that would shut the world away from us, I stopped suddenly in mid-step. Keeping hold of her wrist with my good hand, I slowly pulled my Lady toward me to embrace her. Looking into the glow of her beautiful face, I smiled and held her close.

"You know," I said, "I think I'll stick around this time. I'm getting tired of the stars."

She looked up at me as tears welled in her bright eyes.

"I'd like that very much," she said and our smiles became kissing.

When we were finally alone behind closed doors, we touched. She had that old sense of intensity for our love-

making again. It was a feeling we'd once shared, and that I'd
thought had been lost forever.

The End

More Books by B. V. Larson:

LOST COLONIES TRILOGY
Battle Cruiser
Dreadnought

UNDYING MERCENARIES
Steel World
Dust World
Tech World
Machine World
Death World

STAR FORCE SERIES
Swarm
Extinction
Rebellion
Conquest
Battle Station
Empire
Annihilation
Storm Assault
The Dead Sun
Outcast
Exile
Gauntlet
Demon Star

Visit BVLarson.com for more information.

Made in the USA
Las Vegas, NV
18 December 2020